GEARS OF WAR®
ASPHO FIELDS

BY KAREN TRAVISS

STAR WARS: REPUBLIC COMMANDO:

Hard Contact

Triple Zero

True Colors

Order 66

STAR WARS: LEGACY OF THE FORCE:

Bloodlines

Sacrifice

Revelation

STAR WARS: CLONE WARS

GEARS OF WAR

Aspho Fields

WESS'HAR WARS

City of Pearl

Crossing the Line

The World Before

Matriarch

Ally

Judge

GEARS OF WAR®

ASPHO FIELDS

KAREN TRAVISS

BALLANTINE BOOKS
NEW YORK

Gears of War: Aspho Fields is a work of fiction. Names, places, and incidents either are products of the author's imagination or are used fictitiously.

A Del Rey Trade Paperback Original

Published in the United States by Del Rey, an imprint of The Random House Publishing Group, a division of Random House, Inc., New York.

DEL REY is a registered trademark and the Del Rey colophon is a trademark of Random House, Inc.

ISBN 978-0-345-49943-1

Printed in the United States of America

www.epicgames.com
www.delreybooks.com

2 4 6 8 9 7 5 3 1

Book design by Christopher M. Zucker

For the 2nd Battalion the Mercian Regiment, and all British service personnel in Afghanistan. Because real heroes in the real world are the ones we should be reading about.

ACKNOWLEDGMENTS

My grateful thanks go to my editor at Del Rey, Keith Clayton, for indulging my love of outlandish armor and unfeasibly large weapons; to Gears producer Rod Fergusson, Epic president Mike Capps, and—of course—Gears designer Cliff Bleszinski for making Gears such an intelligent, emotional gut-punch of a universe; Jim Gilmer, for sharing his invaluable ER experience with chainsaw injuries; real-life sniper Ray Ramirez, for friendship and technical advice; to Jerry Holkins and Mike Krahulik of Penny Arcade, who promised me Gears was "Traviss Town," and made up my mind; and to all the men and women in uniform who've generously given me their time and wisdom over the years, and who continue to leave me humbled by their courage and quiet professionalism.

GEARS OF WAR®
ASPHO FIELDS

PROLOGUE

TIME: FOURTEEN YEARS AFTER EMERGENCE DAY. PLACE: SOMEWHERE BENEATH THE SURFACE OF SERA.

For a time, the humans of Sera knew the illusion of peace . . . until Emergence Day.

At that moment, our people broke free from our subterranean world, erupting into the domain of these groundwalkers, and wiping out whole cities. We fought and killed the humans on their fine boulevards, in their homes, on their battlefields.

And they fought back.

In time, their valiant defense was crushed. With billions dead, humans denied their enemy control by destroying their own civilization. They launched devastating attacks on their own territory—sacrificing their own citizens—so that we could not possess it. Such is their loathing and fear of us.

Understand what a world must do to survive—what humans must do, and what we *must do. But survive we must.*

Now the humans' long struggle against overwhelming odds approaches the final, desperate stand . . .

(QUEEN MYRRAH OF THE LOCUST HORDE, ADDRESSING NEW LOCUST TROOPS WAITING TO GO INTO BATTLE FOR THE FIRST TIME.)

URBAN PATROL IN EPHYRA; 14 YEARS AFTER EMERGENCE DAY, ONE WEEK AFTER THE LIGHTMASS ASSAULT ON THE LOCUST.

I swear I can smell barbecue.

I don't mean scorched flesh—that's a stench I know pretty well. I mean *meat,* proper meat, the bitter tang of charcoal at the back of your throat, smoky fat, spices, *juices.* I'm point man today; I raise my fist to halt the squad.

See, smell *matters* when you're on patrol. It's part of the picture you build up, as much a clue as anything you see, hear, *feel.* It tells you plenty: dead bodies, how long they've been dead, discharged weapons, leaking fuel, fresh air from a distant vent when you're looking for a way out. And, of course, it tells the enemy plenty about you.

So how many Locust are left?

Marcus looks around slowly, not blinking, like he's a machine scanning the buildings. "What is it, Dom?"

"Smell it?"

Someone's probably trying to carry on a normal life in this city, pretending it's an ordinary summer day like we had years ago, wars ago. Even with billions dead, humans get on with life. Even me. Even without my wife and kids. Humans always find something to hang on to.

Marcus pauses, inhales slowly, then lets his rifle rest on its sling.

"Dog," he says at last. "Yeah, dog. Overdone."

Cole chuckles. "Save me a leg. *Two,* if it's one of those little yappy guys."

"Shit, those Stranded eat *anything,*" Baird says. He's got no time for the bands of refugees living outside government protection. Has anyone? Me, I try to remember they're our own. "Maybe they'll end up eating each other and save us a few rounds."

It's their choice to stay outside. The Stranded could sign up, do their military service with COG forces, and get fed like the rest of us, but the dumb bastards still want to play the independence game—like it matters a damn now.

"Yeah, very public spirited," Marcus mutters, and carries on picking his way through the rubble.

But Baird's got a point. We all have a choice. It's dumb to keep this tribal shit going when humankind is close to being wiped out. If we had any sense, we'd all unite.

No, it's *worse* than dumb. It's suicidal.

Then it starts; the faint vibration beneath my boots.

Marcus says smell's our most basic sense, the one that grabs you hardest by the balls and gets your attention. His dad was a scientist, so I guess he knows. But not here. In the city, it's that trembling from deep beneath the ground that blots out everything else. It tells you the Locust are coming. You feel it in your guts. The grubs are boiling up from underground.

There's still plenty of them around, even after we bombed the shit out of their tunnels. They have to be the last ones standing.

"Here we go," Cole says. He checks his Lancer casually,

like he's just waiting for kit inspection, not that we bother much with that kind of stuff now. "Damn, I was hoping those Stranded bums might even have some beer to go with that dog . . ."

Forget the beer. The ground starts moving fifty meters ahead, a slow dome rising, shrugging off the paving that's been smashed into mosaic a dozen times already. I react. We all *react.* There's no *think.* My body's been here before a thousand times, and it gets on with the job without asking my brain if it has anything to say about opening fire.

The paving cracks bulge wider as a bunch of Locust drones break through. Big, ugly, gray bastards. How can anything with two arms, two legs, and a head look so alien? We all concentrate our fire on the same spot before the things can steady themselves and take aim, and in that narrow canyon of a street, it's deafening. A single grub goes down. The rest boil out and come at us firing.

One minute I'm ducking down behind a burned-out car to fire from cover—the next I've got a vise around my neck and shoulder, and a drone is hauling me over the rusted metal, scraping my arm raw. I try to bring the Lancer's chainsaw up into its gut. But the thing's got me so close in a rear stranglehold that I can't move the damn rifle. I'm trying to grab my knife with my free hand. I can hear hammering gunfire, Cole yelling, Baird breathless like he's punching the crap out of something, and just a silence where Marcus is—except for rapid fire. Something wet sprays my face. I'm losing consciousness, but I'm taking that Locust bastard with me, you bet I am, and I ram the blade into any part of the drone I can reach.

That's for my kids. *That's* for Maria. *That's* for all my buddies. *That's* for—

Then it's like a grenade's gone off next to my ear. I'm breathing again, and I'm soaked in something warm and sticky. The drone drops, I mean, it *drops.* But it's still got a tight hold on me and nearly pulls me down on top of it as it collapses. It's got half a head left. I freeze, look around in the sudden ringing silence, and then realize none of us fired that shot.

Marcus sticks his hand in its skull and fishes out a round. "Sniper," he says, wiping blood from his face. The drones are dead. We're not. That's good enough, I suppose. "And not one of ours. This kind of ammo hasn't been used for years."

I *hate* surprises. Even ones that save my skin. Anyone who can shoot like that had better be on our side.

CHAPTER 1

I swear I thought the place was a museum when I walked in. I mean, it was huge, full of books and old paintings. And deserted, you know? That kind of dead silence that says just shut your mouth and feel the awe of history. And then Marcus's mom came through the door like she hadn't seen us, reading some papers she had in her hand, and she says, "Hi sweetheart, you brought some friends home? I'll catch up with you later." Then she was gone. I saw the look on Marcus's face, and knew right then that the guy needed a brother a whole lot more than he needed a library.

(CARLOS SANTIAGO, DESCRIBING HIS FIRST VISIT TO MARCUS FENIX'S FAMILY MANSION AT THE AGE OF TEN.)

EPHYRA, PRESENT DAY—14 A.E.

Dom Santiago decided that there was one good thing about a phantom sniper blowing a Locust's brains all over his face. It took his mind off worrying how many Locust were still around.

His legs were shaking as he moved to the edge of the pit

that had opened in the paving and aimed his rifle below, just in case the grubs had backup on the way. The shakes were just the aftershock of the adrenaline, but—

Liar. I nearly shit myself. The grub was choking the life out of me, a round missed my brain by inches. That's fear. Forget the adrenaline.

No, it never stopped being terrifying. The day it did, he'd *really* be dead. In the tangle of broken pipes and cables below, nothing stirred beyond the clicking of settling soil and stones. Dom couldn't feel anything under his boots now except the slight rocking movement of broken paving. The vibrations from deep in the planet had vanished for the time being, and the smell of chargrilled dog had been overwhelmed by shattered bowels and pulverized concrete.

"Hey, smart-ass," Baird called to the empty street. "Nice shot. Now show yourself."

"Better shout louder," Cole said. "He could be a mile away."

It was always hard to spot a sniper. But in this maze of destruction and shadows, there were a thousand places to lay up and wait for trade. Marcus squatted down and examined what was left of the Locust's skull again. Then he looked up and gestured in the general direction of the south side of the street.

"No, a lot closer. The round went in near the top of the skull. High angle, and a lot of kinetic energy left."

Dom looked where Marcus was pointing, trying to work out where the sniper would have had clear line of sight. Marcus backed slowly to the nearest wall and pressed his fingers to his earpiece. Dom listened in.

"Delta to Control, any sniper teams to the south of Embry? Any Gears at all?"

"Negative, Delta." It was Lieutenant Stroud: Anya Stroud, still on duty after eighteen hours. The woman never seemed to sleep. If Delta Squad was awake—so was she. "Need one?"

"Not anymore."

"Don't leave me in suspense, Sergeant . . ."

"We've got a joker loose with an obsolete sniper rifle. He's helpful now, but he might not stay that way."

"Thanks for the heads-up. I'll put out an advisory."

Cole was still focused on the roofline. Baird lowered his Lancer and started walking again. "Let's get out. Maybe they got a sudden dose of patriotism and realized they owe us, now the war's nearly over."

"Maybe," Marcus said, "he was aiming at Dom and missed. And it's not over."

"Stranded never fire on us. They're not that dumb."

"Old rifle. Great shot." Marcus reloaded, casual and apparently in no hurry. "So I'm curious."

Baird didn't look back as he picked his way over fallen masonry. "Plenty of Stranded are good shots. Doesn't mean we have to go find them and enlist them."

Baird had a point. As long as nobody was shooting at them, it wasn't their problem. But if someone had a sniper rifle, Dom knew it was stolen. Obsolete or not, the things were scarce. A handful of factories struggled to produce spares, let alone crank out new weapons. Every operational piece of kit, from Ravens to Armadillos to assault rifles, was a losing battle between maintenance and decay. Like all Gears, Dom cannibalized parts from anything he could grab. Baird was a master at it.

"Yeah, we need to know," Dom said. "Because if the rifle isn't stolen, that means the owner's one of us. A veteran."

Baird paused to pick up something. When he held it closer to his face to examine it, Dom could see it was a servo part of some kind. "It's old kit and they're thieving scum." Baird pocketed the servo. "Because no Gear is going to hang around with street vermin if he's capable of shooting."

Again, the cocky little bastard was right. Dom wanted to see him proved wrong someday, if only to shut his mouth for a while. Yes, veteran Gears reenlisted after Emergence Day, even some *really* old guys, because there were two choices for any man worth a damn: fight with the COG forces, any way he could—or rot. The only excuse for not fighting the Locust was being dead.

"Every rifle counts," Dom called after him. No, the war *wasn't* over. "And every man." He turned to Marcus and gestured toward the likely direction of fire. "Give me ten minutes."

"You've got me curious, too," Cole said, resting his Lancer against his shoulder. "I think I'll join you."

Marcus sighed. "Okay, but keep your comm channels open. Baird? Baird, get your ass back here."

Half of this city block had been a bank's headquarters, surrounded by snack and coffee shops that lived off the army of clerks. It was all derelict now. Dom could just about remember how it had looked before E-Day, the ranks of neatly wrapped sandwiches in the window displays, filled with the kind of delicacies nobody could get hold of now. Food in the army was . . . adequate, better than anything that Stranded had. But it wasn't fun.

Dog. Damn, who'd eat a dog?

The glittering granite façade was just a shell now, with a few hardy plants rooted in cracks in the ashlars. Nothing much grew here. It didn't get the chance. Dom and Cole edged inside the burned-out bank and looked up to see that there were no floors, and nowhere to hide. It was a big empty box. Everything that could be hauled away and reused—wood, metal, cable, pipes—had been scavenged long before.

"Well, shit," Cole said cheerfully. "I had my fortune stashed here."

Cole had been a pro thrashball star, a rich man in a world long gone. Wealth was measured in skills and barter now. He always treated his worthless millions as a big joke; he could find humor in just about any situation. But there was nothing much left to buy that a Gear needed. Dom decided that when life returned to normal—even after fourteen years, he *had* to think that it could—he'd follow Cole's example and treat money as easy come, easy go. *People* were what mattered. You couldn't replace them, and they didn't earn interest. They just slipped away a day at a time, and you had to make the most of every precious moment.

When I find Maria, I won't take a single minute for granted.

Dom scanned the interior and peered down into a deep crater where the polished marble counter had once been. Nothing moved, but he could see the old vaults, doors blown open. "Yeah, better cancel the order for that yacht."

"Hey, Dom, you won't find no snipers down there." Cole shoved him in the shoulder. "Heads up."

The back of the bank building was a sloping mound of rubble and debris, like scree that had tumbled down a mountainside. Above the ramp of brick, stone facing, and snapped joists, the rear wall rose like a cliff and the top row of empty window frames formed deep arches. Now *that* was a good position for a sniper—depending on what was behind the wall, of course. Dom slung his Lancer across his shoulders and scrambled up the slope for a better look.

"Nobody home, Dom." Cole followed him. "Don't you get enough exercise?"

"Just want a look-see from the top." Dom grabbed at a rusted steel bar and hauled himself up the stumps of joists that jutted from the wall. His oversized boots weren't ideal for climbing and he had to rely on his upper body strength more than momentum from his legs, so getting down again was going to be interesting. "Because he'd have to be at this height to get that shot in."

Dom heaved himself onto a windowsill and stood with his hands braced against the stone uprights on either side. It was a big solid wall, built like a bastion, and thick enough for him to stand on comfortably even in a Gear's boots. On the other side, adjacent buildings in various states of collapse provided crude stairs down to ground level. If anyone had been up here, he'd had a relatively easy route down.

"See anything?" Cole called.

"Usual shit." Dom scanned one-eighty degrees. "Not exactly a postcard to send home. Unless you live in an even bigger cesspit."

Below, the city still looked like a deserted battlefield, sterile and treeless. Smoke curled upward in thin wisps from domestic fires Dom couldn't see. There was a visible demarcation between the parts of the city that stood on thick granite—the last COG stronghold—and the outlying areas where fissures and softer rock let the Locust tunnel in. The line lay between a recognizable city, buildings mostly in one piece, and a devastated hinterland. The line itself—well, that was the margin in which most Stranded seemed to live, the unsecured areas where they took their chances.

Their choice. Not ours.

It wasn't the view Dom was used to from the crew bay of

a King Raven chopper. It was static, deceptively peaceful, not racing and rolling beneath him in a sequence of disjointed images. He had a few moments to think. Even after ten years, he found himself trying to visualize where Maria might be now. Then he began wondering how they'd ever rebuild Sera, and the idea was so overwhelming that he did the sensible thing and just thought about how he was going to get through the next few hours alive.

"Dom, stand there much longer, and somebody's going to shoot your ass off for the hell of it," Cole called. "Let's commandeer a vehicle and cover some ground."

Dom wasn't so sure the sniper had gone far. It was hard to move fast across terrain like this. You had to crawl, climb, burrow, duck. And that made it perfect to hide in. Whoever he was—Dom was sure he'd hang around.

"He'll be back." Dom tried not to think about the drop below. He just turned around and jumped, relying on the give in the loose rock and the thick soles of his boots to cushion the impact. It still shook him to his teeth. "He's making a point. Not sure what, but . . ."

But Marcus had news to take his mind off the sniper. "Move it, guys. Echo's got grubs surfacing three klicks west. Means they might still be moving along the Sovereign Boulevard fissure. We can get there before anyone gets a Raven airborne."

Marcus's voice rarely varied from a weary monotone. Even when he had to shout, all he did was turn up the volume. There was seldom any trace of anger or urgency, although Dom knew damn well that it was all still battened down, and there certainly wasn't any hint of triumph now.

"Numbers?" Dom asked.

"A dozen."

"But that means they're thinning out," Baird said. He fancied himself as the resident Locust expert, and he was. "Looks like we did it. We bombed the shit out of them."

Dom prodded Baird in the chest as he passed him, friendly but pointed. "You mean *Marcus* did it. He's the one who shoved the Lightmass down their grub throats."

"Well, maybe Hoffman will hand him back his medals after all . . ."

"Knock it off." Marcus turned and jogged in the direction of Sovereign. Most patrols were on foot, out of necessity; APCs were in ever shorter supply. "The stragglers could still outnumber us. Do a head count."

Dom prided himself on hanging in there, just like his dad, just like his brother Carlos. You didn't lose heart. You didn't lose hope. *Resilience,* Carlos called it; a man had to be *resilient,* and not crumble at the first setback. But after fourteen years of fighting, there were only a few million humans left, and Dom was ready to grab at any prospect of the nightmare coming to an end.

No, it'll be a different kind of nightmare. Restarting civilization from scratch. But it beats thinking every day will be your last.

The only thing that bothered Dom about dying now was that it would end his hunt for Maria.

"Right behind you," he said, and ran after Marcus.

OFFICE OF CHAIRMAN RICHARD PRESCOTT, COG HEADQUARTERS, JACINTO.

Colonel Victor Hoffman arrived five minutes early for the meeting and diverted to the bathroom to tidy his uniform.

It wasn't much of a uniform, and this battered building

wasn't much of an HQ, but if he started treating anything as not mattering—anything at all—then the rot would set in. *This* was how civilization was maintained. *This* was how a culture survived. Museums and art galleries could be reduced to rubble, and human society on Sera would carry on unscathed. But the way a man conducted himself, the basic rules of every moment of each day—*that* was all that stood between the last humans on Sera and chaotic savagery. It had to be maintained at all costs.

So Hoffman checked for stubble on chin and scalp, straightened his collar, and tried to disguise the signs that—yet again—he hadn't had a chance to sleep in thirty-six hours.

What's going to kill me first? This job, or the Locust?

The door opened behind him, just a crack judging by the muffled voice. A woman's voice; he froze, then checked his zipper.

"The chairman will see you when you're ready, sir."

A man couldn't even take a leak in peace these days. Hoffman didn't turn around. He replaced his cap. "Thank you. Give me a minute."

He counted silently to sixty, contemplating his reflection in a mirror that had also seen better days, and then turned on his heel to walk the few yards down the corridor to Prescott's office. It was a room that hadn't been refurbished since before E-Day. That, at least, won the politician a few points. He was taking the shortages like everyone else.

"Victor," Prescott said. He stood in front of a makeshift display board covered in sheets of paper, studying each in turn, then glanced over his shoulder. "Take a seat. Are things as hopeful as they look?"

Hoffman folded his cap and tried not to gaze longingly at

the coffee on Prescott's desk. He picked up the briefing notes that were always crisp and ready for him at these pointless monthly meetings, and leafed through the digests. Food stockpiles—10 percent lower than target. Munitions—a third below target output. Utilities—domestic power supplies less than twelve hours a day.

Business as usual . . .

"All I can say, Chairman, is that since the Lightmass detonation, we've seen mainly Locust drones, and in considerably reduced numbers. Normally we'd encounter the full spectrum of Locust types over the course of a week—Boomers, Nemacysts, Reavers, you name it—and a *lot* more drones."

Hoffman stopped. That was all he had to say. Prescott stared at him as if he was waiting for him to continue and give him some good news to announce. In the brief silence, an antique clock ticked with a sound like stones falling off a ledge.

Prescott's patience held out six slow seconds. "So did it work? Has the bomb *worked*?"

Hoffman didn't like hope these days. It always tended to get crushed. He pinned down his thoughts in the realms of the measurable and predictable as much as he could.

"It destroyed the Locust citadel," he said carefully. It wasn't quite how he'd felt when the Lightmass bomb ripped the guts out of the Locust tunnels, but there was no reason to bullshit Prescott. "We're seeing a lot fewer on the surface, and it got rid of most of the Kryll. But short of strolling down their tunnels and doing a head count, I don't know what the overall effect's been. Time will tell."

"People need good news to keep going, Victor."

"And when we get some, sir, you'll be the first to know . . ."

"Morale's a commodity."

"For the army, too. Equipment failures went beyond critical a long time ago." Hoffman had this same conversation with Prescott every month, like clockwork. "We're going to have to think about diverting more civilian resources to arms manufacture."

"How am I going to justify that with fewer Locust incursions?"

Shit, I can't win either way, can I? "With respect, who do you need to justify it *to*?"

"The population. They're running on empty, like you."

"Without an effective army, they'll be running on *dead.*"

"I don't want any more riots over rationing and power cuts."

"Look, Chairman, for the moment, my Gears aren't as *busy* as usual. It's a good time to divert some resources into replacing as much equipment as we can. Even if the Locust *have* been defeated, you'll still need a strong army during reconstruction. Once certain groups think the pressure is off, you'll have a whole new bucket of problems on your hands. Top us up *now,* while we've got breathing space."

It was all true, all solid doctrine, but Hoffman knew how to play politicians. They were short-term thinkers; but flag up a good threat to focus them, and they'd drag their eyes to the more distant horizon. Hoffman actually didn't have the luxury of thinking beyond keeping his men fed and armed for the next day, week, month. So if Prescott got off his back and concentrated on civil unrest and reconstruction, it was one less hassle to deal with.

"I do understand," Prescott said. "I've worn the uniform."

For eighteen months. For appearances. Ever been under fire? No. "Then you'll know society's deal, sir. Gears put their lives on the line, and civilians make sure they've got enough kit and support to do the job. Anything less is morally unacceptable. And it's also a recipe for defeat."

Prescott wandered over to the window and folded his arms, staring out over the city. The grime on the glass—there was no maintenance these days, none of the trappings of a less brutal war—gave the broken Jacinto skyline a softer, more flattering focus.

He let out a long breath. "The average adult male citizen is getting by on two thousand three hundred calories a day, which is about a third of a Gear's intake, women on eighteen hundred. Power's off for more than twelve hours in every twenty-six. Water processing can't keep up. If we didn't tie family food rations to keeping children in school, we'd have feral packs of kids roaming the streets. My job's to keep society running, Victor, any way I can. I have to think past wars. My job is *tomorrow.*"

"Well, I'm just a warfighter," Hoffman said carefully. "My job is making sure there'll *be* a tomorrow."

"Okay, it's been easy to motivate people against this enemy," Prescott said. "It's not the Pendulum Wars. Locust aren't remotely human. Nobody's got a grub relative overseas with a different side of the story to tell. They're the antithesis of humankind, real monsters. But hate and tribalism only unite a society so far."

"We've lasted fourteen years." Hoffman stood up to put on his cap. Long practice made him line the badge up with his nose almost unconsciously, running the edge of his right forefinger down over the metal while his left hand positioned the back of the cap. Sometimes, when he felt the death's head emblem, it made him wonder if the badge was a boast or a prediction. "This is a siege. I'm good at sieges.

Give me an objective, and I'll tell you if I can do it with the kit and men available."

"I'll see what I can do," said Prescott.

Hoffman knew *get lost* when he heard it.

It *was* all men now, near enough. The Pendulum War days of women in uniform were largely over. As Hoffman left, a girl in a sober blue business suit—maybe the girl who opened the bathroom door—stood at a filing cabinet with her back to him. When she closed the drawer and turned, he could see she was several months pregnant. That was a priority job now; not just replacing engine parts and weapon components, but replacing *humans*.

Longer lead time, though . . .

"Ma'am," he said politely, touching a finger to his cap, and walked out into the square.

It might have been his imagination, but the sky was less heavily clouded than usual. He looked up, and saw nothing. Nothing was good news.

His radio crackled. In his earpiece, Lieutenant Stroud's voice sounded a little more strained than usual.

"Sir—two more drone incursions. Delta are heading for Sovereign to RV with Echo Squad."

"Thanks, Lieutenant. Now get some sleep. You're not the only Control commander we've got. Tell Mathieson to get his lazy ass in that seat."

"Yes sir. Stroud out."

The link went dead. Anya Stroud didn't fool Hoffman. Delta got extra attention from her, and it wasn't thanks to their refined taste in the arts. If she thought she could mend Marcus Fenix and make a decent man out of him, then Hoffman had overestimated her intelligence, but it wasn't his place to lecture her on pining after grossly unsuitable men. As long as she didn't let it interfere with her duties, it was her private problem.

And she wasn't her mother, poor kid. It must have been damned hard to grow up in the shadow of Helena Stroud.

Or Adam Fenix, come to that. Hoffman brought himself to a halt just short of actually feeling sorry for the man's son.

"You still got a lot of ground to make up with me, Fenix," Hoffman said aloud. He made his way down the road to headquarters, suddenly wanting to pick up a rifle on the way. He hadn't reacted that way in a long time; now he felt naked with only his sidearm, even in the defended heart of the city. "A *lot*."

SOVEREIGN BOULEVARD, JACINTO.

Dom could hear firing long before Delta reached the junction with the boulevard. Marcus broke into a faster run, then sprinted toward the sound.

"He's going to get us killed," Baird muttered, maintaining a steady jog. "Asshole."

Cole gave him a playful shove in the back, which was a hefty blow from a guy built like a brick shithouse. Baird almost fell. "Come on, baby." Cole overtook him. He could still sprint like a pro. "You don't want to get an ugly one."

There was only ugly and uglier to choose from when it came to Locust. Dom switched comm circuits to pick up Echo's sergeant, Rossi, swearing a blue streak as he emptied his magazine.

"Delta, you took your frigging time."

Marcus's voice cut in. "Yeah, well, we're here now. Want a hand?"

"We're two men down. What d'you think? We're holed up in the mall. *Soon* would be good."

They said the world was divided into those folks who ran away from danger, and those who ran toward it. It was funny how you could overcome that instinct to get the hell out if you were trained hard enough. Dom's legs were moving independently of his brain, and as he rounded the corner behind Cole, he saw what was giving Rossi's men problems: it was the biggest Boomer he'd ever seen, and a squad of its drone buddies.

The boulevard was a big, open space with precious little cover. Dom and the rest of Delta made their way up the road by darting from doorway to doorway, and laid up for a moment behind an overturned dumpster.

The whole area south of the House of Sovereigns had once been full of manicured trees, expensive stores, and pavement cafes beyond Dom's pocket, but he'd window-shopped here with Maria before the kids were born. It was hard to tell that it had ever been a nice place except for the shattered stone façades. All the white marble statues that stood in the wall niches had gone; Dom couldn't even see where the raised flower beds had been.

The Boomer and accompanying drones were preoccupied with the entrance to the mall, another converted period building.

Its weather doors were long gone. But the security shutter—a huge steel portcullis suspended between fluted columns—had been lowered. The Boomer was rattling it as easily as a night watchman checking a flimsy door. The shutter wasn't going to last much longer.

Marcus had his don't-say-anything-I'm-calculating face on. "Rossi," he said, finger on his earpiece. "Rossi, is the mezzanine floor above the entrance still intact?"

Rossi's voice was almost drowned out by gunfire. "Yeah. All the way around the atrium. Height's about five meters."

"Have you got control of the shutter?"

"Sphincters—no. Shutter—yes."

"Raise it on my mark."

"We've got grubs *inside,* too. I wasn't planning on letting reinforcements in."

"Just raise it when I say."

"Want to share?"

"Let the Boomer in and leave the rest to us. We'll go in from the top."

Rossi went silent for a moment. Dom heard a voice in the background urging someone called David to hang in there; they had wounded to evacuate.

"Haven't got much choice, have we?" Rossi said. "Standing by."

"Keep your channel open." Marcus turned. "Okay, we've got two exits at the rear of the mall, accessible from the loading bays. Up the fire escape, along the mezzanine, and then Dom and I drop the Boomer from above."

"What do I do, then, catch up on my knitting?" Baird said. "And how do you know the layout?"

"My mom used to go there a lot when I was a kid," Marcus said quietly. "I *explored.*"

"And that's what we're banking on? Your mom's shopping trips?"

Dom was certain that Marcus was going to punch Baird out sooner or later. He'd never seen Marcus lose his temper, but *nobody* could take Baird's whining every day without wanting to kick the living shit out of him. The longer Marcus took it in silence, the bigger the eruption Dom expected.

"Yeah," Marcus sighed. "So you and Cole give us covering fire if the grubs spot us moving. Once we're in and the shutter lifts, close up and go in behind them."

Baird was still muttering over the comms channel about what a crap plan it was, while Dom followed Marcus back the way they'd come and slipped down a side road to circle around the block. Just as Marcus had said, there was a rear entrance to the mall. The walls were still intact. The doors were missing.

Dom checked his Lancer and followed Marcus into what was obviously familiar territory to him. "When you say *drop the Boomer,* Marcus, define *drop.*"

"Jump him. Take his head off."

Boomers were so big and powerful that they could carry small artillery pieces. They were also as dumb as planks, nowhere near as smart as drones, so one way to beat their sheer power was to outthink them and get close in so they couldn't use their weapons.

As long as they don't rip your head off first, of course . . .

Marcus shot up the stairs two at a time, running on some childhood map that was obviously still vivid in his memory. Dom had spent much of that childhood with him, but he'd never been *here.* Maybe it hadn't been a happy place for him.

"Yeah, I thought that's what you meant," Dom said. "Close quarters."

"He'll break our fall."

Yes, Marcus meant *jump,* too.

What the hell am I going to do if he gets killed?

Losing the kids had been bad enough. But when Maria went missing, Marcus had somehow held Dom together, whether he realized it or not. The guy was his friend, and his last link to happier times. He wasn't replaceable; not in a ravaged world like this. The only upside was that everyone, absolutely everyone, had lost family and friends. You didn't grieve alone. You were *understood.*

I'm not going to let him get himself killed.

Marcus, oblivious to Dom's worries, kicked open a door at the top of the stairs. The two men stared into pitch blackness.

"Lights," Marcus said, sounding as if he was talking to himself. He always did, from the moment Dom first met him. The corridor had no natural light. "Why can't they give us a damn flashlight? Okay, this passage runs past the management offices and opens onto the mezzanine by the elevator."

"What if they changed the layout since you were last here?"

"It's a protected historical building. They had to preserve the internal walls."

It was the kind of obscure stuff Marcus was good at remembering, and it always came in handy. After fifty yards, feeling their way with their hands against the walls, they turned hard right. Dom could see a bright rectangle ahead. The corridor filled with the noise of an intense firefight.

"Doors onto the mezzanine," Marcus said. It was just an empty gap now, without even the hinges left intact. "You okay?"

"Fine."

"You think I've got a death wish."

"No." *Well, maybe . . . sometimes.* "Hey, we do this together, okay? We always have, always will." Dom held up his fist, fingers extended. "Okay . . . one, two . . . *three.*"

Dom was first through the doors this time, even though

he didn't know the layout. The noise hit him like a brick wall. Once he was on the mezzanine, it all became clear. He could see the whole ground floor of the mall from here, from the carved drapes that flanked the interior entrance to the blackened shells of shops that lined the ground level, lit by sporadic muzzle flash. Rossi was crouched behind a retaining wall of stone by the stairs to the basement level, and a Gear—David?—was slumped on the ground near him, surrounded by dark stains. Marcus sprinted to the far end of the floor, overlooking the entrance.

"Rossi," he said. "Rossi, raise the shutter. *Now.*"

"Shit, can he get to the controls?" Dom put one hand on the stone balustrade, preparing to vault over the edge. It was only five meters. *Yeah, but it's onto a frigging Boomer.* He was so pumped with adrenaline now, so set on sticking with Marcus no matter what happened, that everything he looked at was sharp, intensely colored, and somehow both slow-motion and flashing past him. "Can he reach them?"

"*That* used to be the security desk," Marcus said. He had his rifle in his right hand; he leaned on his left hand and slid his left leg onto the edge, gaze darting between the entrance and Rossi's position. "He's right on top of the hand-operated controls."

The shutter shook. It started to lift.

"Stand by," said Dom.

"I go first, and you cover me, okay?"

"Okay." Boomers took a lot more stopping than drones. "And if you don't take him out in one, I'm backup."

The entrance was way too close to Rossi's arc of fire. As Dom got ready to drop over the edge, it occurred to him that he could easily be caught in crossfire, but by then he was too pumped to stop. The shutter lifted high enough for the Boomer to enter. It crouched under the barrier, almost squatting, then paused for a split second to look up.

Marcus put a burst of fire through it. It didn't even slow the thing down. Boomers didn't seem to feel pain. Then he crashed down onto its back.

This was a two-man job. Dom jumped too, boots first, and for a moment he wasn't sure if he'd hit Marcus or the Boomer, but either way it felt like slamming into concrete. The Boomer went down, face-first. The force of the impact winded Dom; he tasted blood in his mouth.

As the Boomer rose to its knees to shrug them off, Dom was aware of deafening fire over his head, but nothing else. He caught the Boomer in a choke hold, his arm closing around its squat neck, while Marcus emptied a clip into its gut.

He fell back to reload. Dom jumped clear and carried on firing. Shit, those things really *did* take some stopping. Not even chainsaws did the job on them.

Ordinary grubs, though . . . that was another matter. A drone came at them out of the rubble just as the Boomer sank to its knees, riddled with rounds. Dom turned to fire, but the grub jumped Marcus first.

"Shit—" Dom couldn't get a clear shot as Marcus struggled with the grub. He revved up the chainsaw instead. *Down through the shoulder, right through the main plumbing. Get off my buddy, you bastard.* "Marcus, *hang on.*"

But Marcus was already doing some carving of his own. His chainsaw screamed and stuttered against armor. There was a precise technique to the saw: you had to put your weight behind it, or else the blades skidded and didn't bite. The best action was a downward slice, leaning into the target, but Marcus was pinned on his back, cutting upward, and the grub was still thrashing around, even though it couldn't use its weapons close-in. Dom sliced into its shoulder—and *still* the thing kept moving.

But the Boomer was out of the game now, just a shaking mound of meat on the floor. Somehow, Dom kept it in his peripheral vision as he sliced into the grub on top of Marcus. He was sure it was never going to die until it bellowed and threw back its head, hurling him clear. As Dom scrambled to his feet, he saw a spray of arterial blood, Marcus rolling clear, then everything ground to a sudden, silent halt.

The Boomer was down. It still wasn't dead—how *could* it hold out like that?—but it would be very soon. The things bled out like any other creature.

"Any more?" Marcus said, jumping up. "Is that all of them? Baird? Cole?"

"I'm mopping up, baby."

Cole rose up from behind a shattered column and opened fire almost casually, aiming his Lancer one-handed. Dom turned in time to see a drone falling backward a few meters away, still firing in a neat arc that tilted up to punch into the vaulted ceiling.

"Nice." Marcus wiped his chin and stared at his palm. "Shit . . ."

Cole looked down at the dead grubs with faint distaste, and prodded one with his boot to check for movement. Then he inhaled.

"I *hate* that smell." He sounded muffled, but it was just Dom's ears recovering from the noise. "It ain't putting me off my dinner, though. Are we done here?"

Marcus looked around. "Everyone okay? Rossi, you still there?"

"Yeah." Rossi stood up. He was spattered with blood, and it could have been anybody's—even the Boomer's. "I've called for casevac. David's in a bad way. Abdominal wound. And I need to find Harries's rifle."

It was a fact of life, driven by shortages; they had to retrieve what kit they could. Rossi and the last Gear left from Echo Squad carried David out into the open to wait for the King Raven, then went back for Harries's body. Dom, caught in that weird limbo between fighting for his life and instant boredom, found he had to keep moving. He kept seeing shadows that just weren't there. It happened when he'd pushed himself too far on too little sleep. He could have sworn he saw someone go into the mall.

"I'll look for it," he said. "Won't take long."

Baird was rummaging through his pouches and pockets, fishing out ammo to reload. "The chopper's going to be here in a minute."

"I said I'd look. Right, Rossi?"

Rossi had a tight grip on David's hand. It didn't look like the guy was in any shape to grip back. "Thanks."

Dom picked his way back through the mall, wondering what happened to the dead Locust if there wasn't a pile of corpses to be set alight to prevent disease spreading. Sometimes, when he returned to a site, bodies were decomposing, and sometimes they were gone. Maybe the packs of feral dogs and cats scavenged them. It wasn't an appetizing thought.

But he was sure the Locust didn't come back for their dead; they weren't like humans. They didn't pride themselves on leaving no grub behind.

He took another look at the Boomer. Shit: it wasn't dead. *It still wasn't dead.* Its eyes followed him as he moved around it, baleful and accusing. After all that, the thing was still hanging on, just like David. Dom aimed his Lancer, then paused to flash Marcus on the radio.

"Ignore the firing," he said. "Just finishing a job."

He emptied his clip into the Boomer. He wasn't sure if he was doing it to make sure it didn't get up again, like the manual said, or if he was doing the decent human thing and ending its misery.

It might have been a waste of valuable ordnance. But at least it was dead now. He waited for its chest to stop moving, and then cast around looking for the Harries's Lancer, ignoring the bodies. He'd been able to see some common ground with enemy troops in the Pendulum Wars, because they were soldiers just like him, but Locust—they were like everything that was rotten in people, with none of the saving graces. There was nothing to pity or love or recognize.

And they smelled bad. That smell clung to him until he showered it off, along with smoke and weapon residue. There was no sign of the Lancer. Another flicker in his peripheral vision made him turn, even though he knew it was just fatigue. There was a retail unit right ahead of him, its doorway partly blocked by rubble.

It was crazy, but he had to check.

As Dom stepped through the opening, rifle raised, he thought he'd walked into a slaughterhouse. The debris on the floor from the collapsed ceiling was littered with bodies. In the smoky gloom, he could pick out limbs jutting from the debris, and his first thought was that a bunch of Stranded had been living here when the place came under fire.

For a second, he recoiled, thinking he'd stepped on a

body, but the loud crack beneath his boots didn't sound like bone, it sounded like . . .

Plastic.

Now he could see the bodies were just old display mannequins stripped of every reusable material. He picked up a stray forearm. Even the small metal ball joints at both ends were missing. He felt stupid, but he knew he wasn't the first guy to make the same mistake in the heat of the moment.

Dom could now hear the staccato sound of an incoming Raven. He picked his way back toward the exit, squinting against the daylight from the mall that plunged the rest of the space back into relative darkness. His gut rumbled, and he reached in his belt-pouch for some dry rations to tide him over. It was then that he looked up, the edge of the foil packet still clamped between his teeth as he started to rip it open, and found himself staring across the beam of a rifle's tactical lamp.

He aimed before he'd consciously worked out what was happening. He fired.

CHAPTER 2

I shall remain vigilant and unyielding in my pursuit of the enemies of the Coalition.

I will defend and maintain the Order of Life as it was proclaimed by the Allfathers of the Coalition in the Octus Canon.

I will forsake the life I had before so I may perform my duty as long as I am needed.

Steadfast, I shall hold my place in the machine and acknowledge my place in the Coalition.

I am a Gear.

(OATH OF THE COALITION, SWORN BY ALL RECRUITS.)

SOVEREIGN BOULEVARD.

Dom fired because no Gear would walk up on a buddy like that.

He heard ricochets, but he couldn't see a damn thing. The afterimage of the lamp and the light from the door blinded him.

"You bloody idiot," a voice boomed. A *woman's* voice, a

strong accent—South Islands, or somewhere close. "You could have killed me."

The spotlamp went out. Dom realized he'd dropped the ration bar. He didn't lower his Lancer. "Yeah? I still might. Identify yourself."

"It's Bernie," she said.

"I don't know any Bernie." His eyes adjusted to the light again, but he still couldn't see her. "Lady, cut the crap and step out where I can see you."

"Next time, I'll let the frigging grub pull your head off."

So this was his phantom sniper. She must have been trailing them all the way, and that thought bothered him more than the Locust.

"Yeah, I appreciate the help, but I still want you to step out here." Marcus and the others must have heard the shots, but he'd already told them not to take any notice. "Move it."

Dom had been decoyed once, when he was too young to know the score. It was a Stranded game; get a woman to keep a guy busy, then send the man to do whatever thieving he needed. The bastards had even tried to steal weapons, fuel, and vehicle parts from Gear patrols, which was a good reason for leaving them to fry. Not that the women were any less trouble than the men, but in a species on the brink of extinction—and humans *were* that species—nobody took risks with their females. They were hope, the future, the survival of society—not cannon fodder.

Dom was cut short by the thud of boots hitting the ground hard to his right, like someone had jumped from a height. He swung around.

It was the rifle that got his attention first, a really old model Longshot, a Mark 2, followed by the woman holding it.

"Shit," he said.

She was bigger and older than he expected—although he wasn't sure exactly *what* he expected—and wore a motley assortment of COG body armor. No youngster, that was for sure; her close-cut dark hair was mostly gray, but she didn't look like anyone's doting mother. She looked like a smack in the mouth waiting to happen. She clipped the rifle back on its sling—shit, she had a Lancer, too—and stood there waiting. Dom stared at the rifle.

"Yeah, I found it," she said. "Didn't have these in my day."

She turned her back on Dom, strode to the doorway, and stuck her head out. Dom could see the tattoos on her arms now. "Hey, Marcus. Don't tell me you don't remember me."

Marcus appeared in the entrance, Cole and Baird behind him. They looked wary, but they were taking Marcus's lead, and he had his arms at his side.

"I know who you are," Marcus said. "And I thought you were dead."

Dom struggled with the name. Bernie? Bernie . . . *Bernie* . . .

"I'm not finished yet. Got a lot of catching up to do." She looked over everyone as if it was parade inspection and she wasn't satisfied with the degree of spit and polish. "Who's running the show now? Is it still Hoffman?"

"How the hell did you get here?" Marcus talked straight past her question. It was incredulity rather than bad manners. It didn't show on his face—nothing much did—but Dom always knew when something had shocked him because he blinked more frequently. She *definitely* had. "You got a vehicle?"

"I walked."

"For fourteen years?"

"Yeah. Try covering a couple of continents that all look as good as this place. And remember that wet stuff called *sea*?"

Her accent sounded a lot like Tai Kaliso's, but she didn't have any tribal tattoos on her face. That was still enough for Dom to decide to give her a wide berth. South Islanders were all crazy, and that was by Gear standards, which allowed for a lot of crazy even at the best of times.

"Anyone going to introduce us?" Cole held out a massive hand for shaking. She took it. "Private Augustus Cole, ma'am, and the *really* ugly bastard here is Corporal Damon Baird."

"Bernadette Mataki." She gripped his hand. "Bernie." Baird just nodded at her, surly and working hard on being unimpressed. "Marcus and Dom already know me."

"Wow, lady, you got a handshake like a Boomer. I *like* that in a woman."

"You're a cheeky bugger, but you'll do. Come on, Marcus, take me to Hoffman."

Marcus made a faint grunt and jerked his head in the direction of the boulevard. Outside, the King Raven had already set down and the winchman gave them an irritated get-a-move-on gesture.

"When you ladies are ready, we've got wounded on board," he said sourly, seeming not to notice Bernie at first. "Just because there's not many—shit, you *are* a woman."

"Hey, don't talk about Baird like that," Cole said. "He's *sensitive*, bein' blond and all."

Baird didn't rise to the bait. Bernie swung herself into the crew cabin and fixed the winchman with a stare, which made sure he didn't say another word. The Raven lifted clear, and Dom caught a fleeting glance between Marcus and Bernie that bothered him for a moment. It was the kind of look that might have been a question or a warning or both.

I've known this guy nearly all my life. We've lived in each other's pockets since we were kids. Is there something I don't know?

"I'm not *a woman,*" Bernie said pointedly, resting the ancient Longshot across her knees. "I used to be Sergeant Mataki. And I can still do the job."

"Yeah," said Marcus, staring out onto the cityscape beneath. "She did. And she can."

Mataki.

Dom found himself trying to erase five, ten, fifteen years from her face without looking as if he was staring. But she caught him looking anyway, and didn't seem offended. If anything, she looked . . . sympathetic.

But she still didn't look like anyone's gray-haired mother.

Mataki. Mataki, Mataki, Mataki. Oh shit, yes.

Now he knew who she was. It came back with all the force of being shaken awake from a deep sleep. She'd fought at the Battle of Aspho Fields.

She'd fought alongside his brother, Carlos.

And, like Marcus, she'd been there when he was killed.

Dom held out his hand. "Thanks," he said at last. "Nice shot."

FORMER WRIGHTMAN HOSPITAL, BARRACKS BLOCK.

It was the first half-decent bathroom Bernie had seen in years.

The fact that the building had once been a mental asylum for the crazy rich didn't trouble her at all. The rows of washbasins stretched to the far wall, and the tiles were the ones she remembered from every COG base she'd ever been in. The novelty of running water would take some getting used to. She filled a basin, plunged her head in, and savored the simple joy of fresh water before straightening up and focusing on the mirror. There was a bittersweet feel of home about it all.

She'd forgotten the smells; smoke, blood, shit, machine oil, discharged weapons, regulation carbolic soap. They filled the locker room. Marcus stood cleaning Locust guts off his armor, looking mildly annoyed. Then he took off the do-rag he always wore and rinsed it in a basin. Without it, he looked like a totally different man.

"God, is that the same one you were wearing last time I saw you?" Bernie asked.

"No." He wrung it out, then tied it back on his head without looking in the mirror. "I got a new one when Dom sprung me from jail."

"Yeah, that's what I was meaning to ask you. Aren't you curious about why I was trailing you? I've been shadowing patrols for weeks."

He shrugged. "Okay. Why?"

"To make sure you weren't with the Stranded. I heard some weird shit about you when I got here, Marcus. Is it true?"

"Depends what you heard."

"That you deserted your post, cost a lot of lives. That they court-martialed you."

Marcus shrugged. "Can't argue with that."

"Not you. Never."

"True. I got forty years. Served four. It was going to be a death sentence, but Dom spoke up for me. And got me out a few days ago."

That was Dom all over. The man would die in the proverbial ditch for anyone he believed in. But Bernie couldn't imagine Marcus Fenix running away from a battle. There had to be more to it than that—a *lot* more.

"You ever going to tell me what really happened?"

"Maybe. Are you going to tell me why you decided to come back now?"

There was an unspoken question in there. She'd put it out of her head so many years ago—deliberately, carefully—that for a moment she thought she really had forgotten what it had all been about. But it only took a glance at Dom Santiago's face to remind her.

He was a good lad, dog-loyal and humblingly brave, the spitting image of his brother right down to the neat black goatee beard. She'd found it hard to look him in the eye.

"Don't worry, Marcus," she said. "I'm not going to dredge up Aspho again." No, Dom didn't need to know the details about Carlos then, and he didn't need to know them now. "We agreed, didn't we? It's been sixteen years."

"He's lost both his kids. And his wife's been missing for ten years."

Everyone had lost someone since E-Day, but that still sounded like too much for one man to take on top of losing his brother. "I bet he's still looking for her."

"Yeah. You know Dom."

"What about his folks?"

"Missing, presumed dead."

"Poor sod. I thought he'd remember me better." Just as well he didn't. He'd only start asking her questions. "Is your dad still around?"

"No."

"Sorry."

"You've been out of the loop a long time."

"You bet. I went back home when I was invalided out of the army. The island was totally cut off on E-Day, so it was eight years before I even heard about the recall to Ephyra."

Marcus looked blank for a moment as if he was calculating. "Is there *any* good news out there?"

The global communications network they'd all grown up with had collapsed, most of it within days of the first Locust emergence. "I came across a few survivors from time to time, usually in fishing villages. Harder for Locust to get at them when they put to sea."

"That's one way of avoiding them."

"I had a hell of a job getting hold of a boat, but there's a lot you can persuade people to do if you've got a rifle."

Marcus looked Bernie over with a wary eye. "You're serious, then."

"I'm too old for breeding stock, but I can still fight. Don't tell me I can't hack it."

"Wouldn't dream of it."

Bernie knew that as long as she could hold a weapon, she had a duty. Any civvies who stood in her way were a threat to everyone's survival. There was no room for neutrality or going it alone, no choice of sides to be on, and she'd lost too many people she cared about.

But everyone's lost someone. Every human, our whole species, is in mourning. What's that going to do to us? What kind of society is going to come out of this? What are we going to be like after so much loss?

Thinking that far ahead was a luxury nobody had, except maybe the politicians. But she thought it anyway.

Marcus continued cleaning up, and Bernie tried the showers. Even with cold water, it was sheer luxury. She was never going to set foot in a bloody boat again.

The main door swung open. She heard Dom's voice as she was getting dressed.

"Hoffman's on his way," he said. "Anya says it was like someone shoved a firecracker up his ass. Just said 'shit' and took off."

"Anya said that, did she?" Bernie called. "Never knew she learned that kind of language . . ."

"Sorry, didn't realize you were there, Sergeant."

"I'm still a civvy until Hoffman says otherwise."

Bernie waited a couple of seconds before coming out of the shower area. The last time she'd seen Dom Santiago before today, he was crying unashamedly for his dead brother, and the victory at Aspho Fields meant nothing. Six months after that, she was stuck in a hospital bed with a shattered leg, and then she was out of the army for good. It was too easy to lose touch with people.

And then—you found the people had gone forever.

She wanted to kill grubs, to wipe them out like they wiped out her world, and being a Gear gave her the best seat in the house to do that.

"I remember you now," Dom said, looking a little guilty. "It's been a long time."

"It's okay. It wasn't like I was in the same company."

"You were in Carlos's, though."

It's a normal comment. Don't start blurting stuff out. What else did you expect him to say?

"Yes," she said. "Good man, your brother. A bloody fine Gear."

That was all it took; neutral, honest, inviting no questions. Carlos was a brother anyone could be proud of. Dom just smiled to himself for a moment, a little sadly, and started singing under his breath while he took off his body armor. Fighting Locust was a messy business. Bernie thought of the chainsaw bayonet, and realized that stripping down and cleaning a rifle was a whole new game these days. Marcus was using an old toothbrush on the blades. He'd disassembled the whole chainsaw feed and was digging out connective tissue that had wound itself around the chain.

"So has Hoffman mellowed?" Bernie asked.

Marcus made that *unhh* sound under his breath. Bernie recalled it all too well. It wasn't actually a sigh; it was just an escape of disappointment, disgust, and disillusionment that he was too tired to hold in any longer. "No, he's still the asshole he always was. But he's top asshole now."

Dom, out of Marcus's eyeline, gave Bernie a meaningful glance. *Long story, don't go there.* But she didn't recall Marcus ever having that much to say. She took that as a guide to just how bad the blood was between him and Hoffman.

"Okay," she said carefully. "I'll try to stay on his least offensive side."

Marcus went on cleaning his kit. Bernie gathered her belongings—one change of clothes, three changes of weapon—and sat in the lobby area waiting to be summoned. Things had changed a lot since she'd left the service. The Gears walking past her were all men. And they looked wrung out in a way that the guys she'd served with never had, however bad things had been.

The Pendulum Wars were different, somehow. After the best part of eighty years' fighting, a kind of saturation level had been reached. Nobody really believed it was the end of the world, even if global disaster was actually around the corner.

This time, though, it was probable, and everyone knew it.

Maybe she'd just come eight thousand miles to die somewhere worse than home.

Well, at least I'll die with a square meal inside me and a decent pair of boots. And take a few more of the grub bastards with me.

"I know I said I'd take anything I could get that could hold a rifle, but you're pushing my limits, Mataki."

The voice boomed from behind her. Passing Gears stopped to stare for a second and then wisely went about their business. No, Hoffman hadn't changed much at all; solid, short, square, lips set in a thin line. She stood to attention and turned as if the last sixteen years had closed up without a single day's gap.

Actually, he *had* changed. His age showed, more around his neck than anything, and his piercing dark eyes looked somehow faded. But he still stood as if he was going to take a run at her, arms loose at his sides, weight slightly forward.

"Sir," she said, "you look like shit."

Hoffman wavered on the edge of a smile. She knew he wouldn't dare grin and look happy to see her again. "Good to see you, too, Bernie. You're not exactly combat-fit yourself."

"I know. But I can still function in full armor and hit a moving target at eight hundred meters. That's how I got here."

"Take the oath, then go see the Quartermaster." Hoffman surrendered to a faint smile, but it was brief and almost embarrassed. "Welcome back. And remember not to kiss Fenix's ass, because if I had my way, he'd still be the last man left in the Slab."

"Arse, sir," Bernie said. She didn't understand the reference to the prison—the Slab. "They're arses where I come from."

"Well, whatever it is, don't pucker up to it."

Hoffman turned and strode off. There was no point telling Marcus that she'd always liked Hoffman and that he was a proper soldier, not a useless chair-warming tosser like some she'd known. And there was no point telling Hoffman that Marcus didn't have it in him to abandon his men, and that there would have been an unselfish reason for anything he did, however stupid the decision.

She wasn't here to referee a grudge match between the two of them. She was here, she reminded herself, because she was human, and being a Gear again was the best chance she had of taking back her world.

Dom walked up to her, reeking of carbolic soap. It was bloody hard to scrub off that Locust smell.

"Come on, I'll take you to the adjutant's office," he said. "You need anything, you got any problems—you just let me know. Carlos thought a lot of you."

"Thanks. You're a good lad, Dom."

"Tell me some stories about him sometime, will you? I bet you two got up to all kinds of shit he never told me about."

Dom grinned. Bernie did her best to smile back, and followed him down the corridor. She'd tell him what she could, but she knew right then that sooner or later, he'd ask her to recount the story she swore she'd never tell.

He'd ask about the day Carlos died.

OPS CENTER, WRIGHTMAN HOSPITAL, JACINTO.

The reports of Locust incursion always came in thick and fast, but they'd slowed to a comparative trickle in the last couple of days.

That didn't mean they'd stopped.

"Sir, we've got a problem." Lieutenant Mathieson got Hoffman's attention by shoving a printout in front of him. The kid was stuck in CIC after losing both legs. "Look at this chart. Look at the direction the new incursions are moving in."

Hoffman scanned the line of short arrows formed like a figure four and the times written against them. Yes, there was a definite progression; Locust were moving north in an area they hadn't reached before, cutting between the outlying Stranded settlements and what was euphemistically called farmland. It was still shown as an optimistic green on charts. The reality wasn't anywhere near as rural—there were few crops grown in the open air, but plenty of industrially ugly hangars full of hydroponics, mycoprotein farms, and poultry units. A lone city of humans still took a lot of feeding.

The incursions weren't advanced enough to form a definite pattern, though. Not yet.

By the time they are, though . . . it'll be too late.

"What's your take on it, then, Mathieson?"

"It might just be coincidence, but if you extend that line . . . well, you can see where they're heading."

"If those things cut off the food production areas, we're screwed," Hoffman said. "The geologists swore that that was solid granite bedrock."

"It might have been the Lightmass bomb."

"What, opening new fissures?"

"Shove that much energy into confined spaces, and it's got to go somewhere, sir."

The ops room, a shadow of the lavishly manned center it had been in earlier years, had fallen silent except for the occasional radio transmissions from Gears in the field and the rhythmic grass-cutter sound of printers spewing out updates. When Hoffman looked up, all eyes were on him; young men too disabled for active service, reserve Gears too old to deploy, and women from eighteen to don't-ask. It wasn't the uniform that made them look alike at that moment. It was the blank dread in their eyes.

Give me a straight battle. Shoot, don't shoot. Advance, fall back. But every time I do this . . . every time feels like I'm going to balls it up and let the whole damn world down.

Without food supplies, the city wouldn't last more than a few months—at best. Securing water pipelines was hard enough. The Locust looked like they'd seized the opportunity to start a siege.

"They're going to try to starve us out, aren't they, sir?" said one of the retired men.

"You're old enough to remember Anvil Gate," Hoffman said. "So you know how I deal with sieges." It had been the defining moment of Hoffman's career. He was no longer sure whether it defined him for good or ill, but it wasn't something he wanted to do again. "Get me the Chairman."

Prescott, to his credit, was always available, day or night, and Hoffman cut him extra slack for that. He called back within a minute. Every back in the ops room was turned as officers returned to their duties, but Hoffman knew everyone was listening intently.

"What's the problem, Colonel?"

Mathieson passed an updated printout to Hoffman in silence. Another four-shaped mark indicated where more Locust had broken through.

"Looks like the grubs have a new strategy. They're cutting us off from the North Gate food production zone."

"What kind of numbers?"

"Numbers don't matter if they concentrate what they've got on creating a no-go area there. We've got two options—counterattack, or start clearing that sector."

"So what are you recommending?"

It wasn't a military option, but Hoffman couldn't guarantee saving the zone, nor the food stockpiles there. They'd had years of practice at evacuating populations and withdrawing into secured areas as the Locust advanced across Tyrus.

"Clear the area, Chairman. At the rate they're moving, we've got three days to shut down production and move everything out. Not many people to shift, but a lot of equipment and stores."

Prescott sounded as if he was counting under his breath. "That means we need to ship people in to do the heavy lifting."

"We'll take in an escorted convoy, and bring it back. But we've got to move fast."

"Okay. I'll put the emergency management unit on this as top priority and they'll get back to you with the details inside the hour. How many Gears can you spare?"

"Not as many as I'd like," Hoffman said, "but the faster we do this, the sooner they get back to combat duties."

"Keep me in the loop, Colonel," Prescott said, and the line went dead.

"Okay, people." Hoffman slapped his hands together to get attention, as if he needed to. He could have heard a rat fart in the silence. "Dust off the contingency plan. You know your jobs. As soon as we get the vehicle numbers, plan me a route in and out, put times on it, and tell me how many assets we need to reallocate. Mathieson, put three squads on standby."

"Very good, sir."

It *sounded* fine. Hoffman could stand outside himself sometimes and listen to his own performance, because command was almost as much about presentation as soldiering. Gears—and civilians—needed to see decisive strength when the shit was on an intercept course with the fan. He just couldn't convince himself half as well as he convinced them.

I didn't earn this position. I just didn't manage to get killed.

Earned or not, though, he held it, and there was nobody else suitable to hand it to. It was his duty. He'd do it.

And he'd pray that he didn't screw up humanity's last chance.

CHAPTER 3

The COG isn't a soul-crushing machine, dumbass. It's society. *Mutual support, mutual dependence. Individuality might sound all noble and free, but it generally means crapping on your neighbors, and if you crap on your neighbors—don't expect them to help you. Rules hold humans together. And it's* together, *or* die.

(PRIVATE DOM SANTIAGO, EXPLAINING TO A FORMER STRANDED WHY HE SHOULD STOP WHINING ABOUT BEING DRAFTED AS PART OF OPERATION LIFEBOAT.)

TWENTY-SIX YEARS EARLIER: OLAFSON INTERMEDIATE SCHOOL, EPHYRA, 12 B.E.

He was a rich kid, he was different, and he was *new*.

Carlos Santiago felt really, *really* sorry for Marcus Fenix. He took refuge at a desk without looking around, as if not meeting anyone's eye would stop him from being noticed. He didn't *look* rich—no fancy clothes, just a school uniform like everyone else's—but everyone knew who his dad was, and where he lived.

He was also tall and skinny, very pale, with spooky light blue eyes that didn't go with his black hair. He might as well have stuck a target roundel on his back.

The math teacher, Major Fuller, was as old-fashioned as the school building and ran classes as if he was still in the army. He even had one of those short brass-topped sticks like the sergeants who drilled Gears for parades. Every man in the Santiago family had served in the military, so Carlos knew all about that kind of thing, but the army was everywhere, part of life itself, and especially at school. This, Carlos's dad said, was where the military *ethos* made a man of you. Carlos had to look up the word.

"Introduce yourself, boy," Fuller said.

Marcus stood up at his desk and didn't look around. "Marcus Fenix, sir."

"Age, parents, siblings?"

"I'm ten years old. My parents are Professor Adam Fenix and Doctor Elain Fenix. I'm an only child."

Oh, Fenix was dead *for sure.* Carlos's heart sank a little farther. Marcus didn't even talk like the rest of them. He had a posh accent. He was going to get *creamed.*

Fuller looked as if he was waiting for Marcus to go on, but there was a tense, empty silence, and Fuller gave up. "Class, you will make him feel part of the team," he said stiffly in his major's voice, "and you will treat him with courtesy. You will *not* behave like street ruffians. You will behave like *citizens.* Are we clear?"

The response was a mumbling chorus. "Yes, Major Fuller."

Joshua Curzon raised his hand. "Sir, if he's *rich,* why is he here?"

"You think this is a *poor* school?"

"Well, *we're* all poor . . ."

Fuller brought his stick down on the lectern with a crack like rifle fire. "Fenix is here because society is formed from people pulling together, not breaking away into separate groups. *Unity.* Because no man can exist on his own. No country can, either. That's why we have the Coalition of Ordered Governments." Fuller repeated this speech so often that Carlos could recite it, and maybe that was the point. It made perfect sense when he stopped to think about it. "If you look after your neighbor, your neighbor will look after you. Previous generations left a rich world for you, so you'll leave a rich world for those to come. Nobody who stands on the sidelines and thinks only of his own needs can ever be a *man.*"

Yeah, that made sense too.

But Carlos understood all that, so he was more interested now in finding out how much stuff Marcus had, and how big his room was. He probably had a whole wing of a mansion to himself. The Fenix estate was *huge.* Carlos had run around the perimeter once with Dom, thinking of shinning over the walls and seeing what the gardens were like, but he never dared. Getting Dom into trouble would make Mom go crazy. He was supposed to look out for his little brother and set a good example.

The estate looked like a prison, anyway.

"Open your books," Fuller said. "Curzon, seeing as you're so interested in financial statistics, you can tell us what you learned yesterday about calculating averages . . ."

Carlos counted down the hours until lunch recess, watching dust motes circling in the shafts of sunlight from windows set high in the wood-paneled walls. The room smelled of permanence and wax polish. This building was hundreds of years old, and it would be here for hundreds more, war or no war. His grandfather could remember when the Pendulum Wars began, but Carlos couldn't. All in all, war didn't seem as bad as people said. Life went on.

Besides, the real war was here, in Olafson Intermediate. At lunch, Carlos kept an eye on Marcus, just in case. Nobody sat next to him at the long refectory table. They just watched him. He never said a word. Eventually Carlos couldn't stand it any longer, picked up his plate, and moved to sit beside him.

"I'm Carlos Santiago," he said. "What's behind the wall around your house? The wall on Allfathers Avenue."

"Orchard," Marcus said, not meeting his eyes.

"Cool." Carlos nodded approvingly. "Where did you go to school before?"

"Private tutor."

That explained a lot. "This place isn't so bad. Hey, I saw your dad on the news once. He's famous. A scientist."

Marcus turned and looked at Carlos. "He always says he's an *engineer* and my mother's the scientist. He used to be a Gear."

"My dad was a Gear. So was my granddad. And my uncles, and Aunt Rosa. I'll be one, too."

"You decided already?"

"It's great. Like a family, really."

Marcus appeared to chew that over for a while. Maybe the COG officers like his dad—he'd have been an officer, not an ordinary Gear—didn't see it that way.

Carlos stuck with Marcus through lunch, reluctant to give the others a chance to torment him. It *would* happen, but it would be over fast, one way or another. Carlos had a feeling Marcus was going to have a harder time of it than anyone else. He wasn't very chatty. Carlos wondered if Marcus just didn't like him, but it seemed more like he didn't know what to do or say.

Joshua Curzon and his brother Roland—a year older—shoved into Carlos's path as they filed into the main building.

"So he thinks he's too good for us . . ."

That could have meant Carlos, or Marcus, or both. Carlos knew he could handle himself in a fight, so he decided to set Joshua straight from the start. He found himself pitching in to defend Marcus immediately, just like he did for Dom.

"He's okay. Leave him alone."

"You're sucking up to him because he's rich," Joshua sneered. "Snob. You're an ass-kissing *snob,* Santiago."

"And you're a moron. Leave him alone."

Carlos had thrown down the gauntlet. Joshua accepted the challenge. "Take that back."

"Shove it."

"Yeah?"

"Yeah." Carlos pushed past him, but it wasn't over yet. He knew that.

The last hour of the afternoon was usually spent playing thrashball. Carlos suspected it was because the teaching staff wanted to take it easy before they clocked off, but it was also handy for settling any arguments that cropped up during the day. Carlos made sure Marcus was on his team to avoid leaving him waiting to be picked. Joshua fixed Carlos with that "you're dead" stare.

It didn't take long before Joshua made a lunge for the ball in the penalty area and brought his elbow down hard into Carlos's back. Carlos waited for the games master's line of sight to be interrupted and brought his boot down hard on Joshua's instep, forcing a howl out of him.

Yeah, that hurts, doesn't it?

"Stop whining, Curzon." The games master waved play on. Maybe he thought it was all part of toughening them up anyway. "Or I'll transfer you to the girls' class."

Marcus moved in to cover Carlos. He didn't look the athletic type, but he was tall, and he intercepted a pass easily. It seemed to surprise him that he'd caught it; he paused for a second. Joshua tackled him with a lot more force than needed, and Marcus fell headlong. He jumped to his feet, looking more embarrassed than hurt, but Carlos wasn't going to let that go.

Carlos caught up to Joshua as they left the field, out of sight of the games master. "I said, leave him alone . . ."

"Oh, I forgot, you're his best friend."

"It's his first day. Give him a break."

It should have ended there. But it wouldn't, of course. Marcus sat down next to Carlos on the changing room bench. They were the last two there.

"Don't worry about me," Marcus said. "I'll be okay."

"But it's not fair."

Marcus shrugged. He didn't seem to be giving in. It was more like he didn't care. "I better get home."

Carlos stopped short of saying he'd see him out safely in case he thought he was treating him like a little kid. It was hard to explain why he felt responsible for Marcus, but he did, and now that he'd taken on that job, dropping it after a few hours felt cowardly and plain *wrong*.

He left first anyway, just to make sure the coast was clear.

It wasn't. In the shade of the portico outside, Joshua and

Roland Curzon waited, hands thrust into pockets, with one of their buddies. Carlos straightened up and stood his ground.

"You think you're really hard, don't you, Santiago?" Joshua said. He let his arms hang at his sides. Carlos knew what was coming. "You're always taking over and telling us what to do."

"And what are *you* going to do about it?"

"This," Joshua said, like he'd heard the line in a movie, and swung a punch.

Carlos was ready for it, but it still hurt, and it was *loud.* He tasted blood in his mouth right away; the crack of bone on bone made his ears ring. He lashed out automatically, just following his fists, and as he was pummeling Joshua anywhere he could reach, he felt someone behind him.

I can't take two of them. Can I? Mom's going to kill me if I come home in a mess again.

But Roland hadn't jumped him, or the other guy, who didn't seem to be joining in anyway. An unfamiliar hand reached out, grabbed Joshua by the collar, and slammed him sideways onto the ground.

It was Marcus.

Roland Curzon pitched in to defend his kid brother, landing a punch on Marcus just above the eye, and Carlos froze for a split second while he decided whether to go for Roland or pin Joshua down. But he'd definitely got Marcus Fenix all wrong.

Marcus came back at Roland with a single punch to the face, aimed like he meant it, like a boxer, and Carlos heard his grunt of effort. Roland staggered back. There was an awful silence for a moment before Roland straightened up, blood running from his nose, eyes glazed with tears, and

Joshua got to his feet. Their buddy was still rooted to the spot. That wasn't how kids here fought. It just . . . *wasn't.* Carlos had never seen anyone punch like that, except grownups.

Marcus looked completely calm, like nothing had happened. But his hand must have hurt.

"Stay away from me," he said quietly, "and stay away from Carlos. Or I'll do it again."

And it was all over, as fast as it started. The Curzons beat a retreat with their useless buddy, and Carlos was left staring at Marcus, scared by the way he'd just *punched.* He didn't look strong enough to hit anyone like that.

Marcus examined his hand, then felt gingerly above his eye. "Is there a mark?" he asked. "I don't want Dad to start worrying again."

"Nothing yet," Carlos said, wanting to tell him he was really impressed but not sure how he'd react. "Tell him it was thrashball." Why would his dad be worried *again*? Ah, maybe Marcus had been kicked out of school for fighting, and that was why he was taught at home. "Why aren't you at the military academy? Your dad could buy the place."

"He wants me to mix with *people.*"

"What, common people, like me and Dom?"

"I didn't mean it like that. I'm just on my own a lot."

"You would be, in that big house. Did he teach you to punch?" It seemed an obvious question. Carlos's dad had taught him how to look after himself, how to form a fist that wouldn't get his fingers broken, how to stay out of trouble unless he had no choice. "I mean, that was *hard.*"

"No, he didn't." Marcus sounded forlorn. "Anyway, thanks."

"Hey, you did okay. You backed me up. That's what real friends do."

Marcus had stood up for someone who stood up for him, which Carlos felt was the best thing anyone could do. He wasn't afraid of getting hurt. And he didn't think he was special, or that Carlos was beneath him. Carlos hoped Marcus understood he could rely on him, too. Maybe he'd have to tell him that. Marcus came from a different world, and it wasn't going to be easy to work out what he thought about anything.

Marcus just blinked a few times, as if the word "friend" didn't make any sense. "Who's Dom?" he asked at last.

"Dominic, my kid brother. He's eight. But he's okay."

"Must be nice to have a brother."

Carlos felt instantly sorry for him. "Hey, you can borrow him when you're fed up."

"Thanks."

Maybe Marcus would have forgotten all about it by the morning, or by next week when he'd settled in more.

Marcus didn't forget, though. He seemed more at ease when he came into class the next day. He had a big bruise over his eye, and he was still quiet, but he acted as if he had a right to be there and didn't have to apologize for being different.

The Curzons heeded the warning and left both of them alone. Nobody ever needed reminding not to mess with Santiago and Fenix again.

THREE YEARS LATER: CARLOS SANTIAGO'S HOUSE.

"I swear that boy grows every time I look away." Eva Santiago set the table, pausing a couple of times to look out the window onto the yard. "I can't believe he's the same kid."

Dom was torn between helping his mother get lunch on the table and hanging out with his dad, Carlos, and Marcus while they dismantled an old engine. Yeah, Marcus had changed a lot in the three years since he'd started hanging out with Carlos. He wasn't skinny anymore, he didn't talk the same way, and there were times when he even laughed. He was actually bigger than Carlos now, as tall as Major Fuller. He was thirteen, but to Dom he seemed like a grown-up already.

"He likes your cooking," Dom said. "You're the best cook in the world."

His mother ruffled his hair. "What are his folks like?"

Dom shrugged. Visits to the Fenix Estate—he always thought of it in grand capital letters—weren't like going to a friend's house, and Marcus's parents weren't *folks*. The place was enormous, full of expensive antique stuff, but it felt like nobody lived there. Carlos made Dom promise not to knock anything over every time they visited. That wasn't often.

"They're nice," Dom said. "But I don't think they know much about Marcus."

"What makes you say that, sweetheart?"

"They don't treat him like you treat us."

Mom put on her I'm-trying-not-to-worry-you expression. "Are they mean to him?"

"No. They just seem like they're trying to work out who he is, and he's *different* when he's at home. His voice changes. You know, all posh."

She started to smile, but it was one of those sad ones Dom didn't quite understand. "You're very smart about people, Dom. I think Marcus gets lonely, and I'm proud of you and Carlos for being there for him."

Dom lined up the knives and forks, then stood back to admire his handiwork before getting the nod from Mom to go out in the yard. He wasn't just keen to join in the tinkering on the engine; he was curious about new neighbors who'd moved in two doors away, and whose daughter climbed the trees in their yard faster than anyone he knew. He thought her name was Maria, but he hadn't plucked up the courage to talk to her yet. He was working on it.

He kept looking up toward the tree, but there was no sign of her today. Eventually, Mom called everyone in to clean up and eat. She really was a *great* cook. Marcus always had second helpings and even thirds, probably because it was nothing like the food he had at home, and treated it all like a rare delicacy he'd never taste again. Mom seemed delighted that he cleared his plate without fail. Dad was impressed by his capacity for hot sauce.

"You can eat *anything* with hot sauce," Dad said, ladling more rice onto Marcus's plate. "When I was a Gear, we always made sure we had some in our rations, because food sometimes wasn't so good, you know? Good dose of hot sauce—problem solved."

Mom laughed. "Ed, you don't need to *solve* my food, do you?"

"Course not, honey. I just love hot sauce."

"Would you reenlist, Mister Santiago?" Marcus asked. "You sound like you miss the service."

"Yeah, I would. Best times, best friends I ever had. Taught me a trade, too. But I've got a good job, and I'm not a kid anymore, so . . ."

There was a magic in the army. Dom saw how it lit up his father's face every time. He told great stories about the things his squad got up to, and even when he recalled friends who got killed, and his eyes brimmed, it still sounded like he wouldn't have missed a second of it. It was a world of its own. It all sounded so vivid, like the only place you could be truly alive, even if you didn't know if you'd get killed the next day.

"You've done your service." Mom didn't approve. It was written all over her face. "You don't have to apologize for leaving. The country's got to keep going, and keeping transport running is as important as fighting."

Dad smiled but didn't look as if he believed that. "You ever thought about the military, Marcus?" Dad asked.

Marcus paused. "I have, sir."

Carlos cut in as if he didn't want Marcus to continue. "Well, I'm going to enlist as soon as I'm eighteen. Sixteen, even."

"You're not dropping out of school early," Mom said firmly. "You're staying on until you're eighteen. You might get drafted anyway if the war gets worse."

"I don't *need* to be drafted." Carlos was talking about it all as if would happen tomorrow. But it was five years away; that was forever. Dom couldn't imagine what five years in the future would even look like. "I *want* to do it."

Marcus didn't say anything, but however hard it usually was to work out what he was feeling, it looked pretty clear from the short-lived frown as he busied himself with his fork. Dom didn't feel that he could join in this conversation. It was going on over his head, suddenly very grownup and worrying, but one thing was clear: Carlos would join the army, and Dom would be alone.

So would Marcus.

That was the look on his face. He had to go to college because his father wanted him to be an engineer, a *scientist* kind of engineer, not a mechanic like Eduardo Santiago.

He and Carlos would be split up, and Dom could see that the realization upset him. The two of them were inseparable. That was the word his mother used: inseparable.

No. We're like brothers. It's worse than that.

"You don't have to think about any of that for a long time," Dad said. "You're still boys. Enjoy being kids while you can."

Changing the subject lifted the mood a little, but now Dom began to see the war not as something that went on in the background without touching his life, but as a real threat to everything that made him happy. He'd be just sixteen when Carlos signed up, and Mom had made it clear that she wanted them to finish school. The idea ate at him for the rest of the day.

After lunch, they went back into the yard to reassemble the engine. Dom tried to stop thinking about the war and the army, but not even wondering when Maria was going to show up could put it out of his mind.

It took something pretty bad to do that.

Mom came out to the back door, looking wide-eyed as if something had shocked her.

"Marcus," she called. "Marcus, sweetheart, come here, will you? Your father needs to talk to you. It's important."

Marcus froze. His parents never called here, so this was serious. Was he in trouble over something? No, Marcus never put a foot wrong. He laid down his tools and went into the house to take the call, and Carlos went to follow him, but Mom put her hand on his arm to stop him.

"Be there for him later," she said quietly. "He's going to be upset. I'll stay with him until his father collects him."

She beckoned to Dad and they went into the house.

"What is it?" Dom asked.

"I don't know." Carlos walked up to the back door but didn't go beyond the step. He tried to listen, then shook his head. "I can't hear anything. It must be really bad, whatever it is."

Marcus didn't come out again. A little while later, Dom heard a vehicle pull up at the front, and then Mom and Dad came back out into the yard.

"It's his mother," Mom said. "She's missing. His father said she didn't come back from work."

"Missing, like kidnapped?" Carlos said. "Murdered?"

Dad shook his head. "People go missing for all kinds of reasons, son. They usually show up again. It's probably going to be okay. But let's be really careful what we say to Marcus. It's going to be hard for him until she comes back."

Dom followed Carlos's lead and said nothing. His first thought wasn't that she'd been kidnapped, but that she was like Mrs. Garcia in the next street, who walked out because she didn't like her husband anymore. She left her kids behind, too. Sometimes mothers did that.

Carlos gave up on the engine and went to his room. Dom gave him five minutes and then followed him.

"When are we going to see Marcus again, then?"

"I'll call him later," Carlos said. He looked scared. "He's got to go to class, too."

"What if she's not just run away, and she's dead?"

"Then we'll take care of him," Carlos said. "That's what friends do. That's what *brothers* do."

Mrs. Fenix didn't show up the next day, or the next week. Marcus, being Marcus, turned up for class after a day's absence, and never said a word about it. Carlos waited patiently for him to say something, and made Dom promise not to ask him before he was ready to talk.

The three of them sat on the steps of the quadrangle after lunch, textbooks open on their knees, silent.

"She isn't coming back," Marcus said suddenly.

"How do you know?" Carlos asked.

"Dad won't tell me where she was supposed to be."

"What does that mean?" said Dom.

Marcus stared at his hands. "You've seen movies. If someone goes missing, you retrace their steps. I wanted to know where she was supposed to be, but Dad wouldn't tell me. Why would he do that? Because he must know where she went, and he thinks I'd be more upset if I knew." It was a long explanation by Marcus's standards. "So maybe she just left. Maybe something upset her."

He didn't have to say he was worried the "something" was him. Dom could see it on his face. Marcus's relationship with his parents wasn't as easygoing as the Santiagos', but Dom still thought it was weird to think it was his own fault if his mom really *had* walked out. Dom was about to say that it was probably his father's fault, like with Mrs. Garcia, but Carlos stopped him before he even opened his mouth.

"I don't think she'd really run away, Marcus," Carlos said. "Are the police looking for her?"

"Dad reported her missing, so they must be."

Mrs. Fenix stayed missing, and by Marcus's fourteenth birthday four months later, they still hadn't found her. Marcus didn't talk about her again. He spent much more time with Dom and Carlos, though, as if he didn't want to go home at all. Mom and Dad let him stay as long as he wanted, every day, but Dom heard them talking sometimes in the kitchen late at night, about what a rotten shame it was that the boy was so hurt that he didn't want to be with his own father.

They didn't seem to talk things through, the Fenix family. But that was okay. Marcus had the Santiagos, and they had plenty enough time and talking for one more brother.

CHAPTER 4

Despite her mother's warnings, and the calls of her friends, Romily left the safe company of her friends and walked deep into the perils of the forest. She thought they would admire her independence, and respect her brave willingness to break ranks with the others. But she did not walk alone. The six-legged demon that had waited patiently beneath her house since her birth followed her, unseen, and joined the rest of his kind who rose from the depths to embrace her.

(ANCIENT TYRAN FAIRY TALE, ON THE POPULAR AND IMPROVING THEME OF MONSTERS LYING IN WAIT FOR DISOBEDIENT CHILDREN.)

WRIGHTMAN HOSPITAL ASSEMBLY AREA, JACINTO, 14 A.E.—TWO DAYS TO DEADLINE.

"I didn't sign up to deliver groceries." Baird ambled down the long line of waiting trucks, pausing occasionally to kick a tire. "I do *grubs.* Killing grubs. Shit, what's up with Hoffman? Is he getting senile, or what?"

"They're our groceries too." Cole goaded him gently. A

couple of King Ravens circled overhead, returning from dropping a team of sappers at the North Gate food facility. "Maybe *you* prefer dogmeat, baby, but I'm ready for some steak."

"Dogs are more useful alive," Bernie said, leaning against the running board of the nearest truck. "I survived on cat for a while, though. Not bad. Makes good gloves and boot liners, too."

Dom wondered how long Baird would hold out against the newly formed Cole 'n' Bernie tag team. Baird was busy pretending he wasn't listening to the ribbing. "Why can't they airlift the stuff?" he said. "This is just asking for it."

"Because we don't have enough spare Ravens," Dom said patiently. *Come on, Marcus, where the hell are you?* "Some of it has to go by road."

There were various ways of coping with Baird. Marcus blanked him out, Cole matched his griping point for point with noisy cheerfulness, and Dom . . .

Dom realized that he handled Baird almost the same way he handled his son, Benedicto. Four-year-olds always asked why, why, *why*. Over the years, Dom had grown used to a level of pain that might have passed for getting over losing his kids, but occasionally there was an unexpected spike of grief that was as searingly raw as the day they died.

Bennie would have been eighteen now, Sylvia seventeen. Dom could have been a grandfather way too young. And Bennie could have been a Gear himself by now.

You've got to stop this. You know where it always ends.

Cole provided a loud distraction right on cue. "So, you got any good cat recipes, Boomer Lady?"

Bernie just winked. "I'm not joking, mate. Tabby boot liners."

"You're shittin' me."

"See for yourself"

Cole squatted down to look as Bernie unclipped the straps at the top of her boots and folded down the fabric. Dom, who had seen some pretty stomach-churning and uncivilized things over the years, found himself staring with horrified fascination. It was tabby fur, all right. Silver tabby.

"Shit, poor little Fluffy!" Cole burst into loud guffaws and slapped his hands on his thighs. "Hey, Damon, you want a pair of these too? Maybe we can get you a nice ginger tom."

Baird just walked up to Bernie and looked down.

"Yeah, real classy," he said. "I'll pass. But you old folk need to keep warm. We don't want you getting hypothermic in the middle of a mission."

Dom waited for Bernie to punch the crap out of Baird, but there was no crunch of bone. She just stood there, half-smiling at him, unblinking; and he was the one who looked away first. It was only a matter of time before he went too far with her. Baird always had to test everyone's limits until something broke or everyone got bored.

"Everyone up to speed with the SOPs?" Bernie asked. "Long time since we did this in training."

"It's a waste of time," Baird said. "It'd take thirty thousand tonnes of food to feed the city for a month. We can't haul anything like that—maybe ten, fifteen per cent. You seriously think that's going to make much difference in the long run?"

"So you can count." Marcus's voice penetrated the rumble of engines. "Joined-up writing can't be far behind."

Marcus appeared from behind a gun truck with Federic Rojas—Jan Rojas's brother. He'd stepped straight into the gap left by his dead brother. Dom wasn't sure what to say, because *I know how you feel* didn't quite cut it. Dom had lost a brother, yes, but Federic had now lost two.

Shit, how bad must things be when a family *is getting wiped out, and I've lost count? Even in the Pendulum Wars, that would have been news, real tragic stuff. Now . . . it's routine.*

But Baird didn't let the rebuke—or the need to acknowledge Rojas—stand in the way of his demolition of the idea. "Leave 'em to it, that's what I say. Fewer mouths to feed. Balances out."

Marcus let out a long, weary breath. "Do you remember *any* of the values of the Octus Canon?"

"Sure he does," Cole said, still admiring Bernie's feline accessories. Dom found himself having an inner debate about why he would happily eat one animal and not another. "They all start with 'Damon's ass comes first.' "

"We're shifting renewables and irreplaceables," Marcus said. "Seed. Poultry. Hydroponics kit. The myco fermenters. *That's* worth saving."

Myco was the staple protein now that livestock farming was almost nonexistent, and Dom actually liked it. It *had* to be better than cat. It also had the massive advantage that it could be grown in factory conditions, because it was a fungus. These days, every secured section of Ephyra was expected to be an urban farm, with citizens ordered to grow whatever they could on windowsills or in backyards; flower beds and parks had been turned into vegetable plots. Dom had heard that one guy kept pigs in his apartment and took them for walks at night. The more the Locust encroached on habitable areas, the harder it got to feed the population.

There were only so many people you could support in a limited space. Dom didn't fancy dealing with food riots again.

"What are we waiting for, anyway?" he asked.

Marcus checked his armor system, activating lights and power packs. "That," he said, nodding vaguely in the direction of the perimeter.

A black speck grew larger against the backdrop of cloud, then resolved into a familiar shape. The last of the returning King Ravens dropped down into the compound, kicking up clouds of dust.

Hoffman jumped out of the crew bay and strode over to the convoy, followed by a Gear with a distinctive haircut. Bernie chuckled.

"Shit, I hope Hoffman's not planning to ride with us," Marcus said.

Dom shrugged. "Hey, he's been a lot less hostile in the last few days."

"He's just getting his second wind."

The Gear with Hoffman was Tai Kaliso, another South Islander. Dom remembered him from Aspho Fields; it was hard to miss that shaved crest of dark hair and swirling tattoos covering half of his face. His armor and Lancer were lavishly decorated, completely against regs, with tribal symbols scratched into the coating. It struck Dom that there were still a lot of Gears left who'd taken part in that operation—including himself—and somehow it seemed a talisman, that Aspho generally forged survivors.

Generally.

Hoffman took out his radio and flicked the transmit button. "Let's see if they've understood their instructions. Drivers? *Drivers!* Listen up." He paused, stalking down the line of vehicles to peer into the first few cabs. "Rule one—stay in radio contact at all times. You won't be able to see what the hell's going on fore or aft, gentlemen, and if the shit hits the fan, then this is where your redirection will come from.

Let me remind you that standard operating procedures are *not* a *suggestion*—you *will* maintain one-hundred-meter intervals, you *will* clear a kill zone as fast as you can, you *will not stop* in a kill zone to rescue anyone, and if you find yourself *trapped* in a kill zone, you *will* use maximum firepower. Now—listen for your call sign, and start your engines."

The convoy drivers were a mix of civvies and Gears who could only handle light duties because of age or injury. Every truck, junker, and pickup had a gun mounted; with the Armadillo APCs, that meant the convoy had a fair amount of firepower. There was even an old ambulance and a hearse, both cannoned up. But this wasn't an open road. It would bring its own problems, Dom knew, but snaking through a city block by block—obstructed visibility, choke points, tight turns that an articulated truck couldn't tackle—was as risky as it got.

Hoffman clipped the radio back on his webbing and headed for the command Armadillo halfway down the convoy. Then he stopped and turned.

"Kaliso, you're with me. Fenix—lead vehicle with Santiago and Rojas. Mataki—rear, with Cole and Baird. Get moving."

So Hoffman was coming after all, and taking the command vehicle. Well, nobody could accuse him of sloping shoulders on dangerous missions. Maybe he was bored; maybe he had something to prove.

And maybe the COG was just so short of men that it had to be done.

"How far have the grubs advanced?" Rojas asked. "I mean, how long have we got?"

Marcus popped the hatch on the lead Armadillo and tapped Jack's housing. The bot, a self-propelling machine like an oversized and heavily armored thrashball, lifted into the air on its jets and extended arms from recessed compartments as if it was waking up and having a good stretch. "Twenty or thirty hours, tops. Jack can do some recon when we get closer."

"It won't take us more than a couple of hours to reach North Gate."

"It's the loading that's going to take the time."

"Is three Armadillos enough for fifty vehicles?"

"Not really."

"Didn't think so." Rojas scrambled inside and settled happily into the gun position. Dom wondered what he would have done for a job in peacetime; even though he'd lost so much in the war, he seemed to have an oddly innocent enthusiasm for fighting, and he didn't appear to have any vengeance or malice in him. Dom wanted to ask him how he dealt with it all, but he was afraid of shattering what might have been a fragile veneer. Every man had the right to cope in his own way. "Dom, you ever done this before?"

Dom slid his back belt pouches around to the front to settle into the driver's seat, and started the engine. "No."

"It's all the same," Marcus said, climbing in beside him. "Get in, get out, don't get in the other guy's way, and shoot it if it moves."

Marcus had a great way of simplifying apparently complex things. Maybe that science education hadn't been wasted after all.

COMMAND VEHICLE, CENTER CONVOY GROUP.

"What's got into *them*?" Hoffman grunted.

There were a lot of Stranded out on the streets, more than he'd seen in years.

Kaliso tightened his grip on the wheel and slowed slightly to glance to the offside of the APC. The road was wide enough here to run alongside the main convoy for a while. “Maybe they’ve discovered acceptance, sir.”

“Acceptance, my ass,” Hoffman said. “Don’t go mystic on me. They’re loitering.”

The convoy was now clear of the defended city and its invisible but very real boundary, and crossing the no-man’s land peppered with Stranded settlements that took their chances with Locust incursions. Settlements—how the hell *could* these people be settled? Hoffman had once been troubled by the idea of humans—countrymen, migrants, whatever—being left unprotected, but only once. They hadn’t been abandoned. They’d abandoned society—abandoned their own species.

For a moment, Hoffman’s eye saw the road surface ahead of him as pale, speckled rubble that had been hammered down again by time and movement. Then he realized that it was actually white marble fragments ground into the darker debris, the remains of a carved frieze that had run the length of the building to his right.

It had been one of the finest archaeological museums in the world. He’d had his first serious dates here, hoping to persuade Nina Kladry that an enlisted grunt could be as high-minded as any officer cadet. *Can’t be what you’re not, shouldn’t even try. Take pride in what you are.* An identifiable chunk of carved panel lying by the curb—a garlanded hand reaching out to him, translucent and white as death—made his scalp tighten. It was the essence of destruction, the last frantic clutch at life before sliding into the abyss.

An elderly man—a rare sight here, because Stranded didn’t live long—raised a ragged, filthy arm to give the Armadillo a gesture. It wasn't exactly one of support for the troops.

"I think we can rule out gratitude." The man was probably Hoffman's own age, but he looked twice that. "Screw you too, citizen."

"You'd think there was some festival going on."

"Maybe they know something we don't."

Stranded were more an annoyance than a threat to the COG at the moment, but Hoffman still factored them into his plans. Reconstruction was going to be beyond hard; shortages would go on not for months or years but *decades*. He knew even now that the army's first task when the Locust were dealt with would be controlling these huge anarchic gangs. It wasn't going to be pretty. He hadn't been scaremongering when he raised the prospect of civil war with Prescott.

"Kaliso, slow right down, will you? I want to talk to them."

Kaliso fumbled for his sidearm one-handed and tucked it under the webbing across his chest. "Be careful, sir."

Hoffman made sure he had his own pistol to hand. It only took one second to find out that Stranded might risk shooting Gears after all. "I have to know."

The Armadillo slowed to a crawl alongside three women—a mother and two daughters by the look of it—and Hoffman opened the nose hatch. Even in the open air, the smell of body odor hit him.

"Ladies," he called, managing to maintain a neutral tone, "what's everybody doing out on the streets?"

The woman stared at him, as far from his hazy memories of Nina Kladry as a female could possibly be.

"Not for throwing roses in your path, you fascist asshole. The Locust are on the run."

"You reckon," Hoffman said. *Yeah, we're the fascist assholes who die fighting them so you don't have to.* "Based on what?"

"You know damn well. You're the ones who did it."

Stranded had their own ways of keeping an eye on Locust activity. Hoffman added this to his list of rumors without taking any hope from it.

"Have a nice, independent, free-thinking day," he said, closing the hatches. "Step on it, Private."

Kaliso was a literal man when it suited him. He slammed the APC through its gears and sent it screaming up the nearside of the convoy, cutting into the gap between the trucks.

"Hoffman to Fenix, Mataki—the Stranded think the Locust have packed their bags." Hoffman kept his forefinger on the transmit key and pondered on his next comment. "Let's not be that optimistic. Hoffman out."

Kaliso kept his eyes fixed on the tail of the truck in front. The jagged crest of hair gave him a look of permanent aggression, which wasn't far from the truth.

"You think they're right?" he asked at last.

"I'll believe it when I see the last grub laid dead at my feet."

"I'll do my best to make that happen, sir."

Yes, he would.

The total sum of humanity now was just a medium-sized city by Sera's former standards, and Hoffman's army was more like a few brigades. He thought back to the Pendulum Wars—huge, continent-spanning, generously resourced by comparison—and almost felt nostalgic.

Wasting eighty years fighting over imulsion supplies, over damn fuel, *when all this was just around the corner.*

Hoffman had been born during war and he expected to die the same way. There was nobody alive today who could remember a Sera at peace.

He took comfort from the thought that he wouldn't have had any idea what to do with peace anyway.

UNSECURED ZONE, FIVE KILOMETERS FROM NORTH GATE; REAR APC.

Bernie braced herself against the coaming of the APC's top hatch, still trying to balance the muzzle of her newly acquired Lancer on something solid. The teeth of the chainsaw made it impossible. After a while, she gave up and took the weight with both hands. The noise of grinding tires and hammering engines concentrated in the canyon-like street was deafening.

The tail of the last truck loomed; she pressed her mike closer to her mouth. "You're getting too close to the truck in front . . ."

"Shit," said the voice in her ear. "Now you're a backseat driver too."

She cut off the mike and dipped down into the cabin so the conversation wouldn't be heard by everyone on the channel. "You need to give him enough room to back up if we hit trouble, dickhead. He can't do a U-turn in an artic. He'd just have to reverse over us."

Baird let the APC fall back a little, and she didn't need to see his face to guess how he felt about that. Marcus tolerated way too much shit from that kid. It had taken her an hour to form that opinion.

"Happy now?" Baird said.

"There's a good boy . . ."

"Yes, Granny."

If Cole had said it, she would have found it funny. But this was Baird, so she didn't. "Son, if I bounced you on my knee, you wouldn't be able to sit down for a week, so *shut* it."

Cole roared with laughter. "You're gonna get spanked, Damon. Play nice, and open the nose hatch . . ."

He lobbed a few ration bars over the side toward a group of skinny, threadbare kids watching from a street corner like a pack of little animals. They pounced on the food. Bernie felt she was watching humanity *de*-evolve.

Maybe that's the worst thing the grubs have done to us. They've turned us back into savages.

Baird sighed irritably. "Cole, what the hell are you *doing*? You need your calories, man. Don't encourage those parasites."

"Aw, c'mon, they're just kids."

"And you know what they grow into."

"You never been hungry, Damon? You grew up rich. You got *no* idea." Cole rustled through his pockets and threw something else out the hatch as if he was making a point. Baird didn't shut it, oddly enough, as if he bowed to Cole's opinion. "And we get shitloads more to eat than they do—they *hate* us for it. Look at us. I mean, just look at how much meat we got on our bones compared to them."

"That's 'cos we have to friggin' *fight.* They could put on armor and get the same."

"Yeah, baby, I'll tell the next eight-year-old that . . ."

Cole's tone was still genial, still patient, but it must have hit a nerve because Baird shut up. Bernie filed that away for future use.

But it was time for her to lance the boil. "Are you pissed off because I kept my stripes, Baird?"

"Well, a geriatric who's been sitting on her ass since before E-Day wouldn't be my first choice."

It just slipped out. "So, you obviously didn't get on with your mother . . . what about your dad? Did you ever find out who he was? Did *she*?"

Great, you've just shown him he's getting to you.

Baird didn't bite this time. She knew why. She'd crossed the line that this war had drawn, which was that jibes about family, however well meant—or not, in this case—were well out of order. *Everyone* had lost family. A new social taboo had taken hold very quickly.

And it was easy to assume that Baird didn't have feelings.

Bernie wasn't planning to apologize—not yet, anyway. And she wasn't his squad sergeant, just along for the ride while she got up to speed again, so there was probably no point wasting time on reaching an understanding with the mouthy little tosser. He was Marcus's problem.

The radio crackled. "Control to Delta, we have updates on Locust activity. Stand by for transmission of new coordinates." It was a woman's voice; Bernie struggled to place it. "Still two kilometers southwest of your planned position."

Hoffman's voice cut into the circuit. "How long does that give us to load, Lieutenant?"

"Whatever you can move in twenty-six hours, sir. The team at the location is prioritizing."

"Understood."

There was a sound of rustling paper. Cole was refolding his map. Bernie tried to recall the voice on the radio, but had to admit defeat.

"Cole, who was that?" she asked.

"Lieutenant Anya Stroud."

"Oh . . . yeah." *Now* she remembered. Little blond scrap of a thing, half the size of her mother in every way. "Major Stroud's kid."

"Is she sweet on Dom?" Baird asked. "Seeing as you knew everyone when they were still in diapers. She always seems extra-friendly with him."

Baird didn't know about Marcus, then. That was just as well. "Everyone's friendly with Dom. The Santiago boys were always nice lads."

"You going to give us a history lesson, then? How our jailbird sergeant got to be a hero?"

Even if she'd wanted to, Bernie had no idea where to start. And history was never as clear cut as it looked, even if you'd been there in person and thought you remembered exactly how things were.

"No," she said. "I'm not."

CHAPTER 5

I rarely see Marcus most days. I just don't know who he is, and it's all my fault. I lied to him about what happened to Elain, and the longer I lie, the harder it is to come clean. Kids know when you're lying. Then their trust withers and dies.

(ADAM FENIX, CONFIDING IN A FRIEND ABOUT HIS FEARS FOR HIS SEVENTEEN-YEAR-OLD SON.)

THE SANTIAGO HOUSE, JACINTO; EIGHTEEN YEARS AGO, FOUR YEARS BEFORE E-DAY.

Dom sat on the edge of the chair, head lowered, elbows resting on his knees, and waited for the explosion.

It never came. If might have been easier if it had.

"You're sixteen," his father said at last. "You're just *sixteen.*"

"Dad, I can't walk away from this." Dom could hear movement outside the living room door; Mom must have been listening. "I have to do the right thing."

Eduardo Santiago squatted down in front of his son to

look him in the eye. "You really want to be married with a kid when you're still a kid yourself?"

"I'm not leaving Maria to go through this on her own," Dom said. For some reason, his next thought was of Marcus. "And I'm not going to have a kid of mine adopted by strangers."

Dom wasn't sure where that speech had sprung from. He had that out-of-body moment where he could hear himself the way his father might, and he sounded like a little boy repeating something he'd once heard a grown man say, without any understanding of the meaning.

But I mean it. I want to marry Maria. I always have. It's just . . . more urgent now.

"Has she told her folks she's pregnant?"

"No." Dom liked Maria's parents, but he'd never had to test their tolerance like this before. "I plan to be with her when she does. *I* should tell them."

Eduardo stared into Dom's face, silent for a moment, and then smiled slowly. "Yeah, that's what I'd expect a man to do."

"I'm scared, Dad."

"I know."

"Are you angry with me?"

"Not *angry.* I would have liked things to be different, but they aren't, so . . . we'll help you as best we can."

"I'm sorry. I let you down."

Dom wasn't sure why he thought his father would be angry, because he never lost his temper; but this was something so serious that the old rules didn't apply. He seemed more sad and sentimental at that moment, the way he looked when he was remembering dead buddies from the army. He put his hands on Dom's shoulders.

"You *never* let me down, son," he said quietly. "I've never been more proud of you than I am now. It's easy to be brave when things are going okay, but the test of a man is how he handles himself when he's in a tight spot."

Dom didn't feel much like a man right then, and the confirmation that he really was in a tight spot—his father never pulled his punches—made his gut tighten like it did when Maria first told him she'd missed a period. He felt like a kid out of his depth, wishing he could turn back time, wishing he'd done things differently. He hadn't. He'd have to live with that.

It's just time. It's just early. *We would have married and had a family anyway. After three or four years, it'll be like it was meant to be.*

"I'll tell Mom," he said at last. "Then I'll go see Maria's folks."

"Want me to come with you?"

"Thanks, but—"

"You can do the talking. I'll just stand behind you."

Eduardo Santiago always knew how to do things right for his kids. Dom longed to have that same deft touch with his own, always there when he was needed, smart enough to know when—and how far—to stand back. A baby on the way was a problem, but Dom's dread was rapidly giving way to a heady contentment with understanding just how much he could count on his family being there for him, even if he was determined not to burden them.

"Her dad's going to go nuts," Dom said.

Knocking on the Flores' door was close to the hardest thing Dom had ever had to do, and it turned out to be Maria's mother who went the craziest.

"I'll give you full marks for guts, Dom," said Maria's father, patting his sobbing wife mechanically on the shoulder. "You'd better marry her, then."

They needed parental consent. Neither Dom nor Maria were old enough to buy a beer, but then there were soldiers fighting on the front line who weren't old enough to do that either.

This was, Dom swore to himself, the last dumb thing he'd do in his life. He'd continue his studies, get a part-time job, and make something of himself for his wife and kid. It wasn't going to be easy. But maybe that was the point; if you got something wrong, you had to sweat a bit more to put it right, or you didn't learn a damn thing.

And Carlos would be best man at the wedding, wearing his COG uniform. Carlos just seemed to get things right every time; Dom was more determined than ever to learn from his example.

THE FENIX ESTATE, JACINTO; FOUR YEARS BEFORE E-DAY.

There was no way of sneaking up to the imposing front entrance of Marcus's home, even without the security cameras. The gravel driveway crunched under Carlos's brand new army boots.

"Is it true you've got to pee on them to soften them up?" Marcus asked.

Carlos looked down. "That's *leather* boots. No, too many metal parts in these. You just break 'em in before they break *you* in."

"Looks like they're winning . . ."

Carlos climbed the steps with some difficulty. He was

still getting used to the thick soles and restricted movement of the knee-high boots. "You'll see. With full armor, they look the business. And they *work*."

Debating the fashion appeal of army boots was just a distraction from the task that lay ahead. It wasn't Carlos who had to perform it, but his gut was churning anyway. Marcus's old man was going to hit the roof.

Carlos found the Fenix mansion more unsettling every time he visited. It wasn't so much a house as a statement. It said that it had always been here, it always would be, and that insects like him were so temporary that it wouldn't even bother to notice him. Its massive columns and intricately carved tympanum told him to wipe his boots before he crossed the threshold, preferably through the tradesmen's entrance around the back.

This was a mausoleum, not a home. The statues in the ornate formal gardens that stretched as far as a city park now seemed more like gravestones. Jacinto's noises—traffic, distant voices, the steady hum of a city—stayed respectfully outside the high, vine-covered perimeter walls.

It felt like all the life had been sucked out of the place. There probably hadn't been much to start with. Carlos just wanted to stay long enough to back up Marcus and then get out.

"You still want to go through with this?" he said.

Marcus stared at the big double doors as if willing them to open. The dark green paint was glass-smooth and layers, years, *generations* deep. It was the portal to an alien world that Carlos glimpsed and never really understood.

"Yeah." Marcus nodded. "More than ever."

It was easy to forget that Marcus was the last and only son of a wealthy dynasty. Carlos didn't like to think of him that way; he was just Marcus, no airs or graces.

Professor Fenix wanted Carlos to call him Adam, like he was everyone's buddy or something, but he would always be a man with a stack of titles and ranks. Carlos could never bring himself to do it.

"Have I pushed you into this?" Carlos asked. "Are you just doing it because I did?"

Marcus shook his head. "I knew this was the right thing to do *years* ago."

When Marcus closed the doors behind them, Jacinto's sounds and smells vanished, and the two of them were instantly in another world. There was no sign of Professor Fenix. How could you have a normal family life in a huge place like this, where you could easily avoid each other? You didn't need to sort out arguments here. You could just run away and hide from them.

"Dad?" Marcus walked around the marbled hall, calling down the corridors that radiated from it. "Dad? Where are you?"

Carlos could hear footsteps approaching. He counted them; twenty-three. It was a long corridor in a silent house. Adam Fenix emerged from a doorway in an open-necked shirt, a small notebook in one hand.

"I wasn't expecting you back yet." He nodded at Carlos. "Good to see you, Carlos. When are you off to basic?"

"Next week, sir."

Marcus interrupted. He didn't slip back into his posh accent this time, as if he'd finally given up fitting into his father's world. "Dad, we have to talk. I've made a decision."

His father almost managed to keep his reaction nailed down, but, like Marcus, rapid blinking gave him away. He probably knew what was coming next. Carlos fought an urge to just leave them to it, but he had to stand by Marcus, even if he had no idea what backing him up meant in a polite, upper-class family argument that was all raised eyebrows and no yelling.

"Is this what we've talked about before, Marcus?"

"Dad, I'm enlisting."

Professor Fenix took his notebook and flexed it back and forth a few times in both hands, staring at it as if waiting for it to break apart. "Well, you can still take an engineering course at the Academy," he said. No, he hadn't understood what Marcus meant at all. "A military-sponsored education is as good as a civilian one. You could go on to LaCroix for your postgraduate—"

"No, Dad. I'm not going to be an officer. No commission. And I'm not going to university." Marcus took a breath. "I said *enlist.* I'm going to be an ordinary Gear."

"Oh, not *that* again, Marcus . . ."

Carlos said nothing. He almost felt guilty standing there in his uniform, as if he had a notice around his neck proclaiming I'M A BAD INFLUENCE. Professor Fenix didn't even glance at him.

"It's done, Dad. I've got my letter to report to the recruiting office."

"It's not *done.* We've got to discuss this. You're throwing away a brilliant career."

"We've discussed it already." Marcus drew himself up to his full height. It always looked threatening, even if he didn't mean to be, simply because he was so big now. "It's okay for you to develop weapons, but not okay for me to fight? Carlos and others can put their lives on the line, but the job's not good enough for your son?"

"I didn't say that, Marcus."

"Dad, I've *got to do this.* I can't sit out the war."

"There's no *got to* about it. Nobody will think any less of you for not fighting."

"*I'll* think less of me. And it's the only thing that's going to make me feel alive."

There was an awful, awkward silence. Eduardo Santiago would have hugged his sons and said whatever they did was okay by him. Professor Fenix didn't seem to know how. His eyes locked on Marcus's for a few moments as if he was expecting him to back down, but then he turned to Carlos.

"Can't *you* talk any sense into him? You're the only person he listens to these days."

Oh boy. "Sir," Carlos said, "all I can tell you is that I'll make sure Marcus comes back in one piece."

Adam Fenix looked as if he was going to make one more attempt to talk Marcus out of it, jaw muscles twitching, but then his shoulders sagged and he began fidgeting with the notebook again. Carlos felt sweat itching on his back but didn't dare move a muscle. He was . . . *embarrassed.* It was awful to have to watch this.

"Okay, I can't stop you," Professor Fenix said. "And if I try, I'll lose you completely, won't I?"

Marcus avoided the question and rolled right past it. "I'm going to give it a hundred percent, Dad. Don't worry about me. Look, I'll be back for dinner tonight, and—"

"Damn, I have to give a talk at the university."

They both looked defeated. "Some other time, then," Marcus said, as if they were just business associates unable to make a meeting. "Got to go, Dad."

Carlos would have preferred a good, honest brawl, with everything out in the open, dealt with and sorted. But people like the Fenix family didn't seem to work the same way. Carlos followed Marcus back down the gravel path and they walked aimlessly in silence until they reached the center of East Barricade and found a pavement café.

"Dom's getting married," Carlos said at last. "I didn't

want to tell you until you got the thing with your dad over and done with. Maria's expecting a baby."

Marcus lost his glacial calm for a moment, just a flash of shock that raised his eyebrows, but that was a big deal for him.

"Wow," he said. "How did your parents take it?"

"Pretty well."

"How's he going to afford it? Is he dropping out of school?"

"Mom made him promise to finish his exams. You know Dom. He'll make it work."

"He needs money. Look, that's one thing I've got plenty of, and I could—"

"He'll be fine. Thanks." Carlos realized that sounded abrupt, but Dom would never accept money from anyone. He tried to soften the brush-off. "Shit, that was ungrateful. Sorry, Marcus. It's just that Dom won't feel he's a man if he can't support his family without help. Hey, maybe if we time it right, we can both attend the wedding in uniform. Classy."

"If that's an invitation, yes. Thanks."

"You don't need any invitation. You're an honorary Santiago. You're family."

Carlos leaned back in his seat and watched the ebb and flow of civilians enjoying the day. The war was a long way from Ephyra, at least geographically; emotionally, though, the conflict was right here, in every home. After more than seventy years of fighting, almost every family had someone who had fought in the war, who was currently serving, or who worked in the defense industry. The reality of war was understood. Nobody could ignore it. Nobody *wanted* to.

If we hadn't discovered imulsion, would we be fighting over other fuels instead? Water? Minerals? Thrashball?

It didn't seem to matter now. Collecting enemies had its own inertia, and the COG had plenty. Carlos didn't worry much about the future because it was simply hard to imagine, but now the future was actually in his own hands along with an assault rifle. It made him feel different. He was still trying to define how.

Marcus looked lost in studying the surface of his coffee. He never said much about his father, but Carlos suspected he'd probably longed for congratulations and support for his decision, knowing all the time that he wouldn't get it. Maybe his whole life had been like that. It explained a lot. He had to jump through hoops to get a pat on the head.

"Tell me straight, Marcus." Carlos nudged his elbow. The spoon resting on his saucer clattered onto the metal tabletop. "Are you doing this just because I enlisted, or to piss off your old man?"

"You need to ask me that?"

"Well, yeah. It's not like you tell me every cough and spit. I have to fill in the gaps."

Marcus's pauses often told Carlos a lot more than what he actually said. He stared into his cup again.

"Because it's the only place I'm going to feel at home, with people who understand me," he said at last.

"Shit, if anyone understands you, maybe they can explain you to *me.*" Carlos managed a laugh. Yeah, Marcus wanted the general camaraderie of army life, but he wanted to be with his buddy, too. Carlos understood that. It was weird to see a guy whose family had everything still looking for something they couldn't buy for him and didn't know how to give. "It's going to be awesome, I know it."

Getting killed, wounded, crippled—Carlos couldn't dwell on that. It wasn't enough of a reason to stay at home.

Besides, anyone who wasn't ready to fight for their country didn't deserve a damn thing from it. The Santiagos didn't freeload.

The rest of that week became an avalanche of irreversible, life-changing decisions. At the recruiting office, Carlos waited for Marcus to come out of the medical examination. He could hear staff talking quietly behind a row of filing cabinets.

"That's definitely Major Fenix's son," a male voice was saying. Here at least, old man Fenix was still seen as an officer, not a scientist. "He could have walked straight into the Academy. A staff college job, even."

"Maybe he wants to be a *real* Gear," said another voice. "Not every guy wants the easiest path through life."

Yeah, they'd got Marcus about right. Maybe he wasn't so inscrutable after all. He seemed incredibly proud to wear the uniform, and Carlos had to admit the pair of them looked pretty damn good at Dom's wedding.

Dom made one glass of wine last for the whole wedding feast, as if he was afraid of what a few more drinks might do to him. It was weird to see him still as nervous as a kid, and yet also a married man with his own youngster on the way. Carlos knew it was the last time he'd see him in that state of limbo between boy and man.

He's still my kid brother. He knows I'll always be here for him.

"I've got to talk it through with Maria," Dom said, nursing the glass in one hand, "but I'm going to get a full-time job. A real job."

"Mom's going to kill you. Still, nothing wrong with being a mechanic—"

"No, I'm going to enlist."

"Shit, Dom . . ."

"It's the pay," Dom said. "It's good money. I've got a family to feed now."

"Sure it is. I believe you." Carlos gave him a ferocious hug and rumpled his fancy suit. He'd known Dom would join up sooner or later, but this soon—well, at least he could look out for him now. "You're all about the money, right?"

At the beginning of Frost, Maria gave birth to a son, Benedicto. By Thaw, Dom had dropped out of school and enlisted. There was the same inevitability about it as the seasons, Carlos decided. Some bonds could never be broken.

The Santiago brothers—by blood or honorary membership—were going to be together for the rest of their lives.

CHAPTER 6

A military life attracts young people for many reasons—duty, comradeship, purpose, the opportunity to test life to the limits, to learn a trade, escape from home, adventure—even patriotism. But for the youngster lacking a stable, caring home, it provides family, *with all the security and meaning that goes with it. They crave the structure, approval, attention, and clear rules that their parents should have given them; and we can supply it.*

(COLONEL GAEL BARRINGTON, HEAD OF RECRUITING.)

GROUNDS OF POMEROY BARRACKS, SOUTH EPHYRA, REGIMENTAL HEADQUARTERS OF THE 26TH ROYAL TYRAN INFANTRY, SEVENTEEN YEARS AGO, THREE YEARS BEFORE E-DAY.

"Stand easy," said the sergeant, stacking mesh cages on the ground. The name tab on her fatigues said MATAKI. "I'm going to teach you how to live off the land. Because you lads are going to have to survive in some pretty hostile places without the catering corps."

Sergeant Mataki was a tall woman in her thirties, built like a sprinter, hair scraped back under her cap, with a hint of an accent that Dom couldn't place. She opened the cage to haul out a live chicken and tucked it under her left arm. It clucked indignantly.

"If any of you are vegetarians," Mataki said, "it's tough shit. We'll do edible roots and fungi tomorrow."

Dom had busted a gut to get into commando training as soon as he turned seventeen, the youngest they'd take him. He'd relished the punishing course; he'd found hard-fighting aggression he'd never known he had. Maria was proud of him. Carlos and Marcus didn't look at him as the kid brother who needed taking care of any longer. He was, as one of the South Islanders put it, *nails,* as in *hard as.*

And now he was brought to a nervous standstill by a small black chicken.

The dozen or so men with him were completely silent as Mataki stroked the chicken's head. It seemed quite relaxed in her grip, which Dom found disturbing. She wasn't one of the usual instructors; the badges on her arm indicated she was a sniper, but everyone said her bushcraft skills were the envy of the commando training unit. Someone said she could make a six-course banquet out of two dead rats and a pile of grass cuttings.

"I'll show you how to trap birds and small animals later," she said. "That's the easy bit. For most of you city boys, *this* is the hard part. Because if you can't do this, your survival chances are shot to hell right away."

Dom *was* a city boy. Poultry came in sealed white plastic trays from the grocery store, already unrecognizable as the free spirit of nature it had once been. Poultry didn't look at him accusingly with pinprick pupils set in vivid orange eyes.

"You're all *very* quiet," Mataki said. "Come on. You're going to be commandos. You can shove a fighting knife in a guy's throat. What's the problem?"

Like she didn't know. She looked like she'd been here a hundred times.

Georg Timiou was standing just in front of Dom, and he could see the guy was edgy by the way his hands were clasped tight behind his back. "The recruitment posters never said anything about strangling chicken, Sarge."

Mataki wasn't remotely like Major Hoffman. She had a sense of humor under that death's head badge somewhere. Dom saw a brief twitch of her lip as she looked down at her boots for a moment.

"We don't *strangle,* Private," she said at last. "We snap the neck quickly and humanely. You've already been trained to do that to a human. Chickens don't usually pull a knife on you."

City boys. Dom saw his baby son's toy animals in his mind's eye and felt deeply uncomfortable. But she was right; they'd all come from the infantry ranks, and they'd all been under fire—and returned fire. Poultry shouldn't have fazed them.

Mataki rearranged the bird head-down. "Right, take both legs in your left hand like *this,* and hold the head between your right index and middle fingers. Other way around if you're left-handed, of course. Then you push down and turn your wrist like so—"

It was the faint *crack* and the flapping that got to Dom.

"Ohhh *shit* . . ." said Timiou.

"Just involuntary reflexes," Mataki said.

She made it all look easy. She plucked the carcass, showering glossy black feathers everywhere, and then drew a hunting knife to prepare it, impressing on the assembled trainee commandos that rupturing the bowel was a *really* bad idea, and that disposing of the feathers helped conceal their presence.

"Make sure you find the liver," she said, displaying the alleged delicacy skewered on the tip of her blade. "Now, your turn. All of you."

They got a chicken each. Dom was mortified.

I can do this. How hard can it be?

"Let's get this right before I hand you back to Hoffman," she said kindly. "I don't want him taking the piss out of any of you. I've never had a trainee fail yet."

It was pretty motivating. Hoffman wouldn't tolerate any squeamishness, and he certainly wouldn't have had the patience to do what Mataki did then; she walked up to Timiou, stood embarrassingly close behind him, and clamped her hands hard over his, right on right, left on left.

"And . . . push," she said.

Crack.

She stepped back. Timiou stared at the bird, dead but still flapping wildly in his hand.

"That's all the force you need to use," she said. "Or else you'll pull its bloody head off."

It got a lot easier after that. Dom still kept checking his dead chicken to make sure he couldn't feel a heartbeat before he started dismantling it. Mataki bent over him.

"It's not first aid, Santiago," she said. "The bloody thing isn't going to respond to CPR. Now pluck it, gut it, and cook it. Because that's the only lunch you're getting today."

Yeah, it was dead.

Dom fried the carefully dissected, bowel-free portions over a campfire in the wooded grounds and made himself eat it, but he didn't like liver. Mataki strolled past, speared it on her knife, and ate it as she walked away. Timiou watched her go as if he didn't quite believe she existed.

"Why was that so hard?" Dom said. "Killing it, I mean."

Timiou gnawed on a thigh. "Because the chicken isn't the enemy and it isn't trying to kill us. It's like having to shoot your pet dog. Always harder to kill something innocent, even for the best of reasons."

It was just a chicken, and Dom reasoned that if you didn't have the balls to kill an animal yourself, you had no right to eat it. But it raised questions he had never considered before, like where the line lay between killing that bothered him and killing that didn't. What was *he* really capable of doing? Commando training had pushed him way beyond what he'd thought were his limits, leaving him with a certainty that he could take absolutely anything, survive anything, tackle any odds. It also made him wonder about the depths he might have to plumb, and whether he'd be able to live with himself if he did.

I'll know the line between right and wrong when I see it. I know I will.

But Dom concentrated on the sense of achievement. With Maria pregnant again, Dom didn't think life could get much better or more perfectly tailored to everything he'd ever wanted, even if he hadn't realized it until now.

He loved being a Gear. He loved it more than he'd ever imagined possible. The very real risk of ending up dead or disabled was simply there in the background, a statistical fact that rarely bothered him.

But he wasn't the only one who'd found his vocation in uniform. Marcus—now Corporal Fenix—had changed. He would never be the life and soul of the party, but he was as happy and at ease with himself as Dom had ever seen him.

He was *born* to be a Gear. In fact, he seemed happier with army life than Carlos.

Carlos and Marcus were deployed again, back in Sarfuth, where winter was setting in. Dom read their usual joint letter—Marcus would write one half, Carlos the other—and Carlos sounded even more frustrated than he had a couple of weeks ago:

This war would have been over a long time ago if the pen pushers at Command listened to the guys on the ground. Some days I think they want me to put in a written request to take a leak.

Marcus had added a comment below in very precise, small handwriting:

He ALWAYS wants to take a leak. It's cold enough here to freeze the balls off Embry's statue.

Marcus was developing a sense of humor. Carlos would have been happier as a commando, Dom decided. The rules were looser. A man could kick over the traces a little. Dom took out his pen, turned over the sheet of paper, and began writing a reply about the art of handling chickens.

SARFUTH, NORTHERN REGION; FORWARD OPERATING BASE, C COMPANY 26 RTI.

There was cold, and then there was *cold*.

Carlos let the APC idle to reach running temperature, scarf pulled up over his nose while he sat in the cab of the vehicle with his hands tucked tight under his armpits. If the temperature dropped much more, the fuel was going to freeze solid in the engine. Shit, anyone who was crazy enough to go sabotaging imulsion pipelines in this climate almost *deserved* to win.

A shadow loomed in the windshield, blotting out the brilliant orange sunset, and then a gloved hand rubbed away at the layer of ice. It was Marcus. And even at minus-freeze-your-ass-off, he still wasn't wearing a helmet. He swung himself into the passenger seat.

Carlos pulled his scarf down a notch to make himself heard. He didn't like helmets either, but at least he had the sense to wear a thermal cap. "You know how much body heat you lose through your head? Are you crazy? You want frostbite?"

Marcus shrugged. "Ten percent," he said. "And maybe. And no."

He just wouldn't wear a helmet unless there was an officer around who'd stick him on a charge for it. Ever since the barber had given him his regulation crew cut on the first day, he'd taken one line of the COG uniform code to heart; a do-rag was acceptable headgear as long as it was plain black, the ties were tucked away, and the cap-badge was pinned centrally. Now he wore one all the time. Somehow it emphasized the hard angles in his face and made him look like a complete and utter bastard. That wasn't necessarily a bad thing, of course.

"I just saw the KIA signals from HQ," Marcus said. The APC's heater roared like a blast furnace, but wasn't making a lot of difference to the temperature. "Captain Harries is on the list."

"Shit. What happened?" Harries had picked up more decorations for gallantry than some regiments. She didn't seem the type to do anything as ordinary as dying. The news knocked Carlos back. "I didn't think *anything* could kill her."

"She led a charge on a gun position. It didn't surrender fast enough for her."

"Wow. Everyone's luck runs out eventually."

"If they push it."

"Her son's in Logistics, isn't he?"

Marcus puffed clouds of vapor. They froze against the windshield. "Yeah. Same age as Dom."

Dom. Carlos thought of him for a moment. Leaving someone alone and grieving when you were supposed to take care of them was pretty crappy. *Like Marcus's mom. Oh, great.* Carlos, long used to these one-sided, guess-what-he's-thinking conversations with Marcus, was again reminded that what his friend didn't say was every bit as meaningful as what he said.

Carlos changed tack. Dead mothers wasn't what Marcus needed to dwell on today. "Well, our luck's holding out just fine. Let's get moving before my bladder freezes solid."

"They're already talking about awarding her the Embry Star," Marcus said, almost under his breath. It was the highest decoration for bravery, awarded only to those who knowingly faced almost certain death to save comrades' lives. It usually ended up being posthumous. "At least she collected the full set of gongs."

"Yeah, you get a free set of wineglasses in the afterlife for that."

Marcus made a small *hah* sound and half-smiled, scraping away the ice forming on the inside of the windshield. Maybe he was hoping his mother had died heroically too, not just run off and left him in an echoing silence with the stranger he called his father. He never said. He simply wrote a dutiful letter home once a month—from what Carlos had glimpsed—with no questions or recriminations, as if nothing much out of the ordinary had ever happened to the Fenix family.

The APC rumbled out past the checkpoint and headed

for the pipeline that ran close to the border with Maranday, a neutral state with a careless way of letting Indie bastards slip in and out to launch attacks. *Porous border my ass. Complicity.* That meant being careful about where you were standing when you shot them. Carlos was getting increasingly pissed off with the niceties of diplomacy.

"They're a day overdue," Marcus said. He cradled his Lancer in his arms as if he was keeping it warm. "Intel's source is slipping. Still no activity in the town."

"Yeah, I'm never convinced their informant isn't just dicking with us."

"Let's check with the snipers." Marcus fiddled with his headset. "Alpha Five to Three-Zero, sitrep please, over."

"Three-Zero receiving." It was Padrick, another South Islander. All the islands seemed to manufacture snipers in bulk, except Padrick was from migrant stock. He was conspicuously redheaded and freckled. It didn't go with his tribal tattoos, but he still had that Islander attitude, so nobody thought it was wise to mention the fact. "I've been watching some tosser digging animal traps along the pipeline for the last hour. He left twenty minutes ago. Check it out for us, will you?"

That could have been exactly what it seemed to be—a huntsman out trapping game attracted by the relative shelter of the overground pipeline—or it might have been something a lot worse.

"What's your position, Pad?"

"Two-Q-J-oh–zero-three–one-three-four-seven-five-five."

Marcus carefully unfolded a map a section at a time, barely moving his elbows from his sides and folding the sheet back on itself to present the relevant part of the grid. His flashlight clicked on. "You up on that hill?"

"No, not enough cover. We're laid up in a snow-hole next to the descending section of the pipe, elevation about thirty-five degrees from the valley floor."

Carlos glanced away from the snow-drifted road for a moment to glance at the map resting on Marcus's rifle. It was getting dark fast. "They can see anything coming up the line."

"Yeah," Padrick's voice crackled in Carlos's ear. "We're waiting for the second shift. Let's hope they get a move on. Baz wants to watch the thrashball final." He paused. "I have visual on you now. The hole's a meter from the connection numbered five-bravo-nine. See it?"

"Got it," said Carlos. The pipeline was numbered along its length so maintenance teams could identify sections. "We'll take a look."

Baz was Padrick's spotter. The sniper teams could dig into a snow-hole up here and almost make it a regular little home away from home, except for a sports channel. But they *needed* to. Laying explosive devices was done by stages here, and it could take days when it wasn't snowing enough to fill the holes. Carlos was fascinated by the efficiency; one scumbag would dig a hole and leave, then another scumbag would come along later and drop off the explosive. A little later, another would wander by and leave the detonators. Finally, a fourth would show up to assemble and prime the device before nipping off to detonate it remotely at his—or her—leisure.

Nobody was left hanging around exposed for half an hour or more, just asking to be spotted. It was random folks just passing by—and there were a couple of hundred miles of pipeline to choose from in the run from the imulsion extraction facility at Denava to the coastal refinery. All the

COG forces could do was rely on tip-offs, tracking skills, and the psychological deterrent of making it very bad news to get caught.

Carlos stopped the APC and cast around looking for the hole. It was about half a meter deep, and there *was* a wire snare at the bottom. It was just about feasible that the guy was genuinely trapping the local rodents, which burrowed through the snow looking for food.

"Pad, it's a snare," he said on the radio. "But that doesn't mean it isn't a prep for a device."

"You're a paranoid after my own heart, mate . . ."

"Let's recon farther down toward the town," Marcus said. He stabbed at the map with a gloved finger. "If there's a follow-up on the way, then maybe the timing's right."

"Keep the channel open," Padrick said. "The last patrol left the radio on transmit, the stupid bastards. If we'd needed them, I couldn't have flashed them."

"Don't worry, you got the grownups on task tonight," Carlos said. "Fenix and Santiago."

"Yeah, the wankers who don't need helmets 'cos they don't have brains to blow out."

"We love you too, Pad . . ."

"Flush 'em out our way."

Carlos killed the headlights and drove parallel with the pipeline at a sedate crawl. Anyone could hear the APC coming, but sometimes Carlos could still surprise the unwary if they were engrossed in a task. By the time they reached the likely entry point from Maranday, it was dark and the pinprick lights of the nearby town were easy to see in the sharp, clear night. It was just two klicks away. The border was a hundred meters on the other side of the pipeline.

Marcus put on his night vision goggles. "Pad's got a point about the thrashball."

"You bet anything on the score?"

"I'm not a betting man. Especially since the Eagles signed that new guy, Cole. Cole Train. Yeah, that's about right."

"He's a *machine.* I'd hate to run into him in a dark alley. He'd rip your head off for a laugh."

Normal life went on, and it kept you sane. Even war could be boring when you weren't fighting and close to shitting yourself. It swung between the extremes. Carlos understood perfectly how some guys needed the adrenal buzz, even when they knew they were shortening their odds of survival, and he thought of Marcus telling his dad that the army was probably the only place he'd ever feel alive. It was true, and it wasn't about cheap thrills; it was about knowing you'd used every cell that life had given you to its limit.

Carlos had felt exactly the same way when he listened to his own father talking about his time as a Gear. Cocooned civilian life never let you find out what you could really do or pushed you hard enough to understand exactly who you were. It was a terrible thought that so many people could die having lived around the half-full level, never knowing more, never trying more. And there was no second chance. This was the only life you ever got.

"Easier on foot." Marcus jumped out and waded into the snow in the shadow of the pipeline. It stood a couple of meters high, supported on concrete trestles at intervals. He pulled the hood of his snow-camo weatherproof over his head. "And this is just to stop you from nagging me . . ."

The area was a big shallow valley, a gentle scoop out of the landscape, and they were looking slightly downhill for what seemed like kilometers. Carlos slipped his NV goggles down from his forehead and looked around. They waited for nearly an hour, walking in small circles or up and down the line of the pipe to keep warm.

Then something made Carlos hold his breath to listen. He put his hand out to get Marcus's attention and gestured; *quiet.*

"Vehicle," Marcus whispered. It was a higher-pitched sound than a car, a smaller motor. There weren't even any roads to speak of, at least other than the track they were on. "Snow-bike of some kind."

That didn't make it suspicious. Lots of locals had snow-bikes. They stood looking in the direction of the sound and Carlos eventually picked out a small wobbling point of light with a darker shape around it. As it got closer, it resolved into a heavily clothed figure on a twin-ski bike. Marcus slipped into the cover of the pipeline and Carlos dropped down onto one knee, shoving his goggles onto his forehead to use the rifle's optics. He tracked the guy as the bike whined past, following the parallel line of the pipe inside the Maranday border.

Could just as easily be a woman, of course.

Marcus radioed Padrick. "Alpha-Five to Three-Zero, possible trade for you. Ski-bike heading your way, parallel with the pipeline."

"Roger that, Alpha-Five."

Carlos started up the APC again, but killed all the lights. "Baz might get to see the game after all."

"Let's not be too hasty." Marcus called in to base to report the possible contact. "Might just be some poor jerk going home after a night in the bar."

The chances were that the noise of the ski-bike's motor

would deafen the rider to distant sounds behind him. And he was wearing a thick hood. Carlos kept it in as high a gear as he could while Marcus leaned out of the cab to follow the rider through his rifle's optics. The upward slope of the valley meant Marcus could see him over the top of the pipeline. The bike hugged that line all the way.

"If Intel is right," Marcus said, "this guy will be the explosives drop."

"We could just stop him, of course. Check what he's carrying."

"Not while he's on the other side of the border."

"Who's going to get out the measuring tape and check?"

"We've got our ROEs. No cross-border stuff."

"He's got to come this side of the line to plant the explosive."

"And *then* we can blow his brains out." Marcus checked his scope again. "Legitimately. Satisfied?"

It sounded stupid to Carlos, but then diplomatic rules usually did. That border jurisdiction shit was for cops, not wars. Eventually Marcus gestured to slow down and dismount.

They ducked down under the pipe and came out on the other side within five hundred meters of Padrick's position. The ski-bike had stopped almost level with the hole dug earlier in the day, and the rider was crouched down, checking through his pannier, still on the Maranday side of the border.

"Three-Zero, can you see anything?" Marcus whispered.

"Negative, Alpha-Five. He's still just a dickhead messing with his bike until he makes a move for that hole."

And then maybe he's really *going to check a snare . . .*

Carlos kept his rifle trained on the man. The night was

silent except for the wind and the faint sounds of the guy handling something in his pannier.

He had to have heard the APC come to a halt. He was far enough ahead when he switched off the bike's motor to notice the noise in the sudden silence. But he carried on rummaging.

Maybe he was a genuine hunter after all.

He had his back to them now, but not to Padrick and Baz.

"Alpha-Five, whatever it is he's taking out, there's a lot of it." Padrick's voice was hard to hear even in Carlos's earpiece. "I've seen the things they hunt—they're tiny. You could stun them with your toothbrush."

"Got him . . ."

"I've got a shot now. Tell me when I'm clear to take it."

It was Marcus's call. Bike Guy was standing upright now, still on the Maranday side of the border, still oblivious to three rifles trained on him, any of which would spoil his entire day. Carlos could understand why it would be a bad idea to leave a harmless Maranday citizen with a COG round in their skull, but he thought it was worth the risk—Maranday was an enemy in all but name, so how much worse could things get, other than pissing off a few diplomats and politicians?

And they didn't count for shit.

"Let's see what he does," Marcus whispered, lowering himself on one arm to prone position and taking aim.

The scope's NV filter gave Carlos a pretty clear view of Bike Guy, but explosives didn't usually have a nice clear label on them. Whatever the man was handling, though, there was a lot of it. It looked like he was removing a stack of books or small sandbags. That was good enough for Carlos. The hard part was always deciding when to slot the bastards.

"It's Pad's shot," Marcus whispered.

"You're a mind reader."

"You're not big on patience."

Bike Guy turned with his arms full and walked toward the pipeline—across that invisible line that made him fair game—while Carlos watched. He heard Padrick inhale a few times before letting out a long, final breath. He was steadying himself to fire.

Any second now.

Bike Guy knelt by the hole, the last time he was ever going to do anything. Carlos had as good a close-up of his face as he was ever going to get. It was almost completely swathed in a ski mask and goggles, so there was no way of making a positive visual ID even if he'd had that level of intelligence detail.

Go on, Pad, take him . . .

Then Bike Guy stopped dead. He looked up, glanced to his left—he couldn't possibly see or hear Padrick from there, so what the hell had spooked him?—then got to his feet. He was still holding some of the objects he'd taken from his pannier.

He headed back toward the bike. It looked casual for a few steps, as if he'd forgotten something, but then he picked up speed.

"Pad, abort, abort, abort," Marcus said, abandoning radio procedure. "Leave him. We're pursuing."

Carlos was off even before Marcus finished the sentence. He put a burst of fire through the bike that chewed up its fuel tank and ripped through the steering, then plunged through the deep snow in pursuit.

You're not going anywhere, asshole, and I can out-run you . . .

He could hear Padrick saying "I've still got a shot, I've still got a shot . . ." Marcus was yelling at him to get back. Bike Guy darted away at a right angle from the bike, heading for the border. Once he was over that, there wasn't much they could do, and Carlos wasn't going to let an Indie sit there laughing at the COG like some kid playing tag.

Maybe Bike Guy thought Gears were too old-fashioned to shoot a saboteur in the back.

Marcus was almost level with Carlos. It was like running in tar, forcing Carlos into a high bounding movement to clear the clinging snow. Bike Guy dropped something but neither of them were going to stop now to check what it was.

"He'll be handy for Intel to play with," Marcus panted. The chase was almost in slow motion. It could have ended instantly with a single shot. "Don't drop him unless we have to."

The guy kept going. If he was armed, Carlos couldn't see a weapon. That didn't mean much. The imaginary line that Carlos had superimposed on the featureless snow was getting closer. He had his rifle, his sidearm, his knife—

"You're over, Carlos, you're over, *you're over.*" Padrick's voice filled his head. He had a better fix on the coordinates from his static position. "Carlos, you're *over the bloody border.*"

"Tough shit," Carlos said, suddenly realizing that Marcus had fallen back. When he glanced over his shoulder for a second, Marcus had taken up a firing position and was aiming. "I can get him—"

The guy wasn't a Gear; he was fit, but he wasn't Gear-fit. Carlos tackled him from behind, more as an accidental and desperate lunge than a calculated move, but he had to stop him.

Like a few more meters was going to make it any worse. Who was going to see this anyway? Who was going to file a complaint?

Bike Guy struggled in Carlos's grip and made the mistake of reaching into his jacket. Carlos had always wondered how he'd react to having to kill someone up this close. But he didn't even have to think about it. All that went through his mind was that it wasn't going to be *him* doing the dying. It was going to be the other bastard. There was no room for any other thought. He plunged his knife into the guy's neck before he even realized he'd drawn it.

COG COMMAND, HOUSE OF THE SOVEREIGNS, EPHYRA.

Hoffman realized something big had shifted in the course of the war when he walked into the basement briefing room at HQ.

He took off his cap and wondered if he'd been given the wrong location. It wasn't unusual to be summoned to briefings with minimal information for security reasons, but this was the first time he'd been given no information at all, and he could see he was seriously out of place and out of rank here.

It wasn't just a gathering of army officers; navy and air corps top brass were waiting in the lobby, too, glittering with seniority. And then there were the suits—the intelligence staff and COG political advisers. It was a small gathering, but in terms of sheer authority, this was a summit.

A bit rich for my blood. Maybe they want me to clean the latrines.

"You too, eh, Victor?" said a voice behind him.

He turned to see a naval officer he'd met a couple of years before. Michael? Mitchell? His first name was Quentin, as far as he could recall, and he hadn't been the full captain he was now.

"Quentin . . ." Hoffman said, extending his hand. He jerked his head in the direction of three admirals. "What are we, then, the hired help? Bag carriers?"

Michaelson. That was it.

"I'm not sure my boss even knows." Michaelson's collar bore the distinctive twin shark emblems of a submariner. "And I don't know why I'm here either. I'm just Captain D Flotilla, so when told to front up, I face aft and salute."

D Flotilla was amphibious assault and special maritime operations. That told Hoffman something, although he wasn't quite sure what; for as long as he could remember, COG doctrine had been built around land warfare—artillery, armor, and infantry. All other assets had been a sideshow. Now two small elements—special forces and amphib—seemed to have front row seats for a big show.

"Okay, so it's spec ops and frogs—any other orphans here besides us?" Hoffman asked.

"Only the orbital technology division, as far as I can see. Odd cocktail."

The big carved doors to the main conference room eased open, and a secretary in a dark blue business suit latched them open. A polished island of tables gleamed beyond in a windowless room.

"Chairman Dalyell will be with you shortly, so please take your seats."

It was the first mention of the Chairman that Hoffman had heard; he'd assumed this was a Chief of Staff's meeting, or a minister's. This raised the stakes enormously. Michaelson followed him in and they looked for their names on the tables.

What the hell am I supposed to contribute to this?

Hoffman had no problem telling the Chairman what he thought of the COG's defense policy or any part of it, as long as the Chairman didn't have a problem with being *told.* But part of him was afraid of being unable to supply answers. All he had with him was his wallet, ID card, pen, and keys. His attaché case—empty except for a pad of paper—had been taken by security, like everyone else's. That was unusual to say the least.

Even the generals looked apprehensive. Hoffman took some comfort from that.

Dalyell was a small, balding man in his fifties who would have passed for an accountant if he hadn't worn such sharp suits. His voice, though, could halt a battalion. He sat down, flanked by two assistants, and gestured at one to shut the doors while the other readied a projector.

"We're soundproofed in here, ladies and gentlemen," Dalyell said, "and soon you'll understand why we *need* to be. This briefing is on an absolutely need-to-know basis. Get the lights, will you, Maynard?"

The display panel flooded with light, and a map filled the frame—the coastal plain of the Ostri Republic, an independent state with a lukewarm alliance with its much bigger and more aggressive neighbor, Pelles. The room fell completely silent—no fidgeting, no coughing—as Dalyell let the location sink in.

Shit. The thought hit Hoffman between the eyes. *We're*

going to invade Pelles via Ostri. About damn time. That'll bring it home to them. RTI special forces inserted to prep the battlefield before the amphib assault. Got it.

He felt better already. He glanced at Michaelson, but the man's eyes were fixed on the map as if he was thinking something else entirely.

"I want you to note a feature on the map," Dalyell said, swiveling his seat to peer at the assembled officers in the gloom. "You're going to be hearing a lot about it, at least within the confines of this room. It's called Aspho Point, and if we don't do something about it, it's going to be the end of the Coalition. Agent Settile, would you like to bring us up to speed?"

Bang.

That was the problem with assumptions. They were short-lived, fragile things. Hoffman's few moments of thinking he'd worked out what was coming had evaporated. Settile walked up to the side of the display and reached in with a battered metal rule to indicate the desolate coast. The key to the map showed the area as a mix of clay wetlands and salt marsh, with pockets of grazing land and woodland; the only features of military interest were a couple of small army bases, a string of gun batteries a long way to the north, and an avionics facility standing on a finger of land jutting into one of the many inlets—Aspho Point.

There were plenty of targets just like this in the Union of Independent Republics. There were much bigger and more strategic ones, too. Settile turned to face the room, squinting against the light from the projector.

"These wetlands around Aspho Point were originally drained for farming a few centuries ago," she said. "They're still called Aspho Fields, but it's so isolated and inhospitable that it's of more use for secure defense installations than crops these days. The research facility at Aspho Point has been developing weapons guidance systems and avionics for the UIR for twenty or thirty years, so no surprises there. But now something's changed. Intelligence shows that routine avionics work has been farmed out a chunk at a time to other places, and Aspho Point has been turned over to a single project. It's now developing a satellite weapons platform—we're giving it the code name *Hammer of Dawn.*"

Well, shit. Hoffman's scalp prickled. *How far ahead of us does* that *put the damn Indies?*

Settile paused for the communal rumble of dismay that rolled around the table. Dalyell gave her a nod and took over.

"If you think *that's* bad news," Dalyell said quietly, "then chew on the fact that they could be ready to deploy it within a year. Our satellite platforms are still sitting in computer modeling systems. *Theory.* So now you know what you're here for. It's not enough to deny this technology to the enemy. We have to *take* it."

That ruled out an air strike. Hoffman glanced at Michaelson again, and this time their eyes met. They both knew what they were there for now. It seemed that a decision had been made long before anyone in uniform was asked for their assessment. COG Intelligence was driving this.

"General Iver," Dalyell said, "before anyone leaves this room today, I want a plan for taking Aspho Point, seizing the technology, and neutralizing the facility, personnel included. And that plan has to be carried out within the next six months. This technology will end the war—for us or for the UIR, but it *will* be the end of it."

Iver didn't miss a beat. "I'll want your priorities spelled out, Chairman. Because, with due respect, stealing a research facility minus the bricks and mortar—which is what you're asking us to do—is a much taller order than putting it out of action."

"You just summed up my priorities in one, General."

Dalyell took his leave of the meeting. Iver got up from his seat and stared down at something he'd scribbled on the notepad in front of him.

"Let's crack on, then, people," he said at last. "This is where we start Operation Leveler. In all the years the Coalition has been fighting, there's never been a more critical mission."

Hoffman had often felt he'd been born into the wrong era and might have been happier in the more rugged and decisive days of Sera's past. But this—*this* was what he'd been born for, even if he didn't yet know how it might turn out, or even what it was. He felt oddly happy.

He knew better than to believe that a single victory could stop decades of fighting in its tracks. War wasn't that clear-cut: politicians weren't that smart. But they could *hasten* the end.

He tried to imagine what a world at peace would be like, and if there would be room or purpose in it for men like him.

CHAPTER 7

I don't know why you're whining. Yes, Gears do *deserve more rations than the rest of us. They're fighting to protect us, all day, every day. It's a hard, heavy job. You want skinny runts defending us from the Locust? We'd all be dead now. Pregnant women get extra rations because they need them too, but the rest of us just* don't*—people live longer on fewer calories anyway, and before E-Day, that was how a lot of Sera lived. Why don't you all shut up and thank God you're still alive?*

(ANGRY JACINTO CITIZEN AT PUBLIC MEETING ON CHANGES TO FOOD RATIONING LAWS.)

SARFUTH, NORTHERN REGION, THE WRONG SIDE OF THE MARANDAY BORDER; SEVENTEEN YEARS AGO, THREE YEARS BEFORE E-DAY.

Marcus dropped down on the snow beside Carlos. "Shit, let's move him. Come on."

It seemed crazy to be worried about such a small detail in a war that had spanned decades and killed so many millions. But wars pivoted on the small stuff, the assassinations, the footnotes. Carlos was on autopilot as he grabbed Bike Guy's ankles while Marcus took his shoulders, but he remembered to pull his NV goggles back into place.

The few meters to the border were harder than running ten klicks. While they heaved the body through the snow, Padrick was scoping across the landscape with his NV filter, keeping an eye out for activity and muttering that he could have dropped the bastard on the *right* side of the border.

At least Carlos had done it *quietly*.

They bundled the body under the pipeline and squatted in the cover of the APC, staring out into the darkness. There was nothing they could do about the ski-bike or the blood, but as far as Carlos was concerned they didn't need to. It wouldn't do the Indies any harm to know they'd get slotted if they tried to sabotage installations in COG territory, and that they weren't even safe across the border.

"I'm going to check whatever he was placing in that hole," Marcus said, without needing to add that if it wasn't explosives then they were in deep shit. "Check the body."

I killed a guy.

It wasn't the first time Carlos had used what the instructors delicately called lethal force, but this was different; it was *personal.* It felt like a bar brawl getting out of hand. His heart was pounding through his chest and he didn't feel the way that he had when he'd returned fire on an enemy position, or launched a mortar. And this wasn't the moment to try to make sense of it. He opened Bike Guy's jacket and felt around in the pockets. If it hadn't been for the wet fabric—blood, not water—it would have been like searching a drunk. He pulled out papers, a key ring, and a small pistol, not that firearms proved anything in this part of the world.

Carlos turned the keys over in his hand. *Shit.* The key ring was a cartoon character of some kind—a bird. Long use had worn and battered it so much it looked like it had been chewed. But when he pushed back his NV goggles and shone his flashlight on it, he could see that the figure had been painstakingly repainted at least once.

Whatever it was, it meant something to this guy.

Carlos switched off the light and replaced his goggles before pushing back the guy's hood. Clean-shaven, maybe in his thirties. He put his thumbs under the edge of the snow goggles and forced them up.

Carlos was caught off-guard by the effect in his night-vision. Bike Guy's eyes were staring up at him, just bright disks. He'd seen it a thousand times on night patrol in living faces, but for a fraction of a second it froze him to the spot. He turned the head to one side to avoid the gaze. But the face was still a face; and he didn't look foreign, alien, different. He looked pretty much like anyone Carlos would have passed on the street at home.

"Shit, why can't you look *enemy*?" he muttered. "Why don't you make it a bit easier?"

Bike Guy's documents didn't tell him anything except that he had a fishing permit and an identity card, both of which matched.

Marcus crunched back and stood over him.

"So," he said, dropping a couple of objects in the snow next to Carlos. They looked like packets of sugar. "Good call."

Carlos picked up a pack and squeezed it, but the faint smell told him all he needed to know. It was a massive relief. Explosives—military grade. He hadn't killed a hapless civvie out trapping animals.

"Well, his blowing-shit-up days are over," Carlos said,

trying to sound like he knew all along. He knew just how close he'd come to causing the sort of incident that easily snowballed into something much bigger. "We're shifting the body, right?"

"Can't leave it here." Marcus was pissed off at him. It was a subtle thing, but Carlos was used to reading all the near-invisible signs; the way he finished the sentence on a falling note, the way he stood with his weight equally on both feet. "Come on. Let's get on with it."

Carlos could hear noises in his earpiece, the sound of Padrick puffing as he ran. He'd left his channel open. The two snipers were coming down the hillside, darting from outcrop to outcrop. They always assumed they were being observed. By the time Carlos had helped Marcus heave the body into the back of the APC, Baz was standing there waiting to mount up.

"Well, nothing else to hang around for," he said. He was a square-built guy in his forties, with a strong north Tyran accent. Carlos got the impression he never gave a second thought to the targets he dropped with Padrick. "I'm freezing. The novelty wore off about two days ago."

Padrick appeared behind him. "Shit, you're not taking your work home with you, are you? Leave the bastard."

"It's not a combat situation," Marcus said. "There'll be some regulation to cover this."

They returned to the FOB in silence, Marcus driving. Yes, there *was* a procedure for dealing with dead guys like that, as well as signing over the recovered explosives. The intelligence officer attached to the base moved in to take over. He seemed especially pleased with the ID papers, for reasons he didn't share with them.

"Hey, the pipeline's still intact," Padrick said as he walked into the barracks block. "Cheer up, Santiago."

Carlos cleaned out the back of the APC and went back out on patrol, this time with Marcus driving. They found more holes dug around the pipeline a few klicks south; but their edges were weathered and irregular, as if they'd been abandoned. They might even have been dug by animals. There were no more snares, just lots of tiny pawprints. It hadn't snowed in days.

Marcus switched on the civilian radio on the dashboard, one hand pressed against his ear so he could still monitor voice traffic on his headset. "Want to listen to the game?"

Carlos nodded. They listened at low volume, and it sounded like the Eagles were winning. "Are Islanders interested in thrashball?"

"Some of them. The Islands aren't all one country, whatever we think." Marcus, jaw muscle twitching, seemed to be shaping up to say something. "Okay, I take the corporal thing too seriously."

"What?"

"You were right. If you'd listened to me, we'd have lost him. Too much focus on SOPs."

It was a Marcus-style apology. But he didn't have to say sorry. Orders and procedures were there for a good reason, and Marcus was the one responsible if the thing had gone wrong.

Carlos felt guilty. "I still crossed into a neutral country and killed one of their citizens, even if his ID *was* fake and he was loaded with explosives."

"Yeah, well . . . it's not always in the manual."

"If I'd run out of luck like Harries, I could have dragged Maranday into the war for real." Carlos thought about it for a moment, not really hearing the thrashball drama that was unfolding on the radio. He didn't feel as good as he should have. He felt he'd let Marcus down by doing something dumb and rash. "Y'know, Dom would be so much better at this. He really loves the covert stuff. I'm built for basic soldiering. Give me a rifle and let me assault a target."

Marcus might have smiled, or it could simply have been a grimace. "We'll be okay when the weather warms up and the fighting season starts."

Yeah, Marcus took his corporal's stripe very seriously, and seemed to think it made him personally responsible for the safety of every last Gear in the COG. He was going to be pure obsessive hell when he made sergeant.

But he was nineteen. They *both* were. Carlos thought of the guys their age who hadn't enlisted, and what they considered to be a hard time or a difficult decision, and realized they didn't have a clue. He felt better about himself; but he also realized he lived in another world.

Who wouldn't want to serve, though? How can they live with themselves?

Slotting Bike Guy was just a single incident in a long conflict, nothing special. The imulsion was still flowing; one more bad guy was out of circulation.

But there'll be another Bike Guy along soon. And another. And another. It's like taking your hand out of a bucket of water. There's nothing to show you ever did a damn thing.

"I really want to make a difference," Carlos said.

Marcus stared ahead. The APC bounced over rockier ground as the Eagles scored again and tinny cheering filled the cab. "How do we ever know which thing we do is really the one that changes history?" Marcus asked.

"I'll know," Carlos said. "I'll feel it."

They lapsed into silence and listened to the rest of the game. That guy Cole was like an avalanche, flattening everything in his path. Carlos wondered how much he was getting paid for this game. Did he ever wonder what it was like to be nineteen and freezing, with a dead guy's blood on your uniform, the most important, things on your mind being a hot meal and calling your kid brother?

Maybe he did. But Carlos doubted it.

DOM SANTIAGO'S APARTMENT, LOWER JACINTO.

Dom turned the key in the lock and waited in the hallway to listen for activity.

Two in the morning wasn't the best time to wake Maria, but he'd caught the first train he could get from camp, without thinking too much about the time he'd reach Jacinto. He placed his kitbag on the floor and found something soft and squashy; it was a toy, Benedicto's fluffy dog, its ears chewed to rags.

That meant his son could get to sleep without it. It also meant he was growing up fast.

Dom switched on the lights and got halfway up the hall before he heard the bedroom door creak open. Maria stepped out into his path, clutching her bathrobe around her bump.

She put her finger to her lips. "I thought he'd never go to sleep. Why didn't you call to say you were coming?"

"I just jumped on the first train. Miss me?"

"Dumb question . . ."

"I've got fifteen days' leave."

"You sure?"

"Yeah." Dom hadn't queried it. He'd learned fast not to make too many plans in the army. "Maybe they gave us a few extra days for being good boys."

"Is that your way of telling me something?"

Dom had been busting a gut to tell her. He wanted to just *show* her, to take his combat jacket out of his grip and reveal the commando insignia now sewn onto the shoulder, but that was too slow for a dramatic flourish. He simply reached into his coat and presented her with his fighting knife, hilt forward. Maria just stared at it.

"You passed."

"Yeah, I passed," he said. "I don't know how I kept my mouth shut this long."

She took it in two fingers as if she didn't want to get fingerprints on it. "You never *said.*"

"I wanted to surprise you."

"It's real?" She handed it back. "I mean, you *use* it?"

"Yeah."

There were still moments when Dom felt he was a kid, wildly unsure of himself; yet here he was with a commando knife in his hand, and frontline combat experience, and a pregnant wife, and a baby sleeping in the next room. He wasn't even eighteen yet.

Sometimes, just sometimes, it all scared the living shit out of him.

"I'm really proud of you," Maria said. "But does this mean you won't be serving with Carlos and Marcus now?"

"Not necessarily." Dom opened the nursery door—a grand name for the box room he'd decorated—and leaned against the frame to watch Benedicto sleeping. "It just means I've got the skills there to call on if the battalion needs them. It's not like I'm in a permanent special forces unit."

Dom missed his brother—and Marcus—more than he'd ever thought possible. But he couldn't trail around after them any longer; his reason was asleep in the cot. Once Dom had really understood the fact that he was a father, that he was now solely responsible for three other people whose needs wouldn't end for years, he found himself preoccupied by very different things. Part of him felt as if he'd abandoned his brother. Maybe that was what growing up actually felt like.

"You want some coffee?" Maria asked. "Have you eaten?"

"I'm fine."

"Then we ought to get some sleep." She slipped past Dom to check on Benedicto. "I'm all wiped out."

"I thought your mom was giving you a hand."

Maria went back into the bedroom. "I'm happier doing it myself. You know how it is."

Maria liked to do things her way. He couldn't blame her, because he wouldn't accept any help, either. But babies were a lot of work, especially when you were expecting another one, and she didn't hang out with the other army wives. She needed support when Dom wasn't there.

He lay awake for most of what remained of the night trying to work out tactful ways to have his folks keep an eye on her. It was hard to offer to babysit for a woman who didn't want to go out anywhere.

Well, he had fifteen days to try to coax Maria into a different way of doing things. She was an only child, like Marcus. They didn't always come to terms with having a bigger family around.

Fifteen days, of course, would vanish fast. Dom found himself caught up in routine stuff like fixing shelves and buying stuff for the new baby. Carlos and Marcus got a two-day pass. When the round of errands and visits was done, there was nowhere near enough time with Maria, proper husband-and-wife time.

But they'd been inseparable since they were kids. Time wasn't really an issue. It wasn't as if he was still getting to know her. And he had no intention of getting killed, so the time they had ahead of them stretched into unimaginable infinity.

The Pendulum Wars had reached some kind of equilibrium, however bad the individual battles were, and everyone got on with life as best they could. Human beings could adjust to any damn situation, Dom decided.

With four days' leave left, Dom sat in his parents' yard with Benedicto on his knee, and wondered if he'd see out his time as a Gear, a thirty-year man. The army had never been demobilized in living memory.

"Has Marcus been to see his dad?" Maria asked.

"I think so."

"Sad, isn't it? Just the two of them, and such a gulf between them."

"He'll be fine," Dom said. "He's a survivor. And he's got us."

The tree where Dom had first seen Maria climbing the branches almost seven years before was in full leaf, casting shadows on the Santiago's yard. Dom shut his eyes, reflecting on just how heavy babies could be when you carried them around for a while. He almost dozed off. He was sure he was still awake.

But he wasn't. His father's voice jerked him out of a dream that he forgot as soon as he opened his eyes, and Benedicto wailed. Dom sat bolt upright, heart pounding.

"Sorry, son." His father leaned over him and picked up Benedicto. "Call for you. It's the adjutant."

Shit.

Dom knew what he was going to hear even before he picked up the phone from the hall table.

"Private Santiago?"

"*Dominic* Santiago. It's me you want, Sarge, yes? Not Carlos?"

The adj didn't say. "You're recalled to RHQ immediately. Report by twelve hundred tomorrow. Sorry about cutting the leave short, but there you go."

"It's okay, Sarge. I know you can't tell me why on the phone, but—"

"I don't even know. All I know is that all the commando-qualified personnel have been ordered back to base."

Dom didn't even remember if he said "Okay" or not. He walked back into the yard, trying to work out if he was elated, terrified, or triumphant, or if he should call Carlos first or break the news to Maria. It could only be a mission. The thought that he could roll right out of training and into a live op was . . . frightening.

But that's what he'd done before; a sixteen-year-old infantry soldier, straight out of basic and into the front line. It was how things were done. He had faith in his training, and in himself.

"I knew it was too good to be true," Maria said, but she managed to smile. She was getting used to being a Gear's wife. "Let me know if you're going to be back in time for the birth."

If I can. Made it back for Benedicto, didn't I?

"I called Carlos earlier," his father said. "The whole Twenty-sixth seems to be moving. Not just you."

Dom told himself that there must have been hundreds of recalls like this in the past, maybe even thousands, but nothing much had changed the course of the war. He had no reason to think his task—whatever it was—would be different. He just believed that it would.

He had to pack now. He *hated* packing.

26 RTI SPECIAL TACTICS GROUP, RHQ, EPHYRA.

Hoffman now knew the internal layout of Aspho Point better than he knew his own house.

He spent more time immersed in it, so it was hardly surprising. If he'd ever struck lucky with Nina Kladry, she'd have left him by now for neglecting her, so once again he was reminded that it was never meant to be, and that he had his just desserts in his wife Margaret.

No, dear, I won't be home tonight.

Sorry. It's work again.

The saddest thing was that she didn't suspect him of having an affair, and she was absolutely right. She knew how thoroughly the military had devoured him. Hoffman paced around the briefing room table, inspecting the sole focus of his existence at doll's house size.

The Aspho Point building had evolved from map to ground-plan to a cutaway scale model, painstakingly constructed and detailed. The intelligence folk added little details all the time; Hoffman wondered if they actually *enjoyed* it. He caught himself staring at the tiny models representing troops, his arms folded on the table, chin resting on his right forearm, and found it oddly funny.

A cup of coffee appeared beside his elbow. Agent Louise Settile, jangling with security passes strung from her belt like battle trophies, slurped her cup in a remarkably unladylike way. He hadn't actually heard her come in.

"When you find yourself going 'Pew! Pew!' and making aircraft noises, Major, you'll know it's time to get some sleep." She was young and not especially pretty, but she was damn good at her job, so she passed muster as a goddess as far as he was concerned. "Aren't you going to need more men for this?"

"Not *inside,*" Hoffman said. "Pour in too many, and they end up log-jamming each other. It's securing the exterior that's critical. Buy time, delay discovery, secure the exfil route." He straightened up and reached for the coffee. "It would really help if we didn't have to extract any guys in white coats, though."

"You really do have a problem with *alive,* don't you?"

"Are the scientists that important? I know I keep asking, but it's one more complication for us."

"We're trying to get a parallel technical team up to speed here, or as close as we can. We've got big gaps in our knowledge. We don't know how the UIR is handling global positioning—targeting—and we don't know the detail of the launch vehicle, the fuel system in particular. Our best shot on paper can't develop enough thrust to achieve the optimum orbit, and we haven't worked out acceptable accuracy for hitting targets."

Hoffman wasn't sure if that was a yes or a no, but Chairman Dalyell was clear: he wanted the key personnel in one piece.

"You're assuming they'll cooperate with you," Hoffman said.

"There's a chance." Settile took a folder out of her briefcase. "But if they're mashed to slurry, then they won't have the opportunity of seeing sense. Anyway, here's the latest aerial reconnaissance images. Nothing much has changed."

Hoffman took the folder and laid out the images on a free space on the table. There were coils of wire strung along the high water line, but they seemed to have been partly covered by material swept up the beach since the last recon run. It was a ferociously stormy coast.

"Given the value of this target, they don't seem to be maintaining adequate beach defenses."

Settile raised an eyebrow. "If I didn't know you better, I'd say you think we intelligence folk are a bunch of incompetents."

"I would never offer that opinion to a lady," Hoffman said. "But you do have more than your fair share of useless assholes."

"Aspho Point *is* what we say it is."

"We'll take it anyway," he said, "because those are my orders."

"You're such a free thinker . . ."

"It's my lack of *free thinking* that ensures there's still a civilian government running the show, ma'am."

Settile looked at him as if she was dismantling the sentence for hidden meaning. But she didn't take the bait. "It'll still be pretty bad weather in Ostri when you insert. They won't expect a raid of that kind until their summer, if they expect it at all."

Hoffman was only responsible for the assault on the facility itself. Landing the troops to secure the wider area, naval gunfire support if needed—that was someone else's job. By noon, he had to have a better plan on paper for General Iver.

"Captain Michaelson's going to be here in a couple of hours." Hoffman got up and walked over to the chart table to look again at the landing area. It all looked so straightforward; a deserted coast, no cliffs to worry about, and a long way from any serious reinforcements. "What made you look here, anyway?"

Settile laid the aerial images on the chart, trying to line them up with the features. "Production of gyroscopic components suddenly starting up in factories where we'd never seen it before. It's taken four years for us to get this far. I wish it were a matter of quiet industrial espionage, just copying their data and plans and getting out. But it's not enough to be first with this capability. We have to be the *only* power with it."

"I understand."

"You're going in personally, aren't you?"

"Of course."

"You feel left out?"

"No, I feel I've got twenty-five years' experience, and there are boys of seventeen I'll be asking to get themselves killed, so it seems kind of *lacking* not to be there with them."

Hoffman rarely let any comment get to him, but these spooks were good at sowing seeds of doubt. It was their job. They probably didn't even know they were doing it, not even the likeable ones like Settile.

Am I going to be a liability? Am I really doing it because I can't face watching this from an ops room?

There was nothing worse than a commander who didn't know when to stand back, to delegate. Hoffman didn't think he'd reached that sorry state. It was about faith; about having it in others, and letting them have it in you.

"Who was it who said there was nothing like the occasional dead general for improving troop morale?" Settile asked.

"I'm a major," Hoffman said.

"So you are," said Settile.

CHAPTER 8

Maybe I don't want no COG protection. Maybe I'm worried that you assholes gonna make me give up too much to get it. And if we ever get back to normal, I ain't sure I'm even gonna like your kind of normal.

(FRANKLIN TSOKO, ONE OF THE STRANDED, DECLINING ANOTHER INVITATION FROM DOM TO JOIN THE COG FOLD.)

NORTH GATE AGRICULTURAL DEPOT, PRESENT DAY, 14 A.E.

It was the chickens that started bringing back the past to Dom.

As the Armadillo rumbled through the security gates into the compound, he could smell them, but he couldn't see them. Cage-farmed poultry smelled of sour, ammonia-saturated shit, an unfamiliar smell to his urban nostrils, but he knew exactly what it was.

A sapper jogged up to the APC as Dom dismounted for instructions.

"Follow the marshals, chainsaw boy," he snapped. He looked older than Hoffman. His name tab read *PARRY L.*, and he was a staff sergeant, a man not to be messed with. "Keep the loading area clear. The trucks need room to maneuver. Park up your 'Dills by the gates." Parry executed a piercing whistle, thumb and forefinger clamped between his lips. A bunch of men and women in scruffy COG fatigues appeared out of nowhere. "Okay, people, fast as you can."

This was the COG's engineering corps, soldiers that Dom rarely saw, let alone spoke to. They didn't look like they got three square meals a day, and he was suddenly conscious of how thin and frayed they were compared to Gears like him. There was, as Hoffman put it, a hierarchy of need even within the army; frontline first, support second. Dom wondered if they were as resentful of the combat Gears as the Stranded were.

He jumped back into the driver's seat and reversed the APC against the perimeter fence, nose out for a quick exit. Marcus jumped down and stood surveying the compound. It reminded Dom of the flight deck of a carrier; the sappers had a plan, and however chaotic it looked to him, it was tried and tested. The area gradually filled with a motley assortment of vehicles, all directed to an exact position and made to re-park if they didn't get it just right.

He could see why now. The forklifts could barely squeeze into the gaps. Where there weren't forklifts shifting palleted crates, there were human chains manhandling boxes and sacks. He got out and climbed onto the hood of the APC with Rojas to get a better view.

"Shit, that's *choreographed,*" Rojas said. "Awesome." A massive crane swung polished steel vats onto the flatbed of a sixteen-wheeler. "I never see these guys. How the hell did they pack all that stuff in a couple of days?"

A sapper walked past the APC. "By not sleeping," he

said. "How the fuck do you think the city keeps running when the grubs trash the water mains?"

Yeah, they were resentful. It was a shitty job, invisible and unsung. Dom watched Marcus walk a few paces with the sapper, saying something Dom couldn't hear, and took something from his belt pack to hand to him. Dom could have predicted what he'd do. There was a glint of wrapping. Ration bars weren't just informal currency; they were communication, apology, encouragement, comradeship, sympathy—and even guilt.

"Do they want a hand?" Dom called. "Eight guys here with good pairs of shoulders on them. I'm counting Bernie in that." She could hear him on the link, of course. "No offense, Sergeant."

"No, they say they're okay. The truck crews can take up the slack." Marcus ambled back and motioned Dom to get off the hood so he could release Jack. The bot lifted clear of its housing and hovered patiently, testing its extending arms and waiting for instructions. Marcus pressed his earpiece. "Delta to Control, we're secured at North Gate. How are we doing for time?"

"Delta, the last reported Locust incursion was an hour ago. Also receiving reports of subsidence two klicks east of you."

"I'm deploying Jack for a recon. Handing over control to you, Lieutenant."

"Thank you, Marcus . . ."

Dom didn't say a word, and Rojas didn't seem to notice the slip into familiarity. Dom caught Marcus's eye just as Hoffman's APC pulled up and backed up next to them.

"Too much water under the bridge, buddy," Marcus murmured. "It's kinder that way."

For her, or for you? Dom didn't ask. Hoffman stalked over to Marcus and watched Jack turn in midair to vanish over the perimeter fence. The last section of vehicles rolled through the gates, with the third APC bringing up the rear.

"The grubs are moving at ten to fifteen meters an hour," Hoffman said. "That gives us a lot longer than estimated. But they're devious bastards, so we'll plan for the worst. They can rip up ground a lot faster than that."

Baird walked into the conversation. "Maybe they're tunneling deeper."

"You got a theory, Corporal?"

"Yeah, Colonel. I have. We're making a lot of assumptions about what they're doing. Just because they're moving this way doesn't mean this is the objective. That's us thinking like humans, not like grubs."

Dom sometimes needed a reminder of why Baird was worth the daily food ration of three nice, normal people. He was actually an asset. He could fight hard, and he was an exceptional mechanic, but he also knew plenty about Locust. Cole claimed it was because he'd dated one once. However he managed it, Baird *had* been right about the grubs as often as the scientists. He was still alive to prove it.

Hoffman looked him in the eye for a long, silent moment. Baird pulled his goggles down again and stared back.

"Even more reason to get out of here fast, then," Hoffman said, and walked off in the direction of Parry, who was standing on the tailgate of a truck checking off a clipboard. "Staff, you got a minute?"

Delta Squad's normal working day was usually an uncomplicated one that left almost no time for thinking. Dom was either waiting to see what might kill him around the next corner, killing something around the next corner, eating as much as he could stuff down his throat before the next enemy contact, or falling asleep from exhaustion so overwhelming that he seldom woke up without someone shaking him or an alarm screaming in his ear. He wasn't sure what to do with this idle moment. Spare time, whenever he could steal it, was spent looking for Maria, walking the rubble-strewn streets, talking to Stranded in the hope they might have seen her.

Ten years. Fuck, ten years. What does she even look like now?

But he would *not* give up.

Bernie Mataki had surfaced again *fourteen* years after E-Day. Dom found himself adding that margin and giving himself the hope of extra time to find Maria, because *that* was how long people could survive. *Fourteen years. Four to go.*

But Bernie's a survival specialist.

Maria was younger. She was in her home city. She might have—

Shit, he'd done this bargaining with himself too many times before. He found he was staring down at his rifle as it hung on its sling, rubbing his fingertips along the points of the chainsaw. Bernie put her hand on his wrist.

"You can borrow my nail file, Dom."

Sometimes it helped to be interrupted. "Hey, I remembered. You and the damn chicken."

"I was wondering how long it would take you." Bernie laughed. "Who was that lad with you, the one I had to help? Georg something or other."

"Timiou," Dom said. "He was killed a year after Carlos."

She shook her head sadly. "I don't know why that still crimps my guts. Chances are that most Gears I trained or served with are dead now. I just don't like letting it become routine. If I can shrug it off, it's like pissing on their graves."

Dom caught a glimpse of Marcus, Rojas, and Cole heaving crates into a small armored truck, probably feeling bored and guilty. They looked like another species of human alongside everyone else. Baird watched the spectacle, leaning against a fence. Kaliso was watching Baird as if he was going to stroll across and deliver one of his weird philosophical pronouncements on life, death, and Locust guts. That couple of seconds told Dom all he needed to know about his squad.

But there was plenty he still didn't know about Bernie. "How hard was it surviving on the road all that time? Or do I get the prize for the most dumb-ass question of the year?"

"Hard," she said. "Even for me. Even for a Gear."

"In what way, exactly?"

"Not knowing who else was out there. Not having comms. Realizing how fast humans turn into shit-houses and rapists and vermin when there's nobody around to kick some civilization back into them." Bernie flexed her right hand a few times, as if testing it. "But on the plus side, I ate a lot of interesting wildlife."

"You know why I'm asking."

"Your wife, yes?"

"Yeah." He swallowed hard. "She got really bad depression after our kids died. I mean *bad.* Weeks without speaking, eating. And then when I got back one day, she wasn't there anymore."

The look on Bernie's face said it all for a fraction of a second, but she swallowed it like a pro and exuded solid confidence. Sergeants were universally good at making you feel you could do anything. Even Marcus could do that, even if he didn't do it with cheery reassurance.

"Okay, I'll help you look for her," she said. It was that simple. "You'll find her."

Even after ten harrowing years, that lifted Dom's spirits like nothing else. "Thanks," he said. "Carlos really rated you. He was never wrong about people. Promise me you'll tell me those stories about him."

Bernie nodded. "Yeah, course I will."

She didn't seem inclined to tell any right then. Lost for anything else to say, they helped out loading a truck. It was like cross-loading ammo; the sappers made sure every truck had a mix of supplies.

"In case we lose some vehicles," one of the corporals explained. "That way, some of everything gets through."

Even Hoffman was getting stuck in, shifting sacks of grain. Cole nudged Dom as he passed. Colonels didn't do that stuff.

"Shit, can't ever accuse that guy of sitting on his ass or being too grand to sweat a bit . . ."

But he left Marcus to die. His *orders. Leave him in the prison, don't evacuate him.*

Dom was still waiting for Marcus to mention that.

It was all going fine until Anya Stroud's voice suddenly boomed in his earpiece and made him jump.

"Control to Delta. I've got visual coming in from Jack—there are drones on the surface, heading in your direction. I have a Raven inbound to intercept."

Hoffman cut in. "Divert it here, Lieutenant. Pick us up and we'll engage them."

"Yes, Colonel. Five to six minutes. Stand by."

Hoffman seemed to come alive, like he suddenly remembered who he'd been at Aspho Point. It took years off him. "Rojas—you stay with the APCs. We'll need those mobile. The rest of you—with me."

His tone was almost kindly—by Hoffman standards, anyway. Dom's immediate thought was that he just didn't want an inexperienced kid with him, but then another thought crossed his mind. Maybe he thought the Rojas family had already lost enough sons.

Shit, I'm still *finding I don't know anybody like I thought.*

The man could be scrupulously *fair.* And that made his attitude to Marcus all the harder to fathom.

KING RAVEN A-108, TWO KILOMETERS EAST OF NORTH GATE.

"Colonel," said the crew chief, leaning on the door gun, "we *can* put you right on the ground. All part of the service."

Hoffman checked his rifle. "No need to expose yourself to unnecessary fire, Barber. Just stand by to extract us."

Hoffman didn't get to use a Lancer half as often as he needed to. He knew that the Gears were staring at him, probably thinking he was a sad old bastard trying to prove that he could still hack it like the younger guys.

Maybe only Mataki actually understood what it was all about. A similar compulsion had brought her halfway across Sera. When you knew there was more life behind you than ahead of you—not the possibility of death in combat, but the imminent certainty of final decay, no deal to be struck with fate—things looked different.

"Sir, are you sure about this?" The pilot, Sorotki, joined in. He obviously didn't want a dead colonel on his watch. "Really?"

"What's the matter, worried that humankind finally evolved something crazier than a Raven jockey?"

Sorotki twisted in his seat as far as he could. The cabin was solid with Gears, a tight fit for seven men, even if one of them was a woman. Hoffman could just about see the crown of Sorotki's helmet.

"That's not biologically possible, sir," Sorotki said, and dipped the Raven sharply below the roofline.

He followed what had once been the line of the main road south to the coast, skimming the stumps of office blocks, and dropped to five meters to fly between the buildings for a while. It wasn't always easy to spot Locust from the air; Control was relying on Jack to recon the area and transmit back coordinates, but even that wasn't foolproof. The small bot could only cover so much ground. If it got too close, it was as much at risk as flesh and blood of attracting a stream of fire, and it was impossible to replace the machines now. Hoffman could remember a time when those flying buckets of bolts came by the crateload. COG technology was now sliding backward in time.

"Colonel, you think we've seen the turning point?" Barber asked. "The Stranded seem to think so. They're like rats. They sense stuff long before we can. And we're not seeing grubs in anything like the numbers we're used to."

Hoffman longed to say something hopeful for a change, but couldn't. "I've been asked that a lot in the last few days. And my answer's still the same. *I don't know.* I thought the Pendulum Wars would be over when we got the Hammer of Dawn technology, but it went on for another couple of years and another God knows how many casualties."

"Thirty thousand," Kaliso said quietly. He had his Lancer resting stock-down on the deck, muzzle held two-handed, like an honor guard at a funeral. "Thirty thousand, five hundred, and ten."

Nobody asked him why he could quote that number so easily, but Hoffman felt he should have known it too. He glanced around the crew cabin, wondering again what the hell was going on in Fenix's head. It wasn't just that the man didn't say much. It was his eyes. They were unsettling, even predatory, but not *angry*. That was what baffled Hoffman.

He was still expecting a knife in the ribs.

If I'd spent four years in that shit-hole of a prison, and some bastard had left me locked there with hot and cold running grubs for company, I'd be looking to insert something sharp. Damn right I would.

The court martial in the House of Sovereigns had spent days hearing how and why Fenix had abandoned his post to help his father. Hoffman had sat through it all; Fenix, a damn war hero, decorated with the highest honors, ignoring his orders and ultimately costing lives. Hoffman *still* didn't have an explanation. Reasons given were not the *why* he was looking for.

Fenix just looked away from him, not a trace of emotion visible, and seemed more interested in Kaliso's impressive but nonregulation lip piercings. Cole was studying them thoughtfully as well, with the frank gaze of a kid.

"Does all that metal shit make it hard to get women?" Cole asked at last. "I mean, no lady wants her mouth stapled shut, right?"

Everyone laughed, and Hoffman wished for a moment that he was still part of that camaraderie. It formed instantly. It held armies together a damn sight more effectively than any flag.

"Hey, Tai." Bernie held out her hand, palm open. "Let me borrow those things. I want to pin Baird's gob shut so we can all get some frigging peace . . ."

"Why ain't you got face tattoos, Bernie?" Cole asked.

"Different island." She seemed to be looking at Santiago's right bicep. He had his wife's name tattooed there. Hoffman had never thought of immortalizing Margaret that way, and now he never would. "Different culture."

"You wouldn't be able to read 'em through the wrinkles," Baird sneered.

"And you won't be able to sit down for my boot up your arse, Blondie."

"Contact dead ahead, visual, five hundred meters," Sorotki said. "Group of grubs, maybe ten or more, moving west toward us."

The Locust would know they were coming, too. "Just set us down here and stand off," said Hoffman.

The Raven couldn't land because of the uneven rubble filling the road, but Sorotki held it a meter above the debris so the Gears could jump clear.

"You're crazy doing this," Fenix muttered as he landed with a thud next to Hoffman.

Hoffman rapped his knuckles against his chest with a hollow *thunk*. "I've got plates, Sergeant."

"I'd hate to have to do the paperwork if you didn't make it."

Fenix probably meant exactly that. It wasn't code for caring.

They formed an extended line to walk down the street, picking their way over fallen columns and shattered glass dulled by years of dirt. On a left turn from here, somewhere ahead, there was a military cemetery. Hoffman didn't want to see the state that was in these days, because he didn't need to hate the Locust any more than he already did. It was hard to recognize the area except for a few rusted wrought iron balconies that had once been elegant and covered in flowering plants. Most hung at an angle by a single bar, threatening to fall. Only one still clung grimly to the remaining brickwork.

Hoffman cupped his hand to one ear, the signal to freeze and listen. Rubble rattled and skidded as if being kicked ahead. The grubs couldn't tunnel here. They'd lost the element of surprise. He could still hear the low-level voice traffic in his earpiece.

Yeah, why am *I doing this?*

Because there was no aging gracefully in the new world order. Whatever Prescott said, the definition of what was civilized had shifted. You were useful, or you were dead.

Delta Squad melted into alcoves and dropped behind solid cover. Hoffman knelt on one knee beside Bernie. She kept putting a nervous finger on the chainsaw switch as if she didn't trust it to work. Fenix squatted on the other side of her, as if he didn't want Hoffman muscling in on his team.

"You haven't dropped a grub at close quarters before, have you?" Fenix whispered to her.

"Anything under six hundred meters is CQB for me."

"Trust me, close is more satisfying."

Hoffman thought it was Fenix's equivalent of reassuring banter for a moment, but the set of his jaw said otherwise. This wasn't normal soldiering. This was personal vengeance.

Then the first three grubs came into view.

"Mine," said Fenix.

But there were more than three. There were more than

ten. There was a whole shitload of them, almost on top of the squad now, just meters away. Hoffman counted at least twenty. He sighted up from the cover of a shattered wall.

And it felt *good.* He was scared and his heart was pounding, but he felt *alive* for the first time in ages.

"Let's ruin their day," he growled, and opened fire.

The first five grubs went down like bricks, and then the rest were suddenly, instantly, overwhelmingly in Hoffman's path, hideously distorted gray parodies of faces freeze-framed in the bright light of muzzle flash, seeming silent in the deafening wall of noise. He emptied one clip and dropped back to reload as Baird poured fire from a doorway. Hoffman couldn't see Fenix or Cole when he turned back again, but Kaliso vaulted clear over a pile of rubble, firing as he landed, then brought his chainsaw down in a practiced arc as he cannoned into the Locust drone. Both fell, Kaliso on top, with his chainsaw embedded at an angle across the grub's sternum and its motor screaming. No; it was *him* making the noise, *him* screaming rage into the grub's face as he cut it apart.

Bernie was halfway down the road now, moving from cover to cover, keeping up a solid wall of fire. It couldn't have taken long. Part of Hoffman's brain somehow said *the clips don't last that long, this is only seconds,* but it was like a series of vivid, detailed images, unconnected as pictures in a gallery, light and noise and stench. By then he was aware of running into the melee, aware of rounds rattling like hail on the walls, aware of the fact that he might have been hit but feeling absolutely *nothing.* A grub dropped in front of him with its head gaping open, but he paused to use the bayonet anyway.

Hoffman didn't have conscious control now. This was the familiar possession of primal hormones, still shocking and exhilarating and awful every time. His body said *leave it to me.*

He did.

Suddenly a drone was right in front of him and Fenix was behind it. Fenix just grabbed it around the neck and spun it around with him, using it to shield himself from fire. The impact of the rounds set him back a few steps, but he fired around the dying grub and took out its buddy, too. Cole, face and armor shiny with blood—not his, surely not his own—grabbed Fenix's arm as the dead grub slid to the ground.

"We lost a couple of them," Cole yelled. "I hate leavin' a job half done. Just going to finish the paperwork . . ."

Hoffman came to a halt. It felt as if the road and buildings were moving around him. Baird and Dom jogged around the rubble, kicking over grub bodies and firing bursts occasionally to make sure they were finished.

Baird sounded personally offended. "Die, you bastard," he kept saying. "I want to roster out. Just frigging well *die.*"

Job done.

It was only then that Hoffman glanced down and found his pants leg and boot were wet and peppered with holes. It pissed him off. Not because of the pain—he'd feel it later, back at the base—but because even a colonel had to jump through hoops these days to get new kit issued.

He activated his radio to call the Raven, pausing to try to get this breath. Shit, he needed to be *fitter* than this. But suddenly he couldn't see Bernie.

"Where's Mataki?" he panted. There couldn't be that many places to lose a goddamn Gear in a deserted road like this. "Where the hell is Mataki?"

Bernie could still see the Locust drone ahead. The things could move fast when they felt like it, and this one was a champion sprinter over rubble. She stopped to fire again. But the Lancer stuttered to a halt and stopped spitting spent cases. By the time her hand went to the dump pouch on her pants leg, she knew she was out of ammo.

And so was the grub.

It stopped, looked back, and then came at her, retracing its steps.

"Come and have a go, then, tosser," she yelled. "And see how far you get."

Bernie had never used a chainsaw bayonet in anger. The drone came right at her and she was still buoyed up on a wave of animal aggression and fear.

Me or you, you ugly bastard, and it ain't my time . . .

She hit the power control and the saw buzzed into life. The drone didn't stop. She stepped into its reach, one hand on the Lancer's grip, the other hand guiding the muzzle, and tried to dig the chain down into the grub's chest. It swatted at her with a massive arm and hit her in the mouth. For a second she was stunned to a standstill, but something completely instinctive boiled up from her gut and drove her blindly at the thing. She didn't have a male Gear's weight; she didn't have the height, either. But she was instantly and insanely enraged, and that made up for a lot. She rammed the saw into the easiest spot she could think of, to one side of the neck and down through the collarbone into the chest, sending debris flying.

The damn Locust seemed to keep flailing its arms forever. The debris coming at her was dark, metallic. Then it changed color. The grub's arm dropped to its side. A shockingly strong spurt of blood hit her full in the face, hot and oddly sharp, like a spray of needles; the saw skipped and screamed as if it had hit metal, kicking her back. But she didn't dare stop. She couldn't. She didn't *want* to. She wanted annihilation, destruction, the end to this animal roar that was venting out of her. She couldn't see anything now except the drone's gaping mouth, and then it sank to its knees and hit the ground.

"Bernie!" someone yelled. *Cole,* it was Cole. "*Bernie,* grub on your six!"

She turned, trying to pull the chainsaw out of the Locust, but all she could do was draw her sidearm left-handed to realize she was out of ammo with that, too. Then Cole vaulted from nowhere, like he'd jumped clean over a wall, and opened fire. Blood plumed from the grub's chest as it fell, firing. It was all over.

For the first time, Bernie could hear herself, the *uh-uh-uh* of labored breath.

"Shit," she said. She couldn't think of anything else to do except try to free her bayonet. She still had the Lancer's grip in her right hand. "Shit, what *is* this?"

She spat to clear her mouth. Her chin felt wet. It was only when she holstered her pistol and wiped her free hand over her face that she felt the shards of something hard and sharp.

"Bernie, you're learnin' to *cook,*" Cole said approvingly. "That ain't your blood, by the way."

No, it wasn't. She could smell that. Something pricked her finger like a splinter.

"This is fucking *bone.*"

"Yeah, they do that when you slice 'em . . ." Cole fumbled in his belt for something and pulled out a grubby rag. He went to wipe her face as if he was dealing with a kid's snotty nose, then paused and handed her the cloth. "Be careful you don't get bone in your eye. Ain't fun, believe me. See the doc when we get back."

"Shit, I don't usually get sprayed by my kills." She felt suddenly elated that she'd instinctively got it right. She knew where to place a cut for the quickest kill even in one of these utterly inhuman creatures; down through the big arteries, through the chest cavity, through the thoracic triangle. "I'd forgotten the personal touch . . ."

Bernie rocked the Lancer back and forth with her boot on the creature's chest until the chainsaw came loose with a sudden jerk. She should have realized what a mess it would make. You couldn't put a high speed chainsaw though metal, flesh, and bone and not expect some flying object damage. *Goggles.* Now she understood why most Gears wore goggles.

No bastard told me that. Thanks, Marcus . . .

But the thing that really shocked her was that she wanted to do it *again.* She wanted to carve every last grub on the planet, all of them, right *now.* It shocked her because her job was taking a calm, passionless shot at long distance, nothing personal, just doing the business after a long and patient wait. *One shot, one kill.* This was something entirely different, against an enemy that was much harder to drop than a human. She had trouble slowing her breathing and calming down again.

"Thanks for watching my back, Cole." She patted his massive, sinewy forearm. He was simply the biggest human being she'd ever seen. Maybe that was why he could afford to be such an easygoing lad. For most people, his bulk would have been intimidating, but she simply felt as if she was in the welcome shelter of a huge, amiable oak tree.

With a rifle. "This is seriously hard work, this chainsaw business."

"We got to get some weight on you, lady. You need *mass.* Don't worry 'bout how big your ass gets, you need *mass* to lean into this thing." He demonstrated the optimum position with his Lancer. "I am *personally* goin' to see your diet improves. No more snackin' on cats and rats. Ain't enough calories."

"There's thirty calories in a mouse," Bernie said, adrenaline ebbing at last. She could hear the *chakka-chakka-chakka* of the King Raven heading back, but movement caught her eye and she turned to see Marcus. "What the hell has he got *now*?"

Marcus jogged up to them with some unidentifiable pieces of circuit board half-sheathed in metal casing. There was also a severed Locust hand jammed in it.

"Asshole wouldn't hand it over," Marcus said, holding his Lancer away from his side. It looked like he'd minced steak with it. "I don't even know what it is, but Baird can play with it."

"Is everyone okay?"

"Not if you include grubs. And Hoffman's got a big chunk out of his calf that's going to need fixing."

Bernie listened for some satisfaction in his voice, but there was none. She still couldn't gauge how he really felt about Hoffman now.

The King Raven threw a shadow over them and sent dust and grit whirling as it set down twenty meters away. The squad came running around the corner, except Hoffman, who was limping along with Dom's support and cursing to himself.

Corporal Barber leaned out the door, one hand gripping

a tether and his other arm outstretched to them. Even when she didn't need extracting in a hurry, Bernie always felt that same flood of relief when she saw the crew chief. The Raven's door was an instant portal to safety from a killing, burning, screaming world. It was *home*.

Dom gave Hoffman a leg-up into the Raven. "You old folks," he said to Bernie, grinning. "Always got to prove how damn tough you are."

The flight back to North Gate was that giggling, shaky aftermath of a close brush with oblivion. One nudge could have tipped the mood over into something darker. Dom squeezed into the seat next to Bernie, almost crushed by Cole on the other side.

"Come on, Mataki," Dom said. "Tell me all about my brother."

"I will," she said, dodging the inevitable again. She caught Marcus's eye: he turned his head away, resigned, grim, and the mention of Carlos obviously still hurt somewhere. "I'll tell you anything you need to know. And you need to know that some of it might upset you."

It was her bargain with herself as much as with Marcus. How much did *any* brother need to know?

"I realize that," Dom said.

Bernie doubted it. He had no idea what she had to tell him.

CHAPTER 9

Infantry, armor, artillery—we're all about guns, bigger guns, ships to carry even bigger guns, and aviation to support those guns and the Gears carrying them. We've never moved much beyond the model of the primacy of land forces; we've grown comfortable with the war. The time's coming when we'll need to work smarter, to develop aviation and maritime assets in their own right, and maybe even move onto the turf the intelligence community guards so jealously. We've got to be more flexible to be ready for whatever the future might throw at us. Because the next enemy may not think like us.

(PROFESSOR ADAM FENIX, ADDRESSING DEFENSE PROCUREMENT EXECUTIVES AT A SEMINAR AT LACROIX UNIVERSITY.)

MERRENAT NAVAL BASE TRAINING AREA, NORTHEAST COAST OF TYRUS, TWO YEARS THREE MONTHS BEFORE E-DAY—SIXTEEN YEARS AGO.

Carlos judged the depth of the water *wrong.*

He stepped off the ramp of the landing craft expecting

to sink a few inches, then there was absolutely nothing under his boots, and he fell.

It only took a fraction of a second to lose orientation in the dark.

The water wasn't that deep. He was almost on the beach. He'd seen the drifts of wet pebbles along the shoreline glinting red and green from the landing craft navigation lights.

And still he ended up pitching forward and going under, inhaling shockingly cold seawater, desperately thrashing around with one hand for something solid to push against while he struggled not to drop his rifle. This wasn't like the swimming pool. It was filthy, pitch-black water swirling with weed and mud churned up by ships. His pack was so heavy that he couldn't get up. He was going to die, an experienced Gear dying on a fucking *exercise,* and somehow the shame of that was uppermost in his mind as he started to drown.

"I got you, Carlos, I got you. Okay, *I got you.*"

The voice was distant. Then something caught the rear neck section of his armor and his head lifted clear of the water.

Carlos realized it was four fingers hooked firmly under the rim, lifting him back to life. He inhaled a wheezing, desperate breath that didn't seem to suck in any air at all. Marcus half-dragged, half-lifted him upright. He choked and coughed, legs moving automatically until his feet found solid ground. He managed a few more steps, crunching into shifting shingle.

Gears ran past him, seeming in slow motion as they struggled against the bank of pebbles.

It felt like the worst vomiting Carlos could imagine. He

coughed and retched until he thought his guts were going to burst out through his nose.

"Fenix! *Fenix!* Did I tell you to damn well stop and have a damn picnic? *Did I?*" It was Major Stroud. She had a cut-glass posh accent that sometimes just didn't go with her colorful language. Carlos managed to straighten up, eyes streaming, just as she reached him and shoved him hard in the shoulder. "Santiago, you'd be lying dead on this god-damn beach with *a hundred frigging rounds in you.* Shift it before I put my boot up it."

In daylight, Stroud was a good-looking woman for her age, blessed with a wide smile and that luminous kind of skin that hyper-fit people always had. Now her features were blurred with dark camo and she wasn't pretty at all. She was soaking wet from the waist down and as angry-ugly as any hairy-assed sergeant.

It was shaming. He wasn't some new recruit, and he wasn't her awestruck little daughter, either. He decided he'd rather die than fall behind and look like a complete asshole in front of Marcus. That bothered him more than Stroud yelling about what a dick he was. Marcus kept pace with him up the shingle bank until they reached the laying-up position behind it and dropped prone to check their rifles.

Carlos heard the *click-click* of rifle catches in the darkness and spat saltwater into the muddy sand.

"You okay?" Marcus asked.

"Yeah. Thanks." Carlos reached for his night vision goggles. He tested his earpiece, surprised that it still worked. "Shit, it was only waist-deep. Knee-deep, even."

"Hey, it's the first time we've done this at night. You probably hit a hole or a rock or something. We'll all be fine on the day."

"Okay, move out," Stroud yelled.

Fine on the day. What day? Carlos got to his feet and sprinted for the next cover and the next, following a zigzag course across short tufted grass to a knot of small trees beyond. He was on solid ground now, the kind of terrain he understood. *What day?* They'd been told nothing except that it was an amphibious insertion, and that they would have to take and hold an area for an unspecified period.

What day?

Whatever it was, Dom was involved too. Carlos hadn't seen him since he was recalled from leave, and his calls and letters were completely devoid of any clue about what he was doing. That wasn't like Dom at all. It didn't take a rocket scientist to work out that this was something big, even if the numbers involved didn't appear to be significant.

But would we know? No. We just know what we're doing, our small chunk of the op. We won't know where we fit in with the bigger picture until the last minute.

He hated that. Okay, there was always need-to-know, but a bigger picture always helped focus him better. Didn't they trust Gears by now?

Carlos moved through the trees and into open ground, expecting enemy contact. It came in a sudden flurry of dummy pyrotechnics and smoke bombs that re-created a minefield. Carlos was still coughing up water, or at least he felt he was. Marcus slowed to whack him hard between the shoulder blades a few times.

"Okay, fall out and see the medic," he said. "You don't sound too good."

"I was only under water for *seconds.*"

"You damn well do it, or I'm not having you in this squad."

"Marcus, I only inhaled some frigging seawater."

"Secondary drowning. Read the safety manual. I'm not taking you home in a body bag."

"Yes, Mom."

"I mean it. Fall out." Marcus had his serious I'm-your-corporal voice on. He called for a medic on the radio. "You must have got a lungful."

"Yeah. I didn't exactly lose a leg."

Stroud came on the radio. "Santiago, you heard the man. *Now.*"

Carlos was furious. The medic actually came and got him, which was even worse, but at least they let him walk off under his own steam. He knew he should have been grateful that Marcus had saved him, but all he felt right then was humiliated and useless. He kept turning to see the flash-grenades and smoke bombs as the exercise developed into a full-scale firefight in the wooded area beyond the shore.

In the medical tent, he submitted to the doctor's examination with bad grace.

"This is frigging dumb," he said. "*Sir.*"

"Yeah, you really should have had your ass shot off," the lieutenant muttered, percussing his back. "Go try again, and don't come back until you're properly maimed."

"I didn't stop for shrapnel in my face on a real op, so—"

"Heard it all before. Shut up while I'm listening to your lungs."

Carlos got the full lecture about deaths within twenty seconds of immersion, secondary drowning after aspiration of fifteen ccs of water, and a whole raft of shit that was probably supposed to make him feel better about himself and less angry at Marcus.

"If you're not dead in four hours," the lieutenant said

briskly, "you're in the clear. Stay on that gurney and call for aid if you get any chest pain or shortness of breath."

Carlos found it funny that he was almost casevacked for falling in a meter of water, but that the COG was fine with him having live rounds part his hair. He spent two miserable hours—*two,* he counted—staring at the roof of the tent and listening to the distant battle.

By the time it was over, the sun was coming up, and the medic relented and pronounced Carlos not dead so that he could get to the RV point for the washup. It was a hundred meters from the dockyard accommodation blocks; Carlos caught a seductive whiff of breakfasts frying behind the wire fence. Marcus wandered over to him, rubbing his nose on the back of his hand, eyes bloodshot with smoke and lack of sleep.

"It's just an exercise," he said, shoulders braced as if he was expecting an argument.

"I could have carried on. You know I could."

"Yeah. I just didn't think it was worth the risk of losing you for the real op."

That was pragmatic, and true. But Carlos knew Marcus was like one of those Islander poems that sounded as if they meant one thing but could be read another way entirely; Carlos's close call had shaken him. Marcus never worried about his own ass. He only worried about what happened to Carlos and Dom. And it worked both ways.

There was a shitload of meaning in the word *friend.*

"Yeah, you need a Santiago there, or it's not a real battle," Carlos said.

The fragrant navy breakfast continued to tantalize at a distance, unreachable and forbidden. The Gears weren't allowed to hang out with the fish-heads; they gathered in the cover of the woods and dug self-heating rations out of their packs. Whatever they were training for, it was obviously not for discussion even with other services. Carlos rejoined the company, feeling like a fraud.

Mataki squatted down, heels flat, and shook her ration pouch to mix the contents.

"What you got, Sarge?" Kaliso asked.

"Chili dysentery," she said. "You?"

"I think it's curried diarrhea."

"Swap?"

The two Islanders exchanged rations. Marcus didn't even look at the label on his and tucked in. Carlos wondered what old man Fenix would think of his boy now, eating shit rations with a bunch of grunts, talking like he'd come from the dog-rough end of town and not from serious money, and visibly, utterly *content.* Marcus was one of life's doers. Just because he was smart didn't mean he would have enjoyed spending his life in a laboratory. Carlos understood that from the first time he'd seen him throw a punch. That memory still surfaced occasionally, and it reminded him that there was a desperate fighter inside Marcus that didn't do anything by halves.

"You'd think they could put the bloody ramps down on the dry bit," Mataki said, poking her fork into the foil pouch. "I just *hate* water. Water should come out of a shower or a glass. Rivers—fine. Bigger than rivers—sod that for a lark."

Carlos took it as a bit of sympathy. "I thought you came from the islands."

"Exactly," she said. "The dry bits. Not the wet bits. I'd rather parachute in, thanks."

The washup was conducted where they sat, huddled

among the trees while an icy rain bordering on sleet started to fall. Stroud had brought her daughter with her, presumably to toughen her up after all that fancy accelerated training at the Academy. There was another young cadet trailing her too, but Carlos didn't know who he was. Not family, that was for sure. Stroud gave no indication that Anya Stroud was her kid from the way she treated her; not hostile or gruff, just . . . distant and professional. It reminded Carlos of the way Marcus's dad behaved.

But Stroud was no cold fish like the Professor. She filled any room she entered, and it was impossible *not* to want to charge after her into a melee with complete confidence. She oozed *winner.*

Her daughter only oozed competence. Carlos felt sorry for her, a scale model of her mother, paler and smaller, but that was what happened to seedlings that grew in the shadow of a much bigger tree. She didn't even seem to know she was beautiful. That was how far her mother towered over her. Other good-looking women always seemed to have that I'm-nature's-gift-to-men kind of confidence, but not Anya.

"I've always said we should take amphibious ops more seriously," Stroud boomed. Carlos was sure some of the guys were holding their breath. "It's never been part of COG doctrine. Sera's a world of contiguous landmasses, so it's always been all about moving Gears over land and using maritime elements for aviation and gunfire support. Well, that oversight is finally going to work in our favor. The Indies won't be expecting us to insert from the coast."

Coast. Well, that was obvious. They'd been training to deploy in landing craft, and there was plenty of coast on Sera. It didn't tell Carlos anything he didn't know already.

"Ma'am." Marcus raised his hand. He'd switched back to his old voice, posh Marcus, son of a dynasty. "Are we allowed to ask operational questions?"

"No, but you'll ask anyway, Fenix."

"What's the objective beyond establishing a beachhead? Is this an invasion?"

"You don't need to know that," she said quietly. "And I'm not sure now if I'd even have an answer."

The posh-Marcus voice seemed to get more results. Maybe it said to Stroud that she was talking to one of her own class, someone who knew which fork to use at the regimental dinner. But Carlos still knew shit about the operation.

No, he knew *less*.

They transferred back to camp by bus. Apart from the brief forays onto landing craft—how to board the things, how to debark, how not to drown yourself—the Gears' contact with the navy had been kept to a minimum. The brass definitely didn't want to draw attention to special maritime training.

There were, of course, UIR intelligence agents operating everywhere, or at least the COG told them to assume there were. *Walls have ears.* It made sense. Everything the COG said usually did. Carlos could hear Stroud holding court at the front of the bus; no fancy staff car home for her, no sir. She was lecturing her two visibly terrified cadets on the virtue of getting out of CIC and seeing what the Gear on the ground had to endure before daring to deploy men. Ah, so that was the point of all this. It was meet-the-noble-Gear time for the kids in despatch.

"She's a psycho," Marcus whispered.

Carlos caught Anya's eye for a moment as her fix on her

mother's face wavered, and it said *I am not worthy.* But her gaze came to rest on Marcus for the time it was allowed to escape, and not on Carlos. He felt crushed and guilty at the same time.

Well, shit. What did I expect? What would she see in me?

"We *need* a psycho," Carlos said, comforting himself with the thought that an impossible date with Anya Stroud would only mean savage scrutiny from her mother, and fraternizing would end a couple of careers. She was a prize for the likes of Marcus, not him. "A psycho who wins."

He had to call Dom as soon as he got the chance. Maria was due soon. She was going to be mad if Dom was away for the birth, or at least she said she was, so Carlos read that as being scared instead. She was seventeen with a second child on the way. Dom was eighteen in a few weeks. That sounded scary enough to Carlos when he added the fact that Dom was now—much as he despised the phrase—on a secret mission.

But the Santiagos were lucky. Nothing would happen to Dom. And if it did—

No. Carlos wasn't even going to *think* it.

BRIEFING ROOM, HOUSE OF THE SOVEREIGNS, EPHYRA.

"I hear good things about your boy, Professor." Hoffman held out his hand to Adam Fenix. He didn't look much like his son except for those mad-dog eyes. *That* was what they reminded him of; it hit Hoffman at last. It was those black-and-white guard dogs with the manic blue eyes, all ferocious intelligence but likely to take your balls off if you turned your back on them. "Natural-born Gear."

Fenix shook his hand with an impressively strong grip. "Thank you. Marcus makes a success of anything he turns his mind to."

Most fathers said they were proud, every time, always that—*proud.* But Fenix seemed to measure his words with a micrometer. *You wanted your boy to be an officer, didn't you?*

Hoffman nodded politely. "Yes, he does. You know the Santiago brothers, too, don't you? Dominic's in one of my squads. Smart, gutsy boy. Steady under fire."

"They've been very close to Marcus since they were children."

So Professor Fenix was a man who restated known facts in lieu of a conversation. Okay, he was steeped in secrecy as part of his job. So was Hoffman. But if Hoffman had had a son, he'd have said something about him straight from the gut, he knew. Maybe Fenix saved it for Stroud. She was the one with his son's life at her personal disposal.

"I assume your son isn't aware you're working on the Hammer project," Hoffman said.

"Of course not. It's on a need-to-know basis."

That was the point at which Hoffman decided he didn't like Adam Fenix. It never took him long to make up his mind. Agent Settile slipped into the meeting room with a folder under her arm and began pinning sheets from it on the display board on the wall.

The number of people in these meetings had dropped drastically. Now it was down to Settile, General Iver, Hoffman, Michaelson, and the recent addition of Fenix. Whatever went on in other meetings connected to Op Leveler, Hoffman had no idea; this was purely about Aspho Point itself—the job the raiding party had to do.

I just hope some bastard has a good overview.

General Iver walked in and indicated the aerial photographs on the wall, now building up into a bigger picture of the eastern Ostri coastal plain and taking in a couple of towns.

"Change of plan," he said. "Look."

The satellite images still showed a largely uninhabited area dotted with the remains of long-abandoned farmhouses and three military targets—Aspho Point itself and two UIR army camps, both about the size that suggested single company strength, nothing more. But there were also clusters of dots scattered along the roads—army vehicles—at the entrance to the largest channel forming the estuary.

"Want me to interpret this for you in a timeline context?" Settile asked. "We've monitored activity at intervals over the last couple of years, and this level isn't normal. Basically, they're reinforcing north of Aspho Point, and the two most likely reasons they'd do that is that they're stepping up operations there, so they have something even more significant to defend . . . or they know we're coming."

There was a long pause. Hoffman could only see months of intense preparation vanishing. Michaelson got up and wandered across to the board to examine the images more closely.

"How the hell would *that* leak?" Hoffman said. "The whole op has been compartmentalized. We've isolated the training as far as we can without making it totally damn useless. We've shaved the numbers of personnel involved to the bone. We've not procured special equipment. This op is as closed as it's possible to make it."

Iver shrugged. "It's possible the Indies have finally realized how vulnerable the facility might be, and they're close to making Hammer operational. The line between advertising that you have a high-value target and protecting it adequately is a fine one."

The most direct route to Aspho Point was heading south along the coast, past the port of Berephus and into the estuary. A steep shelf offshore meant the water was deep enough to drop two small raiding craft close in, with minimal exposure. The other routes meant shallow water and a longer infiltration, time during which the raiding party would be very exposed.

"So how are we going to play this now?" Michaelson asked. "We can't reassure them that we haven't noticed Aspho so they can relax, can we? So we adapt. We've still got to prevent their using that technology, at the very least. But seizing it now might be a tall order. What exactly are we trying to lay hands on? Data, hardware, scientists?"

Settile sifted through another pile of papers and handed a sheaf to Fenix. "That's the latest technical assessment we have. Apologies for the gaps. It's being gleaned from phone taps, and that's patchy at best."

Fenix was the only man in the room—and possibly the only man in the COG—who stood a chance of understanding whatever was on that paper. Hoffman still felt uncomfortable and would have preferred to see it. He watched Fenix reading, mad-dog eyes darting from side to side as he scanned each paragraph, and Hoffman wondered how the man would reach a judgment on what needed doing.

Fenix would have to put it in plain language that a troop of commandos could understand and interpret. They needed to know exactly what they were looking for. They weren't scientists. They'd have just their common sense to guide them, in a big hurry and under fire.

"Make it *achievable,* Professor," Hoffman said. "If we guess at this, we might as well simply line up the navy and get them to sink the whole coast."

Fenix didn't look up. Even Iver waited for him. The entire intelligence operation and the military were simply the errand boys now, hanging on a shopping list from the technical experts.

He's probably known about this since Intel started monitoring it. Why does that thought piss me off so much?

"Make sure you pack a few bots, then," Fenix said at last. "Because you're going to need to strip the Aspho mainframe, as well as hoping they don't have all this backed up off-site. If they're *that* paranoid, they might not have, because that doubles their security problem. Once you've done that—*if* you can do that—then destroy the site."

"I thought you needed *live* boffins," Michaelson said. It was his word for scientists, but Hoffman had never worked out if it was affectionate or dismissive. "If you don't, then it removes one problem for the Major. He doesn't have to worry about extracting civilians."

Fenix's jaw worked for a few moments. He seemed to be staring at the papers without reading; his eye movement had stopped.

"Are you asking me as a human being, as a scientist, or as a soldier?" he said at last.

Settile saved Michaelson the problem of answering.

"We're asking you as a loyal citizen who doesn't want to see the UIR able to target any COG state from orbit. Because if you don't need the personnel along with their data, they come under the heading of asset denial."

"Shoot them, you mean," Fenix said.

"Could they reconstruct the satellite program from scratch?"

"It's not like a list of numbers you can memorize." Fenix was definitely uncomfortable with the idea. His pauses and blinking gave him away. "But nobody forgets their methodology, and so, given a little time, they could recover the program, yes."

"That's all we need to know. Thank you."

"They're *civilians,* Agent Settile."

She gave him a completely cold smile, a mere exposure of teeth. "They're building a weapon of mass destruction, Professor Fenix."

Iver didn't offer an opinion, and neither did Michaelson. They looked at Hoffman.

"Are you asking me to add assassination to the task list?" Hoffman asked.

"I'll need to run that past Chairman Dalyell, Major." Iver had never been a squeamish commander, as far as Hoffman knew, but he had political ambitions, and he probably didn't want a decision like that lurking in his file to be used against him at the most inconvenient time, as such things usually were. "It'll require his explicit authorization."

Hoffman rarely needed reminding why he would never reach the highest ranks. He simply didn't think like Iver and his ilk. His first fear wasn't what issuing an order to assassinate civvies would do to his career, but what *not* removing them would do to his world and everyone else's.

"We'd be killing civilians," Fenix said again. "Presumably *unarmed* civilians at that."

"Maybe you blinked and missed it, Professor," Hoffman said, "but these unarmed civilians are building the biggest fucking gun on the planet."

Iver cut in. "Gentlemen . . ."

"Okay, maybe it's because they've got qualifications and white coats, not uniforms." Hoffman stopped short of asking what Fenix would have done if he'd still been a Gear. "Does it make you feel uncomfortable because they're doing what *you* do? Because I'd have thought you'd dealt with the shoot-or-be-shot thing when you were a serving officer."

"It's wrong," Fenix said quietly. "It's simply *wrong*."

"Why? You think they don't know that what they're building kills people? Where's *their* responsibility in this?"

"If this is an exercise in logic, Major, you've won, but I still don't like the idea of executing civilians for having dangerous knowledge."

"That's all right," Settile said sweetly. "*We'll* kill the intelligentsia. You just concentrate on developing things that kill soldiers and the uneducated."

Hoffman almost didn't believe he'd heard her say it. Iver shuffled uncomfortably, but he didn't seem willing to dare to rap her over the knuckles. It wasn't just because she was a spook. She was remarkably intimidating in a way that Hoffman completely admired; she didn't give a damn about being liked or promoted, as long as the job got done. That was *his* kind of colleague. *Good girl.*

Fenix just smiled back, unflappable—on the outside at least. "I'll do that, Agent Settile," he said.

Iver defused the situation as best he could by getting up and slapping the back of his hand against the panorama of overlapping images. "I do appreciate this is getting to be intolerable pressure for everyone. So . . . our approach now will be to identify an alternative route as quickly as possible."

"If they think we're interested in the Berephus dockyard, let's oblige them," said Michaelson. "Set it up so they think we're aiming at a back door invasion of Pelles. Heavy-handed recon of the appropriate route, mutterings about Pelles's vast imulsion stockpiles, increased naval activity to the north of Aspho."

"That puts a lot of their troops in the area when we want to stroll in," Hoffman said.

"But they won't be keeping such a close eye on Aspho Point, will they?"

"Not unless they think we're aware of its importance."

"We can test that," Settile said. "And misinformation is no problem. But it's going to cost a little to make it look as if we're preparing for an invasion. A credible buildup, at least for the benefit of their reconnaissance."

Hoffman studied the map. It didn't leave him much choice. It was flat ground, and the assault team needed to spend as little time on it as possible, which meant picking a long route through channels shrouded in reed and grass. "We'll have to insert from the south, through the salt marsh. Minimum is still three teams—one to overcome the security measures, one to do the rummage, and the other to neutralize the personnel and lay the charges. We can still do this at night, I assume?"

"The staff still live at the site during the working week," Settile said. "We time this for a weekday evening, same as the first plan."

"And we have to transport bots. That's going to put a lot more strain on the men."

"You've got a troop of Pesang hill-men drawn from the allied forces and special duties Gears from Two-Six RTI," Iver said. "They're supposed to be the COG's finest."

Hoffman raised an eyebrow. "They've still only got two arms, two legs, and one ass each, General."

"Indeed, and once they're ready to go in, C Company

Two-Six RTI under Major Stroud will isolate the Aspho site and hold back any unwelcome attention from the land side."

Hoffman wondered how Fenix felt listening to this. His son was in C Company. Marcus Fenix wouldn't even know where he was going to be deployed or why, until the very last moment. But his father knew right *now*.

"We need an hour," Hoffman said. That was an eternity in special operations terms. But he wanted a big safety margin for problems; he hadn't done the recon personally. All the data he had came from Settile's teams in the field, scraps and crumbs pieced painstakingly together. He didn't even have a complete, up-to-date floor plan, just an extrapolation from reconnaissance images and fragments culled from building contractors, cleaners, unwitting civvies who answered innocent questions without thinking where those innocuous pieces of the information puzzle might be assembled. "And then we need to get out faster than we came in."

Hoffman said *we*. He meant *we*. He wasn't a kid anymore, but he stayed fit, and there was no way he was going to sit this out.

"I've got an idea," Michaelson said. "But we've never tried it for real. General, I take it I can borrow a cargo Sea Raven and let my engineers loose with a welding torch, yes?"

"Budget no object." Iver almost winced. "And I've never said that in my career."

Fenix gathered up his papers and gave a cursory nod to everyone. Settile stepped into his path and held out her hand.

"Those papers don't leave this building, sir," she said firmly. "But any time you need to come back in and read them, any time at all, just call my office. We're on permanent three-shift rotation."

Fenix didn't look offended. He hadn't told his own son about this, after all, and Marcus Fenix was going to be one of the men providing a cordon for the raid. That was the nature of this business. Hoffman found himself in an empty meeting room with Settile.

"I'll do it myself," he said. "I'll take the Aspho staff."

Settile looked as if she was about to put her hand on his shoulder. *Shit, she thinks I'm sacrificing my goddamn soul for the patriotic cause.* But she hesitated and folded her arms tight across her chest.

"There's no moral case to answer, Major," she said. "If I fight, I fight to win. I don't actually believe it matters *how* you win in the end, because being sporting and fair is okay for thrashball, but it's an irresponsible way to run a war. Minimum loss of COG life. Everything else is secondary."

Hoffman shrugged. He had his own personal limits, but taking out enemy scientists was, he thought, well within them. "Just make sure you give us enough information to identify them, because I don't want to exfil and find we shot the janitor and left the head honcho intact."

"Iver *could* deal with this with an air strike once your men are clear."

"Agent Settile, people can survive pretty extreme bombardment, but they usually don't survive a cranial vault shot."

She looked embarrassed. Hoffman hated the thought that she was elevating him into some sort of hero. It had to be done; so he'd do it.

He sure as hell wasn't going to ask a kid like Dom Santiago to do it, even if it was one of those things a commando had to do.

"You're an honorable man," Settile said at last.

"No," he said. "I'm a commander who never asks his men to do what he wouldn't do himself. No more, no less."

And maybe it's because the day I do, I won't have anything left worth living for.

Hoffman walked out into the grounds of the House, surprised as always that it was still daylight after a meeting, and cut through the Tomb of the Unknowns. The mausoleum commemorated unidentified fallen Gears, but there were also monuments to great battles, like Anvil Gate, as well as the graves of the most highly decorated war heroes, holders of the Embry Star. There was a kind of easy comradeship about it all; generals and enlisted men lay side by side in death. Hoffman liked—*needed*—to look at the graves regularly, so that he didn't just understand calculated risks and acceptable losses, but also *felt* what he was doing at a level beyond language.

He studied one elegant granite headstone: **SERGEANT MAJOR GRAME, J.** It wasn't that he was a decorated man that mattered. Grame was simply here, a stone's throw from the place where the decisions had been made that had ultimately put him in this grave.

Forget the medals. Am I prepared to swap places with you, Sergeant?

Yes, he was. The day he wasn't—he didn't have the right to lead men any longer.

MARITIME OPERATIONS TRAINING AREA, UNDISCLOSED LOCATION: COG WARSHIP CNV *POMEROY.*

Dom stood on the helicopter deck of *Pomeroy* and decided things were looking up after all.

A Sea Raven settled onto its mark. It was a heavy lift variant, the naval version, but it was still the basic aircraft he wasn't just used to but also positively *loved.* Every Gear did. Ravens reassured you that the good guys had arrived and were either going to give you something you badly needed, or get you out of somewhere you didn't want to be. There was nothing *not* to love about them. Their *chakka-chakka* engine note alone was enough to make hearts leap. Their rust streaks were sacred. And their pilots were all uniformly insane.

This Raven looked a bit different. Its cargo doors had been widened. The rest of the squad—Young, Morgan, and Benjafield—and the two teams of Pesang hill-men clustered around it as soon as the rotors stopped. Dom found himself looking down on the Pesangas' heads and wondering how any guys so small—and who didn't wear much armor beyond light body-plates—could have such a reputation.

"So we're going to fast-rope in, sir?" Timiou asked. "Change of plan?"

Hoffman shook his head. "No, you're still going to infiltrate in Marlins." He gestured to the naval officer who climbed down from the Sea Raven's cockpit. "Captain Michaelson thinks he has a better solution for minimizing the time we need to spend on the surface without advertising our presence with ships."

"I suggested they'd need this capacity years ago," Michaelson said. He shook the Gears' hands, something Dom wasn't used to from an officer. "But now we can turn necessity into a virtue. The Marlin's range is something like sixty klicks at best, but you're carrying a lot of equipment, so that reduces it farther, and that'll mean a launch vessel standing off far too close to the Aspho coast. We could deploy you from a submarine, but it's too shallow. So the best solution is an airdrop."

Dom thought that meant lowering the small inflatable boats into the sea and then fast-roping down into them. Okay, he was up for that. If it was rough and pitch black, it was going to be hairy, but they only had to get it right once. The Pesang troops watched in reverent silence. They were infantry, just like Dom and the others, and playing a seagoing role was alien to them as well. This was a new departure for the COG.

Michaelson had something to prove, then, that the navy could do more than play ferryboat for big guns and big aircraft. *His* part, anyway. Dom had started to learn that politics—job politics, small P—was rife in the COG forces. That depressed him. It wasn't supposed to be that way. It was supposed to be a team effort; the oath he'd taken said so, that he was a part of the great machine of society like everyone else, joined in common cause.

Great. We're a frigging experiment so some guy can build his department.

"Okay," Hoffman said. "I expect to get the go order any time. I don't know how long we've got to exercise this."

"It's the pilots who need it," Michaelson said. "All you have to do is launch the Marlins. They'll get you where you need to go."

"Plural," Hoffman muttered.

"One Marlin per Raven," said Michaelson. "Twelve men per boat. That's the best permutation, given what you've got to carry. Can I suggest that we just load ballast in place of the bots and ordnance for the dry run? If it goes wrong, then you've lost a lot of technical kit that isn't easily replaced."

Timiou made a noise that might have been a suppressed cough. It wasn't like they could replace commandos in a few hours, either. "I still don't get it, sir."

"The Ravens have been adapted as docks," Michaelson said, smiling slightly as if he was repeating something for the hard of understanding. "Like landing ships. You know, the bow doors aft. The Raven slides the Marlin straight into the sea."

Dom thought that was insanely low flying even for a Raven pilot. He'd be a meter above the water, maybe. Dom thought he got it. He really did. The drop wouldn't be any more dangerous or painful than riding heavy waves, but it was still risky.

They manhandled one of the shallow-draft vessels up the Raven's rear ramp and into the cargo bay. The two Raven crew inside were wearing survival suits, the bright yellow kind for ditching over water.

"Get a move on, then," the crew chief said, gesturing at the Marlin. "You sit back. We'll do the hard stuff. Do you know how to drive this tub, kid?"

Malcolm Benjafield had volunteered to train as coxswain. "My dad's got a powerboat."

"Oh, that's all right, then. You'll drown faster."

Marlins were designed to be easy to handle, if easy meant understanding that the sea wasn't a road and that it had a mind of its own. Dom had been trained in the basics. But this was Benjafield's baby now.

"Shit," he said, peering over Dom's head to the open ramp. "Are you going to do what I think you're going to do?"

"Ooh, I don't know," said the crew chief, hooking up his safety tether. He was clearly a windup merchant, as the captain called it, a smart-ass. "Maybe we won't drown you this time. Got your flotation jackets secure? Good. Let's see how this bird takes to water."

The Gears piled into the Marlin and took up positions with crates and other heavy objects doubling as equipment. The six Pesang troops who jumped in seemed like they grinned a lot anyway, even when things were descending into total rat-shit. Dom settled in behind Hoffman and decided it was going to be a great story to tell the kids when they were old enough to understand.

It's going to be a hell of a story to tell Carlos and Marcus, too . . .

Keeping this mission from his family tested Dom to the limit. Not even Maria knew anything beyond the fact that he was training for something that took him to sea. It bothered him, because part of the appeal of being a Gear was to be able to share everything with Carlos and Marcus, but now he couldn't, and even if they fully understood why, it still made him feel uncomfortable.

"Okay, if we go down, the bay floods up before we can escape, remember?" Benjafield said. Dom still found it disconcerting to have the driver sitting behind him, another thing that reminded him he would never make a sailor. "Ditch procedure. Got it?"

"Shit, Mal, do you *have* to?" Morgan said.

"Yeah," Hoffman growled. "You're goddamn commandos. You'll take this in your stride and bore your girlfriends senseless with endless tales of how hairy-assed you were."

If the old bastard was scared, he never showed it. Dom quite liked him. Hoffman wouldn't have been half as reassuring if he'd been sweetness and light, or paternal, or even cheerful. The fact that he was bad-tempered and didn't give a damn who he offended was his thick layer of plating over a natural, honest fear like everyone else's, although Dom was sure his anxiety was more about coming up from the ranks than getting killed. The "late entry" commissions like him had to prove everything to their fellow officers and nothing to their men.

"Wife," said Dom. "Not girlfriend."

"Another kid due soon, yes?"

"Yes, sir."

"Let's get Aspho done and dusted so you can be there. And get yourself another frigging hobby, or you'll have a whole thrashball team to feed before you're much older."

The ramp closed and the Raven lifted vertically, turning toward the open sea. It was, minus the wet stuff, something they'd done plenty of times before. The view from the cargo bay was limited to snatches of forbidding, choppy gray seas through a couple of side lights.

Then the Raven slowed and hovered, whipping spray and leaving Dom staring through a blizzard of seawater. It was only when the crew chief clambered along the rails set on the bulkheads and the ramp lowered slowly that the sheer insanity of what the pilot was doing became clear. The tail of the Raven was level with the water.

No—it was *in* the water.

All Dom's common sense said that was a bad idea. Sea rushed in across the cargo deck. The noise reminded Dom that he had to start wearing plugs or he'd be deaf in a few years. But the sinus-rattling noise of the rotors couldn't take his mind off the fact that the Raven was *in the damn sea.*

"Holy *shit,*" Hoffman said to himself.

"Glad it's not just me, sir . . ."

The crew chief gestured at Benjafield to start the engine. Dom wasn't sure if the Raven had lifted its nose to slide the Marlin clear, or if there was enough water on the deck to allow the hull to skid, but the two crewmen grabbed the boat's ropes and heaved it down the ramp. Dom couldn't see anything through the storm of spray. A wave slapped him in the face, and for a second he was sure they were going to be swamped. But Benjafield dropped the outboard and they pulled away at low speed.

"Did you know they could do that?" he yelled against the wind.

"I do now," Dom said. Benjafield turned the Marlin in a big circle. They were looking back at the Sea Raven. "Wow . . . *that's* insane."

Dom still didn't believe what he was seeing. The Raven was shrouded in whipping spray, apparently sitting in the water, ramp submerged. Then it lifted clear of the sea, draining water as if it had pissed its pants. Dom knew how it felt.

Retrieval was a lot less exciting by comparison. The Raven winched them inboard one at a time, then hooked up the Marlin and lifted it as underslung cargo.

"That's not as hairy as it looks in the movies," Dom said to the crew chief.

"Try it again in a storm, when it's shipping it green . . ."

There were days when Dom found it easier to understand the Pesangas—who didn't speak the language all that well—than the navy. He assumed *shipping it green* was a bad thing.

"If you can drive the boat off the ramp like that, why can't you drive it back up?" Benjafield asked. "Isn't it a lot faster than winching?"

"You volunteering?" said the crew chief.

"Yeah."

"Maybe we'll try that when we get a pilot who doesn't mind having a Marlin embedded in the back of his skull."

"You never tried?"

"Once. You'll need a lot more training before you try that stunt. Let's see how much time we have."

The Gears stayed on board *Pomeroy* that night. Benjafield was awarded an unofficial Raven's pilot's brevet in the air crew's equally unofficial mess, beer was consumed in modest amounts, and everyone's confidence was sky-high. They were commandos; they could do anything they set their minds to.

"I can only get better," Benjafield said sheepishly. "And Morgan's got to learn to do it yet."

Hoffman, nursing a glass of juice, dropped his guard as far as Dom had ever seen it fall, which wasn't saying much.

"It's taken twenty years to get a commando program together," he said. "Imagine what we could do if we moved away from the old infantry doctrine. More special forces. More cross-service teams. Leaner, flexible, more agile response."

"Heresy, sir," Timiou said. "If you shrink the conventional army, you change Coalition society. It works because the army is part of our social fabric. Citizens know what the price is."

"Damn, who sent me a frigging intellectual?" Hoffman actually laughed. "Yeah, you're right."

Dom was happy. He was busting to call Carlos and tell

him how they could dunk Ravens in the sea. He wanted to tell Maria. He'd get a call to her tonight, but all he could do was confine his excitement to the latest on the baby, and try not to even hint at how he'd spent the day.

There'd be plenty of time later to tell stories. He knew it. They were going to put Aspho Point out of business, and it was going to put an end to the Pendulum Wars.

CHAPTER 10

You may think *they're the government's troops, Chairman, but on the battlefield,* they are mine. *They are my responsibility, my comrades, and my conscience.*

(MAJOR HELENA STROUD,
26TH ROYAL TYRAN INFANTRY.)

FESOR NAVAL BASE, NORTH CORNER JETTY; 0500 HOURS, TWO DAYS BEFORE OPERATION LEVELER, 16 B.E.

Carlos wondered if C Company would ever be allowed out in daylight again.

It was a couple of dark hours before dawn, freezing cold, and the air stank of oil and burning paint. He stared up at the gray steel cliff looming above the dockside, craning his neck until the slab resolved into a warship with CNV KALONA picked out in peeling red paint on the bows.

She wasn't exactly the pride of the fleet. She was small, grimy, and ugly. If it hadn't been for the COG ensign hanging limp from the jackstaff, he'd have taken her for a cargo vessel. *Kalona* looked as if she'd had her backside sawn off and half a ferry welded in its place, because she was an amphibious assault ship—a floating dock for landing craft with a helicopter deck covering a third of her length. She wasn't built to look classy. She was built to land troops and vehicles on beachheads.

"At least it's got stairs," he said, nodding at the gangway. "I won't drown myself this time."

The line of Gears waiting to embark was almost silent. Some of them were asleep, sitting squatted on their backpacks with their heads resting in their hands or on folded arms, ready to be prodded to attention by a buddy if an officer passed, or the line started moving. Gears got everything they needed in lavish quantities—kit, food, benefits—but not sleep. There was never enough *sleep*. They grabbed it when they could.

Carlos debated whether to join them and get a short nap in.

"It's called a brow," Marcus said at last. "Not stairs."

"Thank you, Admiral Fenix . . ."

"Did you get hold of Dom last night?"

"He left a message, I left a message. Whatever he's doing, it's totally locked down now. Maria said she got a thirty-second call from him."

"Shit timing."

"You said it." Carlos leaned forward a little to ease the weight of his pack. "Anything else?"

"What?"

"You're pissed off about something. I can hear it. You called your old man, didn't you?"

Marcus still had his back to him. All Carlos could see was the high curve of his back-plate and the tight knot of the do-rag. "Yeah."

"And?"

"I told him we were shipping out. He went really quiet. End of story, as usual."

Carlos didn't need to remind Marcus that his father couldn't bring himself to say that he was scared for him, or worried, or that he wished that he'd never joined the army. Whatever had made Adam Fenix clam up about Marcus's mother—guilt, pride, pain, some macho shit, who the hell cared—was stopping him from being honest yet again. And Marcus was no better at getting things out in the open than his dad was.

What a fucked-up family.

Carlos knew without asking that his folks would be waiting on the old gun battery at the entrance to Fesor Harbor to wave farewell to *Kalona.* It was a low-key embarkation from a small logistics port, no media and no band, and Gears wouldn't be lined up on deck to start people wondering what was going on. But the families knew. And they'd be there.

"You told him it was *Kalona,* right?"

Marcus paused for a moment, then turned around.

"No, I didn't." Marcus looked puzzled rather than angry. No, he looked *hurt.* "And he didn't ask."

"You can always sort it out when you get back," Carlos said, trying to rescue the conversation from the pit. "You'll be a regular war hero, and he'll be all relieved you're alive. It'll be different."

"Yeah." Marcus turned back to face the ship again. "Like it's been different on every other deployment."

A group of sailors leaned on the ship's rail, staring down at the Gears waiting to embark. "Hey, land-crabs," one of them yelled. "How did you swing the luxury cruise, you lazy overfed assholes?"

There were worse nicknames than *land-crabs,* but cheerful inter-service abuse was reassuring. Chilly politeness—*that* would have been something to worry about. Sailors thought the bulky Gear armor was hilarious, and the wide-legged walk needed to cope with the thigh straps and boots just sealed the deal—they were crabs. The term was applied without mercy.

"What did it say, anyway?" Marcus asked, impervious to taunts. "Dom's message."

"Just some crap about something amazing he did on exercise but he can't tell us what it is. He's totally into this commando thing. *I'm* starting to feel like the kid brother now."

"Sounds happy to me."

Yeah, Dom was happy. He had an instant life; pretty wife, healthy kids—Carlos knew the baby on the way would be fine—and a job he loved, everything tidy and stowed away early. He'd taken a situation that would have been a disaster for most kids his age and made it a triumph. That was typical Dom. Carlos felt immensely proud of him, and just a little overshadowed.

He hadn't bought Dom anything for his birthday yet. He'd have to sort that when they got back.

"She's coming," Marcus murmured, glancing over his shoulder. He took a deep breath. "Gears—ten-*shun*!"

Marcus could hear Major Stroud a klick away. But it wasn't hard. If it wasn't the boots, it was the voice. She strode past the Gears, returned the salute, and then loped up the gangway to acknowledge the officer waiting at the top. It was only then that Carlos glanced sideways and saw who was following in her wake with a group of Command and Control cadets—her daughter Anya again, this time in the Command Corps gray working rig.

"She's like the handy travel-sized version of her mom. They must be running the op from the ship. Shit, that's rough, shoving cadets into frontline posts . . ."

Marcus managed to look without moving his head. He went on looking as Anya teetered up the gangway in regulation high-heeled black pumps. "Why do they make female support officers wear high heels? She'll break her neck."

The Gear in front of Marcus—who hadn't looked as if he was taking any notice—let out a theatrical love-lorn sigh.

"Then you can go give her some hands-on first aid, Fenix, 'cos we all know you're just dying to . . ."

Marcus's tone hardened a fraction and he got even quieter. "I see we've embarked the stand-up comedian."

The guy didn't say another word.

The line of Gears finally began moving, and the brow connecting *Kalona* to the dockside vibrated under Carlos's boots. It seemed to take forever to get to the mess decks. Moving fully armored, laden Gears through narrow passages and down steep, open stairs—*ladders,* Marcus reminded him—took time. They were in 1E2 mess, because it said so on the bulkheads, stenciled in black.

And that was all Carlos or Marcus knew right then. They still didn't know where *Kalona* was going.

"I've been in bigger lavatories." Carlos couldn't even turn around on the mess deck in armor. The bulkheads were lined with racks of bunks that looked like a challenge to squeeze into. "Mind your back, Tai."

Kaliso needed a deck to himself. He looked down his tattooed nose at a ship's rating who was trying to direct the Gears to their allocated compartments. "This ship must have been built for . . . very *short* people."

"Don't mind him," Carlos said. He needed a favor. "He

never makes sense. Is there anywhere we can see the harbor entrance when we sail?"

The sailor pointed down a passage full of Gears trying to stack armor without treading on one another. "Up the ladder, and head aft. The hatch opens onto the flight deck, which you're right *under*, by the way. Don't go on the open deck. Listen for the pipe."

The ship's address system burbled in the background; the whole ship hummed and vibrated. There was nothing to do but wait, inhaling the new smells and trying to translate the foreign language being broadcast through the decks.

"Hands to harbor stations," said the disembodied voice. "Special sea dutymen close up."

"Does that mean we're moving?" Carlos asked.

Marcus grunted, staring at the deckhead from the top bunk like he was trying out a coffin for size. How he'd managed to squeeze into the space was beyond Carlos.

"More or less."

"Come on. I got to see if my folks made it."

It was just about light enough to see detail when they opened the door onto the deck and looked out. There was no ceremonial, no sailors lined up looking smart, just guys in blue overalls clearing ropes and cables.

"Is it a door or a hatch?" Carlos asked.

"Door," Marcus said. "Hatches are in decks. Usually."

"You need to get out more."

"Just look, will you?"

Carlos scanned the docksides and jetties, and then focused on the ancient harbor walls. He could see a small group of about a dozen people huddled against the cold. *Shit, why didn't I bring some field glasses?* He strained to see.

Will they even see me?

"There's your mom," Marcus said. "Look."

He was right. Carlos was elated. His mother, his father, and Maria—damn, what was a woman about to give birth doing out in this weather?—were there with the others. Carlos didn't care about pissing off the sailors. He stepped out to the rail and waved frantically.

Yes, they saw him. *They saw him.* They waved back.

"Shit," said Marcus.

Carlos thought it was just his all-purpose reaction to anything entering the dangerous territory of emotional stuff, but then he saw what Marcus saw.

Adam Fenix was standing to the left of the Santiagos—not with them, just near them—and he raised one hand in a slow, sad gesture of farewell.

Carlos didn't look at Marcus. He needed to drink in every second of his own family; he didn't have time to see if Marcus acknowledged his father. He just heard the rasp of fabric behind him and a faint breath.

So you waved back. It's a start, Marcus.

Carlos watched and waved until the ship passed the cardinal buoys marking a sand-spit, until he couldn't see the people ashore as individual shapes any longer. When he turned around, Marcus was staring back at the land too.

"It's friggin' cold," Marcus said, all denial. His eyes always made him look brutally unfeeling even when every other gesture told Carlos he wasn't. "Let's get below."

"You said you didn't tell your dad where or when. But he found you." Carlos had hope of getting the two of them to behave like regular humans one day, and realize they were *family.* Life was too short for all this shit. "He tries, Marcus."

Marcus vanished into the ship ahead of him.

"Yeah," he said. "He found me. Ain't it interesting how he managed to do that . . ."

HANGAR DECK, *KALONA;* TWO HOURS LATER.

So now, at least, Bernie Mataki knew where she was going.

C Company sat or squatted in rows in front of a big screen on the hangar bulkhead as if they were waiting for the ship's entertainment to begin. The CIC team and landing craft coxswains stood to one side as Major Stroud pressed the button.

"This is output from a couple of UIR news channels," she said. "We have their attention."

All the doors and hatches were dogged shut and guarded. Bernie couldn't work out why there was so much security—security on their own ship—when the whole thing was on the news already. Shaky aerial footage showed COG warships steaming through waters to the north of Ostrini, and was interspersed with scenes of UIR troops mobilizing on the Pelles border. Ostri and Pellesian politicians were pissed off; Bernie didn't need to understand their language or read the subtitling to get the drift.

Major Stroud stepped in front of the screen and switched off the sound.

"That's all complete bullshit," she said in her plummy tones. "You've probably realized that we wouldn't be going ahead with a beach landing if they're already running trailers for it on TV. So while they're busy waving their dicks at us to the north, we're heading south to support an assault on Aspho Point by our commando detachment, which will be a small-scale action conducted in minimum time. Your task is to insert to the north of Aspho Point to cut off any attempt to defend the facility, and give the commandos time to do whatever it is they do when nobody's looking. They bang out, you bang out, and everyone's back on board before the UIR even realizes it's been had over backward. Welcome to Operation Leveler—now gather around and look at the maps."

Stroud was to the point if nothing else. Bernie decided it couldn't hurt to ask. "Ma'am, what's the significance of Aspho Point?"

"Weapons research," Stroud said. "If I had to explain any more, I'd have to get a decent physics education. Let's leave it at asset denial."

Marcus was sitting to Bernie's right, next to Carlos. She heard him let out a breath. Carlos rolled his head as if he was going to shake it, then muttered to himself. "So that's what he wouldn't tell us."

"Tell us what?" she whispered.

"Dom," Carlos said. "That has to be what he's been training for."

The screen now filled with aerial recon images, and Stroud pointed out streams and bridges. The map said *ASPHO FIELDS,* but it didn't look like rolling pasture at all. It looked like marsh, flat as a pancake and with only pockets of cover. Still, the Major said *fast,* and that meant there'd be no spending days in a water-filled hole just waiting.

"Current as of twenty-six hours ago," Stroud said. "If they spot us and respond, they'll have to come down those routes if they're committing land forces. Latest satellite data shows they've moved a brigade about fifty klicks northeast and reinforced the gun battery near Berephus since the flotilla took up position, but that's the most immediate threat so far. The two bases near Aspho are still only company strength at best. But there's always the risk of an air strike. It's going to be all about speed. Get in, do the job, and get out—preferably one hour, definitely within two."

Anya Stroud edged into the briefing. "Met forecast is for high winds and heavy seas, so timing is going to be critical."

Marcus was staring at the aerial view of Aspho Point with a deepening frown. "Ma'am, if we're not detected on the approach, when do they first work out that Aspho Point's under attack? Any time between the first guard getting a round through his head and the charges going off. They could have a few fire teams there in minutes, a helicopter in twenty, so why not just pound the target from the sea and send in a few Ravens to finish up?"

Stroud began marking up a paper map spread on a small trestle table, head down. "Because we want to keep some souvenirs intact."

"Sounds like the kind of *souvenir* my father collects."

He said it almost casually, but the way Carlos glanced at him confirmed to Bernie that there was a lot more to it than that. She wasn't his platoon sergeant now. Maybe she'd have a quiet word with Daniel Kennen, who was, just to make sure there was nothing that was going to distract Marcus over the next couple of days.

She'd known Marcus for two years, in the family-close way of platoon relationships, and she still knew even less about his real family than she did about Hoffman's. Marcus just kept it all locked away.

They had just hours now, not days, to refine the plan. Stroud was putting her faith in the Stomper, the belt-fed grenade gun mounted on each platoon vehicle. She also put her back into it, doing the heavy work alongside her Gears to ready the landing craft and the weapons. It was powerfully motivating. Bernie, who had never really wanted to be a Gear until a recruiting sergeant told her that women made crap soldiers anyway, and especially crap snipers, found herself anxious to do a good job for Stroud.

Motivation. There were a million ways to do it. You just had to judge which lever would move the individual.

"Crafty bastard," she muttered, realizing the lever the recruiting sergeant had pressed in her all those years ago.

Carlos paused with an ammo crate, sweating. It was a good way to keep warm in this freezing tub. "What, old man Fenix?"

"No, some dead bloke. What do you mean?"

"Marcus's dad came to see him off, even though Marcus hadn't told him the where and why." Carlos lowered the box and ran his hand over his forehead, before wiping his palm on his pants. "He's part of the op. Didn't tell Marcus, though."

"Isn't Marcus used to that secrecy shit? Fenix is all classified and eat-before-reading."

"Well, there's a *lot* his dad hasn't told him over the years. Personal stuff. Just rubs him raw, I think."

Bernie took the cue to back off for the while. But she knew enough now; Marcus, for all his apparent maturity and iron discipline, was still a normal lad who could be hurt by his dad. It was the kind of stuff a sergeant needed to know.

"Yeah, crafty bastard," she said.

AIR CREW QUARTERS, CNV *POMEROY*, AT ANCHOR TWO HUNDRED KILOMETERS NORTH OF ASPHO POINT.

"Sir, if I get killed, what will you tell my family?"

Hoffman stopped pressing his jacket and looked up at the kid standing in the open doorway. Ludovic Young didn't look particularly anxious; lads could think about the possibility without imagining it would actually happen to them. Young was just a methodical character who liked to have everything in order.

"I'll tell them the truth," Hoffman said. He always avoided trotting out the reflex reassurance that nobody was going to die. He'd only ever said that once, and he'd been agonizingly wrong. "As far as the secrecy of the mission allows me. And if we pull it off, it won't be very secret."

"Thank you, sir. I wouldn't want them to get a shock years later."

Hoffman decided his uniform could live with a few creases. It was time probably better spent on getting the team together for a morale session. He wasn't good at that kind of thing. He didn't know how to lead. All he could ever do was stand up and tell those under him what he thought of them, what he wanted them to achieve, and then become one of them while they did it. It seemed to work.

"Young, assemble everyone on the hangar deck," he said. "I'll be along in a few minutes."

Hoffman wasn't good at waiting, either. He went to the ops room to find Michaelson and check on the progress of the decoy fleet and the landing ship. The place was quiet and dimly lit; ratings sat at their screens, intent on whatever data or plot was in front of them. It took Hoffman some time to work out which section was dealing with charts. It all looked the same to him.

"So where's *Kalona* now?" Hoffman asked.

Pomeroy's first officer, Fuller, pointed him at a screen and tapped anonymous-looking dots with numbers superimposed on them. A cluster was forming a few kilometers north of them, looking for all the world as if it was gathering for an assault on the coastal cities of Bonbourg and Berephus, and the canal that cut through Ostri's northern territory to Pelles beyond.

"Well, I'm convinced by that, Commander," Hoffman said. "Any idea if the Indies are buying it? I've not heard a damn thing from Iver yet."

"There's a satellite pass in forty-five minutes. We'll have updated aerial images then."

There was no substitute for a full recon on the ground, done by Gears. The best they'd been able to do was get intelligence via Settile's team, and Hoffman still didn't know a thing about them. He had to trust her network. They'd come up with the layout of Aspho Point and a hell of a lot of technical information, after all.

But in the future—after we prove what we can do—I'll make damn sure we have special forces recon teams. No third-party intel. Gears finding out what Gears need to know.

It wasn't just the end of the war that rested on the success of Operation Leveler. It was a new military doctrine, a different army from the one Hoffman had grown up in. He believed in the power of small specialist teams.

The ops room team sat up a little straighter, eyes still fixed on their screens. Michaelson had walked in.

"*Kalona*'s under way," he said. "She should be on station by 2300 hours tomorrow, and her LCTs will be away by 2530."

"Okay. I better tell my boys now. One of them has a brother and best buddy in C Company. I haven't enjoyed sitting on that fact."

"Might improve morale a hell of a lot."

"Their morale is pretty damn good, actually."

"By the way, my admiral's been asking Dalyell what his final orders are if your team gets taken out," Michaelson said quietly.

Hoffman not only expected the question but knew the answer. There was only one possibility. "And Dalyell told him to throw in every missile and air asset he had and sink the whole area, right?"

Michaelson nodded. "Just thought you ought to know."

"I'd be disappointed if he hadn't," Hoffman said. "Once they know for sure what we're after, there's no going back later. Got to cream the place."

"Of course, it all depends what Dalyell defines as *getting taken out*. In other words, what he regards as a failed mission."

Maybe that was the real message from Michaelson, something he'd overheard, intercepted, or deduced that made him think they all had a nervous boss with a shaky finger on the button.

"I thought it was Iver's operation."

"Maybe Iver still does," Michaelson said. "So much for it not being enough to simply deny Hammer to the UIR."

"Then we'd better leave no margin for misinterpretation of our success." Hoffman had learned all the doublespeak of command, but it wasn't his mother tongue. "I told them to do this from the start. It's always sobering to bite yourself in your own ass."

By the time Hoffman got down to the hangar deck, the commandos were stripping down their Lancers, and the Pesang troops were sitting patiently cross-legged on the deck like a class of well-behaved children.

"As you were," Hoffman said. "It's just the waiting now. *Kalona*'s on her way, and tomorrow night she's going to land an infantry company. They'll have your backs at Aspho Fields if the Indies counterattack. If it goes to plan, you'll all be in and out before the bastards know what's happening." He looked at Dom, whose expression was unreadable for once. "Sorry I didn't warn you earlier, Santiago. It's C Company."

Dom seemed to chew over the news, and then smiled. "Have they been told who they're providing support for?"

"I don't know," Hoffman said. "I'll check."

Well, I got away with that one. Hoffman didn't like being kept in the dark and he assumed it offended others equally. Sometimes it didn't. He couldn't imagine why. He turned to the Pesang troops.

"Anything more you need, Sergeant?"

Bai Tak smiled broadly and indicated the huge leather sheath hanging from his belt. It was so long that its tip extended past his hip and rested on the floor. "We got everything we need, Hoffman-sah."

The Pesangas were small men with permanent grins and almond-shaped eyes, unfailingly cheerful people from some remote part of the COG that Hoffman had never visited. Usually, they herded cattle on mountain slopes, but it must have been a pretty rough kind of farming, because they carried the biggest knives Hoffman had ever seen.

The blades weren't ceremonial. Pesangas were shock troops; their task was killing, fast and silently.

They'd certainly proven their worth at the siege of Anvil Gate.

"Okay," Hoffman said. "I'll be in my cabin. Get some sleep."

The men probably would, but Hoffman knew he wouldn't. He spent the rest of the evening composing his usual letter, as he did before every engagement when he had the time to plan this far ahead, and wrote MARGARET HOFFMAN in capitals on the envelope. He'd hand it to Michaelson for delivery if the worst happened. He'd done it so many times that the words no longer had the same weight that they had when he first realized that this would be the most important thing he ever wrote, words that would have meaning beyond their weight or intention because they'd be his last to her. Sometimes he wanted to let her read one, just to see her reaction; but every time he retrieved it from whoever had been tasked to hand it over, he burned it.

The sentiments had varied a lot over the years. The one he wrote at Anvil Gate had been heartfelt. Those that followed were simply designed not to make things any worse.

She'd probably donate it to the RTI museum one day. Mindful of that, Hoffman made sure that his last words would reflect well on the regiment.

CHAPTER 11

Santiago is an exemplary soldier and one of the most courageous men I've ever met. But even with his outstanding record, I can't recommend his promotion to corporal. His loyalty to Fenix may well exceed his loyalty to the COG. Even if it doesn't, then his decision to testify for Fenix must call his judgment into question. However . . . even if I have to refuse his promotion, I'll state privately that this is a man I can only admire for his refusal to abandon a friend, knowing what it would cost him.

(LIEUTENANT COLONEL JAMES AMSTIN, ASSESSING PRIVATE DOMINIC SANTIAGO SHORTLY AFTER MARCUS FENIX'S COURT MARTIAL.)

NORTH GATE FOOD FACILITY, JACINTO:
PRESENT DAY, FOURTEEN YEARS AFTER E-DAY.

"Wow." Federic Rojas was waiting to meet the inbound Raven. He looked almost cheated when Bernie jumped out with a ripening black eye and a split lip. "Who did *that*?"

"Grub," Dom said. Without his helmet, Federic looked

horribly young and way too much like his dead brother Jan for comfort. "She invited him to sit down and discuss their differences."

"You slugged it out with him? I mean, really? Fists?"

"Much as I'd love that rumor to spread," Bernie said, "the thing hit me while I was carving him."

"Wow. I missed a lot."

Bernie patted him on the head as she passed. "Long may that continue, sweetheart."

Hoffman almost fell out of the Raven and stalked across the compound with obvious difficulty. Lieutenant Barber raised an eloquent finger behind Hoffman's back from the gloom of the door.

"You really should get that looked at, sir," Barber called after him. "That dressing won't hold forever. You sure you won't come back with us?"

"I'll live," Hoffman grunted. "Thanks. Now get back to base. That's a valuable air asset you've got there."

Marcus didn't rush to help him. Cole did. He shoved a hand under the colonel's arm and there was nothing Hoffman could do to stop him. He seemed *embarrassed* about getting shot. Cole sat him down on the running board of an APC and took a pain-killer hypo out of his belt.

He rustled the sterile packaging. "You want me to do this, sir, or you want to do it yourself?"

"I'm not in that much pain. You hang on to it, Cole." Hoffman unfastened his boot, rolled up his pants leg, and examined the dressing. "You'll probably need to stick it in your own ass to put up with Baird on the way back."

"He's ugly, sir, but he's useful."

"Where's Jack? It should be back by now."

Marcus stood with his hand to his ear, listening to the

radio chatter. "Lieutenant Stroud's directing it. She's checking the route back." He paused. "Lot of Stranded about. Two more Locust reports, nothing close enough to the route to worry about yet."

"Is that your *yet*?"

"No, Colonel, it's Stroud's. She's always cautious."

Dom checked his watch and then looked up at the sky. It was overcast; they'd lose the light even sooner. Night movements were something any sane Gear liked to avoid, as much because of the nocturnal predatory Kryll as the Locust. Even though no Kryll had been seen since the Lightmass bombing, the compound was flooded by arc lights as the frantic loading continued. That would be enough to keep Kryll at bay; a crowded compound like this would be an ideal hunting ground for them, all that flesh cooped up with nowhere to run from their razor wings.

He couldn't hear any chickens. He wondered idly if the birds warned each other not to go out in case the predatory humans got them and wrung their necks.

Sergeant Parry walked briskly along a line of vehicles and then headed in their direction, making a gesture at his wrist. He broke into a jog.

"How long, Staff?" Hoffman asked.

"Inside half an hour, sir. We're going to start moving the front section into position now."

"That was fast."

"We haven't cleared everything. Just the priority list and every single spare part we could pry loose. No telling if we'll ever be able to come back and retrieve anything later."

"Good work, Parry." Hoffman eased himself up with a white-knuckled grip on the Armadillo's door. "Fenix, get your vehicle in position."

Dom swung into the driver's seat. Marcus slid in and sighed. He'd settled back seamlessly into being a Gear as if he'd never been away, but it wasn't seamless for Dom. He wanted to know what had happened to him in those four years in prison. In the short time since the escape, there just hadn't been the right moment to even begin to ask him if he'd received any letters or how bad it had been in there. And Dom was conscious of being a whiny kid again, pestering Bernie about Carlos, and now maybe risking cracking Marcus's apparent equilibrium. Nobody could spend four years in the Slab and come out as if nothing had happened.

That was the worst thing about lulls in the fighting. They were best filled by eating, sleeping, or arguing, because thinking just let the dead and lost wander back in, and make you wonder why you were bothering to carry on.

Why?

Because she's out there somewhere.

Because Carlos would never have quit.

Because Marcus needs hope too. And Cole, and Baird, and Tai.

"I think Bernie's pissed off with me," Dom said as they waited for Rojas.

"She's never pissed off with anyone. Except Baird."

"I've asked her twice about Carlos." Dom didn't have to explain what *about* meant. Marcus never wanted to discuss it. "She said she'd tell me what happened."

"Yeah, I heard." Marcus stared ahead for a moment, then turned to face him. "You think that's going to do either of you any good?"

"In all these years, you've never said much about it. And it never got to me until recently. You know how when people think they're running out of time, they suddenly want to see people they haven't seen in years, and get their lives in order?"

"Yeah. But you're *not* running out of time."

"She was honest. She said it would upset me."

Marcus turned back to face front. "He got blown up, Dom. For fuck's sake, you want to hear that frame by frame? He got the Embry Star. If the Locust hadn't shown up, they'd have made a movie about him by now. If—"

The top hatch vibrated as Rojas jumped into the rear seat, all bright enthusiasm. It killed the conversation stone dead. Dom wanted to yell at him in frustration, because this was the longest conversation he and Marcus had had about Carlos's death in years.

"Hey, sorry." Rojas leaned forward between the seats and looked from one man to the other. Now that he had his helmet on, he looked and sounded exactly like Jan, and Dom found it almost unbearably upsetting. The dead wouldn't leave him alone today. "I was just helping Tai move the 'Dill. Some civvie blocked him in with a flatbed, and I was worried he was going to eat the guy alive."

Marcus changed back into the public Sergeant Fenix again. "Tai's usually mellow. Says some weird shit, but he saves the aggro for grubs."

The discussion was as far away as it had ever been. Dom waited for the order to move out, head resting against the side hatch while he tried to imagine what could possibly be worse than the death he had imagined for Carlos so many times over the last sixteen years.

"Control to Delta." Anya Stroud's voice made him start. "Delta, there's some new Locust movement I'm monitoring. Jack's doing a sweep in stealth mode. Just stay sharp when you move out, okay?"

"Yes, ma'am," Dom said automatically.

"Rumor has it the canteen is serving noodles tonight. I just wanted to motivate you. Think meatballs."

"No Locust can stand between a Gear and his meatballs."

"That's the spirit. Control out."

Rojas leaned forward again. "I didn't know she had a sense of humor."

"We go back a long way."

"Oh . . ."

"There's no *oh.* Okay?"

Dom didn't have a sense of humor where women were concerned. There was only Maria: there would always only *ever* be Maria.

It was ten minutes before Dom's earpiece activated again, and this time it was Hoffman.

"Move out, Santiago. Convoy drivers—maintain intervals. No stopping. Be ready for redirection in the event of a breakdown or enemy contact. Use your call signs on the radio, keep your channel open for instructions, and only transmit if absolutely necessary. Hoffman out."

Dom fired up the Armadillo and steered for the gates. The sky was purple now, and the compound lights dimmed into darkness. All he could see was the line of dipped headlights behind him.

He could remember when Ephyra had so many street lights that it illuminated the clouds, and he could see it from twenty klicks. Energy was plentiful. Now the city was almost in darkness with only essential street lighting maintained, and only for a few hours a night. There was no formal curfew, but there might as well have been.

Dom accelerated into the gloom, and turned the corner into the main road back to humanity's last refuge.

And even on these deserted streets, he still looked out for Maria every step of the way.

CENTER CONVOY.

Hoffman's calf hurt like hell.

It was a great way of staying alert. Kaliso kept glancing at him as the APC bounced over debris, as if he was testing him to see if hitting a *really* big pothole could make him scream. Maybe it was time for a shot of painkiller after all.

I'm an idiot. If I'd been killed, guess who would take over? Reid or McLintock. Kiss humanity good-bye. Assholes, both of them.

Hoffman didn't want to go down in history as the guy on whose watch the human species ceased to exist. The fact that there'd *be* no history to judge him by if that happened didn't lighten the load one bit. But he wasn't going to live forever, and the officer gene pool was looking more shallow with every passing day. Succession was starting to preoccupy him: he had to find some bright kid to polish for the future. Fenix would have been a candidate if he hadn't been such an impulsive and surly bastard.

Yeah, I see the irony in that, thanks. Maybe I don't trust him because I don't trust myself.

He realized he didn't automatically think *traitor* now, though.

Why did I do it?

Hoffman had never shirked a dirty job in his life, and he'd had to do plenty. It appalled him now to think that he'd simply left Marcus Fenix in a deserted prison and didn't even do him the basic courtesy he'd have granted a sick dog, of putting a round through his head and getting it over with. In the last few nights he'd found himself thinking through the small details of the kind of death that he already knew too well from another war; that eventually the water and food would have run out—food immediately, water maybe a few weeks later—or the Locust would have broken into the cell. Did any man deserve that? Hadn't Fenix earned a little mercy with his war record? Didn't Hoffman himself have higher standards than that?

It was just a split second's decision. *Open the doors, let the bastards out. Including Fenix, sir? No, screw him, he can rot for all I care.* Just a snarl as he reached for his sidearm and went off to deal with another crisis.

Pressure wasn't a *reason,* because Hoffman made split-second decisions every day of his life. It plagued him now that he didn't know why he'd done it, and he didn't know the man who'd done it, because it wasn't the Victor Hoffman he thought he was. Hoffman realized that when he saw Fenix get out of the Raven, rescued from his cell by a buddy who defied orders and was willing to die for him, and he had to look Fenix—and Dom—in the eye.

And Fenix was still willing to fight. Even after all that shit. Even after I abandoned him. He still pulled out all the stops.

Hoffman wondered if it was Dom Santiago's opinion that troubled him most.

You did it. Live with it. Learn from it.

The road ahead was dead straight; no bends or underpasses, no blind spots, good visibility even in the patchy street lighting. Without the visible damage to buildings, it could have been any run-down neighborhood before E-Day. Groups of Stranded leaned against walls or sat on doorsteps, smoking or drinking, savoring the novelty of being outdoors and able to relax for once. Even their raised fingers of contempt as the COG vehicles passed by seemed almost genial.

It wasn't the place for an ambush.

Even so, Kaliso's fingers tightened on the wheel. Hoffman found himself looking from side to side at more than the unkempt rabble loitering there. He could see no combat indicators, the telltale signs of trouble coming that he'd been so thoroughly trained to look for as a young Gear that the awareness was an extra, everyday sense as natural as seeing or hearing. The street hadn't emptied of people. There were no vehicles parked that the convoy would have to skirt around. There was nothing tangible to blip his radar, but he still knew, felt, tasted, *understood* somehow that trouble was imminent.

Kaliso had one hand on the wheel and the other resting on his sidearm. He knew it, too.

Fenix's voice filled Hoffman's head. "APC-One to all vehicles, we're getting vibrations up here. Stay sharp."

It might have been nothing. It might have been more aftershocks as bedrock settled after the Lightmass bombing. It might have been just a collapsing sewer somewhere; but the Stranded were suddenly vanishing, thinning out into the buildings, and Hoffman trusted the wary human animal in all of them more than he trusted technology. But that had its place, too.

"Convoy Command to Control," he said. "Stroud, possible contact. We're getting shakes. Run a check for us."

"Already on it, Colonel. Jack's been route-proving ahead of the column. I've sent it to double back."

Anya was smart. She understood ambushes. She understood that they could hit anywhere along a—

"*Shit!*"

The shout was so loud in Hoffman's earpiece that it hurt. He couldn't tell where it had come from; no damn call sign. *Civvies—no friggin' discipline.* Kaliso held his speed. If you weren't driving into an ambush, you *kept going.* If you *were* driving into one—you slammed on the brakes and backed out fast.

"Two-twenty-five—we're hit, we've rolled." That number meant that the vehicle was to the rear of the command 'Dill. A big chunk of convoy was following it. "Shit—grubs—"

Gunfire rattled, both in Hoffman's earpiece and echoing off the buildings outside, followed by multiple explosions that sounded like a Boomshot. He caught sight of Jack as the bot shot past head-height at high speed toward the rear of the convoy. The line of trucks was spread over at least a kilometer, spaced at twenty-meter intervals now that it was in a built-up area; he didn't know exactly where vehicle 2-25 had stopped, or if there was an escape route for the tail following it. Only Jack could see that. All Hoffman could do—all any of the drivers or escorts could do—was to listen to voice traffic. They were blind. Only Jack could see the bigger picture, and, through Jack's electronic eyes, Anya Stroud.

"Stroud, what can you see?"

Her voice cut in. "Control to two-two-seven, go left, left, left, left. All vehicles, follow two-two-seven." So 2-26 must have been hit as well; she'd taken over the redirection, routing the remnant of the broken convoy in a loop around the ambush. It was best guess time now. If the grubs had broken through here, they could come up anywhere. But the convoy had to keep moving to stand any chance of making it. "Two-two-seven, I've only got one bot airborne, so call in your position at every intersection, so I can direct you."

"Control, this is two-two-seven, turning left onto Parkway." The voice was a woman's, tight with fear but still controlled. *Not bad for a civvie.* "It's grubs, we saw them. We're all clear ahead."

The woman could have been driving into anything. "Stroud, keep Jack with the lead serial," Hoffman said. Kaliso backed up and swung the 'Dill back down the convoy at high speed, shaving past the line of trucks to his left. "We're heading back to engage the grubs. Casrep?"

"Jack's over the ambush point, sir. Both two-two-five and two-two-six are stopped and badly damaged, two-two-six is on fire. I can see . . . the driver and gunner . . . they're still in the cab. Two-two-five . . . driver and gunner both dead—the vehicle's overturned on its near side."

"*Definitely* dead?"

Anya didn't pause. "You won't need to check for a pulse, no. Fragmented."

Sometimes the Control observers had a worse time of it, and in close-up.

But there were rules; there was keep-moving-and-clear-the-kill-zone, and there was engage-the-bastards, and Hoffman was clear he and Kaliso were doing the latter. He twisted as far as he could to reach behind him to feel for the grenade launcher on the rear seat. His leg wasn't troubling him now. It was good stuff, this adrenaline. As the headlights zipped past on his left, he readied the launcher and reached forward to raise the APC's canopy. The last truck in the line passed them and they were suddenly staring down a dark road with a flickering yellow light at the far end—a blazing truck.

"They won't be hanging around," Kaliso said. "But they won't have moved far."

He brought the 'Dill to a halt a few meters from the

wreck. There were bodies, but they couldn't retrieve them yet. A couple of dead grubs slumped in a pool of dark liquid that Hoffman thought was oil from the truck, and when he got out for a closer look, it was blood. Headlights came straight on at him but peeled off as trucks took a left as directed. Somewhere down that road was the trail APC with Cole, Mataki, and Baird.

"Control to convoy, we've got Locust drones on the surface, coming down the Avenue on a heading toward Parkway," Anya said. She must have sent Jack to hover over the crossroads at high elevation to get a wider view. "Numbers—looks like thirty at least. They're moving in and out of the buildings."

The drivers could hear every word. Hoffman hoped the civilian ones didn't lose their nerve and try to scatter down the side roads. They'd done pretty well so far and stayed off the radios.

Baird's voice cut in. "APC-three to Hoffman, you want us to divert and engage? If we turn left at Canal Walk, we can cut along behind them and intercept them at the Rotunda."

Tunneling took time and energy the grubs didn't always seem to have, and when they were moving on the surface like that the odds were better. But the problem with an enemy that moved *under* you was detection. The convoy had no radar or sonic resonator that could track grubs as they moved. So it was a gamble. And maybe it was a decoy before a full-scale assault.

But Baird could often think like a grub.

"The tail of the convoy is clear, sir," Anya said.

"APC-three, divert and pursue." *We should have had more APCs on this, if we had enough of the damn things.*

Day by day, fight by fight, the COG's technology was wearing out, breaking down, or going up in flames, and it wasn't being replaced. Hoffman climbed back into the cab. "We'll take over as trail vehicle. Time it right, and we can give them a good hosing from both sides."

"Got it, sir."

"I don't want to worry you, Colonel," Fenix said, "but if the grubs turn right at the end of the Avenue, they'll be heading for the bridge."

Kaliso sent the 'Dill racing to the end of the line of trucks and did a rapid three-point turn in the road to loop back behind the last one. There wasn't much farther to go; once the convoy was across the river, they were on proven granite, no fissures, and the grubs would have to cross via the bridge to attack.

"Fenix," Hoffman said, "don't let them reach that bridge."

Sometimes, a simple phrase out of nowhere could drop-kick Hoffman back into another world.

Don't let them reach that bridge.

"Bridge" meant one thing to Hoffman when Dom Santiago was around: Carlos Santiago's heroic death at Aspho Fields, killed on the bridge there as he and Marcus made a desperate stand to give Hoffman the time to complete his mission.

Maybe the words triggered the same memory for Fenix. Maybe it didn't. Hoffman would have bet that it did.

"Understood, sir."

In the light from the APC's instrument panel, Kaliso's face looked like violence personified, another species entirely. The metal piercings and the swirled tattoos broke up the lines of his features into an alien face. When the APC reached the turnoff before the ambush point, he slowed down to stare at the wrecked trucks. Stranded had already emerged to scavenge what they could from the truck that wasn't on fire.

There were bodies still in those trucks, bodies of people who took a risk for humanity's survival, and paid the price.

We can't stop. You know the procedure, and why.

But if Kaliso didn't, Hoffman damn well would.

"Sir, permission to dismount," Kaliso muttered.

They were supposed to be defending the living. They'd lose precious time. "Granted," Hoffman said.

Kaliso brought the 'Dill to a halt, grabbed the grenade launcher from Hoffman's lap, and stalked over to the trucks, gesturing to the Stranded with his free hand to move clear. Hoffman slid out of the 'Dill and stood by the open hatch, weapon ready, just in case.

"Stand away from the truck," Kaliso called. "You're defiling it."

Shit, he was on one of his flaky philosopher trips again. "COG property," Hoffman yelled, just to make sure the scumbags got the idea. "Get away from it, or we open fire. Understand?"

It was the standard challenge for looters, but the Stranded rarely encountered it. They stared. Some ran for it, but the others went back to trying to drag crates from the vehicles, as if an angry South Islander with a loaded RPG and a Lancer slung from his shoulder was nothing much to worry about. One man—suicidal bastard—was even draining fuel from the tank.

"It's all covered in oil and shit, man," one of the other men said. "You're not gonna be eatin' it now, are you? We're starvin' out here."

"It's a *temporary war grave,*" Hoffman growled, taking aim at them. "And we're *dying* out here."

The Stranded sprinted for cover. And Kaliso fired.

But he aimed at the truck. A ball of smoke and flame boiled skyward. Kaliso waited and watched the fire take hold, his brow creased in concentration, then turned toward the buildings where the Stranded had fled.

"I'll come back later," he called out. "Don't defile this again."

He got back in the 'Dill. Hoffman stared at him.

"What the hell was that about, Private?"

"It's a war grave, sir, like you said." Kaliso started up the APC again and slammed his boot on the accelerator. "Cremation is the proper thing to do. Permission to retrieve the casualties later?"

There was little to retrieve, but Hoffman understood why the thought of those parasites rummaging around next to the bodies of better men really got to Kaliso. He just had a very weird way of expressing it.

It stopped those Stranded shits from looting the truck, though.

"Granted," Hoffman said. "Nobody gets left behind. Dead or alive."

It was a pledge Hoffman had always tried to honor. In times like these, preserving decency was as important as saving lives, because if humanity survived at the cost of descending into barbarism, then there was no difference between men and Locust.

He'd peered over that precipice more than once. If he fell again, he'd never come back.

LEAD APC, APPROACHING THE RIVER.

"I frigging *hate* this," Dom said.

The voice traffic between the vehicles, Hoffman, and Control formed his only picture of the convoy. It wasn't so much what was being said that rattled him as what he imagined happening in the pauses between the sitreps and diversions. If you couldn't see, you filled in the gaps. It was like listening to a radio play with most of the lines missing, knowing the cast really *would* get killed if anything else went wrong.

"What did we lose back there?" Rojas asked.

"Two civilian drivers, two retired Gears." Marcus was studying a strip map balanced on his thigh. "And a few tons of food."

"Two-forty-five to Control," said a driver. "I've got a problem. Transmission. It's pissing fluid. The warning light's come on."

"Shit." Marcus didn't look up. "That's the flatbed with the fermentation vats. Wide load."

"Can you pull off?" Anya asked the driver.

"Negative, and if I stop, I'll block the route. I've still got a couple of tankers and the trail APC behind me."

Roads might have looked passable on maps, but there hadn't been a highway repair program outside the heart of Jacinto for years; a street could be blocked by Locust activity or a building collapse at any time. Anya was relying on Jack's video feed to recon new routes.

"Two-forty-five, there's a right turn a hundred meters past College Green that'll take you back onto the main route," she said. "Have you got enough room to turn?"

"I can try. This rig's going to grind to a halt at some point anyway, so I don't have a lot of options."

Marcus cut in. "Anya, you could divert the other vehicles around two-four-five, extract the crew, and recover the truck later."

"If he can pull over, I can fix it," Baird said over the radio.

The driver paused for a moment. "Okay, I want to give it a shot. They'll steal anything that isn't nailed down, and we need the truck's parts probably even more than we need myco vats. I'll stand guard on it until we get a repair crew out if need be."

"I said I can fix it," Baird repeated.

"I'm coming up on the turn."

"Okay, two-four-five, turn right at College Green, following vehicles hold your course."

"APC-three changing drivers," Baird said.

"Baird, what are you doing?" Marcus asked.

"Dismounting to assist two-four-five."

"Control, I got it," Cole said. "Damon's given me the keys, but he says I got to be home by midnight."

There was no point arguing with Baird now. And he was right—if anyone could keep the truck mobile, it was him.

"Baird stopping to help a guy out?" Dom said. "He must have had a blow to the head or something."

"I heard that, asshole . . ."

"He just wants to show what a big wrench he's got," said Cole.

Hoffman cut it short. "Keep this channel free of social chitchat, ladies."

Dom could see the lights across Timgad Bridge as a double row like a runway dead ahead. The first trucks in the convoy would soon be home and dry, and then he could double back and deal with the stragglers. "Anya, how we doing?"

"Jack keeps losing the drones. They're moving up through the buildings."

"Any indication that they're making for the bridge?" Marcus asked.

"Not yet."

Just drones. No Reavers, Nemacysts, Berserkers, not since the Lightmass detonation. Dom never allowed himself to get his hopes up too high, but it was starting to look as if the Locust *had* been dealt a massive and lasting blow.

But they won't turn off like a tap.

Stragglers. Unless they've got a new plan . . . and they've not been big on those for the last fourteen years.

"Control, we're coming up to the Rotunda now," Cole said. It had been a cultural center, two crescents of museums and art galleries around a huge sunken amphitheater that was the setting for open-air plays and concerts in the summer when it was closed to traffic. Dom didn't do plays, but it had been a lovely place for a walk and an overpriced fancy beer in the evenings, and now it was an equally lovely place for a counter-ambush if the grubs were obliging enough to walk that way. "They got to go this route now."

There was a grunt of expelled air and Dom heard Bernie swear in the background. Cole was obviously taking a very bumpy shortcut.

"APC-three, we're coming up to the south of you," Hoffman said. "We see them. Damn—" There was a burst of fire. "And they've seen us."

"Race you, sir," said Cole. "Mataki thinks those grubs might be *edible.*"

Now Dom knew how Anya felt. His heart was pounding

with sheer frustration at not being there to add some fire support. "This is driving me crazy."

"Jack's detected more drones, sir," Anya's said. "No sign of e-holes, but they're coming from somewhere."

"We should go back and help them out." More trucks rolled by Dom's door toward the bridge as they waited, the rhythmic, slow *voom . . . voom . . . voom* of engines counting down to the completion of the mission. "We can't just sit here."

"Fifteen minutes, and they'll all be across," Rojas said. "Working on average speed."

Baird called in. "I'm with the truck now," he said, sounding breathless. He must have sprinted after it. "It's a seal that's failed. I'm going to pack it with self-curing tape because that's all I've got, and then top up with—oh *shit*."

"Contact, contact, *contact*. Two-four-five, contact. Grubs emerging ahead of us."

It was 2-45's driver, sticking to the rules on how to report an attack, but *shit* did the job just fine. Dom heard grunts of effort from Baird and then bursts of fire.

"We've got grubs everywhere," said Hoffman.

"Sir, I don't think they're targeting the convoy itself," Anya said. "I think their priority is Gears. It's a lure."

As soon as Anya said it, Dom knew she was right.

"I hate to disappoint," Marcus said. "Get down there, Dom."

Grubs might have looked like grunting brutes, but they were smart, and they'd pulled yet another flanker on the convoy. They knew that humans—humans like Delta and Hoffman—would counterattack an ambush rather than run and let the enemy keep control. And that meant they could pull another ambush elsewhere.

Dom sent the APC screeching back down the highway, skimming past trucks as he tried to visualize the fastest route to the Rotunda and College Green. They were both within a couple of blocks. The rest of the convoy was now on its own.

"Stay where you are," Hoffman said. "Shit, Fenix, did you ever stick to plan in your life?"

"Anya can alert us if we're needed elsewhere."

"Damn, where are all those bastards *coming* from?"

Everyone had kept their channel open, as ordered. But they were all on two-way, and so every gasp, every breath and curse, was in Dom's head and there was nothing he could do to shut it out.

"Been here before," said Marcus. He had to be remembering the same thing as Dom; he knew it. "And I'm not making the same mistakes again."

CHAPTER 12

I've never met a soldier who knew he was a hero. It's not false modesty. They simply decide to do something that they know they must *do, usually for their comrades, because if they don't, those people will suffer in some way. For them, that compulsion is far stronger than any fear. The fact that we find that exceptional is a sad indictment of the human race. I'd like to live in a world of heroes. If we did, there would be no wars.*

(GENERAL JOLYON IVER, COMMANDER, COG LAND FORCES.)

CNV *POMEROY*, SOMEWHERE OFF THE OSTRI COAST; FOUR HOURS BEFORE OPERATION LEVELER—SIXTEEN YEARS AGO.

The cabin looked like a shrine, one of those impromptu street memorials made of pictures and candles that people created when an earthquake or a flood had struck.

Hoffman's cabin bulkhead was adorned with photographs not of the dead, but of the living whose time was about to run out. They were UIR weapons scientists. He tried to memorize every face. When he opened that dormitory door, he had to know he was taking down the right people. It was much easier than he thought to look these strangers in the eye.

I'm going to shoot civilians. Again.

The words made it all wrong. The threat, though, made it unavoidable.

Maybe not. He wouldn't know until he stood there for real.

Someone rapped on the frame of the open doorway. It was Bai Tak, clutching a cup.

"You want coffee, Hoffman-sah? We brew up."

"Thanks, Sergeant."

Bai Tak handed him the cup and stared at the pictures. "This bother you, sah?"

"Maybe." Some of the scientists were women. Women could kill you just as stone-dead as men could, and one of them was about to lead a company of Gears in Op Leveler. Hoffman was courteous to ladies, but he had no illusions about their lack of sweetness and light. "I was raised on rules. Rules of engagement. Assassination—well, it never used to be part of the job."

"Ah, *we* do it for you, then." Bai Tak's people were historically recent recruits to the COG empire, and they still did things the old-fashioned way. "Your rules are dumb."

"Rules are all that stand between us and chaos. Mostly."

"Someone with a small gun aimed at you, you shoot, it's okay. Someone with a gun so big you can't hold it, but it kill you all anyway—you can't shoot. That *is* dumb, sah."

Bai Tak had remarkable clarity, and a way of making Hoffman reexamine everything he thought he knew. The sergeant saw only threats and ways to neutralize them; Hoffman's world was dominated by regulations and chains of command, the political necessity of justifying his actions. It was probably why Pesangas were natural commandos. Their doctrine was that you did what you had to, any way you could, preferably before the other guy had time to do it to you first. There was an honest morality to it.

And I'm the one who told Adam Fenix not to be so squeamish.

"You're right, Sergeant," Hoffman said. "My job is to protect the COG and its citizens, not to worry about my soul."

The little Pesanga shrugged. "They happy to make satellites to kill civvies, yes? They not worry about *their* souls. Least you got the guts to do it yourself, sah."

Hoffman drained the cup and handed it back to him, and Bai Tak walked away whistling. It really did make Hoffman feel better. He went back to memorizing the faces of the key personnel that Settile had identified as being the ones with the most critical skills. These kinds of scientists couldn't be replaced for years, if ever.

Bettrys . . . Ivo . . . Meurig . . .

He shut his eyes and tried to recall the distinguishing features. Maybe these people had changed since the ID photos were obtained. Hoffman wasn't sure that he'd recognize himself from his COG security pass.

We stack around the door, just in case, and then I open it, and challenge them . . .

In his mind's eye, he ran the route penciled on the ground plan on the makeshift desk in front of him, counting the seconds it would take from the time they breached the main doors to the moment he burst into the accommodation block. They'd rehearsed each stage of the assault. They knew as much as they were ever going to know now.

Comms—destroy aerials and antennae.

Power—leave generator intact to exploit security overrides and enable bots to access mainframe.

Anyone we encounter—they won't be friendly forces, not at all.

There were only twenty-six hours in a day. He didn't have the time to delve into possible gray areas, and the COG didn't have the luxury of leaving anything for the UIR to use to regenerate the program.

This time tomorrow, it'll be over, or I might be dead.

The ship's address system summoned the duty landing crew to receive an incoming Raven. Hoffman took little notice and carried on visualizing the mission, checking the bulkhead clock occasionally to see how much time he had left for a final briefing. But he was interrupted again by a tap on the doorframe.

"Sir?" It was one of the signals officers. "Agent Settile and Professor Fenix have landed. Captain asks if you'd care to join them in the day cabin."

"What d'you mean, *landed*?"

"They're here to evaluate any material you extract, sir. The bots have to be processed immediately. We can't rely on data transmission links alone, in case they're jammed."

It was the only way they'd know what they'd grabbed, of course. They had to know before they pulled all troops and vessels away from Ostri. What they hadn't grabbed, they had to destroy.

"Give me five minutes," Hoffman said.

"One more thing, sir—personal message for one of your Gears. Private Santiago's family is trying to get word to him that his wife went into labor early and the baby is fine. What would you like me to do with the message?"

"Give it to me," said Hoffman.

He read the note and then pocketed it. Common sense said to hang on to anything distracting until after the mission. But the possibility of Santiago dying without knowing he had a daughter wasn't something Hoffman felt he could live with.

So that's where I draw the line these days.

Settile and Fenix seemed to be setting up an operations base in the day cabin. Small steel cases with black handles stood stacked on the floor, and the polished table was covered in folders. Michaelson said nothing, but the expression on his face said he didn't want any scratches on that table.

"The weather's not on our side," Settile said. "It was pretty rough flying out here. Are you willing to go ahead with the mission at this stage, Major?"

"The decision's been made."

"It's up to the Raven crews to say if they think they have a chance of deploying the Marlins," said Michaelson. "Dalyell won't ignore professional advice."

Hoffman looked at the bulkhead clock. "Well, that's a first for a goddamn politician. Sounds like he wants to offload blame. Okay, we wait until the last moment, until high tide, and if the weather hasn't improved, and they're *still* willing to fly, and you think the Marlins have a reasonable chance of making it in and out—then I say we go."

"I agree," said Fenix. "I don't think Ostri will buy a second assault on some third-rate target at a later date. They've got their own intelligence. They'll work it out sooner rather than later."

"I'd launch from this ship if we had the range, but we can't trade off any more fuel against load."

"Is C Company returning to *Kalona* after the mission?" Fenix asked.

"That's the plan."

"Then I'd really like to see my son, if that's at all possible."

Hoffman felt it was all a little late, but he didn't have the time or the patience to argue it. "Not my call," he said, "but I'm sure the respective COs will arrange to cross-deck him if they can."

Hoffman wondered what Professor Fenix had to say to Marcus that couldn't wait until he returned to Ephyra. It wasn't the only domestic business that couldn't wait. Hoffman remembered the folded note in his pocket, and decided it was time to assemble his teams.

He'd start with a quiet chat with Dom Santiago.

CNV *KALONA*, SOMEWHERE NORTH-EAST OF CNV *POMEROY*.

Fleet Met had been right about the weather, but wrong about the time.

The wind had picked up just after sunset. *Kalona* was rolling. Carlos didn't feel sick—yet—but listening to other Gears tumbling out of their bunks and rushing for the heads every so often made him worry he'd start vomiting, too. As long as he didn't *hear* the puking, he was okay. Really. He *was*.

He tried to work out if the motion was less noticeable if he shut his eyes or if he focused on a fixed point on the panel above his bunk. The strip of veneer was covered with traces of peeled paper, as if previous occupants had stuck pictures on it and then carefully removed them when their draft ended. There was no trace of what they'd depicted. Carlos imagined wives, sweethearts, kids, maybe even husbands, because there were some female crew.

We're late.

Maybe it's aborted because of the weather.

He glanced at his watch. He could just about see the readout; it was just after 2430, during what they called *silent hours* here, and it was anything but quiet. Most of C Company—the ones who weren't chucking up in the heads—seemed to be dozing. Steady snores rasped around him, but the ship beyond the open doorway was alive with activity. In a couple of hours, high tide, the landing craft would slip from *Kalona*'s bows and head for the beach just north of Aspho Point.

We're late.

The ship felt as if she was corkscrewing. Carlos couldn't work out if she was riding at anchor or just making way slowly in circles; he knew next to nothing about ships apart from the stuff he'd picked up on a couple of exercises and over the last day. Then he heard the rustle of fabric as someone walked between the rows of bunks, and a hand clasped his shoulder.

"Private Santiago?" A young rating bent down to whisper. He had a scrap of signal paper in his hand. "Are you Carlos Santiago?"

"Yeah."

"Message from *Pomeroy*. You've got a new niece, Sylvia Carla."

"Oh, wow . . . thanks." Carlos forgot his stomach. Poor

Maria; the kid was early, and Dom was stuck far from home, like him, somewhere out on this black ocean. "Can I get a message to Dom?"

"Who's Dom?"

"My brother. The kid's father."

"All I got was a signal from the CO of *Pom.* There's a stop on nonoperational comms while we're at defense stations, so I'm amazed they sent this. I'll see what I can do."

"Thanks, buddy. If you get the chance, say—oh, I don't know, tell Dom the drinks are on me."

The rating slipped away. The bunk above Carlos creaked and Marcus leaned a long way over the side, head down.

"Well, well. Congratulations, Uncle Carlos." Marcus gave him a friendly punch on the shoulder. He wasn't one of life's huggers and backslappers, so it was a big deal for him. "Good start to the mission."

"And you're Uncle Marcus, remember . . ."

"Hey, Santiago!" Maybe the rest of the non-puking guys weren't asleep after all. "Your kid brother's spawned *another* one already?"

"Yeah, a little girl."

The ribbing started, voices drifting up from all corners of the mess deck. "Dom knows all about diapers, seein' as he's still wearin' 'em . . ."

"They give those commando guys too many vitamins."

"What you Santiagos trying to do, breed your own army?"

Dim bulkhead lights started switching on one by one. Only a few Gears were left snoring now. The ship's address system came to life.

"LCT engineering party to well deck. Gears detachment to hangar deck at twenty-five-thirty for briefing."

"Does that mean it's all off?" That was the last thing Carlos wanted. He was past the point of walking away from it happy now. He was pumped up and ready to fight, although it was the prospect of landing on the beach that made his stomach knot more than the combat. "Aw, *shit.*"

If they got this right, they might exfil without firing a single shot.

"No." It was Sergeant Kennen's voice. "It means we're waiting for a go. Weather's crap. Crap as in we can't launch landing craft if it stays like this. And no, I don't know how long we'll have to wait."

Nobody griped, but there was a collective murmur. Carlos wasn't sure what the strategic situation was, or even if he'd understand it if he could see it, but his small corner of Op Leveler meant they'd be stuck here riding it out until the next window—the next slack tide at night. *Twenty-six hours.*

"I don't think I've got enough puke left in me for another day, Sarge," said a hoarse voice in the gloom.

"Stick a cork in it then, son," Kennen said, and walked away. "Anyone else here who's puking their ring—report to sick bay for medication, because I don't want dehydrated Gears falling in the drink and drowning. It makes my paperwork just too friggin' embarrassing."

It was like getting off a crowded train. Carlos waited for the press of bodies and activity in the narrow space to clear before he swung his legs over the side of the bunk and armored up. Marcus dropped down beside him.

"You ever going to take that thing off?" Carlos asked. "I swear I saw you shower in it the other day."

Marcus smoothed his hands over his do-rag, almost defensive. "When the war's over."

"Let's hope Stroud's at peak crazy tonight and decides to go for it. I want to get in there, not dick around waiting for the sun to come out."

"It won't be her decision alone," Marcus said, "but if we don't do it tonight, it's another day for the Indies to work out where we're heading. Then we're screwed."

"You reckon your dad knows all about this, then."

"Probably." Marcus had that slightly distant look that said he was chewing over the situation for the umpteenth time. "It's not that important."

But Carlos could see that it was. What could old man Fenix tell him anyway? Whatever it was that the raid was out to grab or trash, it didn't change a thing for them.

"He saw you off," Carlos said. "That's all that matters."

The hangar deck was a very different place from the one they'd assembled on when they embarked. The Gears had to find space on it now, because it was full of crew and Sea Ravens, sheltering below from the high winds and heavy seas.

"Are the choppers going to be available to us, ma'am?" Marcus asked Major Stroud.

Stroud stood with her helmet jammed between her knees as she pinned her hair into a pleat. "If necessary," she said. "We're just fire support tonight, remember, so we won't be needing them unless things go badly wrong. And they shouldn't."

When women Gears were armored up, it was hard to tell them from the men. The chest plates obscured any curves, and the assortment of plates, webbing, and pouches strapped onto the thighs gave women the same exaggerated walk. Some of them were taller than the guys anyway. There weren't many women in combat roles, but to fight in the front line they had to be fit enough to do what a man could, no concessions or exemptions. Carlos thought that was fair. And he treated any woman who could punch him out with due respect. He had no doubt that Stroud could.

"Listen up, people," she bellowed. Her voice cut through the noise around them, making even the maintenance crews pause. "We still don't know if this mission is on. I'm waiting for orders, but we have a narrow window, so I'm prepared to launch in extreme conditions if Hoffman is too. If it's a go—*Merit* and other ships in the task group will shell the Ostri coast at Berephus as a distraction. That gives us and the raiding party breathing space to get in and out."

"Ma'am, we're not going to be able to counter aircraft from the ground with the kit we're carrying."

Stroud slipped on her helmet. She was suddenly anonymous, just another Gear except for the discreet rank insignia stenciled on her chest plate and that distinctive, room-filling voice.

"They're not going to trash their own aerospace facility," she said. "Because unless we screw up massively, that's all they'll be aware of—the raid on Aspho Point. They'll need to tackle that counterassault with a little care, because it's their asset, not ours. Until we stroll off with it, that is. So once the Aspho raid is over—successful or not—we bang out. It's that simple."

Most battles usually were. Getting minced by gunfire was simple, too. Carlos gave the possibility a thought—an academic one, nothing serious, just a healthy acceptance of the odds—and fell in behind Marcus in the line waiting to step into the elevator down to the well deck. The moment the safety gate closed behind him, that was it. Op Leveler had personally begun for him.

Four landing craft nestled in the well deck, waiting for

the sea to be allowed in and create a miniature dock—if they ever got the go. The ship shuddered with every heavy wave, booming and clanging like a heavy tin box.

Marcus settled on the slats between Carlos and Sergeant Kennen. "You okay?"

"No. But I'll be okay when we land."

Carlos was more scared of the transit to shore than what might follow. On solid ground, you stood a chance. You could run, take cover, lay up; the ground wasn't trying to kill you. The sea, though, was a very different matter. It was an enemy in its own right, something to be defeated and survived before the real battle even began. It could neither be killed nor surrendered to. Carlos felt he had no control over it, and he never liked trusting to luck.

"You'll be fine," Marcus said. "I'll see you ashore, and I'll see you're back on the boat again."

It was dumb. Carlos and Marcus had fought in a dozen engagements. It was only a boat, and if the COGN could cope, then so could any Gear worth his salt.

The troops sat huddled in the landing craft. Stroud was in Bernie Mataki's, and Carlos could see her head moving as she talked to Mataki, one hand cupping her earpiece as if she was in discussion with CIC or someone. Then her head turned; she looked up toward the safety gantry that ran near the top of the bulkhead, and waved. As Carlos followed Stroud's gaze, he saw she was waving to her daughter. Anya, gripping the metal rail with one hand, gave her mother a thumbs-up sign, and vanished again.

"Poor kid," Kennen said.

Carlos glanced at his watch again. It was now, or it was abort, close to slack water when the high tide would allow them closer inshore for a few hours without the need to struggle across broad, exposed mudflats.

"It's a go," Stroud said, standing up as best she could. "It's a go, people."

The lights went out, the ramp began to drop, and the sea rushed in to flood the deck in a wall of wild noise. Bernie Mataki said something that got a laugh from the Islanders in her boat; whatever it was, Carlos couldn't make out the words. The four landing craft slipped onto a bucking, angry sea in complete and terrifying darkness, heading for shore.

Carlos looked back and the ship was in absolute blackness. When the craft climbed the peak of a wave, he couldn't see lights on the shore. He thought that this was what space would be like, except without the icy spray that slapped him in the face and snatched his breath away. It was going to be a relief to stand on something solid and get shot at.

Marcus was facing north.

"Shit," he said. "I think it's kicked off."

Carlos craned his neck. Nothing, just unbroken sea; and then there was a sudden flash of orange light reflected in the clouds in the distance, and another. The diversionary attack on Berephus had started. He couldn't hear anything. It was like distant lightning, seen but silent.

Somewhere out there . . .

"Go on, Dom," he said to himself.

"Yeah," said Marcus. "Show 'em, Dom."

SEA RAVEN SR-4467, INBOUND TO OSTRI COAST.

"This is as far as I go," said the pilot. Dom had to press his finger hard to his ear to hear his radio at all. "Have fun. See you back in the mess."

They were two kilometers from shore, the Raven's engine noise lost in the roar of the storm, and running without lights. Every meter that the helo could carry them was a meter more fuel for the exfil to take them back to *Pomeroy* at high speed.

The pilot seemed to have a special exemption from the laws of physics. He dropped the ramp in seas that threatened to swamp the whole helicopter, but Dom refused to drown, get shot, or otherwise give up and die now.

I got a daughter. I got a little girl now. I'm going to pick her up and hold her. And I'm not leaving Maria to bring up two kids alone.

"Shit, why don't we just parachute in and walk back to Tyrus?" Benjafield yelled over the roar of the wind, water, and rotors. "Cho? *Cho!* You okay?"

One of the Pesangas, Cho Ligan, was coxswain on the other Marlin. He grinned and gave Benjafield a thumbs-up. Dom wondered what it would take to scare a Pesang Gear, because so far he hadn't seen anything rattle them at all. He decided that if he absolutely *had* to do this kind of shit, then he was doing it with the best.

We're commandos. We can do anything. Like that crazy bastard flying this . . .

"Go," said the pilot. "Before I tip you out."

The lead Marlin didn't so much slip out as belly flop a meter into a hole that should have been sea, but Benjafield managed to hold it and steered clear. Dom kept his head down. Huddled in the Marlin with him were Hoffman, Bai Tak, and eight other Pesangas. Timiou, Morgan, and Young were in the second Raven with the rest of the Pesang troop. The two boats came about just as the Ravens lifted and vanished. Suddenly Dom couldn't hear them, and he couldn't see them until he dropped his NV goggles into place. The lenses smeared with salty spray immediately.

But faint lights were visible on the shore.

"Aspho Point," Hoffman said. "How's our bearing, Benjafield?"

"Looks spot on, sir."

By the time they edged slowly along the channels that fed into the salt marsh, the wind seemed to have dropped. It probably hadn't. It was just getting clear of open sea that made progress easier. They beached the Marlins in an inlet, unloaded the explosives, and fired up the bots. The three machines—Frank, Bruce, and Joe—hovered in the darkness, alive with small, dim lights that nobody would notice.

Hoffman looked like he was sinking in the soft ground under the weight of his pack. They all were. Nobody dared squat or bend over too far.

"Time to earn it, Gears," Hoffman said. He fiddled with the radio clamped to his chest-plate. "Cleaner to Longstop, we're in position."

Stroud's voice responded. "Longstop receiving. Ready in five. Still fanning out toward the bridge."

It was a long run from the landing point to the perimeter fence. Dom wasn't sure who they needed to keep out on this deserted coastline, but it wasn't Gears, that was for sure. Aspho Point, a sprawling collection of quick-build structures tacked on to a two-story brick building, sat on a raft of concrete in the middle of the wet, spongy landscape. A dozen nondescript cars were parked at the rear of the facility. With its casual security and generally tatty appearance, the place could have been a weather station, and that seemed to be the idea. It certainly didn't have a label that said BOMB HERE—TOP SECRET.

Intel had done pretty well so far; no surprises. Everything was where they said it would be. The steel lattice radio mast that was Aspho's outgoing link to the world stood in the lee of the building, and there was a separate aerial that looked like the TV receiver. If any security staff were watching their favorite show to while away the night, they wouldn't be alerted by a loss of signal. The Gears crouched by the main pedestrian gate, a simple wire-link door to one side of the vehicle gates, with an electronic lock. Morgan slipped off with six of the Pesangas and one bot to cut through the fence at the rear of the complex. It always paid to have a back door, even if the front door was pretty well left open.

Timiou gestured to one of the two remaining bots. "Frank, bypass the gate lock."

The bot lined itself up with the frame and inserted its probes. One gate swung open in the wind.

"If it's all this simple," Dom said, "I'll be pretty unimpressed."

It wouldn't be, of course. Nothing he'd been involved in ever was. They ushered in the bots and latched the side-gate closed again. The wind was shrieking in the wires and rattling the doors of outbuildings, providing a perfect cover for noise.

"Blue One, how's the radio mast?" Hoffman said.

"Nearly there, sir." Morgan was breathing heavily with the effort. "Okay, we're in . . ."

Dom faced out from the group, goggles raised, and scoped through with his Lancer. Two small lights shone back at him. It was a cat sheltering under a dump bin, but just detecting a pair of eyes—any eyes—made his scalp prickle. Morgan's breath rasped in his earpiece.

Waiting was always, *always* the thing Dom hated.

"We're at the power supply," Morgan said. "Locating the junction box now . . . Bruce, cut the juice . . . there . . . done, sir."

Dom almost expected to see the few lights on the site dim and fail, but bots were reliable. Aspho Point was now silenced. In this weather, anyone awake who'd noticed losing an outgoing link mid-sentence would be cursing the wind, not enemy troops. The raid had just bought extra time.

The doors to the main building were set to the side, at right angles to the shore. The windows of the accommodation block faced out to sea; even scientists liked a nice view when they were stuck out here in the ass-end of nowhere, Dom thought. On a sunny day, though, it might have been a pleasant place to be, at least for a short time.

"Okay, Hoffman said. "I'll sweep the accommodation with Red Troop. Santiago and Green Troop—clear a path in for the bots from the front. Morgan and Blue Troop—you go in from the back and start laying charges. Benjafield, Cho—hold here, and keep an eye out for company."

Dom didn't think for one moment that Hoffman was taking the easy job. It was the first time that Dom—that any of the commandos—were going to be shooting at people who didn't have their firepower, or any firepower at all. It needed a different state of mind. It was the kind of thing Sergeant Mataki would have been good at. Snipers saw the world differently, because they had to.

"Go," said Hoffman, and put a quick burst through the lock on the accommodation doors.

CHAPTER 13

Physically, commandos aren't much different from the average citizen, except they're a lot fitter by the time we finish with them. Mentally, though, they are—or they become—another species. We train them to understand and believe that they can do anything. *It's the mental attitude, the absolute confidence and overriding tenacity, that makes them unique.*

(COLONEL KIMBERLEY ANDERS, COMMANDO TRAINING DIRECTOR, PRESENTING A PAPER TO THE COG DEFENSE SELECT COMMITTEE ON THE NEED TO CREATE A PERMANENT COMMANDO FORCE.)

ACCOMMODATION BLOCK, ASPHO POINT; OPERATION LEVELER, TWENTY MINUTES AFTER LANDING.

I want to find myself staring down a barrel.

That'll be fine by me.

As Hoffman moved up the corridor with Red Troop, checking open doors, the last thing he wanted was to find someone unarmed.

For once, he wanted to burst into a room and meet a hail of fire, because he knew exactly how to deal with that, a clear-cut need to shoot rather than the messy business of working out what to do with noncombatants. The rules on what that meant—they now lay across the line, in the murky black ops world that Settile found so easy to navigate, and that Hoffman didn't. For all his lecture to Adam Fenix on threats, he still wasn't sure he had what it took to shoot an unarmed man, even a dangerous one.

Crash.

The door burst open into a communal lounge along the front of the building, empty and in darkness. He could see a small library area. So far, so good; the ground plan was holding up. Rooms were what Intel had guessed they were. That meant the bedrooms were next left, ten rooms both sides of a corridor.

The menials live locally. The scientists ship in for the week from their nice estates in . . .

He didn't know where they lived. He didn't need to. He just needed to extract Muerig, Ivo, and Bettrys. Anyone else could take their chances.

The wind roared and howled outside. Bai Tak and the rest of his men were completely silent, relying on hand signals and whatever spatial awareness made them as quietly lethal in a building as in the field. *Left,* the Pesanga gestured.

As per the Intel layout—there were the double doors, with a simple deadbolt.

The reflection from a lens flared in Hoffman's NV goggles as he moved to the other side of the passage. It was a security camera, more irony than risk right then. Had *nobody* heard a damn rifle being discharged into the door? It crossed his mind that even if they'd heard it, they might not have realized what it was. Civvies often didn't—maybe even ones who designed the biggest weapons of all. Hoffman held up his hand. Bai Tak and the rest of the troop stacked for entry either side of the corridor. Nothing moved behind the narrow glass panel that ran the full length of the left-hand door.

Three, two . . .

Go.

Bai Tak drilled out the lock and the troop poured in, switching from eerily complete silence to a yelling, door-splintering wall of angry noise, tactical rifle lights full on. They hauled the Aspho staff from their beds and herded them into the passage. Hoffman looked into the faces of men and women who hadn't a clue what was happening, and none of his combat instincts kicked in. He could see their faces, green-lit and terrified; all they could see was blinding white light and dark figures who were all noise and aggression.

And they press a button somewhere, and it's good night Ephyra.

Did they see *their* jobs as using lethal force?

"Into the common room," Hoffman yelled. "Move 'em." In an ideal world, they'd get everyone who wasn't an active threat bundled out the door—threats would be shot immediately—and sort through the live ones later, but it was going to be hard enough to exfil as it was. Extra passengers weren't now an option. "Get them in there. ID them."

There were eleven civilians, all in nightclothes or T-shirts and shorts. The Pesangas lined them up face down on the common room floor. Hoffman now had the worst choice of his life. He'd passed the mental watershed where he might have been able to shoot any of them. His choice had been made for him.

"Names," he barked. "I want your names. Do you understand what I'm saying?" He had no idea if they spoke the same language. Most educated UIR citizens could speak or understand Tyran, though. "You—" he prodded the first man in the row with his boot. "*Names,* starting with you."

"Who are you?" the man asked.

"My turn first. *Name.*"

Yes, they understood him, all right. Hoffman listened for three names: Bettrys, Ivo, Meurig. Two men and a woman, that was all Hoffman had to try to bring back in one piece. But now he felt he was past the point where he could justifiably shoot anyone in cold blood. The others would have to be trussed up until it was exfil time, and then he could let them go—before the buildings were blown up, before an air strike followed later to erase the whole site if his team didn't make a clean job of it. Adam Fenix would probably think he'd made the moral choice, but Hoffman knew he'd never be sure he'd made the *sensible* choice.

"Mauris Ivo," the man said at last.

Bai Tak hauled Ivo upright for Hoffman's inspection—yes, he *did* look like his picture, middle-aged, gaunt, bearded—then handed him off to another Pesanga for handcuffing. Hoffman worked down the line. He recognized some names from hours spent staring at pictures—not all—but he was now listening for only two.

Collun Bettrys had put on a few kilos since Intel last snapped him. He was hauled away too. The others had now grasped what was happening, that they were being separated, and it was clear they thought it was possibly the line between living and dying. One of the women started crying. The next in line—also a woman—didn't answer.

Hoffman still needed to identify Anna Meurig. He was

looking for a woman in her forties, not a kid like this. "Where's Meurig?"

"She's not here." The girl looked a little like her. "She's gone."

Intel hadn't done a bad job so far; he couldn't expect them to have a perfect tally of everyone who'd be here on any given night. "Sergeant, search the rooms and grab any ID you can find. Get the names to Control and see if there's anyone else they'd like."

"Okay, I'm Meurig's daughter." The girl gave in pretty fast. But she looked the kind that wanted to flaunt defiance. "You won't find her. I mean it. She's a long way from here, so screw you."

Hoffman now had leverage, at least. Meurig would care about her little girl. "Okay, we'll take you instead. Sergeant, secure the rest, park them here, and get these three down to the Marlins."

"What are you doing with us?" Bettrys demanded. "Are we hostages? What about the rest of us?"

"Usual deal for enemy scientists," Hoffman said. "A nice new job. A great life if you cooperate. No hard feelings, your past wiped clean. Your call."

Hoffman took two of the Pesangas and went to catch up with Blue troop and lay charges. It was all very unchallenging, the kind of job a civil police officer could have handled, if cops also blew up buildings.

He tried to tell himself it had gone smoothly so far because it was planned—as far as plans like this could go—and executed by good men.

I haven't had to shoot any of them. I didn't have to. So, do I feel better now?

"What we do with rest, sah?" Bai Tak asked.

Hoffman checked his watch again. Nine minutes. Just nine minutes from the time they'd breached the gate. It felt like forever.

"When we're ready to exfil, cut 'em loose and tell them to get as far from the buildings as they can." Had nobody worked out there was something wrong yet? How could a republic at war for so long get so sloppy? Maybe the Hammer of Dawn wasn't the history-turning advantage Dalyell and Fenix thought it was. "I can't give them a better deal than that."

No, he couldn't. And he knew that until the day he died, he would never be certain if he should have shot them or not.

ASPHO POINT, MAIN BUILDING; GREEN TROOP.

So all the wild stories were true.

Pesangas had mastered the art of the silent approach—and they didn't mess around.

Frankbot opened the keypad lock. Dom took three strides into the dimly lit lobby before he was confronted by a guy—thirties, tubby, not very enemy-looking—in a security uniform with his sidearm drawn. Dom didn't even have time to put a burst of fire through him. Shim Kor already had his machete raised, and that was it.

The blows sounded like a shovel digging into wet soil. There wasn't enough adrenaline in Dom to stop him from being transfixed for a moment by the simple, messy finality of it. The security guy didn't manage much more than a few gurgles. He made more sound hitting the floor.

"Shit," Timiou breathed, sidestepping a pool of blood.

Pesangas were usually such *nice* little guys.

Shim wiped the blade on the nearest available fabric, which happened to be the guard's shirt. Then he gestured up to indicate he was ready to secure the stairs. The two bots hovered patiently. Dom hand-signaled along the corridor ahead and Timiou followed; if the intel was correct, the ground floor housed computer servers, machine shops, and stores. There were still gaps in that information. Dom was filling them in on the fly.

A shaft of bluish, flickering light slanted from a partly-open door, not dim safety lighting, but maybe a screen with a changing display. He couldn't hear anything. Timiou stood to the side with his Lancer aimed, ready to rush the room.

Dom had been drilled to meet fire every time he opened a door. And if he didn't, he had to make a split-second decision whether to shoot the first thing that he saw move. The lack of clear targets in this place was unnerving him.

No bastard would leave all this stuff unguarded. Would they?

It's the wrong place. We've targeted the wrong place.

He counted down with a raised hand.

Three, two—go.

As he burst into the room with his finger on the trigger, a young woman was watching the news on TV, feet resting on a low table. No wonder she hadn't turned around; she was wearing headphones. She was watching the live coverage of the diversionary attack on Berephus, probably trying not to wake anyone. It was a split second of weird disconnection. Here was Dom, in the middle of an operation, and there was another part of the same op on the TV screen, digested and captioned for Ostri's public, all very unreal unless you happened to live in Berephus.

Shit . . .

Dom simply stepped in front of her and shoved the Lancer in her face. She didn't so much scream as suck in a terrified wheezing breath that seemed to go on forever, eyes frozen on his. She couldn't see them, of course, just NV goggles that made him look inhuman. He grabbed her sweater collar with his left hand to pin her in the seat.

"Who's in the building?" he yelled. "Who's on duty? Any other security?"

"Don't kill me, don't kill me, don't—"

He hauled her upright out of the seat one-handed. "Get those damn things off." She still had the headphones on. *But I'm Dom. I'm a good guy. I don't threaten women. This isn't me, honest.* "Who are you? What's your job here?"

He thought she was going to shit herself. Timiou walked up behind her and she almost fell back over the chair. She could hardly get her breath, eyes darting from one Gear to the other.

"I'm . . . just . . . the network tech," she panted. "Debrah Humbert. What do you want?"

Timiou looked around the room as if he was counting.

"This looks like the servers," he said. "Ma'am, this is just a security exercise. We have to be ready for anything. What the hell happened to your security?"

Shit, what are you playing at, buddy? Timiou had veered off on a totally unplanned tangent. Dom decided to see where this was going.

Debrah didn't seem to register the fact that Dom and Timiou sounded Tyran. Maybe she thought it was all part of this frigging *exercise,* that they were playing COG Gears so well that they spoke the language and had the accent down pat too. Whatever the reason—maybe she *wanted* to believe this was a game, and there wasn't a real rifle in her face—Timiou's story appeared to calm her down pretty well.

"Sorry," she said, still shaky. "We normally have two guards on duty, and the doors are kept locked. We did what we were told and kept things discreet. It's not as if we're in production yet."

Does that mean we won't get what we came for?

"You should keep the server room locked." Timiou just settled into his role as easily as breathing. "Even when you're here."

"Okay, maybe we got slack because it's backed up off-site."

Oh shit, shit, shit, shit . . .

Timiou didn't bat an eyelid. "Never trust a backup, lady. They always fail, especially if the site's as hot on security as you are . . ."

Debrah sounded suddenly indignant. "I think we can trust Osigcor. It's Army."

. . . shit.

Where the hell was Osigcor?

"Show me around," said Timiou casually, taking her elbow as if genuinely concerned for her well-being. "We'll probably have to call endex on this. I'll send Frank in to check."

As he turned her toward the door, he glanced back at Dom. But Dom was already on it, hand cupped over his mouthpiece, trying to raise *Kalona* before he even tried to interrupt Hoffman. If Hoffman had the channel open—and he should have had it set to interrupt the squad channel—he'd hear anyway.

"Cleaner Green One to Control, urgent request for information." Dom tried not to trigger a panic extraction.

"Cleaner Green One to Control, what is Osigcor? Repeat, what is Osigcor?"

Settile's voice answered without a pause. "It's the acronym for the army base just north of you—Ostri Signals Corps. Shown on your map as Peraspha."

"Well, there's a backup of the Hammer stuff there."

Settile's pause told him all he needed to know. "I think your word for this is *shit*."

"Yes, ma'am."

"Cleaner, are you hearing this?"

Hoffman grunted. "I am. We have two out of three of the live targets. Blue Troop is laying charges now. Michaelson, are you there? Can we call for fire from *Merit*?"

"On it," Michaelson cut in. "She's prepping all her Petrels to flatten the site. Plus there's a company of airborne embarked if needed."

"Data's flowing, sir," Dom said. Frank hovered around the room and surveyed the banks of servers like they were a buffet table. The bot made the quietest of bleeps before plugging into the data ports. Frank, at least, was happy. *Knock yourself out, buddy.* "Downloading and erasing."

"Cleaner, where's the third target?" Settile asked. "*Not* live?"

"Not here. But we have her daughter, which might motivate her when we let her call home."

"Glad to know you speak my language, Cleaner. Strip the place, and we'll update you. Control out."

Dom left Frank to gorge itself and headed down the passage again. That was when he heard the sobbing. Timiou had a firm hold on Debrah's arm, not Mister Nice anymore, and she'd worked out that the security guard on the floor wasn't playing dead for an exercise. Timiou was yelling in her face, demanding to know when the backups were scheduled and where the second guard was. Shouting at point blank range worked even on men if you gave it all you'd got. Timiou did.

"Ma'am, just tell him what he wants to know, because the whole place is going to go up soon," Dom said. "At least you won't be here when it happens."

"He's got two kids," she screamed. "Natan. He's got *two kids*. What are his kids going to do?" She was shaking as she gestured over her shoulder in the direction of the guard's body. "You didn't have to *kill* him, you bastards."

Yeah, and I've got two kids. And I'm going home alive, no matter how many Natans I have to slot.

Dom had fast-roped, ambushed, and learned to snap necks. But dealing with civvies—female civvies—was mired in all that bullshit about rules of engagement and not bullying girls. At any single moment, he was never quite certain where to draw the line. He tried to think of any female enemy civvie as Stroud—potentially lethal.

We're not raiding a kindergarten. They design city-killers here. Don't forget it.

"Okay, forget her," Dom said, and sprinted up the stairs to join the sweep of the upper floor. "Assume that the backup's supposed to be running now, and that someone's noticed it isn't."

The upper story was just offices, most of them in darkness. The two bots were darting around at shoulder height, stopping dead every so often to investigate a computer terminal as they passed it, as if they were being directed. They were; Frankbot down in the server room, could communicate with them. It was probably telling them what was connected to the servers and what was on each machine. Dom still found it hard not to talk to the bots like buddies.

Come on, move it, move it . . .

Dom checked his watch again. A massive gust of wind rattled the roof panels. From time to time, he even thought he felt the floor moving under him.

Yeah, I'm disappointed. I was pumped up for a real fight. And I didn't get one. Just a bunch of scientists and a security guard.

Hoffman's voice distracted him. "Cleaner to Green troop, charges laid in the server room and the machine shop. Blue Troop's moving to the upper story to rig charges now. Red Troop—outside to secure the exfil route."

But you couldn't rush a bot. The word *charges* didn't panic or hurry them, and they just did what they were programmed to do. The machines flashed and chattered to themselves as they robbed the UIR of its most decisive weapon.

Are their power cells going to hold out? We can't recharge them.

And we only made one kill.

But that was textbook, the way it should have been. Commandos were there to slip in and do maximum damage to key targets in the shortest possible time, not to rack up a body count. The hairiest part of the op had been insertion because of the heavy seas.

But if you get complacent—you end up dead. Right?

Dom did one more sweep of the upper floor with the Pesangas, opening every cupboard and drawer. He still expected to be ambushed at any moment, and they still hadn't found the second guard, if he was on the premises at all.

Well, one thing was for sure. The guy would only be

armed like poor old dead Natan down there, and unless he was the luckiest man alive, he'd be minced before he could get off a shot. Wars were full of dumb luck and the other guy's cumulative failures. It was high time the COG got a lucky break.

And one thing Dom was certain of was that he was lucky. However bad things got, he always found a way to fix them.

"Boat party to all call signs," said Benjafield's voice in his earpiece. "Contact just offshore . . . rigid inflatable, looks like six or eight men. Running parallel with the shore, one hundred meters out."

They'd expected any counterassault to come from inland. *Shit.* But at least they were ready for it.

Hoffman sounded as if he'd just heaved something heavy. "Stand by. They might not spot us."

But if the UIR was as good as Hoffman's squad, then they would. Dom made the assumption that they'd be more experienced, too. He had to. Except for Hoffman and Pesangas, everyone here was just out of training.

The war had rumbled on for decades. Dom had to assume that meant the two sides were evenly matched. And that was why the Hammer of Dawn was so critical a weapon.

He'd have the fight he wanted now.

ASPHO FIELDS; OP LEVELER, TWENTY MINUTES AFTER LANDING.

Carlos sat behind the machine gun, staring into empty darkness, waiting for Ostri to wake up and smell the trouble.

"Nothing." Conversation wasn't easy in this wind, a fine

line between being heard and not being overheard. They were a kilometer from Aspho Point, mere spitting distance. "There's nothing going on. No fire, nothing."

"That's special forces." Marcus said. "In and out before anyone knows they've been there."

"You think that's going to be the future of warfare?"

"If it is, there'll be a lot of Gears looking for work."

But Dom and his buddies weren't *out.* C Company was still here, waiting, and they'd stay here until the commandos were clear of the area.

The Gears were spread out along the south bank of the main channel to block any advance, but Carlos had his eye on the bridge and the road leading to it. Only an idiot would try crossing the marsh tonight. He could see groups of trees scattered across the landscape, clinging to a windswept existence on small pockets of drained land.

"How can trees grow in salt marsh?" he asked.

"They build barriers and drain it. Rich soil. And the water probably isn't that saline." Marcus was like a mobile science handbook. Carlos hoped his dad was happy that his education hadn't gone to waste. "I don't know shit about the trees, though. Maybe they're salt-tolerant."

"Okay, you get nine out of ten."

Carlos checked his watch again. To the northeast, he could see the occasional flare of light as *Merit* continued the diversionary attack on Berephus. Kennen and Mataki waded across a ditch with Stroud and squatted down to listen to their radios. They had their right hands to their ears, like a matched set of figurines, all three totally silent and staring at the ground; for a moment, it was an oddly comic sight. Carlos listened in to the channel.

"*Kalona* Control to Longstop," said Anya Stroud. *Shit,*

imagine having to perform right under your mother's nose like that. Carlos could feel the pressure sweating out of her. She'd probably get a report card at the end of the op. "Cleaner has marks standing by for extraction, ordnance is in position, still awaiting completion of data transfer. Possible enemy contact approaching from the sea, small RIB. Cleaner will engage if necessary."

"*Kalona* Control, please advise if Cleaner needs support. We can drop Longspears anywhere he needs them, too. Out." Stroud switched back to the company channel. "Mataki, move your platoon back two hundred meters and see if you can get a line of sight."

Longspear ground-to-air missiles were worth the extra sweat of lugging them around a battlefield. They'd work just as well on a RIB as they would on armored vehicles. Would they get decent targeting with all the spray? Carlos thought it was worth a try.

And it could all end up being nothing. Every operation was full of possible contacts that didn't amount to anything.

But that's my kid brother back there. My Dom.

It wasn't the same as having Dom in the same fire team and being able to keep an eye on him.

"Stop worrying about him." Marcus had his mind reader moments. He was using a Longspear command launch unit to scan the marsh to the north, resting the device on his knee as he knelt back on one heel. "So either the Indies can add two and two, or something's alerted them."

"How long you think it's going to take?"

"How much data have they got to transfer?"

"I don't know."

"Exactly. Neither do they."

"They said an hour."

"That's probably my dad saying Aspho would need a given amount of data and storage based on what he'd use."

"Shit."

"Hey, they'll bang out when they need to. It's not a suicide mission. It's asset denial. What they can't carry away, they'll trash."

Only Marcus could make that sound simple and reassuring.

"Anya Stroud must be crapping herself," Carlos said. "Being able to hear her mom and all that."

"Don't try to patch into Dom's channel."

"Okay, I'm not doing a great job of hiding this, am I?"

"If you listen in," Marcus said, "it'll just make it worse, because you won't be able to do a damn thing. Dom's fine. He's a pro. He's an *adult*."

"But he's got no frigging commando experience."

"He's a Gear," Marcus said. "That's all he needs."

"I don't care if he's a father and all that crap. I just can't stop wanting to take care of him."

"When *you* have kids," Marcus said, eyes still fixed on the CLU, "you're going to be the worst pain in the ass imaginable." He stopped and stiffened, then adjusted the CLU's magnification. The visible range was more than the two-klick targeting limit. "You want to take a look about five degrees left of the group of trees? The ones in line with the bridge."

Carlos sighted up. All he could see for a moment was branches bending in the wind and reeds in the foreground. Then he caught a slight bobbing movement and concentrated on it. The infrared picked up hazy shapes—someone moving. *Heads.* Three or four. They vanished again.

Carlos cupped his hand over his headset mouthpiece.

"Contact, one thousand meters, group of trees, quarter left. Four or more personnel on foot."

There was a pause as others sighted up. Carlos handed the CLU back to Marcus and aimed.

"Steady," Stroud said, but Carlos heard the click of her Lancer. "Confirm the target. Fenix—pop a Longspear in the slot, will you?"

Another voice; Sergeant Kennen. "Contact, APV or light armored vehicle, fifteen hundred meters, right of road."

Marcus was already loaded and waiting. The missile launcher nestled on his shoulder. "Contact, one thousand meters, group of trees, confirm at least six hostiles."

"Contact—two thousand meters, another APV, off road, to the right."

"Sit tight," Stroud said. She paused; Carlos saw her tilt her head, listening to another channel. "Roger that—Cleaner is engaging enemy from the sea, so we're in an Indie sandwich now, gentlemen. Hold . . . hold . . ."

Crack-ack-ack-ack.

The distant rattle of automatic fire behind him made Carlos jump. It was carried on the wind; the battle for Aspho Point had kicked off.

He didn't have time to think before his reflexes took over and his attention was locked on the threat facing him. His gut churned, though, not for himself but for Dom, and then the night sky above him was full of orange light. A flare struggled in the darkness, fighting the wind. The marsh was illuminated for a few seconds. It was long enough for Carlos to see a shitload of Indies heading their way.

Marcus let out a long breath.

"I'm locked on the lead APV, ma'am."

"Hold . . . Mataki, have you got anything south?"

"No, ma'am."

"Mataki, go right and secure the exfil route."

"Yes, ma'am."

Long seconds; the comparative quiet was interrupted by bursts of fire from Aspho Point.

"Okay," Stroud said. "Longstop to Control, we have multiple contacts approaching from Peraspha. Engaging now." She was all certainty, the kind of officer any Gear would trust and follow. Carlos did. *"Fire."*

CHAPTER 14

It's important to know how the enemy plans to attack you. But it's more important to know why. *What do the Locust want? Why are they trying to wipe us out? Why did they choose that particular day to emerge? If we can answer that, Chairman Prescott, we might stand a chance.*

(COLONEL VICTOR HOFFMAN, IN CASUAL CONVERSATION.)

ROTUNDA AREA, JACINTO; PRESENT DAY, FOURTEEN YEARS AFTER E-DAY.

"I see him." Bernie had an extra meter's height advantage riding top cover. She kept hitting the control button on her earpiece, but the bloody thing was just howling static. "Cole, back up. *Back up.* Are the grubs jamming the comms?"

"Yeah, they do that a lot," Cole said, slamming on brakes and whipping the wheel. The Armadillo almost spun one-eighty in its own length. "Hang on, Damon baby, we're comin' . . ."

The plan had been to form up on Hoffman, but they

couldn't raise anyone on the radio. The first thing she saw was the flatbed truck—call sign 2-45—loaded with the vats, and Baird crouching behind one of the huge tires spraying fire at half a dozen drones moving up from the Rotunda.

I remember this place now. Been a long time.

Bernie couldn't see the driver or his escort. She'd worry about that later. Baird was a whiny brat, but he was a Gear, and that overrode any personal dislike, because it made him *family*. It was okay to hate your siblings, but no outsider had the right to dare lay a finger on them. The bond possessed her again as strongly as it ever had; once a Gear, always a Gear. It wasn't even a conscious choice. It just *was*.

Cole brought the APC to a screeching halt that nearly ejected her from the hatch. Bernie laid down suppressing fire to cover his dismount, and he just jumped out like an angry driver whose parking space had been taken, swaggered into the street, then opened up with his Lancer.

He switched instantly from lovely amiable Cole to something else entirely. He seemed to have no sense of danger. He just moved forward like he was mowing grass and almost cut the first grub in half with a sustained burst of fire at waist level. The one behind got it full in the chest. Bernie—effectively stuck in the hatch, feeling exposed—switched the Lancer to semi-automatic and went for the head shot. The ugly bastards were taking fire on two sides now, and it slowed them down just enough to get in an accurate shot. She dropped two grubs. And she didn't feel bad about the *satisfaction* it gave her. Monsters were easy to kill. She knew she'd never wake up in the night worrying about their widows and orphans.

"Baird!" she yelled. "Baird, where's the driver?"

"Been hit," he called back. "I shoved him behind one of the vats."

"Escort?"

"Dead."

The truck didn't matter. Under fire, Bernie's defensive reflex was triggered by humans, not objects, not even really *valuable* objects. She had to get everyone out of there. Screw the truck; they'd come back for it later, even if they had to retrieve the parts one at a time by kicking the shit out of every thieving Stranded who'd stripped it.

Cole dropped into the cover of a doorway, reloaded, and came out firing again. Bernie decided it was now or never and squeezed out through the hatch to jump off the top and onto the ground. It was funny how it never hurt during action. By the time she was up on her feet, Cole had nearly reached the back of the truck. But more Locust were closing in from the sides behind him. Bernie had to close that gap.

Not Cole. No, you bastards don't get Cole.

It was a gamble, as always. Cole was in her arc of fire; she had no choice. As the grubs moved farther across, blocking her view of him, she opened up and emptied a clip into one, then another, and then the third one turned to face her. She was still pushing a fresh clip into her Lancer as the grub aimed its weapon. As she looked into that acid-attack of a face, time just wouldn't move fast enough.

The magazine slid home. She raised the Lancer just as the grub's chest burst in a plume of blood, and another, and another. It pitched forward. Baird, aiming on one knee, was now staring at her across the road. There were no more grubs left standing.

Bernie breathed again. "Thanks. Nice timing, Blondie."

"Didn't see you there . . ." Baird said. "I just like dropping grubs."

He got up and went over to Cole, who was inspecting his left arm but otherwise instantly back to his cheerful self. Baird grunted and returned to the grubs, checking for live ones, and paused to put his chainsaw through one of them.

He beckoned to Bernie. She decided to humor him.

"See, that's why you got a good kill, Mataki," he said. "You did it like this." He squatted down, took out his knife, and prodded the open chest cavity with the point, like he was holding a dissection class. "You saw down at an angle through the shoulder. Blade bites into the meat, then rides down the neck muscles, through the big blood vessels, into the first rib and collarbone, trachea, esophagus, and aorta. Pretty instant incapacitation. No point going for the back or the guts unless you have to—too much muscle, too slow. Or the neck. Groin isn't too bad. Incapacitating, but not exactly instant."

Baird obviously understood mechanisms, whether metal or flesh. In a different world, he might even have turned into a nice lad.

Bernie looked down at the grub. Did *they* have families? Plans? Dreams? What did they see when they looked at humans? Where did they come from? No, she didn't care. She made a point of *not* caring about grubs—for her brother Mick, for his kids, and for everyone in her hometown.

Cole was still peering at his arm. A thin trickle of blood snaked down the skin and ran into his wristband.

"Shit, Boomer Lady." He indicated his biceps and bellowed with laughter. A round had shaved a shallow furrow through his skin and gone wide. "You after some black leather to trim those kitty fur boots?"

She'd clipped him after all. It made her gut ice up and flip over. "Sorry, Cole. I'm not as sharp as I used to be."

"Hell, I don't mind. They're dead and I'm not. Thank you kindly, ma'am. You're sharp enough for me."

Own-goals were a fact of life in combat, but that was no comfort for Bernie. There was a fine line between a calculated close shot and risking a comrade's life, and she wasn't sure on which side she'd fallen. It wasn't a happy thought for a sniper. But Cole was right: he survived. She patted his back. Despite the fact that he was a big killing machine, there was something about him that made her want to pour him a glass of milk and read him a bedtime story.

Baird stood on the flat-bed. "Hey, he's fine. Help me move this guy, will you?"

"Can we move the truck?"

"No time. This guy's going to be dead soon if we don't get him some help."

"Oh, great bedside manner," said Bernie. She hoped the driver was too out of it to hear. "That'll really give him a boost."

But the driver *was* a mess. He'd been shot in the thigh and abdomen, but he didn't seem to be bleeding out as badly as Bernie would have expected. Maybe it had missed the major plumbing. But the man riding escort had taken a single shot right above the nose, exiting near his crown.

"Shit," said Cole. "Come on, baby. You're goin' home."

He bent down and hoisted the dead escort onto his shoulder. Every squad needed a Cole. He made you feel like nothing bad could ever happen as long as he was around, not simply because he was reassuringly, *lethally* huge, but also because he radiated a confidence and generosity of spirit that never faltered. Even the fact that his previous squad buddies *had* been killed didn't dent the impression that Cole guaranteed survival.

Baird and Bernie supported the injured driver between them. He was in a bad way. His name tab said TATTON, J.

"What's the J for, sweetheart?" Bernie tried to get him to focus on her. *Keep him talking, keep him conscious.* "I'm Bernie."

"Jeff." It was just a whisper. "What . . . about the truck . . ."

"Well, Jeff, I say screw the truck, because we can always fix that later, but we've got to get you welded up first. Okay? Not far to go. Come on. Easy does it."

"I'll get a haemostatic dressing on him," Baird said, checking in his belt pouch. "Lay him on the seat. I'll do it."

"Have you finally decided to join the human race, Blondie?"

Baird probably needed surgery to remove that sneer from his face. It never left him. "Easier than having to listen to you bitching me out for not following SOPs."

There was a man like any other in there somewhere. Bernie just didn't know if she had the patience to find him.

They were thirty meters from the APC, no distance at all. But as Bernie put her free hand to her earpiece to check if comms were restored, she was suddenly punched into the air on a wave of deafening noise and heat. The next thing she knew she was staring up at smoke billowing across the night sky, her ears were ringing, and Jeff was slumped across her.

Her first reaction was to put her hand on his neck to feel for a pulse. If the grubs had killed him after the squad had busted a gut to save him, she was going to go on a rampage of blind destruction. But there was movement. She could feel it.

"He's okay," she said to nobody in particular. "He's okay."

A long burst of Lancer fire rang out; Baird was swearing. She could feel heat on her face, see yellow light. She couldn't work out why the sun had suddenly come out.

"That's for my fucking 'Dill," Baird kept saying. He was firing at something. "Shit, we're walking back. *Shit.*"

When she managed to sit up, she realized the APC was a mangled wreck spewing flame and smoke. Cole pulled her to her feet and tapped her face.

"Gotta move, Bernie," he said. "You okay?"

If she wasn't, she couldn't tell. She struggled to get Jeff's left arm across her shoulder to lift him, then Baird took his right. Blood was running down his face, but his expression hadn't changed.

Cole lifted the dead escort onto his shoulder again.

"We're on foot, Cole," Baird said. "You can't haul him home. Leave him."

Cole adjusted the body into a more comfortable position. "I ain't leaving him here for the grubs to eat or whatever shit those freaks get up to. Man deserves a proper funeral."

They still had no radio comms. All they could do was listen for gunfire or vehicle noises.

"You're too frigging soft, Cole." Baird seemed to be taking most of Jeff's weight, though. "Look after number one."

"Yeah, baby, I'll do that."

Bernie wasn't sure how her legs were moving, but they seemed to know where to go, so she just let them have their own way.

As they passed the dead grub with a grenade launcher, Baird paused to give it a hard kick. Its guts flopped out as the blow rolled it onto its side.

"Yeah, that's for my 'Dill, asshole," he said.

FORMER THEATER OF THE MUSES, ROTUNDA AREA, A FEW STREETS AWAY.

"Boomshot," Kaliso said, cocking his head to one side. "Which means it's hit something of ours."

The explosion was close. Hoffman decided that it could only be the vat truck—2-45—or an APC. He and Kaliso were working their way through the lobby of a derelict theater, heading through the buildings to the College Green intersection.

Without comms, they had to check it out.

The grubs had stopped firing, but he could hear them moving around in the rubble, getting closer. Kaliso edged up to the section of fallen balustrade that formed a handy barrier and rested the muzzle of his Lancer on top to check through the scope. Hoffman stopped and faced rear.

"Anything?"

"They're just waiting out there, sir."

And we know why.

If the grubs had hit an APC, then it meant casualties. Wounded. *Bait.*

Hoffman checked himself for thinking impersonally even for a moment. *Cole. Mataki. Baird. My goddamn Gears. The best.*

There was no point dragging this out and losing more. Anya was right. The grubs wanted to take down Gears. Without the army, they could stroll into Jacinto any time they liked without even bothering with tunnels. Gears were all that stood between the Locust and the last of humankind.

And grubs knew that Gears never abandoned their comrades. They used that. They probably saw it as a weakness. It was another thing that reminded Hoffman this wasn't the good old Pendulum Wars. He'd shaken hands with some UIR prisoners, enemies or not, because they'd been gallant. He'd regretted having to shoot some of them to stop them. They were *human.* But the Locust were everything that was depraved and loathsome.

"They breed by rape," Hoffman said.

"What, sir?"

"The Locust. I heard the females—the Berserkers—have to be tied down to mate. They're not exactly willing. It sums them up. They enjoy violence, they don't value their own lives, they enslave. There's nothing to admire about them."

Kaliso was still scoping through the rubble beyond. "They're intelligent."

"So's Jack. Your point?"

"Admiration is not approval."

It was just as well Kaliso was a typically aggressive, hard-fighting Gear. Hoffman found all his spiritual mystic shit faintly disturbing.

"Well, I feel uneasy about an enemy that's so easy to hate." Hoffman wasn't sure why he'd said that. He chewed it over, realizing this was a bad time to have profound thoughts. But an enemy so vile that nothing you did to them felt bad or shameful—*that* worried him. It took away the last personal restraints in warfare. It threatened to unleash the monster within most men—and women. "But that doesn't mean I won't blow the bastards away, and all their children."

"If they're waiting, there have to be survivors. And they know they've managed to jam our comms."

"Agreed. Move on."

Hoffman's luck had survived forty years in uniform, every single one of those spent at war. But it wouldn't last forever. He was torn between sending Kaliso back to the APC to make a run for it—they were two valuable assets the COG couldn't afford to lose—and committing what he had here and now to searching for survivors. Without comms, he was blind and deaf in a city he'd grown up in. The streets were more unrecognizable with every day that passed, and the map shifted. But he had a button-sized mechanical compass. Technology was no substitute for basic fieldcraft in the end.

Hoffman indicated ahead and left. *"Go."*

They ran at a crouch for a gap that should have opened onto the sunken amphitheater, right into the path of the grubs, and opened fire. Instead of returning it, the things vanished into the street beyond. As strategies went, it was transparent; Hoffman started looking for the twist, the double-game, and couldn't think of anything beyond the fact that they were being lured on toward something.

But it didn't matter. He was heading for where he thought the Armadillo had been attacked, simply because he could *not* drive away without knowing he had done everything to try to find and save any survivors.

"You could leave me to this, Private."

Kaliso slowed down with him. "And what if we find them alive? Sir, no disrespect, but one man with an injured leg . . ."

Hoffman was in serious pain, and Kaliso could see it. "One *old* bastard with an injured leg. But I'm still moving."

The right turn onto College Green should have been ten meters away. Hoffman could see the sharp granite-clad edge of the old art gallery wall, and adjusted his mental map of the area. Yes, *right.* They were going to step out of cover into what was, the last time anyone had done a recon, a clear road. He brought Kaliso to a halt with a signal, arm extended level with his shoulder.

"Ready?"

Kaliso looked to what had been the other side of a fine mosaic walkway. "There's a column there, sir—you take up that position and cover me while I exit—"

Suddenly the faint static in Hoffman's earpiece popped and he heard a voice again.

"Control to Hoffman. . . . Control to Delta. . . . Control to Hoffman. . . . Control to Delta. . . . Control—"

"Hoffman receiving, Anya." *Not deaf now, at least, and only partially blind.* "What's happened to Cole's 'Dill?"

"All Gears are alive, sir, one convoy crew killed and one injured, but Cole's APC's been destroyed. They're making their way to an RV point on foot. Sergeant Fenix is extracting them."

"The rest of the convoy?"

"The tail's being escorted in by Gamma Squad, sir."

Kaliso made a triumphant fist. "We're done here, then, sir."

"We are, Private." But Hoffman still didn't know why the grubs were playing this game. "Anya, can Jack get a visual on our location? We thought grubs were laying an ambush for us, but if there are no wounded out there, what the hell are they doing?"

"Wait one, sir. Relocating Jack."

Hoffman looked at Kaliso, baffled. He had the feeling that there was something he'd missed, and it was an uncomfortably long wait. He could hear the chatter between Cole and Dom Santiago, so at least the rest of the squad had managed to rendezvous.

"Sir, I can't see anything," Anya said at last. "They're just waiting in the road, looking toward your position."

Hoffman looked up, searching for Jack, but the bot was either hidden behind a building or in stealth mode. "Then we'll be uncharacteristically generous and return to the vehicle instead of blowing their grub asses to kingdom come. Hoffman out."

Kaliso backed away from the opening, and they picked their way back around the edge of the amphitheater to where they'd laid up the 'Dill. The APC nestled under the cover of an archway.

"Hoffman to Fenix, we're about to pull out," he said. It was bliss to have comms back online. Hoffman still marveled at how the Pesangas could operate in total silence with no radio contact at all. Some of the more gullible Gears had thought they were telepathic. "You've picked up the others? Nobody left out there?"

"All mounted, sir. We're rendering medical aid to the truck driver. I recommend we leave the truck until daylight."

"Private Kaliso will lead a recovery team in the morning," Hoffman said. "Let's be extra vigilant on the way back."

But Kaliso had stopped dead a few meters from the APC. He squatted down on his haunches and looked at the Armadillo. "No sir, let's be vigilant right now . . ."

Hoffman stopped too. It finally dawned on him, and he was furious at his own stupidity.

Who's gullible now?

They'd been so wary of being separated and then picked off by the grubs that they'd had to leave the vehicle unguarded. It was one of the problems of running a 'Dill with only two men. And it was also one of the basic rules of not getting stuck up Shit Creek with no ticket out; the vehicle needed to be secured.

"Shit," said Hoffman.

"I always give every vehicle a quick once-over before I mount," Kaliso said. "Old habit. Comrades of mine learned the hard way in the last war."

Grubs were smart, yes, but they also seemed to have a sense of theater. When Hoffman squatted down to look at what Kaliso had spotted, the device clamped under the 'Dill wasn't that hard to see.

Maybe the grubs got what they wanted either way. Dumb humans mounting their vehicle and getting blown sky-high, or dumb humans finding the device and being stuck on foot, prey for hunting.

"If that's how they want it," Kaliso said, "I'm up for it."

"Sir?" Anya could still hear them. "Sir, are you okay?"

Hoffman looked at Kaliso, and they knew they'd reached a silent agreement. If they let Anya know they were deep in the shit, someone else would have to risk their necks to get them out. And neither of them was ready to let the grubs set the agenda.

"Fine," Hoffman said. "Just fine, Lieutenant Stroud."

He switched his radio to receive-only, and reloaded his Lancer.

Kaliso did the same.

LEAD APC, LEAVING RV POINT EN ROUTE FOR JACINTO.

"Control to Fenix," Anya said.

The 'Dill snaked between piles of debris on the road as Dom tried to avoid bouncing it around. Jeff Tatton was in enough pain as it was without having his guts shaken out before he got to the hospital. Marcus sat in the front, turning occasionally to watch Baird trying to stop the bleeding.

"Receiving, Anya." He looked at Dom, eyebrows slightly raised. She usually said why she was flashing them right away. "You got a problem?"

"Yes. Hoffman's switched to receive-only."

Dom's mind raced ahead. It'd had plenty of practice over the years. Anya had a real gift for spotting anything out of the ordinary, probably honed by years of having only voice cues and data displays to give her a picture of the battlespace—or, more to the point, the Gears in it. Fresh shit was incoming.

"Explain," Marcus said, gesturing to Dom to slow down some more. "Hoffman's having radio trouble, or what?"

"Pure extrapolation. I think he and Tai are in trouble and don't want backup for some reason. I'm going to call in a Raven."

"No," Marcus said. Nobody wanted a Raven out at night if they could avoid it. It was even riskier than daytime flying. "We're only a couple of minutes away. We'll do it."

Baird let out an irritated *fffff* sound. "Not unless you want a dead driver here, jackass. You choose. The asshole who left you to rot in the Slab, or this completely innocent retired Gear . . ."

"Fuck you," Marcus snapped. Dom flinched. *Wow, that's not like him.* Baird had hit a very raw nerve somehow. "Dom, stop the 'Dill."

"Fenix, you're as big an asshole as Hoffman," Baird said. "The Embry Star Club. Or maybe you're still trying to impress him."

"Shut it, Blondie." Bernie tapped Dom on the shoulder. "I'll go back for him. I've known the old tosser since we were both baby Gears. That technically makes him my oldest friend, sad as that sounds."

"No. Won't be necessary." Dom halted the 'Dill. He knew what was going to happen next; he knew Marcus too well, and that meant his own course of action was already set. He turned and reached back to prod Cole. "You're the designated driver, Cole Train. Don't scratch the bodywork."

Marcus opened the hatch and jumped down. "Not you, Dom. Bernie, stay where you are. I can do this."

Dom sighed and ignored him. He dismounted and jerked his thumb at Cole to move up front. "Not alone. No."

"My choice."

"You go, so I go." Dom was already moving down the road toward Hoffman's position. He heard Cole rev up the 'Dill. Nobody was listening to Marcus today, but that only ever really pissed him off if he thought it put them at risk. "You want to stop me? Then put a frigging round in me."

Marcus just sighed. The APC shot off toward Jacinto; they began jogging back to College Green.

"Anya, have you got a fix on Hoffman?"

"Yes, Marcus. He's at the junction of Unity Street and Porto, on the west side of the Rotunda itself. Best fix I can get on his radio. Tai as well."

"Thanks. Fenix out." He caught up with Dom. "You don't owe me anything."

Shit, I swear he's a mind reader. "I didn't do you much good while you were banged up in the Slab all those years."

"Funny, I thought you saved my life."

"We got to talk about it, Marcus. Sooner or later."

"Later."

"What's eating you?"

"And thanks for not asking why I'm bothering to help Hoffman."

"I don't need to ask. But I want to know what Baird said to wind you up."

"Don't you get out of breath, talking while you run?"

"No. I'm fit. Stop ducking the question."

Marcus fell silent for a while. All Dom could hear was the steady *chonk-chonk-chonk* of their armor and boots as they jogged. In the deserted streets, the sound echoed like a bag of rivets being shaken.

"Okay," Marcus said. "I hesitated in the past and cost guys' lives. I'm never dicking around like that again."

Marcus didn't have a hesitant bone in his body, and Dom couldn't believe there was something that serious in his past that he didn't know about. He filed it mentally for discussion later. Whatever it was, it had really stung Marcus.

"Okay," Dom said. They were a couple of blocks from the Rotunda now. Some Stranded had emerged again, and loitered on a corner under a dim street light. When they saw Dom and Marcus running, they melted back into doorways. For them, it could only mean Locust were about. "Okay, but I want you to know that I busted my ass trying to get you out from day one. I didn't forget."

"Don't you think I know that?"

"I hassled everyone who'd listen to get an appeal together. Ministers, officers, the lot. Shit, I even tried to get some asshole to spring you." Dom had traded his own Embry Star for that; even in post-E-Day Jacinto, collectors still wanted them badly. The medal didn't seem to matter when everyone he ever cared about was gone. "Did you get my letters?"

"One or two."

"I wrote every week."

"I knew you would."

"Shit . . ." Dom forgot the grubs. All he could think of was Marcus stuck in that shit-hole with scum that weren't worth pissing on, never getting word from the outside. It broke his heart. "I'm sorry."

"You got me out. Don't sweat it." Marcus slowed to check a landmark. It wasn't always easy to navigate on foot, because the ever-changing cityscape looked a little different from an APC's height. "I knew you'd keep trying."

Dom could feel himself slipping back into an old habit. When Carlos had died, he clung to Maria and the kids, and was scared to be away from them even for a few hours. It was a year or so before he kicked the panic. When Marcus had been jailed, it was like losing his brother all over again. Now he wasn't prepared to be parted from Marcus for any damn reason at all.

If I'd stayed with Carlos . . .

Dom had replayed what little he knew of his brother's last hour more than a thousand times. He knew. He'd counted. He also knew that if they'd been together, all three of them, it would never have ended the way it did.

Yeah, he understood why Marcus had to save Hoffman and Kaliso. He understood completely.

CHAPTER 15

Guns and bombs don't kill people. Clever scientists who want to build a better method of destruction kill people—lots of them. Most of my Gears couldn't make anything more lethal than a blade or a bow. So you'll forgive me if I think it stinks that my Gears get your "baby-killer" crap and your educated colleagues get research grants. And that's before *you start inventing other shit you can't control.*

(MAJOR VICTOR HOFFMAN, DURING A FRANK EXCHANGE WITH A STUDENT AT LACROIX UNIVERSITY CAREERS DAY, FOUR YEARS BEFORE E-DAY.)

ASPHO POINT, SIXTEEN YEARS AGO: HALF AN HOUR INTO THE RAID.

"I can now see *two* machine-gun positions, two hostiles, line of sight with the gates," Benjafield said. "Six more still out there but I can't see them. Cho, you got anything?"

"Three moving to rear of building. Want me to follow?"

Hoffman cut in on the comms circuit. "Negative, Cho,

stay with the boat. Morgan, Bai Tak, go to the rear and sort them out. Cho, Benjafield—stand by to bang out of there with the prisoners if it comes to the worst. The bots are programmed to return to you. Data and key personnel retrieval, that's all we're here for."

Dom, crouching by the entrance of the main building, listened on his radio as Benjafield observed from a hide he'd scraped together in the grass fringing the shore. In the green-and-black world of Dom's NV, Hoffman and a couple of the Pesangas were to his right by the door to the accommodation block, and everyone else was a disembodied voice in his earpiece as he tried to keep them mapped on a 3-D model in his mind's eye.

The first exchange of fire had been short—as if the counter-assault team had suddenly changed their minds about storming the building. Now it was silent again.

Maybe the Indie special forces knew they were outnumbered. But Gears didn't usually give a shit about that, and there was another counterassault coming in from the north anyway. So why would Indie commandos back off?

The only firing was coming from behind them, from the hinterland—Aspho Fields. Dom couldn't see the skyline from this position, but he knew it was lit up. He thought of his hot-headed brother.

Carlos, do it by the book. Listen to Marcus.

"They *have* to know we've got civilian hostages, useful ones," Hoffman said. "So they won't risk getting them killed. That's our edge."

Timiou was in the communal room at the front of the building, tasked with keeping the Aspho staff quiet. Life would have been a lot easier if they hadn't been around, but they were also now a useful human shield. The clean rules of engagement had crumbled in this grayest of gray areas. It was going to be a choice between letting scared civvies loose in a battlefield before the charges went off and the bombing runs started, and not letting them go, which had its own bad outcomes.

They're not bystanders. Remember, armed or not, they're not *innocent bystanders. How would they treat us if it was the other way around?*

"Frankbot is the priority," Hoffman said. He seemed to be working through their worst-scenario plan now. "If we lose the other two, the meat of the data's on the servers anyway, so Fenix will have to reconstruct the Hammer shit from that. Santiago, look after that goddamn machine like it was your new kid."

Shit.

I have a little girl. I forgot. I really did; I forgot her for a while. How could I?

Dom checked the server room. Frankbot was still motionless in front of one of the racks of machines, hovering on a faint haze of bluish vapor, both arms extended and plugged into the ports of two servers. It seemed almost rude to interrupt him. "Frank, as soon as you're done, don't wait for us. Go to Benjafield. Got it?"

Did he expect the machine to say yes? At least he didn't have to worry that the bot would protest about leaving its comrades behind. As Dom slipped back outside, Hoffman waved him to the front of the building.

"Santiago, get the civvies into the lobby," he said. "When we exfil, we take them down onto the shore with us, then let them loose at the last moment."

"Sir, do we use them as a shield?"

"That's not what I planned, but if need be, yes."

Dom darted back into the accommodation block to the communal room where the scientists were trussed on the floor. Timiou had his Lancer resting on the windowsill ready to smash a hole in the glass to fire out. Infrared was no use through glass, so he had to rely on his eyesight to spot a frontal assault, but he still kept looking down at the people on the floor.

The question was visible on his face: *what do we do with them now?*

The Aspho staff were helpless on the floor, face down. Dom squatted and took out his knife to cut the plastic ties on their ankles, one at a time, and as he rolled over the first woman to pull her to her feet—ladies first, without even thinking—he saw the terror on her face. She wasn't looking at nice Dom Santiago, doting father and devoted husband; all she could see was a stranger with goggles for eyes and a massive assault rifle, encased in armor that made him look more like a machine than a human.

"We're walking you to the other building," Dom said. Her mouth was taped and her wrists still bound, so it was an incongruous courtesy. "In case it all kicks off."

"Hey." Timiou's whisper was sharp enough to make the woman flinch. He looked up and took a step back, Lancer raised, pointing to the ceiling. "Up there. It's not the storm. I can hear something moving."

Dom was between the door and the woman, just in case she made a run for it. It was for her own safety. He focused on the window that ran the length of the room, facing out to sea and now glittering with salt crystals from the storm-thrown spray. If some bastard was on the roof, they were preparing to spring the prisoners. Dom made the woman get down again.

"Head down, lady," he said. "Because an Indie round won't ask for your ID pass."

"Cleaner, we have a contact on the flat roof of the common room," Timiou said. "Stand by for multiple breaches."

The Indies would do what Dom had been trained to do. They'd get in a number of positions around the building, and then breach simultaneously. The shit would be flying in all directions.

Maybe they'd drilled for hostage extraction. The Royal Tyran commandos hadn't, not yet. It was a bit late. But they could wing it, Dom decided.

"One guy making his way onto the roof via the radio mast," Morgan's voice said. Radio procedure was slipping as the situation got messier. This was the squad's first real deployment in a commando role, and it was starting to show. Hoffman would make allowances, Dom was sure. "Bai Tak's going to give him a steel surprise. Two more coming our way, ground level, via the generator room doors."

Morgan's radio went quiet for a moment. There was a rattle of fire from inside the building. Voices suddenly burst onto the circuit.

"Two right outside."

"Shit—"

"Roof man, he down now, one down."

"Shim, you okay? Talk to me, buddy."

"Young?" Hoffman's voice said. "*Young!* Upstairs, don't let anyone get to the bots."

"On it, sir."

There were still three Indies unaccounted for. Three was a *lot* of special forces. Dom listened for indicators from the flat roof above.

They know where we're positioned inside.

Nobody's that lucky. Or smart.

They've got someone observing inside.

"Sir, they're getting intel from inside, they have to be—"

Crash. The window that ran the length of the common room shattered just as Timiou opened up with his Lancer. For a moment Dom thought he'd smashed a gap to fire out and brought the whole sheet of glass down on himself, but three Indies burst through the window firing, like they'd swung down from the roof. Dom got a split-second flash of goggles, gas mask, and heavily laden webbing. He put a burst through the first shape that triggered his reflex; a round hit his armor like a punch in the shoulder. One, two Indies went down and the third dived for cover just as Dom and Timiou converged fire on him. The screams, muzzle flash, and hammering rounds stopped dead like a switch being thrown. It was a second, just a second, of held breath—

Dom emptied his clip into the man nearest him on the floor, just a step from one of the prisoners. Timiou did the same. They made damn sure they were down and dead.

As soon as the firing stopped, the sobbing and crying started again.

"Anyone hurt?" Dom yelled. He went along the line as fast as he could, shaking each prisoner and checking they hadn't been hit. Timiou checked from the other end of the row. "*Anyone hit?* Stay down. Don't move."

"All alive," said Timiou. He went to check the Indie troops. "And they're not. Green two to Cleaner, three hostiles down. We're coming out."

Four left. Two on the guns, two engaged out back.

That was still a lot of trouble waiting.

"We're going to die," a man kept wailing. "We're going to die."

Yeah, there was a bizarre irony in that. Dom couldn't find the words for it right then, but they would have been something like *and we'd be going to die, if we hadn't got to you first.* He backed out of the room with Timiou to follow the sound of fire from the rear of the main building.

Hoffman had moved inside to the server room and was trying to check Frankbot's progress. Dom waved Timiou on to back up Morgan and stopped to warn Hoffman.

"Sir, I'm damn certain they've got someone in here," he said. "They knew we were here. They knew where we had the hostages. Might be experienced guessing, might not. We still haven't found the second guard."

"Does it matter now, Santiago?" Hoffman's impatience with Frankbot was visible. His jaw was clenched. "There'll be a backup assault anyway as soon as the Indies realize the first squad failed."

"Has it?"

"Yes. We're about to *make* it fail." Hoffman made for the door. "But let's find that insider and stop him anyway."

ASPHO FIELDS.

The wind was starting to drop; it had also changed direction to offshore. Carlos could now feel it on his face.

He could also hear a lot better. Between bursts of fire and the thump of mortars, he heard a sound from much farther inland, beyond the low ridge that marked the edge of the levels and the start of firm ground that dipped slightly into a basin. The grinding noise of gears carried on the wind. It sounded louder with every second. It was familiar bad news.

"They've got armored cav out there," Carlos yelled. The sound of the Indies' armored fighting vehicles, Asps, was as easily identifiable for Gears as the engine note of a Raven, but they didn't produce that same comforting feel in the gut. "Ma'am, we have cav units approaching from the northwest."

"How frigging inconvenient." Stroud paused. Satellite recons were useless now; old data against a very fast-moving strike force, and in darkness. They were relying on basic soldiering again. "I hear them, Santiago. Anyone got a visual? Anyone?"

"Not yet, ma'am." That was Kennen. "They must still be in the depression. We hear them, though."

"Asps are wheeled and *heavy,*" Marcus said. "They won't be able to negotiate this terrain. They've got to stay on the Aspho access road."

"They've normally got AA and missiles mounted as well as heavy cal MGs," Carlos said. "They don't *need* to come this far."

"We're not the primary target," Stroud said. "It's Aspho Point."

"They've got assets inside." Carlos knew as soon as he said it that it was wishful thinking, bargaining with the unseen divine to bring Dom back alive. "They won't cream their own facility."

"They've got a damn *backup,*" Stroud said. "Unless we take out Osigcor, they can flatten Aspho and lose nothing."

"Key personnel?"

"Let's see how long they're prepared to hold off before they decide that's a price worth paying for asset denial."

Marcus shifted to a sitting position, heels dug into the spongy ground, Longspear balanced on his right shoulder. "The bridge," he said. "Look at the map, Carlos. They'll have to come across this bridge. It's the only point anything that heavy can cross."

"Are they reinforcing Aspho, or getting ready to cream it? They could—"

"Off channel! And use your damn call signs!" Stroud barked. "Tactical voice traffic only. Fuck it, people, can we not maintain radio discipline?"

Carlos moved his mike away from his mouth, chastened. Stroud's wrath made his gut lurch more than the mortars. "I was never much good at that."

"Yeah, they're waiting for something," Marcus whispered. "You're right."

Across the maze of channels, mudflats, and reed beds, C Company was now split into two parts as the Ostri mortars churned the ground between them. On the flat terrain, there was no vantage point to observe from, limited cover for movement except for the small scattered islands of woodland, and a steady stream of fire was pinning everyone down.

We're here to let Dom's squad get clear. That's it. Everything else is secondary.

The problem was working out how best to do that in a battle that was developing in ways they hadn't expected, because the signals base clearly had more hardware at its disposal than Intel had realized, or else they'd started moving up armored units as soon as they realized something was amiss.

How did they pick this up?

Is this just one big ambush?

And now there was something else approaching in the distance; Carlos picked up its hot spots in his NV scope.

"Light AA piece," he said. That *could* negotiate the terrain. "Major Stroud, mobile anti-air setting up two klicks north, pedestal mounted."

Stroud's voice was hoarse. "They must be psychic." She paused as if she was firing at something. "*Kalona* Control, please advise *Merit* that her Petrels will encounter surface-to-air missiles. We'll take that out for you. Be advised we also need Ravens for casevac."

Mortars thudded again from behind the Ostri line, sounding like someone hitting a case of rivets with a hammer. It was such a small noise, Carlos thought, totally at odds with the ear-numbing explosion when it landed behind him. Wet soil blown high into the air rained on him in cold lumps. The accuracy of the Ostri fire was improving, and Carlos could gauge it by the comms traffic, the calls for medics and reports of Gears killed or needing casevac.

If they get that anti-air piece going, we'll lose the Ravens, too.

"Shit." Marcus aimed the Longspear and fired it in top attack mode, lobbing a nasty surprise on a mortar position. The missile arced across the levels and dropped into the grass to end its flight in a ball of flame. "We're burning through these damn things too fast."

Carlos couldn't hear anything from Aspho Point now. C Company's part of the operation had shifted from being a defensive wall for the raid to being a fight for their own survival. Another mortar exploded to Carlos's left.

"Longstop to Kennen," Stroud called. "Sergeant Kennen! Shit, Kennen's down. Medic!"

"Asp in visual range." Marcus hesitated. "Ma'am, second

Asp and more light armored vehicles, extended line from seven-five-seven-zero-zero-one to seven-six-one-three-three-zero. Seven . . . no, eight LAVs."

It was a wall of fast-moving firepower coming down on them. A decent airstrike would have done the job just as fast. Carlos found himself thinking more about that bridge.

"They're going to ring Aspho Point," Stroud said. "They're going to lock it down." Her radio clicked as she changed channels. "*Kalona* Control, we have armored units and AA moving toward Aspho Point, strength around ten vehicles so far. Where's our air support?"

"Longstop, two Petrels, inbound for Peraspha." Anya's signal was breaking up. Then it came in strong again. "Ten to fifteen minutes."

"Take the base out first. Give the Indies a good reason *not* to destroy Aspho Point."

"Longstop, you believe that's their objective?"

"Affirmative. Base first, then help us out with the ground forces."

"Roger that, Longstop."

"Mataki to Longstop." Bernie cut in. She was still tasked to give fire support to Aspho Point itself. "I'm seeing intermittent line-of-sight signals from the facility to Peraspha. Some bastard's got a signal lamp. Can't read the code, but Hoffman needs to know he has company. Looks like a very small machinery space on the roof, rear of the main building. Doesn't look big enough to take a man, though."

Stroud let out a little satisfied *ahh*. "Longstop to Cleaner, you have a hostile on-site signaling manually to Indie forces. Rear of main building, machinery space on roof. Old tech defeats a big defense budget again."

"Cleaner to Longstop, thank you for saving us a search."

"Helicopters." It was Kaliso; he'd been very quiet. "Not Ravens."

They were still waiting for casevac. Carlos couldn't think of a safe landing zone now. It was going to be under fire wherever they managed to touch down.

"Medic," Stroud said. "How's Kennen?"

"He's dead, ma'am."

Carlos heard the sudden silence. It was like every man and woman on that field had stopped breathing for a moment—not a breath on the radio, not a single word. Even in the middle of a firefight, the shock paralyzed them for a moment. It was more than losing a comrade. They'd lost a lynchpin of the company.

Stroud said it for them. "Shit. *Shit.*" She paused. "Mataki? You're senior NCO now. Regroup with Kennen's platoon. Get across that channel and get wide of their LAVs. Take them out."

"Yes, ma'am."

"Longstop, this is Kaliso. I hear Indie choppers, approaching from the sea. Can't get a bearing yet."

Kennen's gone. He practically weaned us. My sarge.

The shock of losing a man who seemed immortal really dented Carlos for a moment. The reality of knowing any of them could be next snapped him back into the fight, but a little corner of his mind kept repeating it; *Kennen's dead, Dan Kennen's dead . . .*

Carlos strained to listen to the engine sounds fading in and out on the wind, hoping Kaliso's hyper-acute hearing was wrong for once and it was Ravens after all, but the guy was right.

Marcus adjusted position and reached for another Longspear.

"I've got two left," he said. "Even if the other platoon's got a stack, we've got more targets than missiles."

"Marcus, Kennen's *gone.*"

"I heard."

"Shit."

"*Focus.* We've got to hold off that frigging cav out there."

Carlos couldn't believe he wasn't gutted about Kennen. But Marcus simply pulled down the shutters, in the same way that he never cried about his mother. Carlos wasn't sure if he could ever find the words for grief, or if he was just too scared to let it out in case it consumed him. So now he just rolled his head back slightly as if he was about to shake it, and shut his eyes for a moment, nothing more. Carlos wondered just what it would take to ever make him weep.

"Okay, we've got to move across that channel and drop in a few grenades," Carlos said. It wasn't deep enough to be a river, but it was wide and boggy enough to be a major barrier. "Take out some of the vehicles the hard way. I can start moving up now."

"We *wait* until Stroud says so."

"Yes, Corporal Fenix . . ."

That was Marcus; model Gear, doing it by the book. Stroud was the best, but even the best couldn't get a picture of this battlefield now—dark, seen from flat on the ground, glimpsed through tall reeds and grasses. The battle was, as always, nothing like the plan. It never was. Instant decisions had to be taken, and hindsight might one day prove them right or wrong, but the one that was *always* wrong was *sit on your ass and do nothing.*

Carlos had developed a sudden personal grudge with the two Asps. They were still standing off on the maximum range of the Longspears, and had separated far enough for him to have to track across with his Lancer's scope to follow them.

I could be across there and dropping ordnance down the hatch in minutes . . .

"Fenix to Longstop," Marcus said. "I can take the Asp on the left. It's just in range."

"Hold for a minute, Fenix . . ."

Chokka-chokka-chokka. Carlos could hear it now. *Definitely not Ravens.* They were Khimera assault helicopters, either coming to churn C Company into mince and save the cav boys the trouble, or they were heading for Aspho Point. Taking one of those down with a Longspear was no easy job.

"Noisy assholes," Marcus muttered, still focused on the green landscape on the small CLU screen. "Come on, Dom, take the frigging data and run . . ."

The storm had subsided. The storm that had moved in to take its place was wholly man-made.

ASPHO POINT.

"Minor change of plan," Hoffman whispered. "We've got a hostile inside relaying our strength and movements. I'll find him. Bai Tak, take out the two jokers on the shore."

So the second security guard was somewhere up on the roof, and somehow he knew where the Gears were located in the building. There'd now be a backup on its way—if it wasn't already in position—to pick up what the first Indie squad didn't finish.

"Sah, ready."

Bai Tak, Shim, and four of the Pesangas drew their machetes again. The tall clumps of grass on the shore shivered in the wind, and Hoffman could see the two machine gunners spaced five meters apart. He could also hear helicopters. Whether they were dropping special forces or missiles, it wasn't good news.

"All call signs—how are the bots doing?"

"Ten minutes, sir," said Dom Santiago.

"Where are you?"

"Top floor, with the bots."

"I'm heading your way."

Hoffman paused for a moment because he suddenly couldn't see the Pesangas anymore. They'd melted into the sedge and grass. Even with NV, he couldn't see them. He certainly couldn't hear them.

And neither would the machine gunners.

He shouldn't have waited any longer, but he did. The next thing he saw was the gunner on the right rear up a little as if something unpleasant had crawled under him, and a hand covered his face; he convulsed and thrashed, but then he fell off to one side. By the time Hoffman looked left to the other man, he simply wasn't there. The two guns stood idle. Two heads, two cammed-up Pesang faces, appeared just above the grass and then vanished again, and the machine guns were dragged silently back into the foliage.

Every time Hoffman saw Pesangas fight, they left him awestruck. They did *nothing* the Gear way.

"Two down, sah."

"Nice job, Sergeant," Hoffman said. "Stay near the boats. Watch for helos."

"Need any help, sir?" said Benjafield's voice in his earpiece. He sounded frustrated. "You've got your hands full."

"And you've got the boats. You know what to do if this all goes to shit. Take the bots and get out."

Hoffman slid back into the main building and through the double doors, stepping over the nonessential Aspho staff sitting on the lobby floor. They were still bound and taped. He could see their eyes, staring up at the ceiling as if expecting something to rain down on them, or tight shut, or looking at one another. At least they weren't screaming their heads off.

I should have shot them. But I just can't.

Morgan and the Pesang troop were still trading fire with two Indies at the rear of the building. Dom had joined them, but Hoffman caught his arm and made him follow.

"It's diversionary, sir," Morgan said. "They're not moving. There'll be a second wave."

"I know." Hoffman sprinted up the stairs at a crouch with Dom. "Humor them for a few minutes."

On the top floor, Young was checking Brucebot. Hoffman's attention was on the ceiling and fire doors, looking for a route to the roof. It wasn't shown on the plans that Settile had given them, and there hadn't been anything on the aerial images to indicate a hiding place. He pulled Dom close.

"The guard's up there in a plant room or something, signaling. Find a route up."

Young tapped Brucebot's casing. "He's finished, sir."

He. Young found it hard to call Jacks *it.* "Okay, get it out to Benjafield. Joebot?"

"Finishing up. The data seems to be stored mainly on the server. This is just local drive stuff, but we stripped it anyway. You never know what you need."

Hoffman beckoned to Young and signaled; *up on the roof,*

hostile, we'll deal, get going. Young nodded. It was funny how the expendable assets, the bots, originally designed to free up Gears from hazardous and time-consuming duties, were now more important than flesh and blood. Dom came back and indicated the swinging action of a door.

"Service stairs," he said.

The two men stood flat against the wall.

"We have to assume he knows we're coming." Hoffman listened again for helicopters. He was expecting a roof assault. "I don't know how, but he's tracking movement."

"You think he's special forces, sir?"

"Well, he evaded us so far." Hoffman had only one plan. "So basic drill. Door down, open fire."

When they reached the top of the single flight of narrow stairs—an awful, cramped corner to be pinned in if they got this all wrong—the flimsy door in front of them looked like the entrance to a kid's playhouse. It was tiny, more like a cupboard than a room if the scale was anything to go by, and the height of the ceiling looked all wrong.

It was a flimsy door, too. Dom gestured with his Lancer. *Spray it from here?*

Hoffman shook his head. That didn't guarantee killing the occupant. A badly wounded man could still return fire or activate a booby trap. The door had a simple lever handle and conventional mortise lock, but Hoffman didn't intend to try it to see if it would open. He indicated the lock, raised one hand, and counted down silently while Dom aimed.

On *three,* Dom blasted the lock to let him burst in. The scene that met his eyes slowed and stretched into slow, fine detail, disjointed frozen images of shocking clarity, as if his brain was making damn sure he never forgot what he did next and could never shut it out.

He fell. He fell *hard.*

Where's the floor? Where's the frigging floor?

Hoffman was suddenly flat on the ground, winded, not where he expected to be, trying to right himself. The beam of Dom's tactical lamp picked out a man in a security uniform; a guy maybe in his twenties, balanced on a pile of crates to reach an open vent right at the top of the wall, a heavy-duty lamp jammed into the narrow opening—a lamp for checking dark corners, a lamp for signaling.

For a fraction of a second, he froze like an animal caught in headlights. He had a pistol in one hand. He managed one more flash of the lamp, and then both Dom and Hoffman opened fire.

He was signaling until the very last moment.

Hoffman and Dom stopped firing. In the sudden ringing silence, Hoffman realized the tiny room was no more than a blocked-off shaft, its floor set well below the level of the doorway. He'd fallen more than a meter; the ceiling was set almost flush with the roof, with only the narrow vent standing proudly out of it. No wonder it was never picked up on the aerial recon.

"So there's the bastard," Dom said, catching his breath and staring at the guard's crumpled body.

"So there's the hero," said Hoffman, realizing his kneecap hurt like hell from the fall.

Training and drill made a Gear's body move independently of slow, conscious thought. Muscle memory and adrenaline kept you alive; no time to debate, think, check the manual, dick around—just *react.* But Hoffman's brain was arguing, yelling at his legs that he couldn't leave this man's body here and where the hell did he think he was going.

In the COG, the young guard would have earned a medal. Now he was just a dead enemy. Hoffman found himself constructing an instant profile; a man young enough to serve in the army, but *not* serving. A man who could use signals. A man with the presence of mind to calmly find a hidden vantage point while all hell was breaking loose, and send information that would enable the Ostri forces to mount an early counterattack.

A former soldier.

Dom caught Hoffman's elbow. "Move it, sir. You okay?"

Former. Because he'd been wounded?

"Yeah, fine." Hoffman stopped. He had to look. He turned the man over and looked into his face because it was the least he owed him. When he searched the room for radios and other equipment, the simple mundane truth became obvious: the guy had been monitoring a simple fire prevention system that registered when doors opened and detected body heat to check if rooms were occupied. It was always the stupid little stuff that caught you out. "He kept his head, used his initiative, and brought down the Ostri army and air force on us."

Maybe there's another explanation for who he was. But I know I killed a hero.

Dom checked the body for any useful documents and keys, but he was a perceptive lad. He'd have been thinking the same as Hoffman. "Time to bang out, sir."

"Yeah." *I'll file a report. I'll let the Indies know what that man did. I have to survive to do that.* "Let's activate the det timers and get out."

The Indies wouldn't get the chance to trash Aspho. Hoffman would do it for them.

CHAPTER 16

Make it up with your old man, Marcus, because we're all a long time dead. Forgive him. Forgive yourself. When he's gone, you'll be ready to give everything for one more minute with him.

(CARLOS SANTIAGO, STILL TRYING TO BROKER PEACE BETWEEN THE FENIXES.)

ASPHO FIELDS; COG FRONT LINE, 0145 HOURS.

Carlos's radio came to life. "*Kalona* Control, Petrels inbound from the northeast. Heads down, people, just in case."

He could hear *Merit*'s two Petrels long before he could see them. They thundered toward Aspho and Peraspha from the northeast, a beautiful long storm of a sound that said everything was going to be all right.

The Indies were going to take a pounding.

"Go cream 'em," Carlos said, straining to look over his shoulder. "Go. *Go.*"

"And they said you couldn't cross a fighter with a bomber," Marcus muttered. "Shit, look at that—"

His voice was drowned out by a burst of fire. Without NV goggles, the battlefield was a chaotic, deafeningly noisy landscape of brilliant flaring lights plunging in and out of pitch black. A huge explosion lit up the sky to Carlos's right for a few seconds. He took a deep breath for a bellowing cheer before he realized that it wasn't COG firepower, but a midair detonation. Fireballs scattered and fell to the ground. The split-second gasp on all the radios made his scalp tighten and his gut cramp.

"It's hit," someone said. "Shit, they got the Petrel."

"Asps," Marcus said.

"We need to take those bastards out, Fenix," Stroud said. "Or everyone's screwed."

The roar of the other Petrel continued, sounding as if it was climbing out of Asp and AA range. There was another *whoosh* of hot gas and a missile streaked high into the night sky. A few terrible unbreathing seconds later, another explosion and a massive ball of fire filled the sky.

"Shit, what have they got?" That was Mataki's voice. "How are they locking on that well?"

"I don't know," Stroud said. She was just meters from Carlos and Marcus now. "Fenix, take the first Asp, left. Jakovs, how many Longspears has your section got left?"

"Two, ma'am."

"Make them count, then. Second Asp and the AA piece nearest you."

Longspears were one-man launchers but Carlos braced Marcus's back with his knee as he aimed and fired. The Asp was already moving before he pulled the trigger, but Marcus was a good marksman, and—

"*Fuck,*" he spat. The Asp was right on the Longspear's limit, moving right again, and the missile went wide by half a meter. It took out something in a ball of flame—a tree, or maybe it just hit ground—and Carlos grabbed the last missile to load it for Marcus. "He's moving out of range."

To the other side, Jakovs wasn't having much luck either. The Asps knew the Gears' limits. One of the LAVs wasn't so smart, though, and took a Longspear up the tailpipe.

Carlos could see other armor moving up to the Asps. As Marcus fired, an APC cut across the line of fire and caught the incoming missile fully broadside. Carlos saw the plating fly off in all directions. At any other time the kill would have raised a cheer, but all it represented now was Marcus's last Longspear wasted.

"Shit. *Shit*. Sorry, ma'am. *Sorry*."

"Okay, Fenix, you did fine. One less threat on the field."

"So, no pressure . . ." Jakovs said cheerfully. The very last Longspear streaked away and Carlos didn't even get time to focus on its jet. But the Asp had fallen back, moving into a knot of other vehicles. The missile detonated and a machine gun position vanished.

The difference between turning a battle and defeat could be a matter of centimeters. Marcus kept cursing himself under his breath, one hand blocking his radio's mike, and Carlos felt terrible for him. But he hadn't failed. It just wasn't doable there and then. All he could do was grip Marcus's shoulder hard and try to move him on from feeling the battle was his sole responsibility.

And Carlos could hear helicopters. He fell back on his elbow to look up at the sky, but he couldn't see any navigation lights. The Khimeras were waiting, circling a little way offshore.

"*Kalona* Control to Longstop," said Anya Stroud's voice. "*Merit* is scrambling the rest of its Petrels, but it's going to be ten to twelve minutes. Cleaner is now ready to exfil. Stand by to pull out."

"What about the medevac?" Major Stroud asked. "The Asps are going to drop them before they're anywhere near the LZ. We've got no ground-to-air left. We're down to RPGs. We're going to have trouble suppressing Asp fire."

Anya sounded as guilt-stricken as Marcus for a moment. "We're working that one out, ma'am."

Stroud paused for a minute and her voice changed completely. She was another woman for just a moment.

"You're doing fine, darling. Really fine. I'm proud of you."

It silenced everyone for a few long seconds. Carlos could always hear when everyone on the net was listening hard. All the background noise and breakthrough of local chatter stopped dead. Stroud never broke radio procedure on comms with personal chat, let alone in the middle of a battle, and it made Carlos hold his breath. There was a definite finality to it. He could guess what she was thinking; she wasn't sure she was coming out of this.

Anya seemed to hesitate for ages. "And you . . . Major," she said.

Carlos couldn't bear it. He cut in one syllable before Marcus. "Ma'am, let me get closer to the Asps. I can put one out of action if I get close in."

"I'll do it," Marcus said, and started to get up.

Stroud grabbed his pants leg at the knee and pulled him down again. She was closer than Carlos had thought. "I've had more practice at this, Corporal. You and Santiago—go right and lay down some fire. Keep as many of them busy as possible." She changed channels. "Alpha, Bravo, and Echo fire teams—regroup on Mataki. Mataki, I want half your troop securing an LZ on the beach, and the other half giving the Indies all they've got from as far from me as possible. We're leaving."

"Ma'am," Mataki said. "If you're thinking of crossing that terrain on your own and doing what I think you're going to do, they'll pick you up right away."

"How well you know me, Sergeant," Stroud said. "You'll just have to keep them very, very busy."

"What are the choppers waiting for?" Marcus asked. The Khimeras still weren't over land. If they were, they could have shot up C Company pretty fast. "They're not after us. They're here for something else."

"Well, I can't fart around waiting for them to choose from the menu." Stroud sounded as if they were just a minor irritation, and loaded more grenades on her webbing. "That casevac's going to land whether they like it or not. Keep an eye on the Asp left of us. Give me a few minutes."

She dashed out from the cover of the grasses and Carlos heard her splash into a channel. She was gone before Marcus could protest.

"She's nuts," Carlos said.

"She's got a point."

"If she has, so have I."

Carlos had served alongside women for two years. They had to be as physically capable as the men. But at that moment, it didn't sit right with him to see a woman of his mother's generation having to wade through shit and mud under fire. The fact that she was an officer was irrelevant. All his instincts told him to protect and respect.

"Come on." Marcus tugged his sleeve and began crawling through the sedge. "You heard the lady."

"Yes, you did," Stroud's voice said. She still had her comms link to the net. "And I can still damn well hear you."

And your daughter can hear you, too.

Carlos could face any risk to his own ass without thinking overmuch, but watching—worse, listening—to someone else do the same was unbearable. He didn't expect her to make it. He fully expected to hear her scream and choke as an Indie saw her coming and put some heavy caliber rounds through her. All he could hear on the radio as she moved through the channels was occasional splashes and heavy breathing.

It was hard to work out where anyone was in this terrain without popping up above the grass for a look-see and risking a head shot. Marcus ended up alongside Jakovs and his fire team, and Carlos almost fell over them.

"So what about the other Asp?" Marcus said.

Jakovs was reloading, feeling around in his pockets for another clip. "What about the rest of the cav out there?"

"It's the Asp that's going to stop the Ravens from coming in."

"I'm up for it." Carlos fought down something rising in his throat. It was an unsettled gut that reminded him he was a man, and hiding in the grass might have been correct procedure for this situation, but it wasn't *right.* "I can reach it if Stroud can."

There was a sudden blaze of light and gas farther down the field, a rapid volley of fire from a couple of the LAVs in Mataki's direction. She'd definitely grabbed their attention.

"Longstop to all call signs," Stroud said. "I'm ten meters from the Asp. It's just idling at the moment, and the guy on top cover isn't looking my way."

Carlos sighted up on it. He could see the faint green-lit shape moving at ground level. "Ma'am, you are—"

"Stand by."

Carlos heard her breathing. He even heard the *sok-sok-sok* of boots thudding into wet soil. A man's voice said one word, nothing Carlos could understand, and then he saw Stroud take a leap up onto the hull of the Asp and drop something—one, two, three—into the top hatch. The guy on top cover dropped back inside rather than trying to scramble out. She didn't manage to slam the hatch and tried to jump clear, but her webbing snagged. She was hanging off the Asp, caught with both boots off the ground. It swung its gun turret. It had seconds to live.

And so did Helena Stroud.

For a moment, she struggled and reached for her knife to cut the straps.

"Shit," she said.

The explosion was bigger than Carlos expected. It blew the Asp apart, flames shooting into the night sky. She'd dropped a shitload of ordnance into their laps.

"Ma'am? Ma'am!" Radio procedure went to rat-shit again. "Longstop, are you okay? *Ma'am!*"

It was the stupidest thing he'd ever said. He knew it the moment the words left his mouth. But you always hoped, always knew that Gears survived when they shouldn't have. He'd seen men survive penetrating brain injury. He'd seen miracles.

But he couldn't see Stroud at all. And the Asp was in pieces. When he finally moved the scope much wider of the target—thirty meters—and made sense of what he was looking at, he knew Major Stroud was beyond any help.

"Oh shit . . . *shit* . . ." Carlos still listened for breathing, insane as that was after what he'd just spotted, but he couldn't even hear static on the comms channel. Marcus caught his belt as he tried to straighten up for a better look. Carlos was ready to sprint across that field, Indies or no Indies, and bring back what he could. "Shit, we can't leave her."

"Down," Marcus said quietly. "I know. *I know.*" He put both hands to his ears this time and spoke quietly on the radio. "Mataki, it's your show now."

"I heard," she said. "Santiago, is that confirmed? Is she a T-four?"

Tango-four: dead, beyond medical assistance. It was a clinical, neutral code for the triage of injuries, from the most urgent treatable case—T1—to the low-priority walking wounded at T3. But a T4 needed no medics.

And Anya was listening on the net.

Carlos fought to get a grip. There was no way he was going to say over the radio that Stroud was in pieces. It was starting to dawn on him that her daughter had heard all of it, and he could imagine nothing worse. He thought of Dom. It was too much.

"Confirmed, she's tango-four," he said. "But so is the fucking Asp. She did it."

Mataki just paused a beat. "*Kalona* Control, Longstop is down. That's a T-four."

The distance and clarity was necessary. Carlos knew that.

"One more Asp," Marcus said. He was talking to Mataki. They were the last NCOs—the last command of any kind—left on the field. "That's our biggest problem. It can take the Ravens."

"You keep your arse right there, Fenix," Mataki said. "Wait one."

Carlos could hear the Khimeras, still circling.

They had to be waiting for Hoffman's party to exfil. They weren't going to trash Aspho Point.

"Poor frigging Anya," Marcus said to himself. He swallowed loudly enough for Carlos to hear. He seemed to be changing in front of Carlos's eyes, one death at a time. "Jakovs, listen to those bastards. I don't think taking out that other Asp is going to be enough."

So Anya Stroud had made her mother proud of her; at least that had been said in time. Most folks never got to say the things they should have before it was too late. But it was a shame the old girl couldn't hear her now. Anya's voice shook, like the signal was breaking up, but she did what she had to do, and Carlos could hardly bear to listen.

"*Kalona* Control to *Pomeroy*," she said. "Longstop is down, tango-four." There was a slight pause, as if she'd swallowed, but not long enough to count as losing it. "I repeat, Longstop is down. Tango-four."

ASPHO POINT, SIXTEEN YEARS AGO; ONE HOUR TEN MINUTES AFTER LANDING.

The ground shook as Hoffman herded the Aspho staff across the soggy turf. They were on their own now.

And there were Khimeras out there, just tracking up and down, not engaging, not doing anything. Khimeras didn't just hang around sightseeing at night. They were there to pin down the exfil. The boats wouldn't get two hundred meters before they strafed them.

So the last thing Hoffman needed was civilians adding to his problems.

"Get going," he yelled. "Go on, run. *Run.* Just get the hell away from this place before it blows." He had to shove the men hard in the back. Timiou pushed one of the women. "You're safer out there. *Run.*"

The scientists, still in nightclothes, were too scared to run into open ground where they had no cover. Where Gears saw a chance to escape being pinned in a corner, unable to see the enemy, the civvies saw only noise, explosions, and imminent death.

Ironic. So frigging ironic. This is what weapons do, folks. This is what your work creates.

One woman just wouldn't move. She was about thirty, rooted to the spot in a striped sports top and shorts, and she was simply too paralyzed by fear to leave the illusion of safety that the doomed building gave her. Morgan and Young came racing out of the entrance.

"Eight minutes, sir." Young grabbed the woman's arm and dragged her bodily across the compound. She screamed, but he just kept going even when she lost her footing. "Timer's ticking down. You're going to end up dead, honey, get the hell out . . . move!"

Hoffman ran for the boats. They'd have to be lucky beyond belief to get past the Khimeras. A heavy sea might have been helpful, making them a harder target to fix on, but the storm had picked the worst time to ease.

Prioritize, prioritize . . .

We've got our own scientists. So the data comes first.

"Cleaner to *Pomeroy,* what's the maximum range of a bot with sixty percent charge?"

There was a pause, longer than Hoffman thought reasonable with live dets ticking down behind him. "Three kilometers, to be safe," Michaelson said. "Why?"

"Ravens can get a fix on them, yes? You can pick up control and direct them?"

"Yes, if you give the pilot a search area so he can get in range of their receivers."

"Then I'm sending them out on their own to a hover point two klicks offshore, grid reference five-nine-zero-zero-six-eight. Get a Raven in to retrieve them."

"Cleaner, just because Stroud didn't—"

"I'm listening to a pack of Khimeras prowling out there, Quentin. Attack helicopters and semi-inflatable craft do *not* play well together. Just humor me, give the damn bots a good home, and then if the worst happens, we've got most of what we came for."

Bots were tiny targets. They could hover offshore and avoid an Khimera's attention where even a small boat couldn't. Op Leveler was *not* going to be marked FAILED, not on Hoffman's watch.

"Roger that, Cleaner. Just don't be a complete gung-ho pillock this time, will you?"

Hoffman took that as Michaelson's wish for good luck. "I'll try," he said. "Timiou? Set the bots to free-fly and hold at this location." He scribbled the grid ref on the back of Timiou's glove. "Do it now."

"Great timing, sir."

"Just do it." He trusted Timiou, but he still watched, knee-deep in the surf, as the bots folded arms and probes into their housings, and maneuvered on jets of vapor before streaking out into the darkness. "Six minutes."

Ivo was in Benjafield's Marlin, bound and gagged, and Bettrys and Meurig's daughter were in Cho's, just in case only one boat made it. Cross-loading cargo was always a sensible precaution. Dom pushed Benjafield's boat out into the surf with Hoffman.

Hoffman could hear helicopters again. He knew he couldn't rely on C Company coming to the rescue with a well-aimed salvo. They were in enough trouble themselves. *Dom's brother's out there. He must be going crazy with worry.* "Everybody in," Benjafield yelled. "Sir, we've got room for a few civvies in each boat now that all the ordnance is gone."

"Negative, Private, this isn't a rescue." Hoffman heaved himself into the Marlin. He could see most of the Aspho staff shambling along the shore now, looking back at the facility as if they didn't believe that it was about to blow, but every time there was an explosion in the distance, they dropped flat for cover instead of running. "Bak Tai? Get your ass in this boat."

Benjafield, hand on the wheel at the stern of the Marlin, gave Hoffman that look, the look that said it didn't have to be that way, and it hurt.

"Screw it, Benjafield, who do we take with us, then? You want to choose? We can't take them all. These are *assets*. You want to pick the smartest ones, the prettiest ones, or the most desperate ones?"

"You leaving it to me, sir?" He turned. "Dom? Dom! Grab some civvies. First six who'll come with us right *now*." He turned back to Hoffman. "If it doesn't matter, sir, we'll take the willing."

Bai Tak waded out to Cho's boat. "I go with Cho," he called to Hoffman. Morgan and Timiou were carrying wounded Pesangas on their backs. "Shim and Lau-En need medical aid, too. I do that."

"Okay, Sergeant. No bastard's listening to me today. Timiou, are those bots away?"

"They are, sir."

Dom didn't seem to have any trouble finding six passengers. Two women and four men edged down the shore, clearly nervous of the water, but Dom and a Pesanga ran out of patience and grabbed them like luggage, almost throwing them into the boats.

Five minutes.

Hoffman reached out to haul Dom inboard, then slapped Benjafield on the back. "Get going."

The Marlin roared away from the shore. Hoffman looked back at the other boat now closing the gap with them. They were a hundred meters clear.

"Cleaner to *Pomeroy*, bots are away, and we're clear of the blast zone."

Poor Stroud. But she was always going to go out that way. And so will we.

"*Pomeroy* to Cleaner—roger that."

The sound of rotors was getting closer. Hoffman kept his NV goggles down and rested his Lancer on the gunwale. He looked around the faces of the men in his boat, and bar a couple of the Pesangas, they were all such *kids*—little boys, unlined faces, lives not even begun yet, and that got to him like it never had before. Dom began taking off his armor.

"Private, what the hell are you doing?"

Dom kept looking out to sea. "Try swimming in this shit, sir."

"That'll be the least of your problems if you get hit."

"Khimera guns can punch clean through this anyway."

Nobody else followed suit, but then choosing the best way to die was a very personal matter. Hoffman was watching the shore now, checking his watch.

And right on time, Aspho Point blew.

It wasn't one glorious movie-scene explosion. It was a neat series of staccato detonations, right to left, like a giant burst of automatic fire along the beach. The flames lit up the water for a good distance—Hoffman saw nobody on the shore, and stopped thinking if he'd done right or not—and then died down very fast, settling into something that looked like a factory fire.

"Claim *that* on your insurance, Indie boys," Timiou said.

That got a laugh, but it was short-lived. The rotor noise was suddenly much louder and close enough to tell that it was moving across their bows to port. They saw the sea around them whipped up by the downdraft even before they could pick out the shape of the Khimera. Then it was almost above them, green-lit and filling the sky. Benjafield pushed the throttle as far forward as he could and tried to steer clear.

"It's okay," Dom said, for no apparent reason. "It's going to be okay."

The bright spotlight stabbed through the darkness and circled on the waves as if searching.

Yes, we got the bots away, assholes.

Hoffman wondered what they'd do with the seconds they'd bought. "Cho? Cho, get away, run for it."

There's more than one Khimera. It's just a gesture. But it's still better than sitting here and making it simple for them.

The beam fell straight down on the Marlin; spray kicked up everywhere. Hoffman couldn't hear a thing now except the throbbing engine shaking right above him. He leaned back and aimed his Lancer anyway, because even a Khimera had vulnerabilities at that range.

Sorry, Dom, what with the new baby and everything.

Across the water, closer than Hoffman had thought, the

other Marlin was caught in the sweep of a light too. The pilot was looking for something. He didn't need a search-light to aim. Then gunfire hit the sea, carving across the space between the two Marlins. Cho's boat was hit. Hoffman saw the explosion of splintering composite, but the Marlin was still afloat.

"You bastards," Dom was yelling. He opened fire, aiming up into the belly of the nearest Khimera. "You bastards, they're *your own fucking civvies*!"

But that was the whole point. Hoffman saw that now.

And there I was worrying about whether it was moral to shoot enemy scientists or not.

Die moral. Big comfort . . .

Dom emptied the clip and reloaded. Hoffman and Timiou joined him. The searchlight veered off sharply. Hoffman heard the engine stutter, and then he could smell fuel. He felt something oily and pungent spray his face.

Fuel. Transmission fluid. *Whatever.* Flammable.

"Shit, we're going to burn to death at frigging *sea*," Dom said.

Timiou kept firing in bursts. "We hit the asshole."

Hoffman saw the Khimera was circling, getting lower, and then it belly flopped onto the sea a hundred meters away in a text-book ditch. All he could think of doing was firing on it, reloading, and firing again. The side hatch was open. If his boys were going to drown, then so was the Khimera crew, and the fellowship of survival could go ram itself up the nearest pipe.

He couldn't even think about Cho's boat. He knew he ought to. The other Khimera broke off the attack and hovered above its stricken sister.

It was amazing how suicidal all rotary pilots seemed to be.

I'm going to die. Shit.

"Cho!" Dom yelled. He dropped his Lancer, kicked off his boots, and the last thing Hoffman saw was him disappearing over the gunwale into the black-ink ocean around them.

CHAPTER 17

I couldn't just sit there and watch them die.

(PRIVATE DOM SANTIAGO, COMMANDO DETACHMENT, 26 RTI, FROM THE OFFICIAL REPORT ON OPERATION LEVELER.)

ASPHO FIELDS, TWO MINUTES AFTER THE DESTRUCTION OF ASPHO POINT.

The pyrotechnics should have marked the end of the op and the beginning of the extraction, but Peraspha hadn't been destroyed, and it looked like the raid had hit trouble.

"What the hell's that?" Carlos could see a helicopter out to sea with a fierce beam of light playing beneath it. "What are they looking for?"

Dom. Dom's out there.

"Nothing you can do," Marcus said. "Where's our air support? They need to take out that Asp."

"*Kalona* Control, please advise on progress of Petrels," Mataki said. Her tone was abnormally *gentle.* Anya was still on watch. Carlos marveled at the capacity of anyone to go easy on urgent requests because yelling might upset a bereaved CIC controller. "We need that Asp shut down. Also, advise on medevac ETA—"

Whoomp.

Mataki's voice stopped dead. A fresh wave of mortar fire started up and it was falling on her position. There was a pause that felt like eternity and then she spoke again.

"I say again . . . I have twenty-six casualties. I have three heavies in position to defend the LZ."

"Longstop Two, *Merit* has launched all six remaining Petrels. They've encountered an Ostri squadron off the coast and are engaging." Anya was carrying on too. She sounded distracted, but she wasn't slowing down. *Would I handle it that well? Would any of us?* "Sea Ravens are going to attempt a landing—they're five minutes inbound. It's going to take more than two drops, you understand that, yes?"

There was only so much room on the deck of a Raven, and with the space and kit required to deal with the most urgent injuries, that meant a lot of Gears waiting on the beach for the next lift.

"Sarge, they're on the move," Jakovs said suddenly. "The Asp is heading back onto the road."

It was too much to expect it to be pulling out. Carlos scoped through and spotted it moving. It was making for the concrete road across Aspho Fields that linked Aspho Point with the world beyond, a single service road that sat like a raft on top of the soft ground.

"It's a bit late to reinforce the facility," Jakovs said. "I'd say it wants a better angle on the LZ. Maybe it's on the limit of its range."

"Or it's been called to back up whatever's going on offshore." That alone was enough for Carlos. "Let's stop the bastard from crossing. Come on, Jaks, your guys up for it?"

"You bet," Jakovs said.

"Don't go racing off half-assed." Marcus grabbed Carlos's arm so hard it hurt. "Think this through. I can get out across the bridge and take it down."

"Like Stroud, you mean." Carlos was already up and moving for the bridge. "We're down to minutes. Just do it."

"Santiago, no heroics," Mataki snapped. The net went quiet. It sounded as if she'd blocked their direct link to *Kalona.* No, she wouldn't want the chaos being heard by the officers. That was Bernie Mataki all over—sort it out inside the tent, so the brass thought it was all seamless and perfect, even now. "Listen to Corporal Fenix. That's an order. And I don't say that too often. What have you got left?"

Jakovs's buddy Marasin assembled an assortment of rounds and ordnance. "Stomper and a few gut-punchers." They were less effective than missiles, but did a good job at close range. "If we get close enough, that's our best chance."

"Do it," said Mataki. "But stand off at maximum range." There was another rapid succession of *whoomp-whoomp-whoomp*—more mortars hitting her position. She paused and then resumed as if nothing had happened. "Because we won't be able to retrieve you. Use your head. Listen to Fenix and do what you've been drilled to do."

"Sarge, we're going to engage the Asp before it gets to the bridge," Marcus said. "Thirty meters, one gut-puncher from each side simultaneously. If that doesn't fully penetrate the troop compartment, it could still put it out of action."

"Go," said Mataki.

The Asp wasn't moving fast, giving the impression that it was wandering around to avoid presenting a stationary target rather than going anywhere. But it rumbled over the uneven ground on its tracks and climbed onto the roadway.

All the Gears could do was jump into the channels and head for the bridge. It was heavy going, but it enabled them to move unseen if they kept their heads down. Once under the bridge, Carlos scrambled up into the grasses that provided some cover on both sides, and ran at a crouch to the left with Jakovs and one of his team, Hurnan. Marcus vanished into the grass on the right with Marasin. They had a couple of minutes to set up.

Gut-punchers could be fired from Lancers with attachments, and at this range it didn't matter if they weren't calibrated. The armor-piercing rounds would smash into the sides of the Asp. They couldn't miss.

The two teams were thirty meters off the road, about fifty meters into Aspho Fields.

"Here it comes," Marcus said. "*Wait.* On my mark."

The Asp was now sharp and vivid in Carlos's NV goggles, every detail resolving out of the green blur, from the rivets in the blast plate over the letterbox slit of a windshield to the regimental identification stenciled on its nose. He could even see a head, a rounded helmet and a pair of goggles just visible above the partly open top hatch. Now he could see it quarter-on, the rims of the wheels inside the track, the indentations on the track plates, the long black gouge in the side.

"Three . . ." said Marcus. "Two . . . *fire.*"

They opened up. Carlos saw a ball of smoke and light; the loud bang didn't sound like a detonation, but the gut-punchers did what it said on the label. A ragged, depressed hole was punched clean through the side plating. The Asp swerved, the top hatch clanged shut, and it ended up with one track off the road surface.

But it was still making for the bridge. It righted itself. Some bastard was alive inside.

"Shit," said Marcus.

Carlos sprang up instinctively and ran for the bridge, with some crazy thought in his head that he could reload as he ran, drop back into the channel just a meter or so below the bridge—up to his knees, easy, so *easy*—and put another gut-puncher up through the floor-pan from the side. He heard Marcus yell at him to get back. When he stopped to turn, he saw Jakovs and Hurnan racing after him. They'd simply reacted. Carlos had a plan; he *looked* as if he had a plan. He was the kind of guy people followed.

But he realized it wasn't a smart plan at all.

Fire opened up from the right just as he looked back. Both Jakovs and Hurnan were hit again and again. Hurnan fell hard on the concrete, and Jakovs, still standing, tried to stoop to grab him and was hit three more times. Then Carlos felt something hit him so hard in the top of the leg that he lost his balance.

He'd been hit once before, in the back of the hand; he knew what a bullet felt like, a hammer blow that didn't actually feel as if it had penetrated. But this was deep, and he knew right away that this was different. His first thought was to roll clear. He fell anyway, toppling into the shallow muddy water.

"Three men down!" Marcus was suddenly not Marcus, not silent and battened-down Marcus, but a stranger bellowing: "Carlos! *Carlos!* Hang on! Where are you, buddy? *Where are you?*"

"Who's down?" Mataki's voice demanded.

I'm not dead. I'm not dead. I'll walk away from this somehow.

It didn't hurt *that* much. It couldn't be serious. Carlos was numb, if anything. It was a miserable cold night.

"I jumped clear," he called. "I'm fine, Marcus. Get down."

"I'm taking it," Marcus said, not making sense.

Mataki came on the radio again. *"Who's down?"*

Carlos heard a scrape of metal and then single muffled shots. Marcus grunted with effort.

"I've got the Asp," Marcus said. "I'm in."

"What do you mean—in?"

"I'm in the Asp and it's drivable."

"Holy shit, Fenix." Mataki said. "Can you fire?"

The engine was still running. Carlos could hear it even above the constant rattle of fire. He managed to haul himself onto the side of the channel by clinging onto the sedges, and got his eyes just level with the flat slab of bridge. It didn't even have safety rails.

The Asp backed up and swung around to face into Aspho Fields again. Carlos could see it trundling toward the Ostri line. For some reason, nobody seemed to react to it; maybe they thought some of the crew had survived the attack and were withdrawing. Their radios had to be down, or maybe they were just as confused as everyone else.

Shit, I feel tired.

Carlos could see Jakov's and Durnan's bodies on the road. He couldn't see Marasin, but he obviously wasn't still with Marcus. Shock, guilt, fear—for Marcus, fear for Dom, for himself. Carlos didn't know what came next. His thoughts were an annoying interruption to a screaming silent voice in his head that said *get the hell out, you're hit, you're in a bad way, you got to do something fast, you fool . . .*

The Asp slowed and stopped. Damn, it was getting *cold* out here.

Carlos folded his arms on the bridge to support his weight. He could feel a raw, oddly distant pain from his hips to his knees. That was good, right? If he was in pain, and awake, it wasn't *that* bad. He looked down to see where he'd been hit.

It was only then that he realized he could see things he didn't recognize. In the green NV image, his pants looked wet, but he knew what guts looked like. And now he could see his own. For a moment, it seemed unreal, that he'd made some kind of mistake, and then he realized he hadn't.

Shit, shit, shit . . . I can do this. Guys get shot up like this all the time. Keep cool. Just pack some dressings in.

Somehow, it wasn't happening to him. He was just observing. But he had to move. He was about to heave himself out of the channel when the explosions started. By the time he dragged himself onto dry ground and found his legs weren't working, Aspho Fields was in turmoil as an Ostri Asp hammered its own armor-piercing rounds into LAVs and fired on its own troops. Marcus was charging deep into enemy lines in a shot-up fighting vehicle with probably no way back.

You promised. You promised you'd play it sensible, Marcus.

Carlos now lay panting on the bridge, unable to move. He couldn't even reach his belt to pull out any dressings. All he could think at that moment was seeing a ten-year-old Marcus come out swinging and land a punch on a bully, a punch that nobody expected.

"Sarge." Carlos managed to press his radio. "Sarge, I'm going to lay up here for a while and keep an eye on Marcus . . ."

OFFSHORE, LESS THAN A KILOMETER FROM ASPHO POINT.

The Khimera didn't matter a damn. It really didn't.

Dom thrashed in the sea, trying to keep his head up. He was going to drown long before a door-gunner got him. But all he could focus on now was the Marlin taking on water, Morgan bobbing face down on the waves, Young slumped over the gunwale, Cho trying desperately to bale out. Two of the scientists were struggling and screaming. They wouldn't be able to swim when the Marlin went down, as it surely would. They were still handcuffed.

One of the six civvies who'd boarded at the last minute was trying to free her colleagues. She'd ripped off the tape gags, but the plastic wrist-ties were impossible. She didn't have a knife.

I got one. I got a knife.

Dom managed to get a grip on one of the rigid seats and fell into the Marlin. It never occurred to him to do anything else but what he was doing now—pulling out his fighting knife and cutting the plastic ties. In the darkness, the prisoners couldn't see what the hell was happening, but Dom could, even with water leaking behind his NV goggles; some of the civilians and Pesang troops were already dead, riddled with rounds that had ripped through the Marlin's hull, and on the deck, at the lowest point of the hull, Bettrys was face down in water that was flooding in. Meurig's daughter—shit, he didn't even know her first name—was struggling to keep her head above it. He hauled both of them into a sitting position, but it looked too late for Bettrys.

You can never tell, not with drowning.

But how the fuck are we going to resuscitate anyone here, anyway?

"Dom, look!" Bai Tak was in the water, gesturing wildly behind him as he clung to the boat. "Move them across!"

Dom looked around just as Benjafield brought the other Marlin alongside. The Khimera was around somewhere—he could hear it—but it wasn't bothering them right then, and that was all that mattered. Hoffman reached over the side and tried to get a line on Morgan, while Dom lifted Young and slid him across the gunwale, boat to boat so that Timiou could drag him inboard. But there were only so many extra bodies a Marlin could take before it was too low in the water to be stable. Now Dom had the terrible choice of who he could save and not save.

There was no Raven coming to winch them to safety. They were on their own.

"Five," Hoffman yelled. "Five inboard. The rest can hang on outboard and hope for the best. Pesangas first. My men first."

Dom hadn't a clue what the next five minutes would bring. All he knew was that he couldn't stop moving, that he had to grab every single chance to stop people from drowning before the Khimera came back and machine-gunned them all.

"We're fine," Bai Tak shouted. "Take the civvies."

There were five of them. Something in Dom clicked and made decisions without debate or conscious deliberation. Bettrys—*too late.* He had no time to check for a faint pulse or pump chests or any of that shit. Meurig—alive, but she could wait. He pulled off the gag and cut the ties. Cho, Sim, and Lau-En were wounded—not urgent, but a priority. He held onto the other Marlin's rope while Hoffman and Timiou pulled bodies across, dangerously close to capsizing themselves.

"Bai Tak, come on," Hoffman yelled.

"You move others. This thing sinking *fast.*"

Two minutes, maybe five in the water in this weather before hypothermia sets in.

Dom couldn't leave anyone. He realized he was crazy, and that any sane man would have taken the chance to get the other Marlin away as fast as possible, but Benjafield and Hoffman had to be as crazy as he was, because they were trying to rescue people too.

The Marlin was taking on water so fast now that Dom could only think of one thing. He had to make sure everyone kept with the other boat. As the vessel sank beneath him and he found himself treading water, he hauled whoever was still afloat to the Marlin and placed their hands on the hull.

"Just hang on there," he said. *"Hang on."*

He could barely see now. Water beaded the inside of his goggles, forcing him to push them up on his forehead. Hoffman reached down and grabbed his collar.

"Enough, Santaigo. In you come."

Dom wasn't even sure now how many people he was supposed to have rounded up. He knew he'd lost some. It devastated him. It wasn't that he felt he owed the Indie scientists a damn thing, but he imagined for a moment sinking helplessly under that sea in the cold blackness, and the thought was overwhelming.

"I can't," he said. He really couldn't grasp Hoffman's

outstretched arm; he had no strength left in his grip. He wasn't a great swimmer at the best of times, and now he began wondering what the hell he was doing in the water at all. "I'm okay, just let me float—"

"You get in," said Bai Tak. The sergeant was bobbing beside him. He gave Dom a shove. "Get your ass in, Dom. You got babies to worry about."

Dom fell into the Marlin head first. When he scrambled upright, hands numb with cold, the Khimera lifted from a hover just above the sea and swung about. It must have rescued the crew of the other helicopter or given up on them.

But now it was heading back their way. Dom grabbed a Lancer from the deck. It was the dumbest and most desperate thing he'd done on a day that was turning out to be all dumb desperation, but he waited until the Khimera came within range. It kept its height. It wasn't going to suffer the same fate as its sister. And then it opened fire.

Malcolm Benjafield, standing at the wheel of the Marlin a meter from Dom, was hit in the chest and face, and thrown into the sea. Dom felt rounds punch through the hull. If the burst hit anyone else, he didn't know, and all he could do was fire back. He wasn't the only one returning fire; he was pretty sure that Timiou and one of the Pesangas were giving it all they had, too. The Khimera suddenly climbed and banked sharply, and for a moment Dom had the idea that they'd driven it off, but it wasn't the Lancer fire that was scaring the shit out of the crew. The Khimera was a couple hundred meters away when something *whoosh*ed overhead, trailing a small wake of smoke and flame, and hit the helicopter in the tail section.

"Shit!" Timiou said. Dom ducked as the ball of flame seemed to roll over them. But it didn't, and debris fell into the sea a long way from the Marlin. They were in instant darkness again, a long way from shore, and Dom felt the water rising over his ankles. Now this Marlin was sinking too.

All that for nothing. No, I'm not giving up. Not now. Bastards. Not after all that.

"Bai Tak?" Hoffman was bent over the gunwale, yelling into the darkness. "Bai Tak? *Bai!*"

He knelt in the bow with his Lancer, searching through the scope. Eventually he lowered the rifle and started punching the shit out of the Marlin in complete silence. Timiou was on the radio, calling *Pomeroy* for rescue.

"*Pomeroy* Control says the bots have been recovered," he said.

"Hoo-fucking-ray," said Dom.

"We're not done yet," Hoffman said. "Bai? *Bai*!"

Timiou went back to the radio. They'd sink before anyone got to them. They'd sink before they could move a couple of hundred meters. Dom went on autopilot again and checked who was wearing life jackets. All they could do was stay afloat in a group and hope *Pom* found them before another Khimera came back to finish the job.

"Where did that missile come from, anyway?" Dom asked. He wasn't thinking fast. The cold was slowing him down. "No frigging Ravens out here."

Timiou paused to check with *Pomeroy*. "From shore. *Kalona* Control reported that Fenix commandeered an Indie vehicle with AA and he's been shooting everything in sight."

Dom couldn't quite take that in. He had bigger problems that wouldn't let him stop and consider that extraordinary fact, or that he had a brother fighting ashore, or that he had a brand new daughter who he hadn't seen yet and now might never set eyes on.

The last thought was the one that brought him instantly alert. He could see Hoffman still kneeling in the bows with his hand to his head for a moment.

"Sir, you okay?"

Hoffman didn't answer.

"Sir?"

"Bai Tak's gone," Hoffman said at last. "Bastards. What's his wife going to do? His kids?"

There was nothing Dom could say. But Bai Tak could have been on board now if he hadn't pushed Dom to safety. It was a hard thought to deal with, and Dom knew it would only get harder as the years went by.

"Young's dead." Timiou was now baling out the Marlin with Hoffman. "Shit, we lost half of us. Shim's in a bad way. Where's that frigging Raven?"

Dom joined in, and so did the civvies. He didn't know how long they'd been baling out when he heard the Raven approaching. He just slumped there, trying to scoop the sea back where it belonged, listening to the Indie civilians talking in hushed voices in a language he didn't understand, until the helicopter was close enough for him to see the crew chief looking down at them through a mist of spray. The water foamed around them in the downdraft. Hoffman was talking to the pilot on his radio, but Dom could only hear Hoffman's side of it. His own comms had packed up.

"It's going to take too long to winch us in one at a time," Hoffman said. "He says they've picked up more Khimeras on their radar. The crazy bastard wants us to dock the Marlin in his cargo bay."

"I'll do it," Dom said, not thinking.

"You sure you can manage it?"

"It's that or have them come back and blow us to bits." Dom wasn't a proper coxswain like Benjafield, but he knew how to drive this thing. He was so tired that he just wanted an end to this, one way or another. "They won't rescue their personnel. They'll just fucking kill them, and us with them."

How hard could it be?

Dom realized just how hard when he stood at the helm, watched the Raven land on the water—yes, it landed, it really set down on the water—and opened its cargo ramp. A Marlin sitting low in the water with water slopping around its deck was a nightmare to steer. Dom managed to get the boat to line up with the cargo bay and tried to gauge the width of the cargo door through salt-smeared goggles. Hoffman handed him his comms headset.

"Just line her up and steer straight," said the crew chief's voice. "And be ready to lift the outboard at the last moment."

Dom's cold-addled brain told him that the rubber bows would buffer a crash if he rammed an internal bulkhead. The Raven seemed to rush at him. "How's that?"

"Keep coming. Hold that course. And speed up."

"You're joking."

"No. You need momentum to mount the ramp. Come on. Trust me."

Dom watched Hoffman's shoulders hunch a little, like he was bracing for a crash. And then he went for it. Dom prayed. He didn't do that often. The open mouth of the Raven's cargo hold came at him like a devouring animal, and all he could think was that if anything went wrong, the last thing he'd see would be Hoffman's hard metal armor neckpiece, which would probably break his nose.

"Throttle back, throttle back, *throttle back,*" the crew chief yelled.

The Marlin hit something hard and smashed down with a loud thud. The stern swung; yellow shiny figures—crew that Dom hadn't even realized were waiting in the cargo bay—seemed to cling to the bulkheads like flies. Then the boat stopped dead, and Dom almost tipped over the wheel onto Hoffman's back.

"Shit," he said.

The ramp clanged shut behind them and the Raven lifted, draining seawater across the deck. Dom simply slumped forward on the wheel and rested his forehead on his folded arms, shaking with fatigue.

Done. Done it. Where's Carlos now? Where's Marcus?

"Santiago," Hoffman said, slapping his back. "Have you any idea what you achieved tonight?"

Only one thing was left in Dom's mind right then. Aspho Point and bots and downed Khimeras receded into the numb distance.

"Yes, sir," he said. "I've got a daughter."

ASPHO FIELDS.

The Asp came to a halt a hundred meters from Bernie's position and rolled slowly to a stop, nose first, in the channel.

It had been hit three times by Indie light armor, and its ten-minute rampage had left nothing on the battlefield that could down a Raven for the time being. Bernie Mataki knew the comparative lull wouldn't last long. *Merit*'s Petrels had hit Peraspha and were coming back for a second run. The horizon was orange with flames, a false sunrise. It was time to withdraw.

"Corporal, get out of there. It's done. You got a frigging Khimera, too."

"Is Carlos back with you?"

She hadn't seen him. He was down by the bridge, and she'd heard him return fire a couple of times, but she couldn't see anything from her position.

"No," she said. "He's still taking potshots out by the bridge."

"Dumb asshole," Marcus muttered. "He doesn't even trust me to shoot up a few cav units on my own."

The hatch opened and Marcus hauled himself out. Instead of making his way back to the rally point—to the beach, to the landing zone where Sea Ravens could now land for a brief, precious time—he started looking around in the opposite direction.

Bernie swore under her breath. Shit, she was never going to get him back here if she didn't drag him away herself.

"Tai, get the stragglers down to the LZ, will you?" she said to Kaliso. "Fenix and Santiago are playing silly buggers. Just make sure that if we're not there in ten minutes that the last pilot knows we're alive and want to go home. I don't fancy having to escape across country."

"Yes, Sarge. You sure Santiago's still out there?"

"Sure."

"I haven't heard any firing from his position for a few minutes, and he's not been on the radio."

"I bet he's run out of ammo." But why wouldn't Carlos call for support? Was he really keeping an eye on Marcus?

"I'll put my boot up his arse five lace-holes deep when I get hold of him."

But she knew even before she said it that something was wrong. And as soon as she moved, fire started again from the Indie positions.

They were still out there, plenty of them. They just didn't have any anti-air capability left.

Marcus was going to hear what she said next on the radio. But she couldn't avoid it. She sprinted for the next available cover, a thick mound of grasses, and automatic fire ripped up the ground a few meters from her.

"Carlos," she said. "Carlos, can you make your own way back to the rally point?"

She waited. She had a feeling she knew what the answer would be.

"Negative." Carlos sounded bad. "I can't move. I've been hit."

Predictably, Marcus cut right in. "I'll get you," he said. "Where are you? What the hell happened? Why didn't you call for a medic? For me?"

"Because I knew you'd do this. Don't, Marcus."

"Shut up. I'm coming."

Marcus was closer to the bridge than Bernie. She saw him scramble up the bank, but as soon as he broke cover, the contact started all over again. Tracer rounds pinpointed him. He dropped flat and kept crawling.

Shit, he's not going to listen to me . . .

Bernie switched to the squad frequency. Marcus had a future ahead of him, and the last thing Bernie wanted was for every man and his dog to hear him disobeying orders and making a general dick of himself. He was the perfect Gear—except when it came to Carlos. That friendship came before staying alive and following SOPs, and although it hadn't landed either of them in trouble yet, it would. He was going to get himself court-martialed one day if he didn't get a grip on that.

"Fenix, stay back. That's an order. Roll into the channel and get to the LZ."

"No, Sergeant. I have to go back for him."

Okay, I better give you a hand. "I'll stick you on a frigging charge."

"So why are you heading his way too?"

Bernie darted along the edge of the channel, zigzagging and dropping flat every few meters. Marcus was moving along the opposite bank. She was certain he was going to get cut down at any time, but he got within a hundred meters of the bridge before the fire was too heavy and he was pinned down.

It was then that she decided to take a second or two to check where Carlos was. The scene framed in the sights of her Lancer made her stomach lurch.

Marcus had to be able to see it too, if he could get his head up. Carlos was ripped apart. He was lying on his side on the bridge itself, one arm extended as if trying to get up, the other hand clutching his guts. The pool of blood had spread around him. She was amazed he was still conscious. No; she was horrified.

"It's okay, Carlos," she said, as calmly as she could. "We're coming, sweetheart. You hang on. We're not leaving you."

"Go back. Don't be so fucking stupid. Leave me."

"Just hang on."

Bernie darted another twenty meters. When she dropped and looked up, Marcus was at about the same point along the bank. Rounds were lifting wet soil all around him. She thought he'd been hit.

"Sarge, just go." Carlos sounded as if he was going to sob. He was struggling to move his free arm. "Please. You're going to get killed. I got Jaks and his mates killed too. Marcus . . . just don't, okay? I'm sorry. *I'm sorry.* I blew it. I didn't think. I let you down."

"You've never let me down. *Never.* Don't ever say that." Marcus lifted his body a fraction but the rounds kept coming. "Sarge, can you lay down some fire for me?"

Marcus was younger, and a hell of a sprinter. Bernie was the better shot. She couldn't argue with the logic.

"Okay. On my signal—"

But fire hit the bridge this time. Someone had heard Carlos. He shrieked as if he'd been hit again. Bernie heard Marcus react—not intelligible words, just a terrible animal sound—and she thought she was going to throw up. There was nothing, absolutely nothing, worse than being able to see and hear a wounded buddy, and yet not reach him.

"You better look after Dom," Carlos panted. "Marcus, you hear me? You take care of Dom. He's your brother too. Promise me."

"Stop it," Marcus said. "Just shut up about it. You can take care of him when we get you back."

It was the first time Bernie had ever heard Marcus close to breaking down. He was always so detached, but he was human, and this was his one vulnerability; his buddy. His *brother.* She put a few bursts in the general direction of fire and got some silence. When she looked back at Carlos, his arm had moved and he'd managed to reach his belt. He'd been hit in the chest now, top right just at the point where the pectoral muscle inserted into the shoulder. It was a fresh wound. But it didn't stop him from rummaging in the pouches. It was a slow and labored movement, but she had a good idea what he was trying to do, and she watched him fumble a grenade in one hand.

Oh shit. I know you both too well.

You and Marcus. Just because you'd die for each other, doesn't mean you have to.

"Carlos, wait," she called. "Hang in there."

Marcus didn't seem to have seen the grenade. Carlos was struggling with the pin. "We're coming, buddy."

The pool of blood was spreading. It wasn't fair that Carlos was still conscious. He should have passed out from blood loss alone. Bernie cursed.

"For fuck's sake, shoot me, Marcus," Carlos yelled. "I'm not going to make it. I can't move the pin. *Shoot me.* I'm not letting you get yourself killed for me."

Marcus froze. Bernie thought he was never going to move again.

Shit, look at the state of Carlos. Poor bastard. He won't make it even if we can get to him. If Carlos can't do it himself, if Marcus can't, then I will.

"Bullshit," Marcus snapped.

Carlos's voice was weaker now. "You're going to get killed. Go back. Please. I can't let you do it. Get out of here."

Bernie was the section sniper. It was her job. And Marcus would never recover from shooting his best friend. She knew it.

Better he hates me than hates himself . . .

She sighted up, settling the reticule of her optics on Carlos's forehead. She was looking at him face on; she wanted him to turn away, and not just because she could hardly bear to look into his eyes. She wanted a clean cranial vault shot. She visualized a line that ran in a band level with his eyes and around the back of his head. A single shot in the back or side of his head would give him instant oblivion. Now she had to try from the front.

Shit.

"Carlos, sweetheart . . . just close your eyes. It's okay."

After a couple of painfully long seconds, Marcus came to life again, with his normal no-nonsense voice.

"Cut the crap, Carlos, we're getting you out."

He didn't even pause or ask for her to cover him. He just rose from his knees into a low squat, waiting for the right moment.

That was Marcus all over. He was going for it.

"You dumb bastard," Carlos said. "You're the best. Can't let you make a dead asshole of yourself."

And, at last, Carlos pulled the pin.

Bernie had misjudged how near they were. Debris hit her—concrete, mud—and the bridge collapsed. Marcus just bellowed, pure anger and grief, not even a word. *But he kept going.* He sprinted for the body. For some reason, as she knelt up and sprayed fire as wide as she could, Bernie found her mind fixed not on the round that was going to kill her, but on what the hell Marcus was going to bring back. She didn't want to look. She just kept firing. The next thing she knew, Marcus was splashing across the channel, and then he was crouched at her side.

"We're going home," he said. "I'm taking Carlos home."

SHORELINE EXTRACTION POINT, THREE KILOMETERS NORTHEAST OF ASPHO FIELDS.

Bernie Mataki had been a Gear since she was eighteen, twenty-one years in armor, and she had seen men and women die any number of ways.

Sometimes it was quick, and sometimes it wasn't. And sometimes—like Marcus Fenix—they only died a little, and still carried on moving for years. The Marcus now kneeling on the shoreline waiting for extraction with his best friend's remains wrapped in a bivvy sheet wasn't the kid she'd embarked with. And he never would be again.

Her radio crackled. "*Pomeroy* Control to Mataki, Raven inbound to your position, ETA fourteen minutes. We're transferring you to *Pom. Kalona*'s doc has her hands full patching up the rest of C Company."

"Roger that, *Pom.*" *Shit. Pomeroy* might have had better facilities than *Kalona,* but it also had Adam Fenix on board. She glanced at Marcus to see if he'd heard or taken any notice. He showed no signs of reacting. "Only one serious wounded left here. Lower leg shredded, lost a lot of blood while we were banging out, but stabilized for the moment."

"We'll advise the surgeon. Nice job, Tyrans. The bots are home and dry, and most of the special forces guys made it."

She had to ask. She couldn't bear to think how Marcus would react to more bad news. They'd all lost close friends that night, and it was going to be hard coming to terms with it, but Marcus had been in the worst position she could imagine.

Yeah, I'd have slotted Carlos. But I didn't. And Marcus

was right to try. And nobody else heard, so . . . the matter's closed.

"Dom Santiago?" she asked. "Did he make it?"

"Damn hero. Rescued some buddies from the water, downed a Khimera, and landed a Marlin in a Raven's cargo bay. He's going to get a medal."

Bernie wanted to sob with relief. "Nobody's spoken to him about his brother yet, have they?"

"Is he a casualty?"

"Yeah, 'fraid so. I don't want Dom finding out from anyone else. Not a damn word, okay? We'll do it. He needs to hear it from us. It's a close regiment." Yeah, she'd break it to Dom personally. Marcus was in no shape to do it. "And Major Hoffman?"

"Cleaning his Lancer at the moment, believe it or not. Weird bastard. *Pomeroy* out."

Weird. No, sad. *Poor old Vic.*

Bernie made it her business to know what would make or break the Gears under her. Marcus wasn't exactly going back to the bosom of close, supportive family. He knelt, one knee drawn up, one arm clasped around it, still frozen in that same position, head down, one hand on what she could only think of as the *package.* She edged across to him and put her hand on his back. It was good news, but it would only cut him more deeply.

"Marcus," she said. "I just heard Dom made it okay. Did a great job, too."

Marcus didn't say anything for a few moments, or even move a muscle. The remaining ten men and women from C Company were laying up in the cover of a crumbling cliff, waiting for the Raven to land.

"Yeah, Dom's a natural Gear," he said at last.

"I'll tell him. It's okay."

"No, it's my job. I'm a Santiago. They always said that. Honorary family."

"You sure?"

Marcus was a big, solid lad, the epitome of a Gear, but however hard he looked, he always struck Bernie as damaged. He seemed to be searching for something all the time, something he desperately needed—approval, acceptance, affection—but whatever it was, he'd had it from Carlos and Dom. Now that Carlos was gone, he seemed to have shrunk to half the size.

"We've been buddies since we were kids," he said. "Him, me, and Dom. I spent more time at their house than I did my own."

Yeah, you were a lonely kid. It's written all over you. "I'm sorry, sweetheart." She couldn't talk to him like a Gear any longer. He was just another broken kid at that moment. "I really am."

Marcus lowered his head onto his knee again, and Bernie waited. She expected him to stay like that until the Raven landed, shut off in his own head, and then get up and carry on as he always did. He wasn't the demonstrative type. But his shoulders started shaking, then his whole body, still in complete silence.

She realized he was sobbing his guts out.

Somehow, he managed not to make any sound at all. She wondered how anyone learned to do that, or why they even had to. But eventually, the dam burst.

"He was my fucking *brother.*" It was just a whisper, still no obvious tears. "And he's gone. He's really *gone.* What am I going to do without him?"

"You're going to be there for Dom," Bernie said, "and

he's going to be there for you. That's what you're going to do. This regiment's *family,* Marcus. We're used to getting through this shit, and you and Dom won't be alone."

It was all the harder watching him with his left hand still resting on Carlos's remains. He wasn't the first Gear to retrieve his buddy's body in pieces, but there was no way that any human being was ever prepared for that, or could deal with it easily. It wasn't even easy for medics dealing with strangers. It was a nightmare.

And we didn't recover Stroud. Shit. It's all the things you don't think about until it happens. Poor Anya. Another kid going through hell now.

"Would you have fired?" Marcus asked at last.

"Too bloody right I would. I was sighted up on him, but he got there first." Bernie wasn't sure if that would make Marcus feel worse or better. Maybe he'd take it as a rebuke for making Carlos pull the pin to stop him trying to reach him. "And I'd expect anyone else to do the same for me."

"I let him die."

"No, you bloody well *didn't.*" Bernie picked her way carefully through a minefield of wrong things to say, and opted for the least dangerous one that happened to be true. "Carlos was a good bloke, a *bloody* good bloke, but he got himself in that shit. He should have stayed put and not tried to take the vehicle the second time. And the others were crazy to follow him. That won't make you feel any better, but you're not to blame for any of them dying. He did it himself."

"He was a fucking hero."

"You were *both* heroes. He fragged himself to stop you from getting shot up. You were ready to die to save him. What can possibly matter more than that?"

"But I should have stopped him. I should have gone out and dragged him back after Jakovs got hit. I should have got to him first before I charged off in the Asp. I should have known better. I'm *supposed* to know better. Aren't I?"

"Marcus, you were on your way out to drag him clear when he pulled the frigging pin. You'd have been killed before you even reached him. Suicidal rescues are for movies."

"I hesitated. And he died."

"It was just timing. And it was Carlos not *wanting* you to die for him."

Shit, it was getting harder by the second.

Marcus wiped his nose on the back of his hand. "This is going to destroy Dom."

"Maybe I better tell him after all."

"What exactly *do* we tell him?"

And now they had to deal with another immediate problem.

Bernie knew how families reacted to KIAs. When they said they wanted to know if their loved ones had suffered or gone clean, they really didn't know what the answer was going to do to them. Some could take it; some couldn't. But they sure as shit didn't need to be told that their son or brother or father had been killed because he did something stupid and took comrades with him. Closure could heal, but nothing was going to bring back the dead. Hard facts were best kept for the historians, revealed long after anyone living could be hurt.

Dom didn't need to know it all. And neither did the families of the others, not this time.

"Tell him that his brother was a bloody hero," she said at last. "Because he was. He put your life first and he blew that bridge. And Dom has to go on living, the poor sod."

"Yeah," Marcus said, still staring at his hand. "That's exactly what happened."

Nobody was going to say any different. Nobody else had heard any of it; they'd only see the official report, the truth minus the shit that was nobody's business but hers and Marcus's. Bernie waited in silence with her hand on Marcus's back until the Sea Raven dropped onto the shore and the hatch opened, and then they made sure that the first casualty on board was Carlos Santiago.

CHAPTER 18

Sir, don't you think we got enough corporals and sergeants? I'm real happy with my buddies, and am I gonna kill grubs any better with a few stripes on my arm? Everyone's job's pretty straightforward these days—kill grubs, kill more grubs, and then kill some more. You don't need no more NCOs to do that. But thank you all the same, sir. It's the thought that counts.

(PRIVATE AUGUSTUS COLE TO COLONEL VICTOR HOFFMAN—TURNING DOWN PROMOTION AGAIN.)

JACINTO, PRESENT DAY: FOURTEEN YEARS AFTER E-DAY.

The grubs came out of the ruins, and Hoffman wondered for a moment what they did with prisoners.

He didn't plan on being one. He had his sidearm, and if push came to shove he would deny the grubs the pleasure of his company, right after he took as many with him as he could.

"They're coming out of that basement," Kaliso said. "We can plug that or wait for them to emerge."

"One try, then fall back," Hoffman said. There was no way into the APC for more ordnance, let alone an escape. "I'll cover you."

Hoffman laid down fire for Kaliso as the Islander moved forward to lob a grenade down the mouth of the stairs. The grenade flew past three grubs that were already at ground level, bounced down the steps, and detonated. Kaliso dropped two of the three drones even before they got close enough for Hoffman to smell them, but there were still half a dozen coming through the rubble.

They didn't fight like men. They were chaotic. They seemed to have no organization, no section formation, nothing Hoffman could recognize—except the classic ambush, hitting multiple points simultaneously and trying to throw Gears into disarray.

The smell. I hate the damn smell.

And they never seemed to get in position and fire. They always went for close quarters battle. It was a psychological tactic, he had no doubt of that, because they must have known how hideous they looked to humans.

But we can get used to anything. And kill it.

Kaliso never retreated from grubs. He went forward into them, chainsaw revving, and sliced the next one that came at him across the face—not a lethal wound, but enough to blind the thing for a moment to let him withdraw the saw and bring it back down into its chest. Hoffman, slowed by a stiffening, burning calf muscle and plain age, had to wait for the grubs to come to him. He fired in bursts at chest level. Maybe, if it all went wrong and he was in the final seconds without hope, he could get them to rush him when he was close enough to the Armadillo to rock its frame and detonate the bomb.

But they were too smart for that. *Way* too smart.

They were jerking him around.

He fired from the hip. Kaliso pulled back and cannoned into him, shoving him behind the cover of a concrete pillar. "They want to play ambush, so maybe they're not ready for a target that wants to stay in the kill zone."

"You're completely frigging crazy, Kaliso." Hoffman aimed the Lancer blind around the pillar and let off a long burst. "Only an idiot wants that. A *dead* idiot."

"We're not fighting human beings, sir."

"I say we charge them." Hoffman believed that every living creature feared *something,* and so it was simply a case of finding it. Failing that, it was a matter of killing the other guy before he killed you, the fundamental essence of war since time began. "I can't outrun these assholes anyway."

Hoffman just kept firing. Kaliso switched to single shots, just like Bernie always did, and they staggered reloads. It took a good few rounds—Hoffman averaged ten, he found—to drop a grub, and that meant only six per magazine. And if he didn't keep a rein on it, he could empty a clip in under five seconds. *I need more time to get back on form with this rifle. I'm a liability.* He'd been using Lancers since he was eighteen, but the older models didn't eat up ammo. He'd see if he could dredge up a few from Stores if he was going to make a habit of this. There was no point having a weapon that was better than you were.

Habit? I'm probably going to end up like Lieutenant Kim. Impaled on the end of a damn grub blade. And I've dragged Kaliso down with me.

It had become easy to think in terms of what men were

worth, measured against his own life. Kaliso was mid-thirties, fit and aggressive; he was worth five or more Hoffmans on the battlefield.

It makes sense to sacrifice yourself to let him fight another day.

Shit, why do I still have this death wish?

Hoffman found himself wanting to let his anger take over and swing the chainsaw into the next grub like a breaching tool. So he did, and the surge of anger alone felt blissful, and the spray of blood didn't shock him one bit. He came out from behind the pillar, and ducked low to fire upward. Kaliso was too tied up with his own grub problem to stop him. The next grub pitched forward on him and nearly knocked Hoffman flat. He fell back against the nearest wall, struggling to push it off.

"Colonel," said a rasping voice in his earpiece, "I know you can hear me, so don't blow our heads off when we come around behind the grubs."

Kaliso grunted, struggling to pull his chainsaw free. "Stay out of my arc, Marcus."

"We're on receive-only," Hoffman said. "He can't hear you."

"My Lancer is speaking for me, sir. . . ."

Hoffman switched his headset to two-way. He was going to direct Fenix's fire, but it all went down too fast. Fenix came running in from the Rotunda end of the building with Dom, and plunged in.

Fenix was always abnormally calm until he got near a grub; he seemed to save all his pain and frustration especially for them. And he'd saved up a *lot,* as far as Hoffman could see. He moved in, Lancer raised, and brought the chainsaw down through the collarbone of the first Locust that turned to face him.

It didn't fall. The chainsaw bit too deep to dislodge one-handed, and Fenix had to raise his boot to kick it off. Another grub came at him; Dom hit it with a burst of fire. It stumbled against Fenix, and he caught it as casually as a dancing partner, grabbing it around the neck to hold it against his body like a shield while he moved toward its comrade with his rifle held around it. The sheer effort was visible; every tendon in his neck, every blood vessel seemed close to bursting, but he made no sound. Rounds ripped into the helpless grub as he finished off its buddy and let both fall together.

Dom just went for a lot of fire and fast reloads. He liked his fighting knife, too. He had more to hate grubs for in many ways, but he didn't seem to need the release of killing them like Fenix did.

It took all four of them to put down fourteen grubs. The ruins finally fell silent.

"Thanks, Sergeant," Hoffman said carefully. *I didn't want to be saved. I especially didn't want* you *to save me. Not after what I did.* "Well done, Dom. You've still got the commando touch."

Dom just nodded, suitably modest. "So what's the problem with the 'Dill?"

"They stuck explosives under it," Kaliso said. "We can't afford to lose another one."

Fenix scratched his jaw, oddly relaxed. "I'm not calling Baird back. Anya? Can we have Jack for EOD work?"

"That's what bots are for . . ."

"Yeah, but that was when we had shitloads of them."

"Not my budget, Marcus. But the budget holder is standing next to you."

Budget. Money had ceased to exist in governance terms. It was a barter economy.

"Do it," Hoffman said. "If we blow the 'Dill *and* Jack, Prescott can bill me."

They withdrew to a safe distance and took cover to watch for more grubs while they waited for Jack to locate them.

"Does Jack have any choice in this?" Dom asked. He'd always seemed to feel guilty about the risks he put bots in, right back as far as Aspho Point. "This always grosses me out."

"Sentience," Kaliso said gravely.

"Grubs are sentient. You don't mind slicing and dicing *them.*"

"That's my calling."

"I love ethicists," Fenix muttered. "I don't get any of this philosophical shit from Baird."

Hoffman watched anxiously. Jack extended both arms under the 'Dill, whirring and vibrating like a food processor. It took longer than Hoffman liked, and he expected the grubs to come back for a second round at any moment. But Jack pulled back after a few minutes, deposited a device in parts on the ground at Hoffman's feet like a loyal dog, and hovered waiting for instructions.

Fenix squatted down to look at the components. "Jack, this is safe, right? Let's give it to Baird. He'll love analyzing it." He gestured to the Armadillo. "Okay, back to base."

The day really was close to over. Hoffman didn't fancy doing this again tomorrow. But, of course, it was exactly what his Gears did, day in, day out. There was a time when he'd known exactly what that felt like. The idea of forgetting terrified him.

I'm getting old. Fast.

And I have to be able to look them in the eye.

"Drop me just outside the security cordon," Hoffman said. "I want to walk through the city."

"You've got a hole in your leg, sir," Dom said. "And you're not a kid any longer."

"Thank you for noticing, Santiago."

"Okay, sir," he said, "but if you walk, I walk."

"If he walks, he'll collapse," Fenix said. "So I'd better dismount when he does. Kaliso, drop us past the Stranded line."

Kaliso shrugged. It was clear they all thought Hoffman was nuts. He just wanted to spend some time outside, breathing fresh air, away from the office and not encased in an APC or in a Raven. He was afraid of that disconnection from the men around him who did it every day.

And he wanted to see how civilians—not Stranded, proper citizens, the society he was tasked to save—looked at him and his Gears.

"After you, *sir*," Fenix said, managing to make it sound like *asshole*.

JACINTO; VEHICLE CHECKPOINT.

They trudged into Jacinto just as it was getting light.

"I think I could eat that dog after all," Dom said. Hoffman was doing his best to walk under his own steam but Dom and Marcus supported him with a hand under each armpit. Dom knew he felt like shit about that, being helped home limping like an old man. "And a couple of liters of coffee."

It was like passing into another dimension. On one side, not even the Stranded were out and about. Inside the secure zone, there were street cleaners and maintenance patrols taking advantage of the relative lull to try to keep the city center running on sweet fuck all and goodwill. Dom marveled at the doggedness of it. They didn't even have the adrenaline of minute-by-minute combat survival to keep them going. The city even smelled different from the outside world. Disinfectant, cut grass, bread from a nearby bakery—small things that said that the place might have been hanging from a thread on the literal end of the world, but pockets of normality survived, and humans weren't wholly beaten yet.

The street crews stopped to stare at them. Dom realized his armor was covered in grub blood and shit, like everyone else's. He waited for comments on the filthy state they were all in, but the civilians simply laid down their brooms and shovels, stood up straight as if they thought it was the respectful thing to do, and broke into spontaneous applause.

It upended Dom completely. He almost cried. It was fatigue, he told himself.

"Rough bar," Marcus said to the street crew. A streak of dried blood ran from his brow to his chin. "Won't be drinking there again . . ."

It was the same all the way through town. The early-morning workers going to factories or offices, in the determined pretense of business as usual, stopped to slap the Gears on the back. One woman—thirties, not bad looking, but nothing like Maria—walked up to Hoffman and gave him a big kiss on the cheek. The colonel looked shocked rather than flattered.

"You've pulled, sir," Dom said cheerfully. "Get your coat."

"It's true, isn't it?" The woman looked delighted. "They're beaten. We've finally beaten the damn things."

"I don't know, ma'am," Hoffman said. He still had his courteous moments. "Time will tell. All we can do is keep killing them until we run out of grubs to kill."

Dom shut the prospect of ending the war out of his mind. But it was good to be able to walk down the street and see the difference a Gear could make, to feel the sense of connection with the people of the city. Now they could actually *see* why Gears earned their extra rations. Hoffman knew what he was doing. The Gears looked and smelled a mess—blood, armor damage, stubble, fragments and splashes of dead grub—and it all said *we're out there dying for you* better than any official COG poster ever could.

And the spontaneous welcome home certainly beat any number of medals. It was worth the long slog to Wrightman Hospital. Dom didn't spend much time around civilians inside the barricade, and it was useful to be reminded what they looked like, and how different their world was from his.

"I hope you think that street theater was worth exacerbating your injury, Colonel," the doctor scolded when they showed up at the medical wing. Dr. Hayman was older than Bernie, but half as patient, and she lifted Hoffman's leg behind him like a veterinarian inspecting a horse's hoof. "And *you,* Sergeant, you get your hairy ass in here for tests as well. Have you any idea of the infections you can get from Locust feces in open wounds?"

Marcus shrugged and checked his exposed skin. "Okay, I'll avoid shooting them in the guts in the future, ma'am."

For Marcus, that was happy and chatty. Dom decided it

was okay to leave him with the doctors and went back to the main barracks. His priority list—after hosing the worst crap off his kit—was a shower, the biggest breakfast he could fit on a plate, and then to find Bernie before she changed her mind.

No, she made you a promise. She'll keep it. She'll tell you the truth.

For Dom, a shower was the difference between civilization and an animal existence. He let the hot water pound the top of his head, palms flat against the tiles. When he looked at his body, he had fresh bruises everywhere, and raw pressure marks where the edges of his armor had rubbed simply because he'd been sweating in it for so many hours.

I'm not a kid anymore either. How long have I got? Shit . . .

All that he could think at that moment was that Maria wouldn't recognize him when he finally found her, or she wouldn't want him because he wasn't the man she remembered.

"You're too tired to make sense," he said aloud to himself. "You're thinking shit again. Go eat something."

It was getting on for 1000 before he finished cleaning himself and his kit. When he walked into the mess hall, a couple of squads—Kappa and Omicron—were eating. Omicron's sergeant, Andresen, beckoned him over.

"Hey, Santiago. Good hunting?"

"Not as many as normal." Dom took a couple of slices of toast from Andresen's plate and wolfed them down. "Enough to be a pain in the ass. Almost lost Hoffman, too."

They all laughed. "You got to try harder, you lazy shits,"

Andresen said. "You reckon the Lightmass cracked it? Have we finished off the grubs?"

"No idea."

"The Stranded say they've all gone from Tollen. Haven't had an attack in days. Lots of ground tremors, but no grubs."

Dom could hear it in their voices. They wanted him to give them good news, to say it was all over, because in their eyes he was part of the inner circle of Hoffman's elite. But he couldn't.

"Let's hope," Dom said.

"We're still keeping an eye out for Maria."

"Thanks." Dom glanced at Andresen's corporal, who'd nodded off at the table with his head propped on one hand. His breakfast was getting cold. Dom slid the plate away from him and tucked in. Wasting food was unthinkable these days—especially today. "If Bernie Mataki can surface after disappearing for so long, all things are possible, right?"

"Santiago, you're a lucky charm for keeping folks alive," the corporal said sleepily, eyes still shut. He wasn't dozing at all. "Even Fenix. How's he doing? Four years in the Slab can't have done his health much good."

If I'm such a charm, how come I couldn't keep Carlos alive? "He's Marcus. It'd take the Lightmass to put him down."

Dom believed it. Marcus was as fit as he ever was, except for a few more as yet unexplained scars, and a lot more lines. He was just less talkative than ever. That was how he coped.

Dom finished the breakfast and went up to the servery for more. He had to face Bernie on a full stomach. She'd already warned him; he was going to hear old, bad news.

WRIGHTMAN BASE, ALPHA TO DELTA BARRACKS BLOCKS.

Bernie sat with her feet up on a chair, and understood what it meant to be staring at sixty while trying to keep up with men nearly half her age.

It hurt. *Everything* hurt, from her eye and her split lip to her knees and wrists. Fitness was one thing: recovery time was another game altogether. Hoffman was a couple of years older than her, so she knew he felt every bit as shitty as she did right then. In the next room, Federic Rojas snored loudly in the obliviously deep sleep of the young. Baird was cleaning his boots. Cole pulled up a chair and settled down at the desk in the far corner.

Okay, Baird's a congenital tosser. I'm probably not going to be deployed with Delta. Does it matter if I get on with him or not?

She'd never given up on a Gear with a bad attitude yet. For that reason alone, she'd try to reach an understanding with the little shit.

"So," she said. "Anya Stroud, Blondie."

Baird didn't look up from the boot on his lap. "What about her?"

"Why's she still a first lieutenant at her age? The kid was a prodigy."

"What's the point in promotion?" Baird muttered. "Only assholes want it and get it. Anyway, since you've been gone, Granny, the choice for women now is breed or do war work. She can't have kids. So she does what she's best at."

He was a target just waiting for a shot. She was a sniper. Despite her best intentions, she just couldn't help herself.

"You made corporal. Did they force that on you at gunpoint, on account of your being a *reluctant* arsehole?"

Baird paused. "How long we going to keep this up, Granny?"

"Until you get bored, Blondie. Never piss about with an old sergeant."

"Boomer Lady's speaking the truth, Damon baby." Cole was writing steadily on a notepad. "You ain't gonna beat a woman who can eat kittens."

"I don't treat you any differently from the rest of the squad, Mataki," Baird said.

Cole nodded to himself. "That's the truth, too, baby. This is as sweet as Damon gets. He just lacks my natural charisma."

That was another truth, for sure. "So what are you doing, Cole?" Bernie asked.

"Writing to my momma."

"I didn't realize your family was still around."

Cole paused, still staring at the page. "They're not."

Bernie took a moment to process that. Cole was probably the sanest of all of them, Mister Solid. It was hard to stay sane in a world that was more dead than alive, though, and maybe the definitions of normal had to change for a society where everyone—absolutely everyone—had lost friends and family in the worst way possible.

She craned her neck to look at Cole. He sat at the desk, two sizes too big for it, writing painstakingly with a big smile and tears streaming down his cheeks. Baird didn't seem to think it was significant. She bloody well did.

"Are you okay, Cole?"

"I'm just fine. I'm always fine."

Bernie got up and went to sit in the chair by his desk. He carried on writing for a while.

"Mind if I ask?" she said.

He wiped his cheeks with his left hand. "Go ahead, baby."

"Why do you do it?"

"Shit, all the things I never said while she was alive, I suppose. Just 'cos she's gone, don't mean I can't say 'em. And they're better out than in." He sat back in the chair, making it creak, and read what he'd written. Then he folded the letter carefully and slipped it into his pocket. "Hell, I miss her. Miss 'em all."

Bernie stood up and patted his shoulder. She didn't want Baird to see she was close to tears herself. "Sorry to intrude, Cole."

"You're not intrudin'. *Any* time." He caught her hand. His fist was so huge that hers was lost in it, and she wasn't a small woman. "You okay? You findin' it hard being back among us good guys after years of mixing with scum? If you ever want to get it off your chest, Bernie, just let it out. I'm here and I ain't got too many pressing engagements."

Cole was so perceptive that it was frightening. Yes, it was hard learning to trust people again. It was hard knowing that she didn't have to sleep with a loaded weapon or a knife not just under her pillow, but in her hand. Just a few days of knowing she was safe again had made her relax enough to make the last few years visible for the hell they were; anarchy, tribalism, violence, all the bestial behavior that lurked beneath the skin.

But not grubs; humans.

Grubs were monsters and didn't know any better. Humans—humans were *worse,* because they had the capacity to *choose* to be civilized. They'd *been* civilized for centuries, millennia. There were no excuses. Humans collapsed into savagery almost overnight, and the only sanity left—the only humanity she saw worth preserving in the last fourteen years—was the COG. She never thought she'd come to see the regime that had invaded and conquered her islands as any kind of haven or guardian of humanity's better values.

But it was all there was left. And it was the need to be among Gears again that had brought her halfway across the planet, not the COG.

"I've done some bad stuff," she said at last. Shit, she'd shut this out for years. A hot shower, long-forgotten flavors, a reminder of the sheer primal power of comradeship under fire, and suddenly the floodgates were swinging open. "It wasn't just cats I skinned."

The rhythmic scuffing noise of Baird's brush stopped for a few beats and then carried on.

"It's okay, Boomer Lady," Cole said. His voice was quiet and serious, a different Cole altogether. "I bet you had a damn good reason for anything you did."

It all made sense now; Cole's loud cheerfulness wasn't his way of keeping his own fears at bay. He was too strong emotionally, too self-aware to need to whistle in the dark. The show was for the squad—to make everyone around him feel bulletproof. Cole was the ultimate team player.

"I just need a pee," she said, desperate for a moment alone. "Five minutes."

She strode down the passage to the lavatory, found a stall at the far end of the row, and sat down to sob. Cole personified all the reasons she came back. He was what humans could be at their best. It hit her hard, and it took ten minutes with a cold wet towel pressed to her eyes before she felt she could walk back into that room with enough control not to smack Baird in the mouth at the next jibe.

But Dom Santiago was waiting for her, with that expectant look on his face, just like Carlos. He stood up when she came in.

"You've been putting me off for ages," Dom said. "I'm not stupid. I can see the look every time I ask. You don't want to talk about Carlos."

He wasn't far wrong. Cole gave her a knowing nod as he got up and diverted Baird.

"Come on, Damon." He gave him a playful swat. "Those boots are *done.*"

"I know."

"Get your tool kit together, then, baby, 'cos we said we'd collect that truck."

Baird took the hint, but he gave Bernie his dead-eyed predator look, the one that didn't impress her one bit. "We'll be waiting in the vehicle compound, Granny."

She waited for the door to close.

"Okay, Dom. What do you want to know that you don't already?"

"The truth," said Dom.

"Truth's not the same as facts."

"I'll have to be the judge of that. You're an honest woman. Just tell me what you saw. There's nothing left that can hurt me."

He reached into his shirt and pulled out a couple of photographs, then selected one to show her. It was shocking in a totally unexpected way, just a regular picture of three young men—Dom, Carlos, and Marcus, Carlos in the middle with his arms around the others' shoulders. It was shocking because Marcus was grinning from ear to ear, minus that do-rag that he never took off, and she had trouble recognizing him even as the young Gear she'd known. The gulf between the present-day Marcus—scarred, unsmiling, restless—was so wide she couldn't even begin to fathom it.

"Carlos never even lived to see my daughter," Dom said, sliding the picture back among the others as if he was handling a holy relic. "Just give me something to make sense of it all. Please."

Carlos was a nice-looking lad. It seemed such a waste now, saving society from one threat when it wasn't the one that was lurking ready to destroy most of humankind.

"Okay," Bernie said. "Carlos was a hero—the best kind, the kind who does it for people, not some idea. If there was a risk to be taken, he'd be first in line shoving Marcus out of the way. He didn't know what it meant to give up. He adored you, and he was proud of you." *Whoa there, girl, this is worse than telling him the bad shit. How far are you going to twist the knife?* "I still miss him. Is that what you want to know? I'll probably remember the funny stories piecemeal, like the time he pissed in the adjutant's—"

"I want to know *how he died.*"

"He got the Embry Star. Doesn't that say everything?"

"No, it doesn't say a frigging thing. It tells me what was in the citation." Dom was cut from the same cloth as Carlos, all right. He never gave up. He wouldn't back off, even knowing he was going to get hurt. "You were there—right there. So was Marcus, but I can't push him to churn over stuff that broke his heart. Tell me what you saw."

They always think they want to know.

And maybe Dom really does.

The trouble was knowing for sure. Once you told someone the truth, there was no way of un-telling it, and they were trapped in a box with that knowledge for the rest of their lives, unable to escape. Bernie liked Dom too much to trap him there carelessly.

"Dom, he died," Bernie said. "You've served eighteen years as a Gear. You know death's not like the movies. You want to hear *that* level of detail?"

Dom had that same expression as Carlos; he jutted his chin out just a fraction, lips compressed in a tight line, frown deepening a little, as if he was thinking hard.

"Yeah," he said. "I have to."

It's his brother. He's got a right. It's not my secret to keep now. What's this about, his feelings or my guilt?

"It's going to upset you," she said.

"Okay. Yeah, I'm okay with that. Thanks." Dom nodded. Bernie wanted to drag Baird back by the collar and make him look at Dom, to see how a real man conducted himself. "Sorry. I don't want to haul up bad memories or anything."

Bernie almost lost it; Dom had that same ability as Carlos to think of the other person first. But after sixteen years, she wasn't going to hesitate and let a brave man do the hardest part of all. She wasn't going to freeze and let another Carlos save her from a tough call.

Sorry, Carlos. But you proved it. You proved you were the real deal, and I didn't rob you of that. And I don't have to see your face with my round between your eyes each time I sight up, and hate myself for doing it.

Carlos had even saved her in the end.

"Your brother," she said, "did something every last one of us does at least once in our lives. He screwed up. But he died to save Marcus, and Marcus almost got killed trying to save him, and both of them would have given their lives for you in a heartbeat. There's not many human beings who can love like that. Gears, mainly. It's why we know what it really means to be human. It's more than family. It's *civilization.* What's best in humanity. Even Baird, the inbred little shit. Funny, that, for a bunch of bastards who'll carve up another living creature with a chainsaw." Bernie put her hands on Dom's shoulders and made him sit down; his face was now more illuminated than stricken, as if he'd discovered a great religious truth that had eluded him. "Now I'll do the decent thing and tell you every damn detail. Because Carlos Santiago was a fucking *hero.*"

CHAPTER 19

What do you mean, Pesang troops aren't eligible for the Embry Star? What kind of xenophobic bullshit is that? You mean you've got to be defeated by the COG before you get recognition? Pesang volunteered to fight with us, as a free country. That makes them twice the men of any of our damn vassal territories.

(MAJOR VICTOR HOFFMAN, TALKING TO THE GENERAL'S ADJUTANT, 26 RTI HQ, WHILE COMPLETING HIS REPORT ON THE ASSAULT ON ASPHO POINT AND MAKING RECOMMENDATIONS FOR AWARDS.)

CNV *POMEROY*, SOMEWHERE OFF THE OSTRI COAST; SIXTEEN YEARS AGO, A FEW HOURS AFTER OP LEVELER.

"Give me an hour," said the lieutenant in Comms. "We'll have a satellite window then. I'm sure we can get a call through for you."

"Thanks, sir," Dom said. "I wouldn't ask if it wasn't important. But my wife doesn't know if I'm alive or dead.

And I haven't been able to speak to her since she gave birth."

"No problem," said the lieutenant. "Anything for a guy who can park a Marlin in a moving Raven first time out."

There was a time when Dom would have been proud to be treated as a VIP—little Dom Santiago, feted by all these officers—but all it did now was make him feel guilty and confused. He couldn't sleep. He was shaking with fatigue, but every time he rolled into that bunk with so many empty ones around him and tried to shut his eyes, some animal deep within said *don't, don't do it, you don't know what you'll see.* He found himself lurching from one emotional extreme to the other. The pure tearful joy about the baby swung to utter grief for the buddies he'd lost that night and left him unable to find a balance.

At around 0230 he walked through the passages to the hangar deck to wait for the inbound Raven. *Pomeroy* was still at defense stations, all her deck lights in darkness as she steamed out of range of Ostri fighters.

I'll be okay when Carlos and Marcus get here.

They'd be able to make sense of it all together. While Dom waited, leaning on the safety rail, deck crew passed back and forth. Some paused to shake his hand. Word got around fast.

Hoffman wandered up to join him.

"No guarantees," Hoffman said quietly, "but I'm recommending you for the Embry Star."

"I'm not dead," said Dom. "I really should be dead to get it, right?"

He was only half joking. His buddies *were* dead. Hoffman didn't reply. He must have been just as gutted to lose Benjafield, Young, and Morgan, and the Pesang troops he'd known for years, some of them from the Siege of Anvil Gate. Nobody could feel triumphant tonight.

"But neither am I," Hoffman said. "Or Timiou, or Shim, or the rest of his boys. All down to you."

"I'm not a hero." Dom just wanted to get home and see Maria and the kids. "And what *about* the others, then? Do they get a gong?"

Hoffman looked as if he was going to say something, but just nodded and leaned on the rail with him in silence. Hoffman was a fair commanding officer, but he wasn't a chummy guy; something was going on.

Dom knew that for sure when he saw Marcus step down from the Raven. He waited for Carlos to emerge, but as the hangar deck cleared and the wounded were taken away, he felt his brain switch off and a terrible distance opened up across the deck as if he'd been catapulted backward against the bulkhead. Sergeant Mataki paused with Marcus for a few moments, talking quietly to him, and then patted him on the back before walking up to Hoffman.

"Bernie," Hoffman said. "Good to see you." He turned to Dom. "I won't be getting any sleep tonight, so if you need to talk—you know where I am."

And Sergeant Mataki shook Dom's hand and held on to it for a few seconds. Yes, something *had* gone wrong.

He's badly hurt. He's lost a limb. They've taken him to Kalona.

Dom didn't want to move from that spot. Part of him felt that if he didn't take that first step, he could put off the inevitable forever. The other part told him to face up to it because it wasn't going to go away. He walked out to meet Marcus halfway.

We'll look after Carlos. He'll cope. It's not the end of the world.

"Dom . . ." Marcus stopped in the middle of the deck. He looked terrible. He peeled off his do-rag and screwed it up in one fist, staring at it and looking as if he was struggling for words. "Dom, I'm sorry. I'm sorry."

That was as far as he got—as far as he needed to get. Dom could hear himself saying, "No, no, not Carlos . . ." but it wasn't real. His face felt numb. His mouth wouldn't function.

He was wrong. It *was* the end of the world.

HOUSE OF THE SOVEREIGNS, JACINTO; FIVE WEEKS LATER.

In the Pendulum Wars, medals were awarded and handed out fast. The Coalition had become very efficient at warfare and its administration over nearly eighty years, and—so Hoffman liked to think—it wanted to award its decorations while the live recipients were still in that condition, and could share their honor with their loved ones.

It was also better for the media coverage. Hoffman noted that as he stood waiting for the awards ceremony.

Most Gears who got the Embry Star weren't around to enjoy the moment. Hoffman joined the list of live specimens with Dom Santiago and Marcus Fenix, and felt not pride but embarrassment that he was there at all. Margaret thought the promotion was long overdue; Hoffman didn't give a shit about it. She was upset that he hadn't wanted her there for the ceremony. But *Lieutenant Colonel, ES,* was just for signing memos, and bringing her along in her best frock was too celebratory for his liking. It didn't change a damn thing. It just took him one more step away from what he signed up to do: frontline soldiering.

Hoffman waited with the other honors recipients in the echoing anteroom, in a forest of smooth marble columns whose rich red-brown colors added to the impression of being lost among sturdy trees. Paintings of the Allfathers in plain gilt frames adorned the walls. Ornate moldings were fine for other public buildings, but here the COG drew the line, and had built a plain heartland of austere self-sacrifice and common purpose.

The Gears gathering in small groups in their best parade uniforms were from various campaigns, not just Operation Leveler. There were also widows and children—and a few widowers—in smart civilian suits, who would follow the stage direction and accept the medals with appropriate stoic pride for the cameras. One of the children was in uniform herself: Anya Stroud. How the hell did anyone cope with having to listen to their mother die like that? She deserved a medal herself, just for being able to carry on for the rest of her watch. She was talking to Marcus and Dom, eyes lowered, ashen, and they both had a protective hand on her shoulders. They moved to block her from cameras. It said it all.

Hoffman swore that if any of the media roving the anteroom took that picture, he'd hunt them down and ram their cameras so far up their asses that they'd be able to film their back teeth.

Shit, without that do-rag, Marcus Fenix looks just a kid. And he is.

Hoffman accepted the media as a necessary evil, like air raids. But that didn't mean he had to like either. The hacks were moving from group to group, getting their interviews done before the medals ceremony, and Hoffman prayed they didn't come to him.

They did, of course. A polite but weedy young man who clearly didn't have anything of what it took to be a Gear tackled him head-on. He had EXEMPTED FROM SERVICE stamped all over him.

"Get lost, parasite," Hoffman said. "Why don't you report on what it's like when the ceremony's over, when you're trying to raise kids on your own?"

To his credit, the baby hack didn't flinch or miss a beat. He must have been inured to abuse at an early age in his job. "You sound as if you don't support the war, Colonel."

"Of course I don't," Hoffman snarled. "I support *winning* wars. The whole point of going to war is to stop it as fast as you can. It's not a damn hobby."

But it's all I know. The only solution I can think of.

Dalyell's PR jackals were prowling. One zeroed in on Hoffman and caught his arm as her colleague fielded the frantically scribbling journalist and headed off an incident.

"Colonel Hoffman, that's not very helpful," she said. "You know how they misquote us."

"I'm sorry, ma'am, did I stray off message?" He stepped just a fraction inside her personal space. He never thought of himself as a bully, but he treated his female Gears the same as the men, and he wasn't going to change that for any civilian pen pusher. "I don't know what got into me. It must be losing half my men."

But Hoffman wasn't what the media really wanted. They had their perfect picture lined up: Dom Santiago, a shockingly young hero accepting his dead brother's medal along with his own, and their equally heroic childhood buddy, son of the saintly Adam Fenix, poor shattered Marcus with his brand new sergeant's stripes and his bloodless, haunted eyes. It was an iconic image of Tyrus's bravest and best with tragedy visible on their faces, a picture that would press every emotional button on the public's panel. They could even add the pretty blond girlie with her heroic mother's Embry Star. It was the five-star jackpot of front pages and prime-time headlines.

But it's true. That's all true. It is *tragic. They* are *good boys, good girls. It shouldn't be that way, but it is, and what they did is already changing the course of the war. They did it.*

The ceremony was quick and low-key. Chairman Dalyell and the Chief of Staff had plenty of medals to dish out, from the Embry Star to the Allfathers's Military Medal. Hoffman looked Dalyell straight in the eye as he came to attention in front of him.

"Magnificent courage, Colonel," Dalyell said, extending his hand. "This is the highest number of Stars awarded for any single operation in Coalition history."

Hoffman didn't shake his hand. He knew at that moment that this promotion was his last, and that it was worth everything to fire this single shot.

"I accept it for all the Pesang troops who didn't get the recognition I recommended," he said, watching Dalyell's face stiffen. "Pesang is a willing ally, not a conquered territory. They *volunteered* for our war. So this is for Sergeant Bai Tak and his countrymen."

Yes, Hoffman's career *was* finished. He saw it in Dalyell's eyes. And he was entirely at peace with that. He marched away smartly to the side, in accordance with the op orders, and then went out into the courtyard and stared up at the clear blue sky, his heart pounding with anger. As he fumbled to unpin the medal, he snagged threads in his jacket, and swore.

"Can you hold up your Star, Colonel?" said a photographer. He hadn't even heard the guy approach, just like a Pesanga. "Just a quick picture."

The poor bastard was only doing his job. "No, I frigging *can't,*" said Hoffman.

And he couldn't even explain why. It was a classified mission. The media didn't know the details of Op Leveler beyond "destroying an enemy facility and saving COG lives, against overwhelming odds," and they wouldn't be told, not until it suited the COG to do so years later. But the media here were used to that restriction. There was a war on, after all. They were used to heroes who couldn't explain, and they'd learned never to ask too many questions.

Hoffman waited on a small stone bench in the gardens of the Tomb of the Unknowns. Across the gravel path, edged by a dense miniature hedge precisely twenty centimeters high, was one of the new graves with its crisply-engraved, glossy granite headstone free of weathering and lichen; PRIVATE CARLOS BENEDICTO SANTIAGO, ES, 26 RTI—FALLEN AT ASPHO FIELDS, OSTRI, 15TH DAY OF BRUME, 77TH YEAR OF THE WAR, AGED 20.

"And that's your lot, Private," Hoffman said. "That's your life, all in six lines."

Carlos's folks hadn't attended; neither had Adam Fenix, nor Dom's wife, but then she had two babies to care for. Hoffman didn't blame any of the Santiago family for wanting to keep their grief out of the news. He sat there watching the sun move across the headstone, until Fenix and Dom eventually walked down the gravel path and looked at him as if he was intruding.

"I'll go," he said.

"No need, sir." Dom had his Embry Star clutched in his

hand in its small red leather case. "We're having dinner tonight. All of us, Cadet Stroud and Professor Fenix, too. You want to come?"

"That's very gracious of you, Private Santiago." Hoffman looked past him for a moment to see Fenix just staring at the grave, face carefully fixed. "I'll have to pass. I'm on wife-placating detail. But I'd be honored to have a beer with you very soon."

Hoffman got up, shook their hands, and walked slowly to the staff car that would still be waiting for him by the main gates, unless he dodged it and walked alone through the city to gather his thoughts, and ponder what he'd do now that he'd completely fucked his chances of ever being promoted or given a decent posting. *So what? So what does it matter? I'd rather be an NCO again.* He stopped to glance back at Marcus and Dom.

Hoffman had never really known what to make of Marcus Fenix, except to conclude that he was a superb soldier. Whatever went on in his head was a mystery, though, and Hoffman was uneasy around people whose motives were unknowable.

Until now, at least.

Fenix squatted down and dug away at the white granite chippings on the grave with his knife until he'd excavated a hole. It took him a long time. The spectacle left Hoffman oddly disturbed and . . . yes, he *pitied* that boy. Hoffman watched until his adjutant came crunching down the path.

"Colonel, your car's waiting—"

The rank was new and uncomfortable. "I know."

"What's he doing, sir?"

Hoffman felt inexplicably protective for an instant. "Look, get back to HQ. I can make my own way back. Just go."

If Fenix knew he was being watched, he didn't seem to care. He dusted off his hands, sill squatting, and bowed his head for a few moments. Then he unpinned his Embry Star and laid it in the hole in Santiago's grave, before scooping the soil and granite chips back into place.

It hit Hoffman like a slap. It literally left him unable to breathe or swallow for a few moments, not just on the verge of tears but on the precipice of losing every fixed point in life that he'd clung to. It confirmed that he'd done what he had to, and that he hadn't been a crazy middle-aged loser throwing away what little he'd achieved.

You wouldn't get it, Margaret. I'm not even sure I can explain.

Hoffman walked back to his office, packed his Embry Star in a small box, and settled down to write to Bai Tak's widow again. The bank draft that he placed in the envelope with the Embry Star would be a fortune to a hill farmer in rural Pesang trying to make ends meet.

REDOUBT HOTEL, EAST BARRICADE, LATER THAT DAY.

It was a painful, miserable evening.

Dom's parents left before the dessert course to relieve the babysitter, and they didn't look as if they regretted it. This wasn't their kind of place at the best of times, let alone when they were still sobbing most nights about Carlos.

It wasn't Dom's kind of place, either; the silver cutlery and starched white tablecloths made him afraid of spilling anything, but it was the deferential waiters who freaked him out most. He couldn't believe anyone would want to do that kind of job for people who didn't even look you in the eye when you served them. He and Marcus sat there in their formal uniforms, just the ribbon of the Embry Star visible to show what the day had been about, and Marcus looked even more uncomfortable about it than Dom felt.

Professor Fenix meant well, Dom was certain of that, but he just wasn't equipped to handle this kind of thing. The meal was mostly silent. There was no other option, because the weight of shared loss was like someone else sitting at the table with them, hogging the conversation with its loud silence and unwilling to let anyone speak.

Glasses chinked at other tables, the sound muffled by the weight of drapes in the restaurant.

"Are you going to loan Carlos's medal to the regimental museum?" Professor Fenix asked.

Dom had no idea such a thing could happen. It was all part of that book-lined, antique-filled world that Marcus had grown up in. "No, sir. I gave it to Mom and Dad." He hoped Marcus's old man didn't ask what he would do with his own. He wanted Benedicto to have it. "It's rightfully theirs now."

"Anya?"

She looked hunted for a moment, sitting between Marcus and his father with no escape from the question. Dom had expected her to fall apart, given what a bag of nerves she always seemed to be when her mother was around, and she was a quiet girl anyway—as far as he could tell from their occasional contact. But something had shifted inside her.

"No, sir," she said firmly. "It's all I have left of her, and I won't let strangers stare at it. I've had enough of public bereavement."

That was a new Anya, all right. Marcus seemed surprised, too. He gave her a slow, careful glance, the kind he did when he didn't think anyone would notice, and Dom wished that the pair of them could just be like anyone else, and go on a date or something.

"I understand," said the professor. "My apologies for being crass."

It was very stiff and formal. Eduardo Santiago would have given her a comforting hug, a father's hug that she had never had. Major Stroud had raised her alone. No wonder she gravitated to Marcus; they both had *lonely smart kid* embedded in their genes.

Shit, old man Fenix can't even talk to Marcus about his mom. And I expect him to let Anya cry on his shoulder?

Dom let himself think about Carlos again, trying not to drown in the endless rerunning of that last couple of days. The last thing he said to him, the last time they actually talked and didn't just leave messages—Dom still couldn't remember what it was.

Bereavement was a double punch. It was a pain that wouldn't leave you alone, even when you dreamed, and then it twisted the knife by whispering in your ear that it had warned you all your life, but you just hadn't listened—*you'll miss me when I'm gone, make the most of every day in case it's the last, you'd give everything for one last chance to tell them how you felt . . .*

It was all true. Nobody could say that they didn't know what was coming. But everyone thought it would never happen to them, or that when it did, it would somehow be different.

It wasn't.

Maria gripped Dom's hand under the table. All he wanted right then was to get home, lock the door, and—

Home, he realized, was his parents' place. Yes, that was where he needed to be, with Maria and the kids, just for a few nights the whole family, everyone he loved. The need filled him with guilt. Because Marcus needed him too, even if he'd never acknowledge it.

"Would anyone like more coffee?" Professor Fenix asked at last. "Maria? Anya?" The table was dotted with confusing glasses, all half full—water, different wines, even brandy—but nobody was really drinking. Anya had managed two glasses of wine, Marcus three. That was a lot for both of them, Dom thought.

"I think I have to get back," Anya said. "Thank you, Professor. It's been very comforting to get together."

We have to go. I can't stand this.

Dom found himself wishing Anya was right for Marcus, because loss was easier to bear if you could lean on someone you loved. Before Aspho, she'd definitely been interested in him, and Marcus spent a little too long staring at her legs when she wasn't looking. Now they just seemed linked by a kind of relief that they didn't have to explain to each other how much they hurt. Maybe extra-talented kids who grew up in the shadow of larger-than-life parents were doomed never to live easily in the routinely intimate moments that lesser mortals took for granted.

She got up to collect her jacket. "Are you going to be okay?" Dom said, cupping her elbow. She'd never seemed comfortable tottering along on high heels, and now that she had a drink or two inside her, she was unsteady. "Marcus, I'm going to get Anya a cab and see her back to the officer's mess."

"Thanks, I'll be okay," she said. "I need to go check out Mom's apartment." She turned to Maria. "Your Dom's one in a million. He really is."

It was an odd phrase for Anya. *Your Dom.* It was almost as if she wanted to make it clear they were just friends, and that she had no designs on him. Maybe everyone else treated her as predatory.

Marcus stepped in.

"I'll see that she's okay, Dom," he said. And, utterly out of character for him, he offered her his arm in a formal old-man kind of way, as if he'd been drilled that was how to treat a lady. "We'll be fine."

Dom called a cab anyway and slipped the driver some bills. "Those two," he said, indicating Marcus and Anya. "Take 'em wherever they want to go."

Dom and Maria went back to his folks' house, and he spent the night curled up on the sofa with her, with Benedicto and Sylvia in their arms. He couldn't bear to shut his eyes or let go of any of them. He wasn't sure how he was going to go back on duty, because he didn't want to turn his back on his family for a second in case he looked around again and they weren't there.

"She's right," Maria murmured, eyes shut. "You're one in a million."

"Hey, it was nothing like that."

"I know."

"We just ended up in that room waiting to get the medals, and it all sort of . . . I don't know. Me, her and Marcus. Friendship. Something fell into place."

"Now, Marcus and Anya . . ." Maria said. "I know it looks like a good idea to you, but those two are never going to last beyond tonight. Don't try to fix it for them. And she's an officer, he's enlisted. They'll end up on a charge."

"Not if they keep it for off-duty hours." Dom hated crushed hopes. He wanted to see Marcus glowing with dumb head-over-heels love tomorrow morning, not keeping his head down so Dom wouldn't nudge him and ask if things went okay. "And things change. People change."

Life was always going to be like that now. There was before Aspho, and after Aspho. Dom now lived in after-Aspho, and it was a strange new land where the only landmarks he recognized were his family and Marcus Fenix.

And even they would never be the same again.

CHAPTER 20

I don't know his name. I don't know anything about him, other than that he was a guard at Aspho Point, his name wasn't Natan, and if he had been one of my men, I'd have been proud of him. Make sure he isn't forgotten.

(A HEAVILY REDACTED OFFICIAL REPORT OF THE ASPHO POINT RAID FROM MAJOR VICTOR HOFFMAN, FOUND IN THE VAULTS OF THE OSTRI EMBASSY, JACINTO; STAMPED *UNCIRCULATED.*)

RECOVERY ROOM, MEDICAL WING, WRIGHTMAN HOSPITAL; FOURTEEN YEARS AFTER E-DAY, THE PRESENT DAY.

"Are you done with me yet?" Hoffman demanded.

"No." Dr. Hayman prodded the back of his calf. It was still numb and he couldn't see what she was doing because he was lying face down, which didn't improve his mood. "Have you ever tried quiet gratitude?"

"Screw that. I've had more wounds like this than you've given enemas."

"That was when we could afford to lose a few Gears," she said. "Now even miserable old bastards like you have to be kept operational. And trust me, I could ruin your entire *week* with one of my enemas." She turned to the next bed visibly angry, not playing for effect. "I don't want any more lip from you, either, Sergeant Fenix. If I'd known you'd just come out of the Slab, I'd have had you in here days ago. You're probably carrying every disease known to man."

"I washed my hands," Fenix said, his voice like a dead grub being dragged over gravel. "Twice."

"Well, you two keep each other company while I go treat a real patient. They've just brought in an eighteen-year-old corporal who's lost both legs, so you two fucking heroes go right ahead and feel sorry for yourselves until I get back."

That news did the trick just fine. Hoffman felt like dirt. But he was now cooped up on his own with Fenix and there was no avoidance, no small talk, nothing to do except deal with the enormity of what still hung between them when there were no more grubs around.

I've got a reputation. He won't expect tact from me anyway.

"I need to know something, Fenix." Hoffman defied Hayman's instructions and rolled over to sit up, because he had to look the man in the eye. "Why the hell did you come back for me after what I did to you?"

Fenix was staring at the ceiling, fingers meshed behind his head. "No Gear gets left behind. Maybe I went back for Kaliso."

"Let's clear the air. I can't abide unfinished business. I left you to die."

"Yes," said Fenix. His tone was matter-of-fact. "You left me for the grubs, while you let the rapists, cannibals, pedophiles, and serial killers go free."

Hoffman still didn't know why he'd done it. Fenix's complete lack of visible anger was actually worrying him. He had to lance this boil right now. "You want to settle the score, then?"

"Nothing to settle."

"I'll bet." *Shit, he's just like his old man. A damn machine. If I hadn't seen him at Santiago's grave, I'd have thought he didn't have a scrap of feeling in him.* "You're okay about it. No hard feelings. Minor misunderstanding and all that shit."

"We get what we deserve in life."

No, you don't. Nobody with your record deserves that.

Hoffman felt swallowed up by guilt. He found himself blurting out his reasoning, feeble as it now seemed, knowing it still didn't justify what he'd done, but his mouth was on autopilot.

I'm scared. I'm always scared. Not death. Worse than that. Getting shit wrong. Getting people *wrong.*

"You dicked around and cost men's *lives,* Sergeant," he said. *Like I never did?* "You cost us Jacinto. Your father just snapped his fingers, and bang, you leave your men and stroll off with the targeting laser. You think that doesn't make you an asshole, at the very least? You've got a buddy like Dom, who'd shit his last drop of blood for you, who put you first even when his wife went missing, and you do that to men *depending* on you?"

"I meant," Fenix said slowly, "that I let someone die a long time ago, so I can't bitch about someone doing the same to me."

Hoffman was completely thrown by that revelation. He had no idea how to come back, or—more to the point—climb down. He wanted to apologize. He really did.

"Just tell me the truth," he said. "Not what you told the

court-martial. I need to know. What did your father have that was so important that you'd leave your post to get it? Because I can't believe Adam Fenix would expect his son to do that just to save his sorry ass."

"He died before I got to him. I'll never know."

"He must have said *something.*"

"He put the COG first. He had his reasons. That's the only thing I could trust about him."

"That's got to be the fucking lamest excuse for running away that I ever heard," Hoffman said. There; his mouth was on rapid fire again, all bluster to cover the real shit, the embarrassment at hearing this hardest of Gears admit that his father was an asshole. Actually, Hoffman believed Fenix. He probably hadn't said that at the court-martial because publicly admitting that Adam Fenix wasn't a paragon of wisdom and virtue was one pain too many to handle. But you could take the stricture against speaking ill of the dead a little too far. "You were too *late.* Your plan didn't work. And people died. And we lost most of Jacinto."

"I *know* I fucked up, Colonel. I had the rest of my sentence to think about it. And it wasn't the first time I was too late. If you want to stoke the self-loathing, you're way too late."

Hoffman's anger—with himself and with Fenix—ground to a halt. "You don't know why you did it, do you? You don't know why you ran to your daddy like he still controlled your goddamn life."

Fenix propped himself up on one elbow and loomed over Hoffman across the gap between the treatment tables. They were almost nose to nose. "You're an asshole, but you're not a *sadistic* asshole. You ever ask yourself why *you* did it?"

"All the damn time," Hoffman yelled in his face. "Every day. Because I can't believe I did it, why I didn't just shoot you and have done with it. Probably because I *couldn't,* because before that day you were one of the finest soldiers I ever knew."

He *had* saved Fenix not long after that, though. The bastard had needed rescuing after he steered the Lightmass bomb to its target; without Hoffman's help, Dom wouldn't have been able to pull Fenix on board the Raven. It was like fate had given him a chance to make amends.

But Hoffman knew that didn't wipe the slate clean, and it never would.

The door suddenly swung open so hard that it hit the tiles and bounced back. Dr. Hayman stepped in with the kind of face she reserved for serious physical intervention. Hoffman knew that expression only too well.

"*Shut up!*" she yelled. "This is a damn hospital, not a bar. Fenix—get dressed and pick up your medications from the dispensary. Any symptoms—get back here, not because I care, but because disease control gets harder every day. Hoffman—I'm going to enjoy sticking this needle in your ass, so turn over again and keep your mouth *shut.*"

Hoffman knew he didn't deserve courtesy because he often didn't give it. He also knew exactly what had made him reinforce that wall of callousness more heavily with each year, and he wondered if Dr. Hayman's job had turned her into this harpy too, her defense against going crazy or—worse, finding that the task she had was beyond her and that she would let down everyone who was depending on her for their lives.

Fenix grabbed his clothes and walked out. Hoffman held her at bay for a moment with a raised hand and called to

Fenix. The place was so quiet that the man had to be able to hear him clear through to the entrance gates.

"I'm sorry," Hoffman yelled. "There, I said it. I'm frigging *sorry* I left you there. You deserved better, you surly asshole."

If Marcus heard, he didn't stop. His boots thudded all the way down the hall without missing a step.

Dr. Hayman held up a hypodermic and checked the vial for air bubbles. "Okay," she said. "Just remember, it's only pain. . . ."

Hoffman braced for impact. The bitch would have been right at home brandishing a chainsaw, but he was damned if he was going to give her so much as a twitch by way of reaction.

She must have picked the bluntest, oldest, largest recycled needle in the whole damn city.

But she was right. It was only pain.

COLLEGE GREEN, OUTSIDE THE JACINTO ENCLAVE.

Kaliso insisted on coming. He'd sworn that he'd retrieve the bodies from the burned-out truck, and that was the first port of call.

Bernie and the rest of the squad, minus Marcus, piled into the 'Dill and set off to gather up what was theirs.

Dom needs a little time alone to think. Just as well.

Nobody argued with Kaliso. It wasn't simply the fact that he took this warrior tradition stuff way too seriously—it wasn't Bernie's island's way, not at all—but also that he was a hard bastard who looked like he had a very short temper.

The real Kaliso was a lot less volatile than his image, but most people liked to give the man the benefit of the doubt.

Bernie understood his compulsion only too well, though. Coming right after a harrowing hour with Dom discussing how his brother died, the principle of gathering remains was now rubbing a very raw nerve, an icon for the last bastion of civilization against savagery. She saw Stranded much as she saw grubs. That didn't make her unique as a Gear, because Stranded were almost universally loathed. She thought it not because the COG had told her so, but because she'd spent so long among them and seen too much for herself. No Gear would do the things she'd seen, not to another Gear—maybe not to anybody.

"You okay, Dom?" she said.

Dom, bless him, had had no qualms about crying his eyes out and hugging her. Like Cole, the childhood foundations of his life had been solid, and let him weather an awful lot of storms.

"Just thinking about Marcus," he said. "Explains a lot. He changed after Aspho. Now I know why. And he's not the same as he was before he went to prison."

"So, are you going to talk to him about it?"

"I've got to. No secrets between us. Funny, I always thought I'd failed Carlos. I really did."

There was nothing more corrosive to a relationship than waiting for the other person to come clean with you. Bernie hoped Dom would cut Marcus some slack. But Dom was all heart, and even if he was hurt, he would never let Marcus know that.

Kaliso banged his fist on the 'Dill's hatch. "Done," he said. He lobbed chunks of charred material into the cargo section, and Bernie did a double take to make sure they really were just pieces of metal for reclamation, not human remains. No, Kaliso was very proper about that kind of thing. "Come on. Let's try starting that trailer."

The huge articulated flatbed had shuddered to a halt near College Green. As soon as the 'Dill reached the intersection, they could see it; and Stranded swarmed all over it like dung beetles. The steel fermentation vats were still on the flatbed, but there were lifting straps rigged to it, suggesting that some tosser had gone off to fetch a crane of some kind. Bernie dismounted from the 'Dill even before Dom switched off the engine.

She wasn't in a sunny mood for anything non-Gear today. She didn't even shout a warning. She aimed the Lancer a meter above head-height and fired off a long burst. The Stranded dived for cover as she strode up to the trailer.

"Boomer Lady," Cole said, jumping down behind her. "Remember, cats is bad enough, but eatin' *people* is just plain *wrong*."

She'd seen that, too, but somehow it was nowhere near the worst excesses of a human race in collapse. One of the Stranded found the balls to venture out from behind cover and confront her.

"You dumb bitch, you could have killed someone," he said. "What the hell are you playing at?"

"Correct, I *could* have killed you." She switched back into a Bernie that she'd been glad to put aside for the last few days, and let the chainsaw run for a few deafening seconds to focus their attention. They'd probably never seen the bayonet operating close-up before. "The law's clear. You loot, I shoot. Now, get your diseased arse back into your hovel, and bring back every last rivet and spring you've stolen, or so help me I'll burn down every house I think is storing stolen goods. Understand?"

Baird swaggered up to stand beside her in a rare moment of solidarity. "What she said." He looked at his watch. "Ten minutes. Move it."

The man looked past them toward the Armadillo. "Santiago? Santiago, this ain't right—tell her. We thought you understood us. After all we done for you."

Bernie listened for a hint of disapproval in Dom's voice as he jumped down from the 'Dill. She really didn't want to offend him. Like Cole, he was her benchmark of decency, and she'd lost sight of that standard so many times since E-Day that the prospect of that blurred line terrified her.

I don't want to be like these savages. I want to stay human, stay civilized. I'm a Gear.

"Do what the sergeant says," Dom said quietly. "We need that thing for food production. And if you'd stop being such assholes and just join us, you'd get to eat some too."

Bernie wasn't sure if he was just distracted by the morning's traumatic memories, or if he was disappointed that she wasn't the same good old Bernie he'd thought she was. She waited with Baird and Cole, just doing the staring act as cans of fuel, truck seats, engine parts, and other prizes already stripped from the truck began piling up in the street.

"I'll know if you're keeping anything back," said Baird. "Because I'm going to put this truck back together again."

And he did.

Bernie had to hand it to him. He had a rare gift for engineering, and he offered up parts to gaps with unerring accuracy. She marveled at it. At last, she saw some common ground to be explored, a possible foundation for the kind of working relationship she wanted. Delta Squad might have been okay with his constant whining, but she was too old and too overrun by the real tragedies in life to tolerate any shit over trivia. She needed to make peace with him somehow.

"You ever repaired a truck like this before?" she asked.

"Never." Baird's expression had relaxed into a kind of intense concentration, almost like a sense of wonder. He straightened up from the engine compartment to reach for a wrench. "But how hard can it be to work it out? It's just a machine."

"You know you're better at it than anyone else," she said. "Don't sell yourself short."

She could have sworn he was waiting for the sting in the tail. When he didn't get one, he looked almost put out. He was completely silent from then until they got back to Wrightman, and then it was clear that he had no idea how to deal with anything beyond the back and forth of low-grade abuse, and didn't even look comfortable playing a harmless game of cards in the mess with the rest of the squad.

He seemed almost grateful when Marcus showed up and sat down at the table. Marcus was clearly his favorite target, much more rewarding than an old bag like her. Maybe it was because the risk seemed higher. Marcus was the dormant volcano that had been known to engulf cities within living memory, and built like a brick shithouse as well.

"Hey, dickbrain," Baird said casually, not looking up from his hand of cards.

"Hey, asshole." Marcus, quiet as ever, accepted a fresh hand from Cole. "I hear we got the truck back. All of it."

"Granny had a chainsaw chat with the vermin."

"Good for her." Marcus gave her one of those looks, the one that said he wanted a word later. She knew damn well why; Dom. "We could do with an enforcer."

"So," Baird said, "you going to tell us what your chat with Dom was really about, Granny?"

Bernie had found a comfortable balance in the last few days, back in a culture she could rely on and still peppered with people she knew from before the time the world as she knew it ended. It was still very fragile, though, offset by fourteen years of basic survival. Baird had now stepped on a mine. It wasn't her issues so much as the fact that he had raised the subject of Carlos in front of both Dom and Marcus.

"None of your business, sweetheart," she said. *Shit, that'll just keep him going. He's stuck in permanent bloody puberty.* "Sentimental stuff."

"It's another major screwup by our heroic sergeant here, isn't it?"

The switch was thrown. Baird could have no idea just how far below the belt he'd hit Marcus, but it was clear to Bernie, even if nobody else—except Dom—knew it. She couldn't sit back and ignore it. Some things had to be said and defended.

"No," she said. "Actually, it's *not.* Do me a favor and stay off the subject."

Cole hummed tunelessly under his breath. "Damon, baby, won't you *please* think of the little kitties?"

"Okay," Baird said, undeterred, "why am I expected to trust my life to a guy who was serving forty years for helping us lose Jacinto to the grubs, but I can't ask questions about his service record?"

Dom didn't even get a syllable out before Bernie dived in. "Maybe," she said, "it's because I'm telling you to show some respect to a real frigging *man,* Blondie."

"Shit," Cole said. "I'm just enjoying the game. Kiss and make up, you two, will ya?"

"No, sod it, let's deal with it once and for all." Bernie got up and stood to one side of the table, feeling her pulse pounding in her throat. "Come on, Mouth Almighty. Let's see what you're made of, other than a big gob."

Baird got up and stood with his hands on his hips, feet apart in his screw-you stance.

"Don't think I'm going to apologize to him and kiss your ass because you got some sergeant's stripes from ancient history, Mataki."

The mess fell silent. There were plenty of Gears around watching the show.

She'd been waiting a decent while for this. Life was still fragile. So it didn't even count as losing her temper—did it?

Baird was twenty-odd years younger, faster, heavier, taller. He was combat-trained. As she came at him, he hunched, clearly expecting a kick in the balls. What he got was a hard right hook to the back of the jaw, just under the ear.

It was an excruciatingly painful punch that worked every time.

Baird almost fell. He hit the wall. He certainly made some interesting noises, and the rest of the mess cheered encouragingly. Dom put his arm out to stop Bernie from going back for seconds, but she didn't really have that planned, and Cole just caught Baird by the scruff of the neck.

"Remember the kitties?" Cole said. "Now be *nice.*"

"Shit," Baird said at last. "*Shit.*"

Marcus sat at the table, still rearranging his hand, looking unconcerned. He wasn't, of course; she knew that.

"If you hadn't shown Jeff a little humanity in the ambush, I'd just be waiting for the chance to frag you now, Blondie." Bernie stepped back a couple of paces. She wouldn't bet on Baird not hitting a woman, even with Cole restraining him. "But you still better mind your mouth with me. Got it?"

She turned her back on him and ambled off, careful not to look hurried, almost expecting a thud in the back as Baird resumed a fight she would almost certainly lose badly. But she ended up back in the locker area and sat down, knowing she'd just shown him how much he could wind her up.

Bad mistake. Never let them find out where the switches are. How did I forget that?

Marcus followed and stood staring down at her as if he'd remembered something. "Good punch."

"Yeah, jaws aren't built for lateral impact. The nerve pain's a showstopper. No lasting damage, though."

Marcus was still standing there as if he was waiting for an explanation.

"What?" she said, embarrassed at her loss of control.

"Just thinking." Marcus might have looked like a slab of dumb muscle, but she never forgot he was ferociously intelligent and, despite a complete inability to drop his guard, a very sharp judge of people. "You must have had a tough time getting here."

You bet. "There were times when I liked Locust better than humans, believe me. A woman traveling on her own has to be *creative.*"

"Baird's a scared kid. He just mouths off instead of shitting himself, that's all."

"He's nearly *your* age, Marcus, and he's been in uniform for almost as long as you have. Are *you* a scared kid?"

Marcus glanced away at the window, its glass reinforced by tape and filtered by a haze of grime.

"Yeah, most of the time," he said. "We all are. The grown-ups don't have the answers, and we can't trust them anyway."

"Okay, you're telling me to make up and play nice with him."

"No. But if he was a genuine asshole, he'd be a Stranded gang lord. He's still in armor, and he's never let us down. It's just his frigging tedious mouth."

"Okay. But I can't have him saying that about you."

"Words," Marcus said, and shrugged. "Heard 'em all."

"So I told Dom what he wanted to know."

Marcus looked suddenly defeated, as if one more cornerstone of his trust had crumbled. "We agreed *never to do that.*"

"That was then. He needs closure now. I warned him it would upset him."

"He's lost his entire family."

"Yeah, and that's why he needed to know."

Marcus's temper never went much further than a grunted expletive or two, but she knew she was on dangerous ground. She was more afraid of leaving him feeling betrayed than anything else.

"Don't forget Dom's my friend." It was *friend,* not *buddy.* The way he said it made it clear there was only one of those, and that no replacements would be considered. "If finding Maria for him cost my life, it's a price I'd pay. Do you understand that?"

"Oh, I think so," Bernie said. "I was there, remember?"

She patted him on the back as she left, wanting him to understand that there were no hard feelings. She was pissed off that Baird had impugned Marcus's courage; Marcus was pissed off that the H word had been used.

He really didn't like the hero thing.

When Bernie resumed her hand of cards, Baird was a quieter, wiser man, at least for the moment. She decided she'd read another human being totally wrong for once, and wondered if she was slipping.

Baird didn't need understanding or a meeting of minds. Like all brats, he just needed a good clip around the ear from his mother from time to time.

"Deal," she said.

DELTA BARRACKS BLOCK.

Dom put it off as long as he could, but it had to be tackled.

He'd come to terms with Carlos's death a long time ago. It went in the queue with Benedicto, and Sylvia, and his parents, knowing he could deal with it like he dealt with the rest of the grieving, but still staggered by the unique misery of each. Every bereavement had its own flavor that left him unprepared.

But knowing the details about Carlos was like losing him all over again. It was another death, a different pain. Dom now had to reorder his world. When he walked into Marcus's quarters, it was like the conversation had already begun an hour ago.

"Why didn't you tell me?" Dom asked.

Marcus, lying on the bed with his hands behind his head,

kept his eyes fixed on the ceiling. It really pissed Dom off when he wouldn't look him in the eye.

"It would have skewed the way you saw him," Marcus said at last.

"Hey, I loved my brother, but I wasn't blind. He could be a crazy bastard. I knew that."

"He *was* a hero. He was a hero from the moment I met him. He's *still* a hero."

Yes, he was. But this wasn't just about Carlos. It was about Marcus. It was about the truth, and why an otherwise brutally honest man decided to lie. Omission was still lying. Dom needed to know the totality of his brother, and now that he did, he felt torn up, and desperately lonely deep in his guts, and also . . . off the hook.

For all the fresh pain, that sickening cold sensation deep in his guts and the weird feeling at the back of his throat from the spike of adrenaline, Dom felt some relief. Carlos was a regular mortal. Dom hadn't failed to live up to him. They'd both done their best, and on the day, Carlos's best just hadn't been good enough. On any other day, it would have been Dom instead. At Aspho Point, in the sinking Marlins, it very nearly was.

"It stinks to find out how he died after so many years, especially when *you* knew for all those frigging years." Dom wasn't berating Marcus. He just wanted to be sure they'd dealt with all the unsaid things, because Dom liked emotions out in the open, and Marcus couldn't manage that however hard he tried. "How do you think I feel now? What else haven't you told me?"

"I *do* know how you feel." Marcus sat up and swung his feet onto the floor. "Dad never told me he knew where my mother disappeared. Remember?"

It was the most shocking thing in Dom's childhood, a real mystery. He remembered the day Marcus was told that his mom had vanished. "Is that what he called you back for, when you left your post?"

"No."

"Well, shit, Marcus, just spit it out."

This was going to be ugly. Dom didn't want to get into some kind of competitive grief. He had to remind himself that Marcus was just explaining, just trying to prove to Dom that he wasn't dismissing his sense of loss, that for all his silences and apparent lack of emotion he still knew what the pain was all about.

"We were in the Locust tunnels looking for imulsion crystals for the targeting laser. We found Mom's body."

"He knew she'd gone there? Shit."

"Yeah. Some field research in off-limits places."

"Why?"

"I'll never know." It should have been a tirade, venting all his frustration and sense of betrayal, but Marcus's tone was as quiet and weary as ever. "He let me think she'd just left us."

Dom never had any problems telling anyone anything. He couldn't grasp how Marcus could sit on so many terrible memories that his friend needed to know to understand him.

"Hey, I'm sorry."

"I'm the one hijacking your shitty day. And you're worrying about my problems instead of your own. Again."

"Bullshit," Dom said. "At least I know why you didn't tell me about Carlos. To protect me. He asked you to look after me, didn't he?"

Marcus just nodded.

"And you always have." Dom gave him a mock shove in the chest. "When you're ready, I want to know what happened in prison. Because you've changed."

Marcus grunted. "It's early days," he said. "I'll tell you. Sometime."

The conversation was over for the time being. Dom still needed to talk, though, so he went in search of Bernie, who could talk about Carlos without pain or guilt. He found her cleaning her rifle.

"Want to see the pictures of my kids?" he asked, knowing that she wouldn't feel creeped out by it.

Bernie put down the wire brush and the small tin of oil. The cloth on the table was covered with fragments of stuff that Dom didn't want to think about right then.

"I'd love to," she said, and put the rifle to one side.

EPILOGUE

We could have cooperated with the groundwalkers for our mutual salvation, but they are humans, and they only understand dominance and ownership. All that we have left is a war to the death. For all their so-called intelligence, humans are blind to the threat right before their eyes. We never stood a chance of enlisting their aid, so now we fight alone. And we will stand on their corpses to do so.

(MYRRAH, THE LOCUST QUEEN.)

WRIGHTMAN HOSPITAL, A FEW DAYS LATER.

The grubs still hadn't come back in any great numbers, and those that emerged were almost all drones.

Dom never wanted to use the word bored when he meant *not fighting for his life*, but there was a definite sense of not knowing what to do with himself, and he wasn't alone.

"Shit, I'm going to have to get a *hobby,*" Cole said. "Where the hell am I going to find one of those?"

"Baird-baiting," Dom said. "It's a spectator sport, too."

Even the dwindling King Raven fleet took advantage of

the downturn in business to ground half the squadron for maintenance. Dom had the feeling of a change, a big one, but he wasn't sure why he wasn't happy about that. Maybe it was because there was no point rebuilding life until he found Maria.

But the first sign that they had fresh problems—environment problems, not grubs—was in the morning patrol briefing, just a casual reference from the geological survey manager who had reports of refugees starting to arrive in Stranded settlements because of flooding in Tollen, two hours south of Jacinto.

"Is this our problem?" Hoffman asked. "Other than strain on the public order situation outside the secure zone."

"Not a problem per se," said the survey manager. "Except we don't know the cause, or the extent. Could be inconvenient, could be catastrophic. Oh for the days of a satellite network." He took a scrap of paper out of his pocket. "We received this message in the emergency management center today. *The whole damn place is filling up with water. Help us, you bastards.* Well, that's pretty clear, if unscientific."

Dom had combed the Stranded communities around Jacinto for a decade. He wasn't averse to taking a look at settlements farther afield, because where there were Stranded, there might be Maria, or at least information.

"Is there anyone left down there?" Baird said. "I thought that was evacuated years ago."

"Stranded," Cole said. "There's always Stranded."

Baird sneered. "Like I said, nobody left there . . ."

Dom had been to Tollen a few times just after E-Day; pretty dull, big grim public buildings, and endless elevated highway. At least, it had been like that before the Locust overran it. It was lost to the COG now.

"Want us to take a look, Colonel?" Marcus asked. Whatever had passed between them, Marcus and Hoffman appeared to have reached an understanding again. Dom hoped it would hold out. "Just in case."

"Remember we can't evacuate civilians," Hoffman said. "That's an airlift we can't handle. So if you go, you go with the express orders that you do *not* return with passengers under any circumstances."

Dom decided to take Marcus aside later and explain that. It was more about the legacy of Aspho Point than Hoffman's belief that Marcus would turn a recon into a humanitarian relief operation. He remained uneasy about his responsibility to those outside the COG to this day.

But Dom had learned to see beyond the angry Hoffman who was never satisfied with anyone or anything. The man behind those eyes was scared of failure, scared of being rumbled as the late entry grunt who should never have been promoted over Academy grads, scared of giving in to his impulses like a normal man in case his ordinariness was noticed by his betters and used against him. He looked like he had the survival of the human race on his shoulders, and on his alone. And, more than anything, he seemed to feel responsible for every casualty on his watch.

Poor bastard. Even after what he did to Marcus . . . poor bastard. But he did help me pull him inboard. He's still the man I knew.

Dom had watched Marcus grow up weighed down by a cargo of expectation too. Hoffman probably loathed Marcus because they had far too much in common. He had a reputation for leading from the front, even when he shouldn't have, and turning a deaf ear to orders that mysteriously hadn't been heard on a bad radio link. Maybe Marcus could see the similarities and it scared him to think what he might turn into as he grew old.

"Sightseeing tour," Marcus said after the briefing. "We'll overfly and recon. You, me, Baird."

"Lightmass?" Baird asked.

"What about it?"

"We don't know how much subsidence it caused when it detonated. Maybe it's diverted an underground river. Lots of water under the surface that we never see."

Marcus shrugged. "We'll find out. Not much we can do for the locals now."

The King Ravens rarely went far from the city. They were too valuable, and too busy. When Dom climbed into the crew bay, he got a definite sense of . . . not *excitement*, but extreme interest from the crew. Barber was crew chief, and the pilot was Gill Gettner. Dom had a mild nightmare that one day he'd be casevacked with Dr. Hayman in a Raven flown by Gettner, and that he'd be traumatized for life. They both came from the same charm school of do-not-question-me-little-man. Barber rolled his eyes silently as they did the preflight checks.

"I haven't been that far south for years," Gettner said. "Not sure I can even find the place on the chart."

"I'm reassured," Baird said.

"Reckon you can do better, chainsaw boy?"

Dom put his elbow hard in Baird's ribs. "No, Lieutenant," Dom said. "Our buddy's just a nervous flier."

"Oh, I'll pack his parachute myself, then . . ."

Barber mouthed *good mood* at them and hooked up his safety tether. From the door, the destruction spread out below them like the concentric rings of a target roundel, with Jacinto as the irregularly shaped bullseye. As they flew south, taking recon images, scattered settlements appeared briefly in clearings and vanished into tree cover again, reminding them just how few humans still clung to a precarious existence beyond the city. As they neared Tollen, ruined suburbs began to replace the trees.

Dom was taking note of the terrain beneath him, just as he'd been trained to in his commando days, and keeping a rough idea of range and bearing in his head. The Raven seemed to be circling.

"Barber," Gettner said. "Check the latest VFR sectional for me, will you?"

Barber reached into a bulkhead pocket for the paper charts. "It's six years old."

"Yes, but cities don't walk . . ."

"Told you so," Baird murmured, but he had the sense to stop there.

Gettner circled again. As the Raven banked, Dom could see a blinding reflection through the broken towers and houses.

"Oh, shit," he said.

Barber spread out the chart on his knees, folded it to the correct strip, and leaned out of the bay to look for landmarks.

"I'm with Santiago," he said. "*Shit* indeed. In fact, I'd go as far as a *holy fuck*."

Gettner's brittle cheer had quietened noticeably. "I'm glad I'm not delusional."

"It's gone," said Dom, pointing. Marcus leaned forward and followed his extended arm. "Look. I'm not crazy, am I?"

The scale of Tollen had confused them. There were still structures on the edge of the city, but the heart of it was a lake that seemed to stretch for kilometers. It was only when the Raven climbed that Dom could get the scale and estimate it was maybe ten klicks across. There was simply nothing there except debris—trees, ad hoardings, chunks of roof—floating on a surface that was less like a lake than a rolling sea.

The city was gone. It was *gone.*

Giant bubbles of air broke the surface foam like a massive depth charge had been detonated deep below. The surface was a boiling cauldron for a few moments, then the bubbles became steadier and slower. As they watched, the bubbles became more vigorous for a moment. Whatever was beneath the surface was collapsing and venting air pockets.

There were also bodies. Most were pretty bloated, so the serious flooding was some days or weeks old. Dom looked automatically for survivors clinging to anything above the waterline, but there was no point looking. Whatever he saw, he would feel obliged to help. But he couldn't, and so all he would take away with him would be a lasting nightmarish guilt at leaving people to die.

The bubbles were pretty impressive.

"Shit. Hang on to your frillies, boys." Gettner banked the Raven sharply and sent it wheeling away from the restless water below. "I mean it. Be ready to ditch if necessary. This is *not* good."

Barber slid hard against Dom as the Raven tilted, still craning his neck to see what the hell was going on. "What are you going on about, Gill?"

"*Methane.* If that's a methane pocket, we're going to go down like a ton of frigging *bricks.* And if it's come up there, if a pocket that opened can sink a *city,* then it can vent *anywhere.*"

"Shit," Barber said. It was just a breath.

Dom didn't have a clue what Gettner meant. He started to reason it out, but the spectacle of a city becoming a lake—no, a *sea*—was too distracting. The farther they pulled back, the more impossible it looked.

And the more *circular* it looked.

"It's not methane," Baird said.

"Oh, shall I go back and test your hy-fucking-pothesis, Professor? If we plummet, you're wrong. Can do."

Baird had finally met someone even more surly and acid-tongued than himself. He shut up.

"Methane makes water and air less dense," Marcus said quietly, leaning toward Dom, as if he didn't want to look like a smart-ass. Of course Marcus knew: he was the one who'd been the top science student when they were kids. "Ships won't float, aircraft won't fly. *Splat.* Sometimes it vents from the seabed during quakes."

"Close enough." Baird was leaning out from the seat as far as he could to watch. "But I still say that's not methane. That's a pretty regular ellipse. Nature doesn't do geometric shapes. Look."

The Raven was at a 45-degree elevation from the basin now, high enough and far enough to get a better overview. Baird was right; it looked regular, almost man-made.

"Circular calderas," Barber said. "Hexagonal basalt plugs. Nature actually *does* do geometry, Corporal."

Baird just shrugged. "So you think the Lightmass shook up the geology around here enough to do that."

"You ever seen major subsidence in a mining area?" Barber slapped one palm flat on the other. "Straight edges. Down like . . ."

"A ton of bricks," Gettner said. "As I was saying. Got enough images there, Mister Observer?"

"No, but you're not going to do another pass, are you?"

"Good guess. Can't replace these birds."

Marcus pressed his earpiece and waited for Control to respond. "Anya, this is Delta. I have some weird shit for Hoffman."

"I'll be happy to relay *weird shit* to him, Marcus."

Marcus's frown didn't shift at all. There'd been a time when it would have softened. "Tollen is now a lake."

"As in seriously flooded?"

"As in *lake.* As in body of water and nothing else. As in the city is *no longer there.*"

Anya paused for just a breath, no more. "Yes, that definitely goes on the Weird Shit form."

At least she seemed more cheerful having Marcus around again. But that wasn't catching. Barber, Baird, and Marcus were all craning their necks for a look at the lake receding in the distance, expressions grimly blank.

"There could be a perfectly natural explanation for this," Dom said. "The planet still does stuff, right? Seismic activity, weather patterns, melting glaciers, all that crap."

"Yeah," said Baird. "It does. But they're back. The grubs are back. Believe me. They're back, but I have no frigging idea how they managed to do *that.*"

It was a big intuitive leap, as Marcus called it, maybe no more than wild imagination from a clever guy who could just as easily have been wrong. But Baird had a scary track record of being *right.*

"It's a long-winded way to try to drive out humans," Barber said. "Unless the Lightmass really screwed them and their weapons production has been so badly hit that they're reduced to damming rivers."

"That's not a flooded city." Baird began scribbling notes

on a dog-eared pad, as if he was working out some relief diagram of the terrain. "That's a city that's *sunk* Look at the elevation of the land around it."

"You're crazy," said Barber.

"Grubs aren't like us. They don't think like us. We don't even know what they want, do we?" Baird had a mind like a razor, especially where grubs were concerned. They were just one more type of machine for him to dismantle and understand. "There's always more motive for a war than just wanting to kill the other guy. We just need to work out what that is."

"And you can, but the scientists can't . . .," Barber said.

"Dumb assholes," Baird muttered. "They haven't worked out an answer in fourteen years, have they? Excuse me if I trust my own brain over theirs."

The cabin fell silent except for the steady, ear-numbing drone of rotors and engine. A Raven sounded very different from inside. Dom watched the glint on the new lake recede into a point of light and then vanish, and then they were passing over trees and derelict buildings again.

"Can grubs swim?" he asked.

"Can they drown?" said Marcus.

Dom could only pray that they did.

Marcus folded his arms across his chest, shut his eyes, and looked as if he was dozing. Dom knew damn well that he wasn't, and that he was just brooding over something he'd never discuss.

Dom's thoughts went back to Maria, and he told himself she couldn't have been in that drowned city, because she was still alive. And he would find her.

Alive. He knew it.

ABOUT THE AUTHOR

KAREN TRAVISS is the author of four *Star Wars: Republic Commando* novels: *Hard Contact, Triple Zero, True Colors,* and *Order 66;* three *Star Wars: Legacy of the Force* novels: *Bloodlines, Revelation, and Sacrifice;* as well as her award-nominated Wess'har Wars series—*City of Pearl, Crossing the Line, The World Before, Matriarch, Ally,* and *Judge.* A former defense correspondent and TV and newspaper journalist, Traviss lives in Wiltshire, England.